STEVE O'BRIEN

The
Ferrari Club

www.steveobrienmusic.com
www.ferrariclubthebook.com

Cover design by Michael Lovett
Author photo by Bob Berg

ISBN: 1463507143
ISBN-13: 9781463507145

The characters and events depicted in this book are fictional.
The cars, however, are very real . . .

CHAPTER 1

It was a gorgeous springtime day in Manhattan—one of those magical days that catch you by surprise a few times a year, when a crisp easterly breeze from the Atlantic blows the smog from the sky and cobwebs from human hearts. People imagine that their lives might change overnight, or even in the next few minutes. It was a day when everything seemed possible and anything could happen. And for Andy Baxter, it did.

He'd just finished his last afternoon class at New York University's downtown Greenwich Village campus and was following a butterfly down Bleecker Street. The butterfly was made of red satin and sewn to the seat of a pair of jeans worn by a tall girl in a scuffed biker jacket strolling half a dozen feet ahead of him. Its wings twitched enticingly with the motion of the girl's hips as she walked, and Andy wondered where she was headed. If he wasn't due at his part time job at Pizza Pete's in a few minutes he might follow her and find out. Maybe she'd step into a coffee shop and he'd have a chance to invite her to the bar where he and his band were playing tomorrow night. Offer to put her on the guest list at the door, maybe even write a song about her and work it up during rehearsal. You never know.

Andy hummed thoughtfully as he walked, trying to come up with lyrics that had something to do with a butterfly. Life was good. He'd submitted his master's thesis last week and his acceptance into the university's fall Ph.D. program looked secure. With a little luck, he'd have a shot at a cushy job teaching English Literature at some nice New England girl's college in a few years. Unless, of course, his band landed a record deal—though there didn't seem to be much chance of that. So far, not a single record company scout had come to a gig. But anything was possible.

When he reached the entrance of Pizza Pete's, he paused to watch the butterfly flutter down the sidewalk until it disappeared, then stepped inside the restaurant.

"What's shakin', Pete?" he asked.

The tiny cafe was empty except for a gaunt man wearing a tie-dyed shirt and sandals. He smiled as he emptied cash from the register into a bank deposit bag.

"Not much, dude, I'm headed to the bank. Keep an eye on things for a while, okay?"

Andy nodded and walked behind the counter as Pete adjusted the bandana tied around his head and shuffled to the sidewalk. Andy rinsed a dozen dirty aluminum platters left from lunch and was loading the dishwasher when two sharply dressed men walked in, laughing and speaking Spanish. One was thirty or so, the other a few years younger, about Andy's age. They sat at a front table and ordered grinders and Cokes. Andy scooped ice into plastic tumblers, grabbed two bottles of soda and turned toward their table.

What happened next unfolded in slow motion, and was a little different each time he tried to recall it—like a movie explosion shot from multiple camera angles, then edited into a sequence that lasts longer than the blast itself. In reality, the whole thing was over in less than a minute.

A motorcycle with two black helmeted riders pulled onto the sidewalk in front of the restaurant. The passenger slid off and pulled an HK MP5 machine pistol with a stubby silencer from under his windbreaker. He pointed the gun at the restaurant's plate glass window and Andy dropped to the floor as the pane shattered. Oddly, he never heard the shots, just the sound of disintegrating glass crashing onto the floor punctuated by the gun's metallic coughing and thuds that rang like blows from a ball-peen hammer. Bullets pummeled the service counter in front of him and ricocheted off the restaurant's brick walls. Andy felt a sharp stab of pain behind his ear and reached to pull a bloody chip of masonry from his scalp.

Then it was quiet, except for the sound of Kim, Pete's Vietnamese cook, running down the hallway and out the back door. Andy's nostrils itched from the smell of burnt gunpowder and suspended brick dust, and he suppressed a sneeze as he slowly peeked over the counter. The two customers were sprawled on the floor in growing puddles of dark blood. The older one's legs twitched and a sucking sound accompanied each rise of his chest. The man from the sidewalk stepped through the broken window and kicked the man hard in the balls. The machine pistol in his hand jerked, and the wounded man's head bounced upward as the back of his skull exploded against the floor tiles. The shooter thumbed a button on his gun and its crescent-shaped clip dropped to his feet. He replaced it with a fresh one from his windbreaker pocket and slowly turned toward Andy as he lifted the smoked visor of his helmet. He was smiling—an ugly Halloween mask of a grin that started at one ear and extended almost all the way across his badly scarred face.

Andy fell behind the counter again, this time slipping and hitting his head hard on the tiles as the gun delivered another round of bullets in a long clanking burst. His leg was knocked sideways, as if it had been smacked with a baseball bat, and he cringed as splinters of Formica and plywood ripped the skin of his exposed arms and neck.

Suddenly, it was quiet again. It occurred to Andy to try to crawl to the back door, but his leg wouldn't respond to his brain's commands. His thinking grew fuzzy. For some reason he was soaking wet. The atmosphere disintegrated in a white hot flash that seared his skin and sucked the air from his lungs like the just-opened blast of a furnace. He gripped the edge of the cooler and pulled himself a few inches across the debris-strewn floor before the heat pushed him into a black void.

CHAPTER 2

Andy woke to the sound of girls' voices.

Being a rock star was everything he'd ever imagined it would be. His band's show at Madison Square Garden had gone even better than he'd hoped; they'd opened for Bruce Springsteen, of all people. The funny thing was, he couldn't remember much about it except for the last song. Something about a butterfly.

Now he was on the couch in his dressing room wishing he wasn't so drunk. He was having trouble seeing. One of the groupies must have pulled her panties over his head. He blinked and tried to focus through the flimsy fabric. For some reason the girls hovering around him were wearing nurse's uniforms.

He closed his eyes and the voices faded.

CHAPTER 3

"You one lucky motherfucker."

Andy opened his eyes. The voice belonged to a middle-aged black man wearing a hospital orderly's uniform. Definitely not a groupie.

"It was the cooler that saved you, that's what the cops said."

Andy closed his eyes. Several moments later he heard a woman speak.

"You're a very fortunate young man."

He turned his head toward a smiling nurse who was handing a medical chart to a slightly built dark-skinned man in green scrubs. The nurse was a large blonde in her thirties. Pretty, but definitely not a groupie either.

"How long have I been here?" Andy asked. His lips felt as fat as polish sausages and he had trouble getting the words out. His arms and legs were heavy, especially his left leg, but everything still seemed to work.

"Three days."

"Have I been out the whole time?"

"Most of it, but that's good," the man replied in an Indian accent. "Your mind shuts down to allow your body to repair itself. By the way, I'm Doctor Radrukshi. As the orderly was saying, it was the cooler that saved you, kept you from being burned too badly. One of the bullets knocked a water pipe loose from its fitting on the icemaker and when the EMTs arrived you were lying in a puddle behind the cooler with water spraying everywhere."

"Am I going to be okay?"

"You're slightly concussed. I removed a nine-millimeter slug from your thigh that barely missed your femoral artery and lodged in the bone below your hip. Nothing was broken but you lost a lot of blood. That's why you went into shock and passed out . . . that and the fact that the fire consumed most of the restaurant's oxygen. We'll have to do have some skin grafts on your face and neck, but most of the burns are minor."

"The femoral artery? That's next to the groin, isn't it? The bullet didn't. . ."

"No, you're going to be fine."

The nurse smiled reassuringly.

Andy tried smiling back, but the bandages on his face pulled at his skin. Dr. Radrukshi patted his good leg.

"And we'll have you looking like a movie star in a few months."

CHAPTER 4

Dr. Radrukshi returned that afternoon with two men in suits. As they entered, Andy caught a glimpse of a uniformed police officer sitting in a chair in the hallway outside his room.

"I'm Special Agent George Baskins with the FBI," the first man said, displaying a shield and extending a freckled hand. He was about forty, short and scrawny with bushy red hair and eyebrows. "And this is Detective Joseph Henry, NYPD."

"You're a lucky guy," Henry said as he approached the bed. He was a big black guy about Baskins's age, with the confident stride and manner of a retired NFL linebacker who knew he was good for a couple of free beers at any bar in the city.

"That's what I keep hearing," Andy replied.

Henry sat by the bed and opened a briefcase.

"Doctor Radrukshi allowed us to ask a couple of questions," he said, withdrawing a folder. "You were semiconscious when the paramedics arrived. Apparently you mumbled something about two guys on a motorcycle, one of them with a badly scarred face. Did he look anything like this?"

Henry held out a photo. The twisted smile in the picture was unmistakable.

"He was grinning just like that when he shot me," Andy said.

"It wasn't a grin," Henry replied. "His name is Tony Bertolini. Smiley Bertolini's his nickname. The scars on his face make it look like he's permanently happy, but believe me, this is one twisted, angry man. He's Roberto Puccini's nephew."

"The Mafia guy?" Andy recognized the name from the papers.

"Yeah, that's his uncle. The firebomb was a giveaway; it's one of Bertolini's trademarks. He uses it after a hit to ensure no witnesses survive. His face got messed up when one exploded a little too close a few years ago."

"Too bad it didn't take him out, too," Baskins added, reaching to calm a twitch in his right eyebrow.

"Yeah," Henry said. "It would have saved us a lot of time and trouble. Bertolini's murdered half a dozen people we know about, probably a dozen more that we don't. But with your testimony, we'll be able to nail him. The local precinct got a tip just before the shooting. We picked Bertolini up a couple of blocks away. Lucky to get that tip, though—doesn't happen often with this mob stuff."

"Who were the victims?" Andy asked.

"One was Miguel Marquez, a Colombian who supplies half the cocaine in Brooklyn. The other was Ricky Glaus, the son of City Councilman Bernie Glaus from Queens. His parents are beside themselves. Ricky was their only kid."

Dr. Radrukshi cleared his throat and glanced at his watch.

"It'll break the Don's heart to see his nephew rot in jail," Henry said as he and Baskins stood to leave.

Baskins smiled. "But with your testimony, he'll be behind bars till his teeth fall out."

CHAPTER 5

"I'm not going to testify."

Baskins and Henry stared at Andy. They'd been smiling when they arrived back in his hospital room a few minutes ago, now Henry was frowning and Baskins's eyebrow was twitching like a caterpillar on a hot skillet.

"But you ID'd Bertolini yesterday," Henry said carefully.

Andy gestured at the IV bag hanging to his left. "I was doped up with painkillers and thought I recognized the guy in the picture. Now I'm not sure."

"Andy, we really need your help. Your testimony could put him behind bars for the rest of his days."

"I'm more concerned about the rest of *my* days. Roberto Puccini's one of the most powerful mob guys in the city."

"That's right," Baskins said. "This could be the beginning of something big. Think of the lives you'll save."

"Dude, I'm twenty-eight years old," Andy protested. "I'd like to hang around for a while."

"We have ways to ensure your safety. Have you heard of the Federal Witness Protection Program?"

"You can't force me to testify," Andy said.

"We've told you what a scumbag Bertolini is." Baskins bellowed.

"That's not my problem."

"He likes knives," Henry said. "A couple of uniforms busted a one-eared hooker on Canal Street last month, told us Bertolini carved her up after she joked about his face. The only way she can make a living now is giving blowjobs to bums coming out of the blood bank. This guy has got to go."

"What about me? I do what you ask and I'll end up dead. Didn't you guys ever watch *The Sopranos?*"

"Calm down," Baskins said. "We need this guy. And the D.A. really wants him."

Henry added, "Here's another thing: Councilman Glaus is offering a hundred thousand dollar reward for information leading to the conviction of his son's murderer. You're the only witness."

Baskins nodded. "And the FBI is willing to add another hundred grand from a special reserve fund we keep for situations like this. Use this right and you'll be set for life."

"How can I spend it if I'm at the bottom of the East River?"

Henry ignored the question. "You won't even have to appear in court. We'll videotape your testimony with your face bandaged and your voice scrambled electronically. No one will ever know it's you. Besides, after your plastic surgery, you won't even look like you."

"I like being me, damn it," Andy said, rising on an elbow in spite of the tubes and wires taped to his arms and torso. "I'm just finishing up my master's program at NYU, I play guitar and write songs for an awesome band—and I've got a career ahead of me that I'm looking forward to."

"We've thought of that and spoke with your advisor at NYU yesterday. Ever heard of Pepperdine University, in Malibu? We can get you enrolled in the Ph.D. program there, NYU will cooperate. Think about it, living on the beach, all expenses paid—with a couple hundred grand in the bank."

Henry smiled. "Southern California lifestyle ain't bad. Wake up early, surf for a few hours, catch a class or two, then hang out at Starbucks and wait for Paris Hilton or Angelina Jolie to drop in for their daily latte or cappuccino. How cool would that be?"

Andy levered himself up further in bed. "I don't give a shit. I just want my old life back."

The door opened and the blonde nurse bustled in. "You gentlemen are going to have to leave."

"Just think about it," Baskins said on the way out the door. "The Witness Protection Program has lots of possibilities."

Andy fell back on the pillows. "Then make me a rock star. Put me and my band onstage at Madison Square Garden opening for the Boss on his next tour."

CHAPTER 6

Baskins and Henry didn't return the next day, or the next. Andy began feeling better, though his thigh throbbed in spite of the meds. He actually didn't mind the pain; it reminded him that he was alive. His plastic surgery was scheduled for next week and he couldn't wait until he was released from the hospital and playing his old Fender Stratocaster in his East Village apartment.

He was dozing when a double knock on the door awakened him. Henry entered, followed by Baskins. Andy noted that the uniformed police officer was still in the hallway.

"How are you feeling?" Baskins asked.

"Better," Andy said.

"Have you reconsidered what we talked about the other day?"

"I've thought about it, but I'm sorry. There's no way I'll testify. Like I told you a couple of days ago, I just want to go back to the way things were before all this happened."

"You can't have your old life back," Henry said, shaking his head. "Your name's in the papers. Don Puccini knows who you are—and that you survived and can ID Bertolini. The fact is, whether you testify or not, he'll think you did. Your ass won't be worth a quarter when you step out of here."

Baskins added, "And besides, we've been researching options for you and think we have something good."

"You're going to make me a rock star?"

"Close. Ever been to Nashville, Tennessee?"

Andy rolled his eyes.

"We may have a job for you with a record producer there, writing songs for his music publishing company. Here's the deal: His name is Sam Solstice and he was implicated in a payola scandal a few years ago, or rather, some of his associates were. We never had any direct evidence against him, but he doesn't know that for sure and would like to stay in our good graces because the case is still pending. We can get him to sign you to a songwriting contract with his company for a year or two. I can't promise your songs will be recorded, but you'd have a decent shot. Solstice isn't a bad guy and he's produced quite a few hits. If music is what you want to do, this is a once in a lifetime opportunity. If things don't work out, there's always Pepperdine."

"He's produced some hit records?"

"Lots."

Andy sighed. He actually liked country music, especially some of the older artists like Johnny Cash and Merle Haggard.

Henry said, "A lot of kids would give anything for a chance like this."

Andy shrugged, but continued to think. He'd been writing songs since he could remember and was responsible for most of his band's repertoire. Writing country music couldn't be that hard. He'd miss the guys in his group, but they were always breaking up and reforming, and they weren't all that close. After his parents were killed in a car wreck when he was six, his only relative—his grandmother in Massachusetts—had raised him. It wasn't an easy job. As a teenager, he'd been more interested in playing guitar than studying. It made him sad, even now, to think how heartbroken she was when he'd flunked out of community college and been busted for writing bad checks when he was nineteen. Since it was his second arrest, the judge gave him two options: prison or join the Marines.

He'd chosen the Marines. His grandmother passed away while he was stationed in the Philippines. He returned to the states a different man—fit, disciplined and with a newly discovered passion for reading he'd developed during long hours alone overseas. He sublet an apartment in lower Manhattan, enrolled in City College on the GI Bill, studied hard and managed to graduate with honors a few years later. Just days ago, he was eager to see what tomorrow would bring. Now, the future was no longer so clear or bright. He thought again about the fact that his name had been in the newspapers.

Baskins spoke again, his voice softer, "You can't go back to your old life. It doesn't exist anymore."

"Word on the street is that Puccini's already got a contract out on you," Henry said. "Fifty large is what we hear. You really don't have any other options."

Andy stared at Baskins and Henry. They were right, he realized. He didn't have any other choice.

CHAPTER 7

Arnie Fortune was a handsome devil.

He'd left Andy Baxter and his old Stratocaster in New York, now he was checking his reflection in the restroom mirror on an American Airlines flight en route to Nashville. Dr. Radrukshi's team of plastic surgeons had done a great job. The deft changes they'd made to the contours of his nose, chin and cheekbones had left him looking GQ handsome and, more importantly, radically different from his former self—almost unrecognizable in fact.

The summer had passed quickly. After his surgery he'd been escorted from the hospital to the FBI's office on West 30th Street, where he videotaped his testimony against Tony Bertolini. Once Baskins and the attorneys were satisfied, he signed a printed transcript and was whisked to the rear entrance of a small hotel a few blocks west of Central Park.

The FBI kept every promise. Baskins presented him with a receipt for two hundred thousand dollars in a Merrill Lynch investment account, plus filled his request for a Taylor acoustic guitar and a Yamaha digital four-track recorder. They even picked up the top twenty CD's listed in *Billboard* magazine's country album chart and a dozen compilation albums of country classics. He'd spent the last four months studying the CDs, watching CMT and GAC on TV and listening to a country music station broadcasting from Long Island. Most importantly, he'd been writing songs. He'd spent long hours with his guitar and recorder and had completed over a dozen tunes, half which he thought sounded at least as good as those he'd been hearing on the radio. He couldn't wait to arrive in country music's capital city.

The plane touched down just after eight p.m. and Arnie followed signs to the baggage claim area. He did a now-instinctive survey of the people around him as he watched for his bags. The aftermath of the recent events and some good training by Baskins had taught him to always be aware of the people who were nearby. He grabbed his guitar case and duffel bag as they came by on the carousel, then turned to find himself facing a young blonde woman shrink-wrapped in a red halter top and blue jeans so tight they appeared to be tattooed to her long legs. She was perched on four-inch high heels, also red, and carrying a cardboard sign with bold letters: ARNIE.

"You must be Arnie."

"How could you tell?"

"The guitar," she said, laughing. "No, just kidding!"

He looked around and noticed half a dozen other travelers with guitars in the crowded terminal.

"I had an idea what you would look like, but the guitar did help. I'm Starr, by the way. I work for Sam Solstice."

"Nice to meet you."

Arnie smiled as he followed Starr's swaying form out the terminal's sliding glass doors. He liked Nashville already. A few steps later, they approached a glistening red convertible parked under a sign that said PASSENGER PICKUP—STANDING ONLY. Two burly security guards were by the vehicle.

"You boys are such darlings to keep an eye on my Ferrari!" Starr said as she slid into the driver's seat and popped open the hood.

Arnie dropped his duffel into the front trunk and settled into the tan butter-soft leather passenger seat with his guitar case crammed between his legs. Starr jammed the gearshift into first, blew the guards a kiss and popped the clutch. Arnie's head snapped against the headrest as the car fishtailed slightly, then darted away from the curb.

"So this is Music City," he said, as she maneuvered from lane to lane on Interstate 40, while simultaneously checking her makeup in the rearview mirror. They were approaching downtown Nashville and it wasn't quite the sleepy Southern burg he'd imagined. Though well past rush hour, traffic was heavy and tall skyscrapers loomed ahead.

"There's LP Field," Starr said, pointing to the right. "Home of our NFL team, the Tennessee Titans." Arnie was thrown against the passenger door as Starr downshifted and cut between two tractor-trailers, then veered left onto the downtown loop. "And that's the Bat Building." She slowed down momentarily while indicating the tallest of the buildings, which sported twin spires from its roof, causing it to resemble the headgear of Batman.

"Is this your car?" Arnie asked. "It's unbelievable."

"No, it belongs to Sam." She exited the interstate at Demonbreun Street and the tires chirped as she turned left at the foot of the ramp and accelerated hard past a row of restaurants to a roundabout. "And this is Music Row," she said as they emerged onto a wide boulevard lined with office buildings. "Most of the music companies in Nashville are located within a few blocks of here."

They drove for a mile or so, then circled onto Sixteenth Avenue South and stopped in front of a one-story horseshoe-shaped apartment building framing a well-groomed lawn. "This is where you'll be staying. Hillsboro Village is a few blocks that way," she said, pointing south. "Plenty of shops and restaurants nearby. And you're in walking distance anywhere on the Row."

The apartment wasn't bad—the small living room, bedroom and kitchen were more space than he'd had in Manhattan. The furniture looked comfortable, if a little threadbare. Starr showed him how to access the phone's voicemail and wrote down the office number and address.

"Leave your stuff here, we're meeting the boss for drinks," she said.

"Sure, give me a minute to clean up."

In the bathroom, he brushed his teeth, slicked his hair back and checked himself in the mirror. He was looking forward to meeting a real record producer. The closest he'd come had been a year before, when his band had made a demo recording and dropped off copies with a dozen record companies. The only response had been from a secretary who said her boss wasn't crazy about the group, but wanted to play one of Andy's songs for another artist on the label. Andy had called back half a dozen times, but the producer was never available to take his call.

Arnie followed Starr outside, his eyes on the lookout for possible danger, and once again admired her driving skills as she threaded the car down a series of side streets and alleys before emerging at the intersection of Broadway and 21st Avenue. When they arrived at a three-story restaurant named Bound'ry, the parking valet motioned her to a spot in front of the entrance.

"Always easy to find a parking space in a Ferrari," Starr said. "Makes the restaurant look good."

Starr handed the valet her keys and headed inside with Arnie close behind. A petite hostess with a French accent led them past the packed downstairs bar to a large circular booth where two men were seated with three attractive women. The man closest to Arnie stood and extended his hand.

"You must be Arnie."

"Mr. Solstice?"

"Just call me Sam," he replied, motioning the slender Asian girl sitting next to him to scoot over and make room for Arnie. "How was your flight?"

"Fine," Arnie replied, taking a seat. The producer was strikingly handsome. He appeared to be in his late forties or early fifties, though it was hard to tell. His hair was dyed a monochromatic chestnut and his face had the taut look that comes with a facelift or two. His eyes sparkled with feral intelligence and he exuded a restless energy that gave him the air of a much younger man.

"Meet Sendy," Sam said, slipping his arm around the Asian girl. "And this is Ruth," he added, nodding to a buxom blonde in her early thirties. "And George and his friend Cheryl." He gestured to the hip looking black-clad couple at the far end of the booth. "George is a song plugger with one of the publishers here."

Starr slipped into the booth next to Cheryl as George tipped his Heineken in greeting.

"Nice to meet you. Sam says you're a new writer for his company. Where are you from?"

"Well, I —"

"Hey," Sam interrupted, "Arnie's just gotten into town and I'm sure he's worn out from his flight. How 'bout a beer, son?"

"Sure," Arnie replied.

"He's cute," Ruth giggled, lighting a cigarette and brushing back her long curls to offer a better view of the two pneumatic breasts popping out of her black velvet dress. "Wherever you're from, I'll bet the ladies are missing you tonight."

"Down girl!" Sam laughed. "Watch out for Ruth, Arnie. She'll eat you alive."

"I can't help it if I like songwriters," Ruth squealed. "Besides, he *is* cute!"

"I agree," chirped Sendy.

"I like Music City already," Arnie said, as Sam raised his glass and prepared to make a toast. He couldn't believe he was here with a real-life record producer and four of the prettiest women he'd ever seen in his life.

As they clicked their glasses over the center of the table, Sam enthusiastically asked, "Is this a great country or what?"

Arnie just had to agree.

CHAPTER 8

Arnie woke the next morning to the sound of traffic whizzing down Sixteenth Avenue outside his apartment window. He rolled out of bed with difficulty and stumbled into the kitchen. The previous tenant had left a half-full jar of instant coffee in one of the wall cabinets. He spooned some into a cup, filled it with hot tap water and stuck the muddy mess in the microwave.

His memory of the previous night was blurred. Sam and his party had stayed at Bound'ry until well past midnight, then gone to another bar until it closed at three. Starr had left at some point with a hockey player who'd just been traded to the Nashville Predators. Arnie vaguely remembered Sam driving him home in the red Ferrari with Ruth sitting on his lap. He realized he had no idea what happened to Sendy—somehow they'd lost her between bars.

He stood in the shower for ten minutes and emerged feeling a little better. Sam had told him he'd see him in the office first thing in the morning and he wanted to be there by nine. It took a considerable effort of will, but by eight-thirty he was on the sidewalk, squinting in the bright sunlight with his guitar in hand and backpack containing his tapes and notebooks slung over his shoulder.

He stopped at a small market for some aspirin and a can of Red Bull, hesitating to check his instincts for safety before he went in. As he was paying, the squat Asian man at the register asked, "New in town—songwriter?"

"How'd you know?" Arnie answered.

"Guitar, no car, easy to spot. Wanna hear joke?"

"Okay."

The man peered through octagonal red tinted glasses at Arnie as he handed him his change. "You know how to get songwriter off your front porch in Nashville?"

"How?"

"Pay him for pizza!" The grocer exploded with laughter.

"Very funny. You're a smart man to get your money before you tell jokes like that."

"Good idea for songwriter too—get money first. Promises cheap in show business."

Arnie was still smiling as he left the market. He popped three aspirin in his mouth and washed them down with the can of Red Bull. After a few blocks they began to kick in and his hangover faded to a manageable level.

He was confident about the songs he'd written during the last four months and felt good about the recordings he'd made of them. His small recorder was an inexpensive piece of equipment, but it had four tracks that enabled him to record his voice and guitar, then add additional guitar and harmony parts to suggest musical arrangements for the tunes. He couldn't wait to play them for Sam.

Solstice Productions was housed in a stately two-story brick building with a small, impeccably landscaped front courtyard. And when he stepped inside, he was taken aback by the décor of the reception area. It was stunning—hunter green walls accented by naturally finished oak woodwork and exquisite antique furniture. Starr sat behind a small kidney shaped desk set on an oriental rug. This morning she was dressed in a subdued outfit of gray slacks, black satin blouse and a simple gold necklace. She looked as fresh and classy as a *Vogue* cover model and Arnie couldn't believe she was the same girl who'd been out with him and Sam for half the previous night.

"Hi Arnie. Oops, gotta get this. . ." Starr grabbed the phone as it buzzed. "No, I'm sorry, Mr. Solstice isn't in yet . . . no, we don't accept unsolicited material, but you're welcome to drop off a CD." She hung up the phone, which immediately rang again. This time she took a message.

"Sam's not in yet?" Arnie asked when she was finally free.

"No, he's never in this early, but he asked me to give you this." She handed him a nine by twelve inch manila envelope. "It's a songwriter contract he needs you to look over and sign."

"He said he wanted me to meet him here this morning to listen to my songs."

"Why don't you review the contract and come back a little later, say about eleven-thirty. He should be able to see you then." Starr made a note in the appointment book on her desk. "In fact, I'll make sure he is."

Arnie slid his guitar case beside a couch and walked out to the street. Though it was late September, the day was already uncomfortably warm. Deciding against trudging back to his apartment, he wandered several blocks north to Broadway, where he came upon a pleasant deli-style restaurant named Noshville. An emaciated brunette waitress with half a dozen earrings in her left ear and a spider web tattooed on the back of her neck took his breakfast order. Settling into the booth, he examined the contract while he waited. The document was two pages long and appeared straightforward. It stated that Arnie would receive a salary of five hundred dollars a week, plus the use of a car and an apartment. In return, Arnie would grant Sam worldwide publishing rights and fifty percent of the income from the songs he wrote during the one-year term of the agreement. Sam had the option to extend the contract for an additional year if he chose to do so.

Arnie had taken a semester of entertainment law at City College and his initial reaction was that the contract was fair. Although there was no guarantee that his songs would be recorded, he recalled that Agent Baskins and Detective Henry had said that would be up to him. He had a few questions for Sam, but decided it would be safe to sign the agreement without consulting an attorney—after all, the FBI had Sam under their thumb and could put the squeeze on him if he didn't treat him fairly. He finished breakfast and chatted for a few minutes with the waitress, who said she'd moved to Nashville with her six-year-old daughter two years earlier to pursue a singing career. So far she hadn't had any luck. When he told her he was working with Sam Solstice she was impressed.

At eleven-fifteen, he returned to Solstice Productions and Starr informed him that Sam was in a meeting. Thirty minutes later, the door to Sam's office opened and Arnie's jaw dropped as an extraordinarily beautiful girl emerged. She was about five and a half feet tall with long brown hair, deeply tanned Mediterranean skin; and was wearing yellow cowboy boots and a tiny blue satin pillowcase of a dress that bulged like a gunnysack stuffed with fighting alley cats as she strutted into the reception area. When she passed Arnie, he caught a subtle scent that he couldn't quite define, a delicate perfume laced with pheromones that froze his nervous system.

"Stefany, this is Arnie Fortune," Sam said, jolting him back to reality. "Arnie's a new writer for my publishing company."

"I'm Stefany," she said. Before Arnie could respond, she turned back to Sam. "I'll be back in town in a couple of weeks."

"We'll start recording then."

Stefany flashed Arnie a quick smile as she walked out the door.

"Come on in, Arnie," Sam said, motioning him into his office.

"Who was that?" Arnie asked, still dazed as he took a seat beneath the dozens of gold and platinum award plaques that adorned the walls of Sam's inner sanctum.

"Stefany Simmons. She's got a great voice and her old man's got beaucoup bucks. For a chick singer, looks are half the battle. She's obviously got that covered, but she's got fantastic pipes too. I'm starting a spec project with her in a few weeks. She doesn't have a deal yet, but I'm hoping to come up with some sides that are strong enough to shop to the labels. Maybe you'll have a song for us."

"I'd love to write something for her," Arnie said, regaining his composure. "I've written quite a few songs. I brought six of my best today."

"Great," Sam replied.

"I've also got my guitar with me in case you want to hear more."

"Let's get that the contract out of the way first. Do you have any questions?"

"A few. I've never signed a publishing contract before and I'm not all that sure how the songwriting business works. I noticed that there's nothing in the agreement about getting my music recorded."

"That's up to you. The five hundred dollars a week is an advance, or draw, against future royalties. If none of your songs get recorded, I'm out twenty-five grand for the first year—plus your demos and other expenses. On the other hand, if you do write something good enough to get cut and your sales royalties exceed your advances, you'll be paid the surplus semi-annually. Plus, if one of your songs is a single, you'll receive performance royalties from radio airplay. That's separate from your draw and paid to you by the performance rights agency you decide to join: ASCAP, BMI or SESAC. By the way, the performance royalties can be quite substantial for a hit song, well into the six figures.

"Wow," Arnie said.

"I believe in win-win business deals," Sam continued. "If you develop into a successful writer, we both come out ahead. If not, I've honored my commitment to the FBI and we can move on. By the way, I don't know where you're from or what led you here—and I'd just as soon keep it that way."

"So you don't know—"

"No," Sam said sharply, raising his palms. "And I don't want to. The less I know the better. In fact, I'd prefer that we not speak of it again. As far as I'm concerned, you're a songwriter like any other. I'll keep my end of the deal. It's a tough business, but I'll do whatever I can to help you. You seem like a good kid, I hope that we have success working together. But most of it's going to be up to you."

Arnie thought it over for a moment. Sam seemed like a straight shooter and he respected his business-like manner. He signed both copies of the contract and passed them across the desk.

"I'll get Starr to notarize these," Sam said. "Now let's hear your songs."

Arnie handed him his CD. When the first notes of his guitar came through the big speakers mounted behind Sam's massive walnut desk, he couldn't help smiling. His song sounded fantastic.

Sam listened with his eyes closed, moving his head slightly from side to side. When the song ended, he grinned. "Not bad."

Halfway through the second song he smiled again. "That's good too. I hope you don't mind. . ." He hit a button and the CD jumped to the next track. He listened to the remaining songs in the same way, playing only the first verse and chorus, then removed the CD and handed it back to Arnie. "They're nice songs."

"So you like them?"

"I'll be honest with you. I do like them, but there's nothing here I can use. You've been listening to the radio?"

Arnie was a bit taken aback. "I have," he replied.

"Well, it shows. These songs sound like what's on the radio—what's on the radio *now*. What I'm looking for are songs that are going to be on the radio a year or two from now. These are structured well, but the lyrics are a little vague. A song's like a movie, it's got to tell a story with a beginning, middle, and end."

Arnie wondered how Sam knew his songs didn't have an end, he'd only listened to one all the way through.

"You need to start hanging with some other writers," Sam continued, "and develop your knowledge of the craft. Start going to songwriter's nights—there's a club called the Bluebird Café that has some good ones. Another good place is Douglas Corner. Most hit songs are simple, but it's hard to write a song that's simple and unique at the same time. You obviously have talent, but you've got some work ahead of you."

Arnie was disappointed—worse than that—but impressed by the fact that Sam didn't mince words with him.

"Why don't we meet again in a week or so," Sam said, standing. "We'll get together on a regular basis and I'll listen to what you've been writing and critique it."

"Sure."

"And remember this: I'll always tell you what I think, but don't let anyone, even me, ever talk you out of believing in a song you truly love. I know what my instincts are—and my instincts have made me a lot of money. But my opinions are my own. Nobody in this business, I mean nobody, knows what a hit song is until it's made it to the top of the charts."

"Thank you," Arnie said as Starr walked in with an armful of FedEx packages.

"Put your heart into what you write," Sam continued. "People don't relate to music with their minds, they relate to it with their gut. Make them feel something and they'll buy the record."

Arnie smiled and shook hands with his new boss. "Thanks for your advice. I'll be back next week."

"I look forward to it."

"So that's your Ferrari Starr was driving last night?" Arnie asked Sam after Starr had notarized his contract.

"Sam's got several Ferraris," Starr jumped in. "The 430's my favorite."

"But she only gets to drive the 355 most of the time," said Sam. "You liked it?"

"Loved it!"

"Why don't you join me for lunch Saturday. I get together every now and then with a group of folks who own sports cars. This week we're meeting at the Loveless Cafe. You'll get to see some pretty automobiles."

"I'd love to. By the way, didn't the contract say I'm supposed to get the use of a car?"

"It's parked out back," Sam replied. "Starr will show you."

Arnie followed Starr to the office's rear exit. In the back parking lot was a blue Mazda Miata convertible with a frayed tan top.

"It's not a Ferrari," she said, handing him a set of keys. "You'll have to write a few hits before you can afford one of those. But it runs, and it's fun to drive. It's more dependable than Sam's cars—Ferraris spend half their time in the shop.

"Oh."

"But when they're in tune, driving one's better than sex!" Starr concluded her sentence with a wink and the twinkle in her eye as she turned and sashayed down the hall left him wondering if she believed what she said could possibly be true.

CHAPTER 9

Arnie grinned as he tooled down Seventeenth Avenue South in the Miata. The car's upholstery was worn and the engine wasn't all that powerful, but the light vehicle's quick steering made it fun to drive. He circled Music Row and headed toward Hillsboro Village, where he found a pleasant cluster of shops, bars and restaurants. It looked like a cool place to hang out and he was glad it was within walking distance of his apartment. Exploring further, he drove past the nearby campuses of Vanderbilt and Belmont Universities, and the surrounding shady streets lined with older houses and apartment buildings. The more he saw of his new neighborhood, the more he liked it. When he came to a grocery store, he stopped for beer, coffee and groceries and picked up a copy of the *Nashville Scene*, the local weekly paper.

He found the address of the Bluebird Café in the paper's entertainment section and noted that a writer's night was scheduled that evening. After an hour or two spent unpacking and settling in, he set up his recorder on the kitchen table and strummed a few chords on his guitar. Remembering Sam's advice, he experimented with arranging them in a sequence he'd never tried. He liked the sound of the new progression and felt himself on the verge of getting a song started, but couldn't come up with words that fit the music.

When he noticed it becoming dark outside he downed a quick sandwich and drove to the Bluebird. To his surprise, the club resembled a New England coffeehouse more than the lusty Texas roadhouse he'd anticipated. The hundred or so people seated at small tables were paying rapt attention to four performers seated in a circle around a cluster of microphones in the center of the room. A round faced girl with a smoky voice was singing and playing an electric keyboard, accompanied by an enormous shaggy-haired fellow in his mid-thirties wearing a plaid shirt and faded denim overalls. His bulk dwarfed the small Martin guitar he was playing and Arnie couldn't believe the languid motions of his stubby fingers created the melodic riffs emerging from the room's speakers.

The song sounded familiar and when the audience applauded at its conclusion, Arnie realized that he had heard it on one of the CDs he'd listened to over the summer. The room quieted and the girl introduced the massive guitarist who had been accompanying her as Bubba Jones, then invited him to do one of his own tunes. Arnie's ears perked up. The song was one of the biggest hits of the past year.

The remaining performers were equally good and they traded songs for the remainder of the evening. Arnie especially enjoyed one writer's song introduction about an experience he claimed to have had in New Orleans several years earlier. He slammed a chord on his guitar and launched into the tune, a raucous ditty about being bushwhacked by an octoroon hooker and her pimp in an alley off Bourbon Street. When he got to the chorus he sang the title line: "*It was a night I can't remember that I never will forget*," and the audience broke into wild applause.

When the show was over, Arnie stood to leave and noticed Bubba chatting with a cluster of people near the front door. He introduced himself and told him how much he'd enjoyed the night's performance.

"Thanks," Bubba replied in a thick Alabama accent. "Glad you could come out."

"I'm a songwriter too," Arnie said. "Just moved here. I'm signed to Sam Solstice's company."

"Really? If you're writing for Sam, you must be good. Give me a call sometime, I'd like to hear some of your stuff." Bubba handed him a business card from the chest pocket of his overalls. "Might even be interested in doing some co-writing."

"Sure."

Arnie checked his watch as he pulled out of the Bluebird's parking lot. It was only a little past eleven. There were other bars and clubs to visit, but there'd be time for that in days to come. Tonight, after his first full day in Nashville, he wanted a good night's rest.

Tomorrow he was going to write a hit song.

CHAPTER 10

Arnie was full of energy and still pumped about his experience at the Bluebird when he sat at the kitchen table with his guitar the next morning. While thinking about how much he'd enjoyed the evening, the phrase "last night made my day" popped into his mind. He hummed a bit of melody over the chord sequence he'd developed the prior afternoon and modified the progression to fit. As he did so, his thoughts drifted to Stefany, the girl he'd met at Sam's office. Lyrics formed as he imagined what it would be like to have spent the previous evening with her. He jotted down lines as they came to him and soon had a chorus:

Woke up to stardust falling
Been dancing on air all morning
Just one kiss got me feeling this way
Suddenly there's a new sun rising
Since I looked into your eyes and
All I can say is last night made my day

Pleased, he hit the record button and sang the completed chorus all the way through while accompanying himself on guitar. After pouring himself a fresh cup of coffee, he listened with the volume as loud as he dared without disturbing his neighbors. It sounded great. Suddenly, he realized that he was hungry—it was almost noon and he could use a break. As he was leaving the apartment, he remembered Bubba's card and left a voicemail message for the writer saying how much he'd enjoyed meeting him.

Arnie strolled down the street humming the melody of his new song while watching the parade of sleek BMWs, Mercedes and SUVs pass by. When he reached the market he'd stopped at the previous day, he pushed open the glass door and entered to the sound of a high-pitched female squeal.

"Arnieee!"

Sendy, the girl he'd met with Sam at Bound'ry, was standing behind the counter next to the chunky proprietor, who was scowling.

"Hi Sendy," Arnie said. "Nice to see you again. So this is your dad?"

"Yeah," her father said. "I tell her to stay away from songwriters—always talking about big hit that never comes. You know what difference is between a songwriter and an extra-large pizza with pepperoni on one side and anchovies on the other?"

Arnie grimaced and waited for the punch line.

"The pizza can feed a family of four!"

The grocer exploded in laughter and Sendy grinned sheepishly.

"Don't you know any jokes that don't have songwriters and pizza in them?" Arnie asked, chuckling in spite of himself. The man needed his own TV show.

"Yeah, but you don't want to hear those either," Sendy interrupted before her father could answer. "Daddy wants me to marry rich doctor or lawyer, but too boring for me."

"Boring can be good sometimes," Arnie said, turning to get a drink from the cooler. "So you work here every day?"

"Six mornings a week. Market closed Sunday. You hungry?"

"Hmmmm, those egg rolls look good. How 'bout two to go."

Sendy removed three large egg rolls from the glass case on the counter. "Extra one on house—to make up for mean father."

"Are you going to lunch with Sam on Saturday?" Arnie asked after paying.

"Yes, you?"

"I'll see you there."

Arnie munched on the egg rolls on the way home, thinking about his new song. When he arrived at his apartment, he realized that he was exhausted. Although he only intended to close his eyes for a few minutes, he slept until the phone woke him two hours later. Bubba had gotten his message and wanted to get together and try to co-write sometime. They set a date a few weeks ahead and Arnie hung up, his new song still rolling around his brain. He picked up his guitar and began trying to create verses to go with the chorus. Several scraps of lyric popped into his mind, and he scrawled them in his notebook.

He mouthed the words softly over and over to himself, and found that they suggested a rough melody. More lyrics occurred to him and soon he had several pages filled. He took a break to make a pot of coffee, then picked out the best lines and assembled them into two verses.

When he played the song back after recording it, he was pleased, but realized that he was too tired to be objective about whether it was any good or not. It was well past dark—he'd been completely wrapped up in his work, almost in a trance, for five or six hours.

It was a balmy evening, so he decided to walk the few blocks to Hillsboro Village for a beer. Halfway there, a dented Toyota pulled up to the curb beside him, the passenger window rolling down as it came to a stop. Instinct took over, just as it had at Pizza Pete's in New York a few months before, and Arnie was halfway through a gap in the hedge that bordered the sidewalk to his right before he realized that a woman in the car's passenger seat holding a baby in her arms was asking him for directions to Vanderbilt Hospital. He emerged from the shrubbery, too embarrassed and shaken to respond, as the car screeched off. After looking furtively to his left and right, he continued on to Hillsboro Village. He passed several upscale restaurants, searching in vain for a gritty working class bar where he could watch a team of Clydesdales prancing across a lighted Budweiser sign, and eventually came upon a tiny place called the Villager Tavern. No Clydesdales, but it would do.

Arnie found a seat at the bar and ordered a draft beer, tossed it back quickly, then ordered another beer and a pastrami sandwich. The FBI had warned him that he would experience incidents like this, and he had received counseling from a psychologist on coping with them. Still, he was surprised at how terrified he had felt when the car had stopped. He shuddered and looked around. What if it actually had been one of Don Puccini's men?

The crowd in the bar ran the gamut from coeds playing Foosball to construction workers at the rear of the long narrow building throwing darts. He considered trying to strike up a conversation with the girls, but ordered a third beer instead; he simply couldn't summon the energy to emerge from his shell. Unable to shake the feeling that enveloped him, he finished his sandwich, paid his tab and headed home. Tomorrow was lunch with Sam and Sendy, and he was anxious to spend more time working on his song before meeting them at noon.

CHAPTER 11

When Arnie sat down to listen to "Last Night Made My Day" the next morning, he was a bit apprehensive, but then pleasantly surprised. It sounded good. However, as he played the song back a second and third time, something began to bother him. He wasn't sure what was wrong, but couldn't shake the feeling that it could be improved. He worked for several frustrating hours without making any progress, then glanced at his watch. It was almost eleven and he was going to be late for lunch.

After a quick shower, he raced to the Loveless Café, a quaint country restaurant several miles from downtown, and slipped the Miata into a vacant parking spot between Sam's 355 Ferrari Spyder and a gleaming metallic blue Porsche convertible. Inside, he found Sam and his entourage seated at several broad tables pushed together. During the quick round of introductions he met Jules, Starr's date, a handsome investment banker in his forties who owned the Porsche. When Arnie complimented his car, Jules promised him a ride after lunch. Sam was seated between two women in their twenties, a tall brunette of either Middle Eastern or Eurasian descent and a pale girl wearing wire rim glasses who wasn't particularly attractive until she stood to go to the restroom and revealed an extraordinary figure. A solidly built man in his fifties with steel gray hair and forearms the size of bowling pins was seated next to Sendy.

Arnie turned to him and asked, "So your name is Vinnie?"

"That's right," he replied in a thick Italian accent.

"Best Ferrari mechanic east of the Mississippi," two fellows sitting across the table added simultaneously. One of the men, Lars, was a nattily dressed black man about thirty. The other, Buford, was a bit older, with a chalky white complexion and several days' growth of beard.

Arnie had expected the lunch to be a gathering of people in the music business and was surprised to find they represented a variety of professions. He chatted for a while about Formula One racing with an ultra-fit attorney in his mid-sixties named Ted, who was the president of the Tennessee Ferrari owner's organization. Arnie noted that Ted's date was the prettiest girl at the table, a redhead in her early twenties who spoke with a Russian accent. Two of the men were building contractors, one was a health care executive and another, who was named Carl, owned a chain of florist shops. Arnie particularly enjoyed speaking with a heavy equipment importer named Robert who had recently returned from a sailing trip in the Caribbean. When the waitress came with the checks, Sam announced to Arnie that the group was going for a drive.

"I'm riding with Arnie," Sendy squealed.

"It's quite a life you have here," Arnie remarked to Sam as he followed him from the restaurant. "I mean the music, the cars, the girls. . ."

"An old fellow once told me 'Make the most of life while you're living—you're going to be dead for a long, long time.'"

"I'll have to remember that."

Half a dozen of the cars parked outside were Ferraris, ranging from an older Testerossa to a stunning new 430 coupe. Several other marques were represented and Arnie was fascinated by Carl's car in particular—a Lotus Seven, which had a low cigar shaped body, open wheels and cockpit like that of a Grand Prix racecar. Carl invited Vinnie to ride with him and the mechanic agreed, jokingly reminding Carl that he had once driven for the Scuderia Ferrari racing team and was looking forward to giving him some driving pointers.

As promised, Jules thrilled Arnie with a quick spin around the restaurant parking lot in his blue Porsche. Then Arnie fired up the Miata and with Sendy by his side, followed the string of cars onto the highway.

"So, how do you like the Ferrari Club?" Sendy asked, sweeping her hair into a ponytail as they accelerated toward the town of Franklin.

"Is that what they call it—the Ferrari Club?" Arnie answered, shifting gears.

"Yep, Sam and his friends and the prettiest girls they can round up."

"Do you think I can be a provisional member in my Miata?"

"Sure. Then write big hit and drive Ferrari like other guys!"

Soon they turned off the main road into an area of expensive homes on multi-acre lots scattered between rolling horse farms. The cars in the lead snaked through the curves and the exhilarating sound of the free-revving engines faded into the distance as Arnie tried in vain to match their pace. Sendy waved both arms over her head like a roller coaster rider and yelled at him to go faster, but the drivers ahead had no regard for the speed limit, and soon were out of sight.

Arnie eased the pressure on the accelerator. It was a beautiful afternoon and he didn't want it to be his last. When Sendy squawked in protest, he reminded her that she needed to stay alive or else her father would lose his business by running off every songwriter who came into his market.

Ten minutes later he had lost contact with the other drivers and was wondering how he'd find his way back to Music Row. Suddenly, as he emerged from a tight, tree-lined hairpin turn, he saw two cows standing in the road in front of him. He slammed his foot on the brake and miraculously passed between the two animals. Shaken, he slowed the Miata and spotted Sam's car doing a U-turn a short distance ahead, and several more cows wandering through a broken section of barbed wire fence bordering the road. The earth around the damaged fence was deeply gouged. Sendy shrieked and pointed to the pasture on the other side of the fence, where Carl's Lotus was lying upside down with one wheel missing and the remaining three canted in different directions.

Arnie jerked the Miata onto the shoulder and ran with Sendy to the Lotus as Carl crawled from the car and staggered to his feet. Blood streamed from a gash in his forehead. Gasoline was seeping out of the tank into the dirt, and Vinnie, who appeared to be unconscious, was still strapped into the passenger seat. Arnie bent and frantically tried to unfasten the safety harness holding the older man in the open cockpit, but the car's roll bar had sunk into the soft earth and he couldn't reach the release. He yelled for Sendy to help and they each grabbed one of the wheels and rocked the lightweight chassis to one side. Sendy leaned against one wheel to hold the car in place as Arnie got on his hands and knees in the muck to unlatch Vinnie's harness.

Though he knew it was dangerous to move an accident victim, the gasoline dripping into the dirt convinced him to pull Vinnie out of the car's cockpit. With Sendy's help, he carefully dragged the husky mechanic about thirty yards. Suddenly, they felt a blast of heat as a sheet of flame fanned rapidly from the dirt around the Lotus. Although there wasn't an explosion, in a few minutes all that remained of the car was a twisted steel carcass bubbling with blistered paint under a billowing cloud of black smoke.

CHAPTER 12

Arnie woke in his apartment the next morning to the sound of loud snoring and looked over to see Sendy lying in bed beside him wearing his old I Love New York T-shirt. He reminded himself to get rid of it soon—after all, he was in the Witness Protection Program. The events of the previous day and evening came back. The drivers had regrouped after the accident and followed the ambulances to Saint Thomas Hospital. Miraculously, both Vinnie and Carl had escaped serious injury. Carl was just shaken up, but Vinnie's condition was more serious: three broken ribs, a dislocated shoulder and a mild concussion. The doctors' prognosis was good and they expected to release him in a few days.

When he and Sendy finally left the hospital that evening, he'd asked if she'd like to stop somewhere for a beer. They'd gone to the Villager and ended up having at least half a dozen, most of them bought by other patrons, as Sendy entertained them with increasingly exaggerated recounts of the day's adventure. By the end of the night the casualties in her story included three totaled Ferraris and two dead cows. Arnie was too tipsy to drive her home, so they'd taken a cab back to his place. He vaguely remembered her emerging from the bathroom wearing his T-shirt and crawling under the covers. He tried to remember whether they'd had sex and decided they hadn't. But he was definitely thinking about it now.

Sendy was on her side, facing away from him. He kissed the back of her neck and she sighed, then sleepily reached behind her to touch his penis, which was prodding the base of her spine. He slipped off his shorts and caressed her stomach, while pressing from behind toward the shadowy triangle where the tops of her muscled thighs parted to meet the cheeks of her buttocks. Sendy moaned again, louder this time, then suddenly woke and sat bolt upright.

"What time is it?" she exclaimed.

"About six o'clock," Arnie answered, trying to ease her back on the mattress.

"Oh my God, I'm late! Market open in half-hour, gotta cook breakfast or father kill me! Twenty sausage and biscuit, ten ham and egg biscuit, twenty egg biscuit."

Arnie tried to protest, but she jackrabbited out of bed and disappeared into her jeans and sweater before he could think of a word to say.

"Since when are sausage and biscuit an oriental breakfast?" he finally blurted. "Don't you have fried robin's eggs or something?"

"Ha, ha. Very funny. I tell father and he poison your fortune cookie." She turned and smiled as she went out the door. "You come by for lunch, okay? Free egg roll and Coke. See you then."

Arnie watched her leave and shook his head. He'd been within an inch of getting laid—and she'd stolen his T-shirt. Oh well, he'd been planning to get rid of the shirt anyway and he'd see her at lunch. Then he remembered it was Sunday and the market was closed. And now she was gone. Shit!

He lay back down and slept till noon.

CHAPTER 13

Arnie spent Sunday afternoon working on "Last Night Made My Day." He still wasn't happy with the way it sounded. It occurred to him that he might feel more inspired if he'd been successful in his attempt to have sex with Sendy. But since he didn't know if anything was going on between her and Sam, it was probably good that he hadn't. As he worked on the tune, his mind drifted back to Stefany, and he found himself imagining once again what it would have been like if he'd spent the night with her. He made some changes to the lyric, simplifying it a bit. Then, almost by accident, altered the way he was strumming his guitar during the verses. Inexplicably, the song came together. Not only did both verses sound great now, but the contrast between them and the chorus made the chorus sound even better than it had before.

Pleased, he recorded what he had, then headed for the hospital to check on Vinnie. Starr greeted him at the door of the mechanic's room and he followed her inside. Vinnie was lying in bed with his eyes closed. An attractive red-haired woman in her early forties was sitting by his side and a young boy was playing with a toy Ferrari on the floor. Starr introduced them as Rose and Joseph, Vinnie's wife and son.

"I thought I'd never have to go through this again," Rose said. "Vinnie wrecked at Monte Carlo right after we got married, spent six months in the hospital. That was twenty years ago; he was driving for Alfa at the time."

"But he's going to be okay?" Arnie asked.

"The doctors want to keep him here another day or two," she replied.

"Arnie. . ." Vinnie opened his eyes.

"Hey Vinnie, you're looking good."

"You saved my life."

"No big deal," Arnie answered, "I just glad I drove up when I did."

"I owe you."

Vinnie closed his eyes and Starr took Arnie by the arm and led him toward the door.

"He needs to rest. Everyone so appreciates what you did for him. By the way, I wanted to tell you. Sam flew to L.A. this morning, but he'll be back Friday. Bring him some songs for Stefany, they're recording next week."

"Thanks Starr, I'll do it."

CHAPTER 14

As promised, Starr set up an appointment with Sam the following week. The day dawned crisp and clear, with the leaves beginning to blaze their autumn colors. Arnie was optimistic. He had three new songs, the best of which he felt was "Last Night Made My Day." He arrived to find Starr on the phone, discussing flight reservations to Antigua. She waved him into Sam's office, where he found the producer leaning back in his leather chair with his feet propped on his desk.

"Hey, hero," Sam said, toasting him with a red coffee mug bearing the Ferrari logo. "Everybody's still talking about what you did for Vinnie."

Arnie shrugged. "I just happened to get there first."

"Whatever—you're the one who saved his life,"

"How's he doing?"

"Great, better than that actually. He may make a pile of money from the accident, Carl was insured out the ass, has a seven figure umbrella policy with State Farm." Sam raised his mug again. "Here's to insurance companies. Starr tells me you've got some new songs."

"Yep, three actually," Arnie replied.

"You've been working hard."

Arnie handed him his CD and Sam popped it in his machine. He listened all the way through without saying anything and nodded politely. "Hmm . . . not bad." At the end of the next song, he hit the stop button.

"These are okay," he said, shaking his head. "But they need work. Maybe I should hook you up with a co-writer."

Arnie was perturbed, though, as before, he appreciated the fact that Sam didn't mince words with him. Still, he'd labored all week and had expected a more positive reaction.

"There's one more song," he said. "It's my favorite."

Sam punched the play button and the first notes of "Last Night Made My Day" boomed out of the speakers. Arnie noticed Sam's foot tapping almost imperceptibly in time to the music. But when the song ended he once again shook his head.

"Better . . . but it doesn't quite grab me."

Arnie fidgeted in his seat. Remembering what Sam had said several weeks before about having the courage of his convictions, he decided to voice his feelings. "I spent a lot of time on that one. I think it's the best thing I've written so far. Is there anything specific I could do to improve it?"

"It's got a good rhythm and an interesting guitar part in the chorus, but the lyrics don't do anything for me." Sam hesitated. "It sounds good, but it's not . . . it's just not a very good song."

"It's not a very good song, it just sounds like one?"

Suddenly, the door to the reception area opened behind Arnie and he caught a whiff of familiar perfume.

"If it *sounds* like a good song, maybe it *is* a good song!"

Arnie spun in his seat to catch the delightful sight of Stefany striding into the office. She was wearing a short denim dress accented by a pink straw cowboy hat and looked even prettier than he remembered.

"I was in the reception area talking to Starr," she continued as she brushed past Arnie to Sam's desk. "I heard that song. I'd like to hear it again."

Sam restarted the song. Stefany listened, hand on hip, smiling and tapping her foot all the way through and singing along with the last chorus.

"That's the best song I've heard in a long time," she announced when it ended. "The only reason you don't like it, Sam, is because it's about being in love and that's something you don't know anything about."

Sam sat upright and his feet thumped to the floor.

"Hearing it a second time, I'm inclined to agree with you sweetie," he said. "If you like it, you should consider recording it."

Arnie couldn't believe Sam's abrupt change of demeanor.

"Listen, Arnie," Sam said, rising. "Stef and I have some business matters to discuss. Hope you don't mind if we cut this meeting short."

"Let me walk Arnie out," Stefany said, taking him by the sleeve.

"I've been singing for a long time," she said when they stopped in the foyer. "And I've learned you've got to follow your heart when it comes to songs. If you don't believe in your shit, who else is going to? Opinions are like assholes, everybody's got one. I don't care what Sam thinks, I love that song and I'm going to record it. In fact, I think it may be special enough to get me a record deal."

Arnie stared at her. His initial impression had not changed. She was possibly the most beautiful woman he'd ever seen in his life. He wondered if a demon hid behind her gorgeous exterior as he struggled for words. "I . . . I don't know what to say," he finally mumbled.

"Well, why don't you think about it and meet me for dinner at the Blackstone Brewery tonight at nine. You're a writer—I'm sure you'll think of something to say by then."

CHAPTER 15

At quarter of nine, Arnie arrived at the Blackstone Restaurant and Brewery on West End Avenue. The brewpub appeared to be an industry hangout, and Arnie thought he recognized a few faces from the covers of the CDs he'd studied in New York. After giving his name to the hostess, he managed to snag a stool at the far end of the jammed bar. He ordered one of the establishments hand-crafted beers, which he sipped while people watching and snacking on pretzels and nuts from a basket provided by a husky barmaid with a Skoal ring worn into the back pocket of her Wranglers.

Half an hour later, there was a disturbance at the front of the restaurant and Arnie spotted Stefany. She moved through the crowd of admiring guys at the bar like Moses parting the Red Sea, somehow looking even more alluring than she had that morning. Several of the people she passed tried to engage her in conversation and she politely spoke with each for a few seconds before arriving at Arnie's barstool.

"Song pluggers!" she exclaimed with an exasperated look as he stood to offer her his seat. "They know Sam's doing a project with me and want to pitch me their songs, but not one of them has any idea what I sound like or what kind of material I'm looking for. By the way, you can call me Stef."

"Well, Stef, I appreciate you liking that song of mine."

"Do you have anything else that you think might be good for me?"

"I've got a lot of songs," he replied. "But maybe I should hear you sing first. That way I won't waste your time by pitching something that's not right for you."

"You learn quickly. I told Sam I'd meet him and some other folks downtown later at a club in Printers Alley. Maybe I'll do a number with the band so you'll have a chance to hear me."

Arnie's pager vibrated, and the hostess seated them at a cozy table near the rear of the restaurant. Stef chose grilled salmon with vegetables and Arnie ordered a rib eye steak and another beer to calm his nerves—he was as shaky as a high school kid on a first date.

As they chatted during dinner, he gradually began to feel more at ease. When she asked about his life before coming to Nashville, he gave her an abbreviated version of the death of his parents and stint in the Marines, then stretched the truth a bit by saying he had attended college in the Midwest. It was a cover story suggested by the FBI because he had in fact, as Andy Baxter, attended a creative writing workshop one summer at the University of Iowa and knew enough background information about the area to be convincing if questioned.

He was glad she didn't press him for details about his past and noticed that she, in turn, was somewhat vague about hers. She told him she was an only child, and her father was a wealthy businessman from the Northeast who'd spoiled her since she was a little girl. As an adult, she'd accepted his help in certain areas of her career, such as financing her current recording project. However, she was determined to be successful on her own and had an aggressive booking agent who kept her busy performing at a series of casino and cruise ship gigs. She made a decent living and even had a small fan club, but her heart was set on becoming a star.

"You know, you're different from these people," she said as they finished dinner. "It's like you don't really belong here—you're out of place or something."

Arnie sucked in a quick breath.

"Not to worry, it's a compliment." She laughed. "So many people in the music business are full of shit. They all want something. In my case it's to sleep with me or get me to cut their songs, or whatever. You're different, like a real person. I like that."

Arnie breathed a sigh of relief.

"But you're too quiet," Stef continued. "You're a voyeur, always looking at people, trying to figure them out."

He didn't reply.

"So what do you think of me?" she challenged.

"Well. . ." Arnie thought for a moment. "I'm not sure what to say."

"Try the truth."

"You present a perplexing problem," he finally said with a smile. "Every guy knows that you should tell a smart woman she's beautiful and a beautiful woman she's smart."

"Yes?" Stef said, raising an eyebrow.

"And you're both extraordinarily gorgeous *and* intelligent. That's why I'm speechless around you."

Stef broke into a loud laugh. "No wonder you write good songs!" she exclaimed as the waitress arrived with the check. "I think we're going to get along just fine."

Arnie reached for his wallet, but Stef had already placed an American Express card on the table.

"My treat."

"Thank you."

"Thank you for 'Last Night Made My Day.'"

Check paid, they stood to leave. Stef turned every head in the room as Arnie guided her out of the restaurant with his right hand gently cradling the base of her delectably curved spine. She didn't appear to mind at all.

They drove downtown to Printers Alley, a cluster of a dozen nightclubs located between Third and Fourth Avenues, and found Sam in one of the smaller clubs seated with Vinnie, Carl, Starr, and several new girls who didn't appear to be concerned about being at work by eight o'clock the next morning. Vinnie was wearing a neck brace and seemed to be getting along splendidly with Carl, who was seated beside him.

"Arnie!" Carl exclaimed, standing. "Our hero!"

Vinnie stood and Arnie noticed that, in addition to the neck brace, the mechanic sported a sling cradling his left arm and had an aluminum crutch leaning against his chair. "Arnie, you saved my life last week. Drinks are on me!"

"What's he talking about?" Stef asked.

Carl smiled. "Didn't you hear about the Ferrari Club fiasco?" He pulled a folded copy of the previous week's *Williamson County Review Appeal* newspaper from a pocket of his cashmere sport coat. "Check out the headline, EXOTIC DRIVE ENDS AS LOTUS CRASHES. We made the front page. Look, there's even a picture."

Stef examined the article, shaking her head.

"Here's to the Ferrari Club," Sam said when the drinks arrived. Arnie raised his beer and everyone clicked glasses in a toast as the band onstage began to play.

Arnie's ears perked up; the four-piece group was incredibly tight. The lead guitarist was a hot dog player about Arnie's age with arms so heavily tattooed that he appeared to be wearing a long sleeve blue pullover under his white T-shirt. He rarely looked down to see what his fingers were doing, and the sounds he squeezed from his battered Fender Telecaster and Vibro King Amp were astounding.

When the band took a break, they came over to introduce themselves to Sam and his guests. The lead guitarist's name was Razor, and Arnie told him how much he admired his playing. All the guys wanted to meet Stefany, especially when Sam mentioned that she was in town to record an album he was producing.

"How'd you like to join us for a number?" Razor asked as the group prepared to return to the stage.

"Maybe something by Patsy Cline?"

A few songs into their next set, Razor motioned Stef to come forward. "We've got a special treat for you," he announced. "Let's hear it for Stefany, who's in town working on an album with Sam Solstice."

Stef hopped on the stage to a smattering of applause, then stepped to the microphone as the band broke into the intro of "I Fall to Pieces." When she started to sing, Arnie was pleasantly surprised, then amazed. Sam was right. Stef had a superb voice. She held pitch perfectly throughout the song's rangy melody, and wrung every possible nuance of emotion from the lyric. When she finished, she thanked the band and returned to the table amid rousing applause and whistles from the crowd.

"You were fantastic!" Arnie said as she plopped down in the seat next to him.

"I say you've got a star on your hands," Vinnie announced to Sam.

"We'll see, we'll see," Sam said. "Arnie's written a marvelous song for her."

Arnie felt Stef's hand gently touch his knee and he smiled. He wondered if Sam really liked the song, or if he was just being polite. Then he realized it didn't matter.

"Thanks," he said with a smile, raising his drink in a toast. "All we need is a great producer like you Sam, and with a little luck we'll have a hit record."

The group laughed in agreement and raised their glasses.

After a few more songs Stef leaned over and said, "I've got to be up early tomorrow, can you drive me back to my hotel?"

"Sure," Arnie said. "Let me run to the restroom." He was washing his hands when Vinnie hobbled in and leaned his aluminum crutch by the wall.

Vinnie winked. "Insurance company," he said as he walked to the urinal without a trace of a limp.

"I see."

"I owe you one, my friend. I could have burned to death last week. Not a good way to die."

"You would have done the same for me," Arnie said, trying to block the thought of how close he had come to a fiery death himself a few months before.

"Someday I'll pay you back, you'll see."

"Well I hope I don't have to be trapped in a car wreck first," Arnie said with a forced laugh.

"Let me tell you something," Vinnie said, his face turning serious. "That girl Stefany, be careful with her."

"Pretty girls are always dangerous; I've had my heart broken before."

"Just don't break hers."

"What do you mean?"

"Be careful, that's all I gotta say."

"I couldn't imagine hurting her," Arnie said, realizing just how true it was.

"That's good," Vinnie slapped Arnie's back with his good arm. "Good for her, good for you. So when are you going to write a song about the Ferrari Club?"

"I didn't know you could put a Ferrari in a country song. I thought country songs had to be about pickup trucks and tractors. You know, how it's better to be poor and miserable than rich and happy, as long as you love Mama, NASCAR and the American flag."

Vinnie laughed and they walked back to the table. Arnie and Stef said goodnight to the group, then headed toward Music Row, careful to stay a few miles per hour below the speed limit to avoid the attention of the swarming motorcycle cops preying on patrons leaving the downtown bars. Ten minutes later, he pulled into the circular drive of Loews Vanderbilt Plaza hotel.

"Thanks for a nice evening," she said, kissing him lightly on the cheek. "I'll be recording all week, probably working late," she continued. "But I'd like to see you again before I leave town. Maybe Thursday night?"

"I'd love to."

"Call me Thursday." She opened her purse and handed him a card with her number. In a flash of perfume and heels, she was gone.

CHAPTER 16

The next few days passed slowly. Arnie didn't want to pester Starr about whether Stef had recorded his song, but it was hard to fight the urge to call the office. On Thursday afternoon he still hadn't heard anything, and decided it was time to call Stef. He was about to dial her number when the phone rang.

"Hi, it's me, Stef."

"Hey, I was just about to call you," Arnie said.

"I've only got a sec, but I wanted you to know that we cut tracks for your song this morning—it turned out great. I'm getting ready to do the vocal."

"Wow," Arnie answered. "That's wonderful."

"Can you meet me for a drink later tonight, maybe around midnight in the bar downstairs at my hotel?"

"Sure," Arnie answered, and the phone clicked dead.

* * *

Arnie arrived at the hotel at eleven forty-five and nursed a beer in the lounge until Stef arrived at almost one o'clock. She looked tired, but stunning as ever in a black fleece workout outfit.

"I'm so glad you're still here," she said, as she took a seat on the stool next to his.

"Of course I'm still here," he said. "I'd have waited longer."

"Only if a prettier girl didn't walk into the bar," she replied.

"Since you're the prettiest girl in Nashville, you don't have to worry."

"I see you haven't lost that songwriter's charm. Your song turned out quite well, by the way. I got the engineer at the studio to burn a rough mix that I can play for you."

"Sure," Arnie said, thrilled.

"We'll have to do it soon though, I'm totally fried," she said. "I've got a CD player in my room."

Arnie paid the tab and followed her to the elevator. On the ride up, she slumped against him and closed her eyes, and he put his arm around her. Once in her room, she inserted a CD in a portable player on the dresser and handed him earphones. Arnie stared out the hotel window at the Nashville skyline as his song began. It sounded fantastic. Even though the volume levels of the instruments weren't perfectly balanced, he could tell that the arrangement was spectacular. And Stef had done an incredible job singing it. When the song was over, he played it again. He'd always dreamed of hearing his music on the radio, and his dream was in the process of coming true. And it was all because of Stef, nothing short of a dream come true herself. He turned and was surprised to see her on the hotel bed behind him with her eyes closed, already fast asleep.

Arnie slipped off her shoes and drew the comforter over her. She stirred and reached for his hand, and murmured so softly he could barely hear, "Stay with me."

He unlaced his shoes and slid under the comforter by her side. Stef rolled over and pressed her back against him. She purred, "Thank you," then drifted back to sleep. Arnie stroked her hair and stared past her at the lights of Music City. He wondered what the future might hold for him, but wasn't worried.

Tonight, he couldn't imagine anywhere he'd rather be.

CHAPTER 17

Arnie woke to the sound of the shower coming from the bathroom. He lay quietly in the dim gray light of first dawn, slowly recalling the prior evening until Stef emerged from the bathroom dressed in jeans and a cream-colored sweater.

"I've got a plane to catch at seven-thirty," she said, pressing her lips to his forehead. "Sleep as long as you'd like. If you're hungry, call room service—everything's taken care of. Thanks for staying with me last night."

Arnie reached to pull her closer, but there was a knock on the door. Stef quickly kissed him again, then stood to admit a hotel porter who piled her substantial stack of luggage on a rolling cart. She turned and flashed Arnie one last smile, then was gone.

* * *

Several hours later, Arnie strolled into Solstice Productions, walking on air. Starr greeted him with a huge smile.

"Sam played me the tracks he cut on Stefany. Your song came out great."

"Thanks," Arnie said. "I heard it last night; I'm really stoked."

"There's still quite a bit of work to do, overdubs and mixing, but I must say I haven't seen him this excited in a while."

The door opened and Sam breezed in.

"Your song turned out fantastic," he announced. "I just had lunch with an A&R buddy of mine and was telling him about it."

"A&R?" Arnie asked.

"Artist and repertoire, the division of a record label that signs acts and finds material for them."

"Did you play him Stef's project?" Arnie asked.

"No, I decided to wait. You have to approach A&R people in a certain way. There's an art to it—they're not as smart as you'd think."

"Really?"

"There's an old story about two A&R guys who pass each other in the hallway of a record company, one is listening on his iPod to an album an artist on the label had just turned in. The second guy asks him if it's any good, and the first guy says 'I don't know, I haven't played it for anyone yet.'"

Arnie laughed.

Sam continued, "Until a record's a hit it's just another song, worthless one day, worth a million the next. I've got a feeling I have something special with Stef and I'm laying the groundwork with a few people now, but I don't want to take a chance on anyone hearing anything less than the finished product."

"Well I know that *I love* what I've heard," Starr said.

"Let's keep our fingers crossed."

CHAPTER 18

The cool fall weather that arrived in Nashville the following weekend gave Arnie a surge of energy, and he threw himself into his work. The thrill of having his first song recorded boosted his confidence; it was hard evidence that he just might be able to make a living as a songwriter. He thought about the strange combination of events that had brought him to Nashville and the struggles he'd experienced with his band in New York, and he couldn't believe his good luck. He was looking forward to meeting Bubba Jones on Monday, though he was a bit nervous since it would be his first attempt at co-writing.

He arrived at Bubba's publishing company at ten a.m. It was located in a renovated older house a block from Sam's building. Bubba met him at the door and started to introduce him to the receptionist. It wasn't necessary.

"Arnieee!"

Arnie looked past Bubba to see Sendy sitting at the front desk wearing wire rim glasses and a long embroidered dress. She looked quite professional.

"Sendy! What are you doing here?"

"New job, baby."

"Who's cooking the egg rolls and sausage and biscuits for your father?"

"Yours truly. I go in early, then come to work here with Bubba," she said.

"I hope you didn't bring your father's jokes with you."

"No, I get fired for sure." Sendy winked. "You guys write big hit today."

Arnie followed Bubba upstairs. His tiny office was furnished with a worn couch, scuffed wooden table, and a Wurlitzer electric piano that looked old enough to have been on the road with Elvis.

As they tuned their guitars, Arnie mentioned that Stef had recorded "Last Night Made My Day." Bubba seemed impressed with the tune when Arnie played it for him, and chuckled at the story of how Stef had come to record it—especially Sam's initial statement that it wasn't a very good song, it just sounded like one. Then Bubba played Arnie a couple of songs he'd completed recently.

"Those are all great. Did you co-write them?" Arnie asked.

"Yep," Bubba replied. "I've written a fair number of songs by myself, but sometimes it's fun to sit down with a buddy because you can come up with something you'd never have thought of on your own."

"I'm new to the process," Arnie said. "In fact, I don't know where to start."

"Let's just toss a few ideas around. If we find one we both like, great. If not, we'll go get a good lunch. Here are a couple of things I've been working on." He played a piece of a melody, then a part of a chorus. "Do you have anything started?"

Arnie strummed his guitar and played Bubba a fragment of a song he'd begun the previous week. Bubba slid over to the piano and started playing along. The big songwriter's stubby fingers picked up on his chord progression and added a bass line that gave it a cool groove and brought the melody to life.

"That's pretty," Arnie said.

"Naw," Bubba chuckled. "It's not pretty, it just sounds that way."

A light bulb went off in Arnie's head.

"What if we used that for a title," he said. "But changed it so it was about a girl? Something like: 'She Ain't Pretty, She Just Looks That Way.'"

"Hmm . . . you might have something there."

Bubba altered the rhythm of the chords he was playing slightly so that it fit the cadence of the words. He appeared to be lost in thought, then said, "Except, I don't know if a girl, or woman, would want to hear that. They buy most of the records, you know. Could a girl sing that about a guy? Like, he ain't pretty, he just looks that way?" Bubba picked up his guitar and strummed the chords he'd been playing on the piano, and sang the title over them. Then he went back to the piano, hit a new chord and laughed. "That was an accident, but it'd be a cool way to start the chorus."

"Yeah, it might," Arnie said, picking an arpeggio pattern on his guitar that complimented what Bubba was playing. They played the chord progression together and tossed lyrics back and forth. Before long, they had finished a verse and chorus.

Bubba smiled. "Okay, let's try it from the beginning and record it so we can see what we've got." They sang it through, then listened back. It sounded great, and only somewhat resembled the original song Arnie had started.

"That's cool," Arnie said. "The chorus sounds like it's going to modulate to a different key, but it doesn't really—that's a unique way to have it stand out from the verse. I never would have thought of that on my own."

"I'm not sure if it's any good, maybe it just sounds that way," Bubba said with a straight face.

"Right!" Arnie replied with a laugh.

"I'm about ready for lunch. How 'bout you?"

"Sure."

They left the office and walked a few blocks to a nearby sandwich shop, discussing the second verse along the way. Arnie had the sense that he'd learned a lot in the past few hours, though he couldn't put his finger on what it was. When they returned to the office, they connected the bits and pieces of lyrics he'd scribbled into a passable second verse and recorded the song from the beginning. Bubba went downstairs to dub a copy and Arnie packed his guitar and met him in the reception area.

"Here you go," Bubba said, handing Arnie his copy. "I enjoyed getting together. We'll have to do it again soon."

"I'd love to. I really like this song—I'll play it for Sam and let you know what he thinks."

"By the way," Bubba said. "There's a great band playing at Tootsies on Sunday night, I think you'd enjoy hearing them."

"Tootsies?"

"Tootsies Orchid Lounge. It's downtown on Broadway."

"I'll try to make it," Arnie said. As he headed out the door, he added, "See ya later, Sendy."

"So long, Arnie. Come back soon!"

CHAPTER 19

Arnie stopped by the office on his way home to play Sam his new song.

"Not bad," the producer said. "You wrote that with Bubba Jones?"

"Yeah, it's my first attempt to co-write."

"You guys should keep working together. When you've got a few more songs like this we can think about setting up a demo session. Speaking of sessions, I'll be in the studio Wednesday working on Stef's tracks. Why don't you meet me at nine at the Pancake Pantry for breakfast?"

"I'd love to."

Starr stuck her head in the door. "Hey, Sam, don't you need to head out to the airport to pick up Bobbie? You don't want to be late, she's got a temper, and she could kick your ass."

"You're right," Sam replied.

"Who's Bobbie?" Arnie asked.

"Bobbie Valentine, a female wrestler from Syracuse," Starr said. "Did you know that one of Sam's hobbies is managing lady wrestlers?"

Arnie started to laugh, then realized Starr was serious. "Her name's Bobbie Valentine?"

"Yeah, but she might need to change it to Busty Valentine after the boob job he bought her last month."

"I can't wait to see my investment," Sam said. "Want to ride to the airport with me Arnie?"

"Sure," Arnie replied, incredulous. There had to be a song in this somewhere.

He followed Sam outside to a white Toyota Land Cruiser.

"Is this yours, too?"

"Yeah, I drive it when it rains or the Ferraris are in the shop."

When they reached Broadway, Arnie expected Sam to turn right toward the interstate, but he turned left instead.

"We've got to run by my condo and pick up Nicole first. Her flight leaves at six," Sam explained.

"Nicole?"

"She's a girlfriend of mine from New Mexico. Be careful not to mention Bobbie."

After driving several miles down West End Avenue, Sam turned into an upscale residential neighborhood and approached an elegant two-story town home at the end of a cul-de-sac. A striking auburn-haired woman who bore a remarkable resemblance to a Victoria's Secret model who had often frequented Arnie's fantasies was standing by the open front door with several suitcases.

They pulled to a stop, and Arnie jumped out to help Sam load the luggage into the Toyota's cargo area.

"Nicole, this is Arnie," Sam said. "He's a new writer I just signed."

"Nice to meet you," she said, flashing Arnie a bright smile as she slid onto the leather seat.

"Nicole's from Santa Fe," Sam said as he pulled out of the condo's driveway and guided the Land Cruiser down West End. "She's a nutritionist at a spa I visited there a few years ago."

"I also do some modeling," Nicole added.

"In Santa Fe?" Arnie asked.

"Wherever my agency sends me."

"I can see why," Arnie said. It was difficult not to compliment her. Nicole appeared to be in her early-thirties, but there wasn't a line on her face and she had the sculpted figure of an aerobics instructor or an NFL cheerleader.

"You may have seen her picture in a Victoria's Secret catalogue or two," Sam added.

Arnie gulped and did a double take. He couldn't believe it—it was the same girl!

"I thought you looked familiar," he finally said. "But you're even prettier than your pictures." It was true.

"Well, thank you, Arnie," Nicole said. "He's quite the charmer, isn't he, Sam?"

"No, just observant," Sam replied. "You're the most beautiful woman I know."

"Oh Sam, I'm sure that's what you tell all the girls." Nicole smiled in spite of herself.

"Only you, Sweetie."

On the drive to the airport, Arnie learned that Nicole and Sam had been seeing each other for several years and had plans to vacation together in Palm Springs in December. When they arrived at the terminal, Sam followed signs to the facility's upper departure level, and pulled to a stop in the passenger drop off lane. He activated the SUV's emergency flashers, and with Arnie's help, loaded Nicole's luggage onto a cart provided by a skycap and tipped him.

"Sorry I can't walk you inside, but I'm due back in the studio," Sam said. "Give me a call tonight to let me know you got back safely. Leave a message if I'm still working and you get my voicemail."

"Okay, baby," Nicole answered, standing on her tiptoes to kiss him. "I can't wait for Palm Springs."

Arnie reclaimed the front passenger seat and turned to Sam as the Land Cruiser pulled away from the curb. "A real Victoria's Secret model. Holy shit!"

Sam grinned and guided the SUV back into the traffic flow leaving the airport. Arnie saw the interstate entrance looming ahead and was about to ask Sam if he'd forgotten about picking up Bobbie, when the producer shifted lanes and took a hard left turn onto the ramp leading back toward the terminal. He followed signs to the lower arrival level where Arnie spotted a tall, hefty girl with a long mane of brown ringlets standing by the curb. As they approached, Arnie realized that she wasn't chubby at all—the enormous breasts under her windbreaker gave that impression.

"Damn!" Arnie said. "So that's Bobbie? You knew she'd be waiting down here when you dropped Nicole off upstairs? I thought you said you had to get back to the studio?"

"Someone, I think it was George Bernard Shaw, once said that any man who doesn't tell a woman an occasional lie couldn't possibly have any respect for her feelings. Besides, I do have to get back to the studio—eventually. But it's just to see how the overdubs are going. Once we cut the tracks, I let my engineer do most of the work. I come back and check on things now and then. It's helpful to me to take a break and have fresh ears. Of course, I'm always there when we do the important overdubs and final mixes."

They pulled to the curb and Arnie switched seats again.

"Girl, you look great!" Sam said as Bobbie stepped in the vehicle.

"What do you think?" she asked. Unzipping her windbreaker, she thrust her chest forward and jiggled her boobs through her sweater.

"Awesome," Sam exclaimed. "You're the most beautiful woman I've ever known. Now you're even more gorgeous."

She beamed and turned to Arnie. "Hi, I'm Bobbie."

"I'm Arnie."

"You like?" she said, continuing to shake her breasts.

"I love!"

As Sam pulled away from the curb, Arnie snuck a glance to the rear to check for Nicole. Evidently, she was safely on her flight, or at least inside the terminal. When he turned back Bobbie was on her knees on the front seat facing Sam with her sweater, blouse and bra pulled up around her neck and two gargantuan breasts the size of swollen cantaloupes swaying between the dashboard and front seatback.

"So, how do you like my babies?"

Arnie's jaw dropped.

"Shit, Bobbie!" Sam said. "They look good to me, but be careful, people can see you!"

"That's why I got them. You'll get to give them a closer look later, Sam," Bobbie said, spinning around in the seat to face Arnie and using both hands to lift her breasts over the headrest and present them for his examination. "How 'bout you, Arnie, what do you think?"

Suddenly, there was a squeal of tires followed by an ear-splitting screech of metal on metal outside the vehicle as a black Mercedes in the adjacent lane swerved into the guardrail to its right. "Bobbie, pull your fucking shirt down!" Sam yelled, jerking the Toyota's steering wheel to the left.

Instead of doing as Sam said, Bobbie spun around to the passenger window and flattened her boobs against the glass, giving the Mercedes' driver one last look as Sam accelerated onto the interstate ramp.

"Might as well give him his money's worth. That bodywork's going to cost him a lot of dough," Bobbie said with what appeared to be genuine concern. "I hope he was wearing his seatbelt." She scooped her breasts back into her bra and smoothed her sweater as she settled into her seat.

"So, you're a wrestler, Bobbie?" Arnie asked once they were safely cruising west on I-40.

"Yeah, I skate with a hockey team up in Syracuse, too. I like violence, anything with violence."

"And what's your schedule while you're here?" Sam asked.

"Tonight I'm all yours. Tomorrow I'll be filming with Trixie all day, then wrestling in Bowling Green. You're going to manage, right?"

"Of course," Sam replied.

"You're filming something?" Arnie asked. "Working on a music video?"

"Something like that," Sam said, interrupting abruptly. "Hey, where do you want to have dinner tonight?"

"I'm feeling more tired than hungry, after my flight and all," Bobbie said, reaching to pinch Sam's earlobe. "I was thinking me and my babies could use a nap. Interested?

"I wouldn't miss it for the world."

When they got back to Music Row, Sam and Bobbie dropped Arnie off at the office. He drove back to his apartment, wondering how he could work the afternoon's events into a song. He finally decided it would be a waste of time, no one would believe it if he did. All he knew for sure was that Sam's evening would be a lot more fun than his.

CHAPTER 20

Arnie arrived at the Pancake Pantry the next morning and found Sam at a window table reading a copy of *The Tennessean*, Nashville's morning newspaper.

"How's Bobbie?" Arnie asked after ordering.

"Great! That girl's something else," Sam replied with a big grin. "She's filming again today, then flying back to Syracuse in the morning. But she'll be back in a couple of months for a match in Nashville."

"You said she's filming, is she an actress, too?"

"Not exactly, nothing that fancy. She and a couple of other girls from the gym where I train do topless wrestling videos; soft porn, I guess you could call it. Sometimes rich guys hire them to put on private demonstrations, too. They make good money. Wish someone would pay me to get naked and roll around on the floor with a pretty girl."

"Me, too!"

"I've never seen any of the videos myself, but there's a website where you can check them out." He wrote the URL on a napkin and handed it to Arnie.

"I'll have to do that," Arnie said. "But right now I can't wait to get to the recording studio."

After finishing their meal, they headed into the sunshine where Sam's red 430 was parked.

"It's a great country, isn't it?" Sam said as they got in the Ferrari, ". . . where a man can have as many mistresses as he can afford and get to spend his days doing what he loves, making hit records!"

After a short drive they arrived at a two story brick building on Music Row. Arnie followed Sam inside and was surprised to find that the structure's unassuming exterior housed a labyrinth of tastefully decorated recording, overdubbing and mixing rooms. As they walked through the facility, Sam described the differences between the studios. The largest featured a spacious forty by fifty-foot recording area with twenty-foot ceilings. Arnie listened as Sam snapped his fingers and clapped his hands to demonstrate the acoustics. Adjacent to the recording area, and separated from it by a large triple-glazed glass window, was a control room housing a twelve-foot long recording console and numerous pieces of electronic outboard equipment mounted in angled cabinets. Although obviously designed to be functional workspaces, both rooms were decorated in subdued earth tone fabrics and polished hardwood trim that gave them an inviting, almost seductive, quality.

"This is where we recorded Stef's project," Sam explained. "The console's a vintage Neve, my favorite brand for tracking. He pointed to several cozy glass-walled rooms on the perimeter of the main recording area. "We normally put the singer and acoustic instruments in those booths. The musicians can all see each other and communicate through headphones, but they're acoustically separated so if one of them makes a mistake or wants to replace a part, we can fix it without re-doing everything else."

"Wow," Arnie exclaimed. "It's like what I do on my little four-track machine, but on a much grander scale."

"It's exactly like that, with a lot more options—sometimes too many," Sam said, leading the way to a smaller studio down the hall. The second facility had a similar control room, but a much smaller recording area, about twenty feet square. "This is where we do overdubs. The recording area is smaller, because we're usually working with only one or two players at a time. But the dimensions of the control room are the same as the first studio, so the acoustical monitoring environment is identical."

Just then a shaggy haired fellow in his early forties with a laptop computer under his arm entered the control room. He was wearing blue jeans and a T-shirt with a large red circle on the back and ZERO printed across the front.

"Arnie, this is Zero Taylor. He engineered Stef's tracks."

"Good to meet you, man," Zero said. He shook hands with Arnie, then settled into a swivel chair behind the console and began plugging cables from its patch bay into his computer.

"Nice to meet you, too. I heard one of the tracks you guys cut on Stefany last week, it sounded wonderful."

"She's a super talented chick. Makes my job easy."

"Zero's too modest," Sam said. "His ears are so good he can hear bugs walk. Tell Arnie how you got your nickname."

Zero pointed to a pair of large meters on the console. These are called VU meters, VU stands for volume units. Zero is the maximum level you can record at before you run the risk of distorting the signal. When I record, I try to cut everything as hot as possible, keep all the needles right up at zero VU, so the tracks go down at maximum level. It's a throwback to the analog days when tape hiss was a problem. But I still keep those needles vibrating right at zero, that way my records sound *loud*!"

"It's like driving a Ferrari," Sam said. "The higher the rpm, the more horsepower and torque. Aim for the red line on the tach and watch out!"

"Which one are we starting with today, Sam?" Zero asked when he was satisfied that his computer was interfaced properly.

"'Last Night Made My Day.' First I want to check some things on Stef's vocal, then we'll do guitar overdubs."

Arnie's song began to play and he watched, fascinated, as Zero's hands flew over the hundreds of knobs and faders on the mixing board's surface to bring the instruments up in volume and adjust the balances between them. The track sounded incredible, even though it was playing very softly through a pair of small speakers set on top of the console. When it reached the end, Zero restarted the tune, and the sliding fader knobs moved up and down on their own accord, remembering the moves he'd programmed.

"What we're doing now is getting up a rough mix so we can hear what kind of background the vocal will have," Sam explained. Arnie couldn't hear much difference as Sam and Zero manipulated the controls through another playback; it all sounded tremendous. When Sam was happy, Zero brought Stef's vocal up in the mix.

Sam explained that Stef had sung the song half a dozen times, and he and Zero painstakingly played the different performances over and over, section by section, and chose what they felt was the best version of each phrase from the several takes available. Then they merged the chosen pieces onto a single track. They encountered several small intonation problems where Stef had sung slightly sharp or flat, and Zero fiddled with his laptop and magically brought them into tune. The laborious process took several hours, but Sam finally was satisfied.

"Let's give Arnie the LFP," Sam said.

"What's that?" Arnie asked.

"The Loud Fucking Playback," Sam replied. "When we work, we listen softly so our ears don't get burnt. But when we're done, it's nice to blast it through the big speakers."

Zero cranked up the volume and switched to the large monitors mounted in the room's front wall, then started the song from the beginning. Arnie was blown away. Stef's vocal sounded sensational. The various pieces combined perfectly into what appeared to be one fluid performance belted out spontaneously on a concert stage.

"I didn't realize you could do all that in the studio."

"Now you know why so many live acts sound like shit in concert compared to their records," Zero said.

"Zero is so good he could even make a Yankee like you sound country," Sam piped up. "He's got a plug-in for the Pro Tools software we're recording with called a *Ruralizer*."

"Really?" Arnie asked, puzzled.

"It can turn a New England twang into a Texas drawl," Zero said. "It's so smart it automatically changes 'are not' to 'ain't,' and 'you guys' to 'y'all.'"

Arnie shook his head, and Zero and Sam burst out laughing. "We're pulling your leg. Things aren't quite that advanced yet, but I'll bet someone's working on it as we speak!"

They took a short break and walked down the hall to the studio's lounge for a cup of coffee.

"What's next to finish the record?" Arnie asked.

"We'll do some electric guitar overdubs this afternoon, and I'll add some strings later in the week before I mix," Sam said. "Sweetening a track is like painting a school bus with a Q-Tip—it's detailed work, but can be a lot of fun."

"It's fascinating to watch you and Zero work—the concentration level and all. Isn't it hard to focus on each individual part, and at the same time not lose sight of what the final product will sound like?"

"You hit the nail on the head," Sam said. "I try to keep an eye on the big picture. My job as a producer comes down to capturing a performance and getting something on CD that people can relate to emotionally. It's the same with songwriting. lot of work can go into perfecting a song, getting every word right and so forth, but you've got to create something that touches people's hearts."

They finished their coffee and returned to the studio. Sitting in the control room was a very skinny man about Arnie's age, and he was removing an electric guitar from a frayed tweed case.

"Looks like my old Stratocaster," Arnie said. "What year is it?"

"It's a '59," the guitarist replied, standing and extending his hand to Arnie. "Robb Lawson."

"Nice to meet you. I'm Arnie Fortune."

Robb plugged his guitar cord into a stack of blinking sound processing equipment by his side and Zero adjusted the console's controls to raise the guitar's volume in the control room speakers.

"Just play what you feel," Sam said as the song started.

Sam liked most of what Robb came up with, but had him try several alternate approaches to the tune, stopping him occasionally to make a suggestion or hum a fragment of melody. Robb incorporated Sam's ideas into his accompaniment and Arnie was again struck by the deep concentration level of everyone involved. The three men laughed and joked as they worked, all while making critical decisions involving musical nuances almost too subtle for him to hear.

After an hour, Sam was satisfied and ordered another "LFP."

"What's next chief?" Robb asked.

"There's one more song that needs some electric on it," Sam said.

"Which one?" Zero asked.

"'Love Drops,'" Sam said, getting to his feet. "But I'll leave it with you guys to finish on your own. Just use your judgment, Robb."

Arnie followed Sam outside after thanking Zero and Robb for their hard work on his tune.

"So you're going to let them finish the next song by themselves?" Arnie asked Sam as they got into the Ferrari.

"They're pros. They can handle it."

"But you were so picky about 'Last Night Made My Day.'"

"Yeah, that's because your song has a chance of being a hit. 'Love Drops' is a piece of crap. It's got a good beat, but the lyrics are idiotic. The only reason I cut it on Stef is that it's published by a guy named Buzz Corbin who runs one of the record labels we're going to pitch her to. It'll help her get a deal if he owns a song on the album. You know, I scratch his back and he scratches mine."

"That makes sense," Arnie replied.

"I should have everything finished and mixed by the end of the week." Sam said as they arrived back at Arnie's car. "I'll let you know what kind of reaction I get."

"Thanks again for letting me watch you work."

"Thanks for the song."

Arnie was elated as he drove to his apartment. When he arrived, his good day got even better. The voicemail light on his phone was blinking with a message from Stef saying she'd be in town in a few days and hoped he'd be available for dinner on Tuesday. He fell asleep feeling excited and content. For once in his life, he was doing exactly what he wanted to do. He knew he had a lot of hard work ahead, but it was work he loved doing and the opportunity to do it was a dream come true. Most of all, he knew he wanted to spend a lot more days just as he'd spent today.

CHAPTER 21

The sound of loud knocking on Arnie's apartment door roused him at seven the next morning. He rolled out of bed, pulled on his jeans and a T-shirt as he stumbled to unlock the deadbolt.

"Hey, songwriter!"

FBI Agent Baskins shouldered past him into the living room.

"You don't want me to spend any more time than I have to on your doorstep, do you?" Baskins said. "Got coffee?"

"Well, sure . . . hang on a minute," Arnie muttered groggily. He started toward the kitchen, then spun back to face Baskins. "What the hell you doing here?"

"Just checking on things—haven't heard from you."

"Haven't you been talking to Sam?"

"We have minimal contact with Sam Solstice. I thought you knew that."

"No."

"We run Witness Protection like Al-Qaida runs its terrorist cells—the less each individual knows, the better. That way if one person is compromised, there's minimum damage to the others."

"Well, I'm doing fine," Arnie said, disturbed by the reference to the terrorist organization. "I thought the idea of the Witness Protection Program was that I start a new life and leave the old one behind."

Baskins frowned. Arnie noticed that he hadn't lost the tic in his right eyebrow.

"Mind if I smoke?"

"Hang on, I'll get an ashtray." He pulled a saucer from the cupboard and handed it to the agent. "Is something wrong?"

Baskins didn't answer at once. "I'm . . . we're not sure."

"What do you mean 'not sure'?"

"Well . . . there may be a problem, your new identity may have been . . ." Baskins hesitated, ". . . compromised."

"*What?*" Arnie exclaimed.

"We have a tap on Roberto Puccini's home phone. Your name came up a few days ago."

"My old name or my new name?"

"The new one. We only picked up part of the conversation—the connection was bad. We heard Don Puccini say: '. . . his name is Arnie Fortune.'" Baskins hesitated. "Then we lost the signal—the other party was on a mobile phone. Must have gone into a tunnel or something. So we don't know what they were talking about."

"I thought you said I'd be safe here!"

"Calm down. You probably are. The Don didn't sound upset. And, realistically, if they were discussing a hit, I doubt he'd be talking on his home phone. I'm sure he knows we've got it tapped."

"And you have no idea what the conversation was about?"

"No. Like I said, the connection was bad. It's possible there's another Arnie Fortune somewhere. But the Bureau thought it'd be a good idea to send me down. You haven't noticed anything funny or suspicious?"

"No, but I'm starting to get suspicious now—suspicious of you."

"Your safety is our first priority. I'm here, aren't I? I flew down to give you a heads up and a chance to bail out of Nashville right now."

Arnie thought for a moment. The past two months had been the best of his life.

"What if I don't want to leave?"

"You like it here that much?"

"Yeah, I've had a song recorded by this girl. . ." Arnie paused, hesitant to mention Stef's name. If he were forced to leave town, he might want to see her again. "A girl recorded a song of mine. I don't know if anything'll come of it."

"Well, it's your decision," Baskins said. "You can stay if you want, but keep on your toes. In fact, it might not be a bad idea if you were to take a little vacation, if you get the chance."

"I'll think about it."

"Good." Baskins pulled a small black object from his pocket. It was about half the size of a cigarette pack and looked similar to an electronic pager. "Keep this with you. It looks enough like a regular beeper to fool people, but it's really a PLB, a GPS enabled Personal Locator Beacon—satellite based, so it works anywhere in the world. Hold down the small button on the side and press the big button on the front if you're in trouble. It'll transmit an alarm with your exact location and we'll get to you ASAP."

"That makes me feel a little better." Arnie tried to keep the sarcasm out of his voice.

"And memorize this." Baskins handed him a card with a Hotmail email address and a password. "Make sure not to access this from your own computer or from Solstice's office. We have to be careful about cookies and shit that could help someone locate you. Check it every few days at a coffee shop or something. We'll let you know if anything comes up that you need to worry about."

"Okay, I'll do that," Arnie said, taking the card.

"Good. I'm out of here," Baskins said, stubbing out his smoke in the saucer and heading for the door. "Keep the beeper with you, and don't hesitate to use it if you even *think* there's a problem. We'll get you out of here and back to the real world as quick as we can."

Arnie pulled back the window curtain and watched Baskins drive off. I'll be back in grad school studying dead authors instead of writing songs, he thought. Nashville *was* the real world, more real than anything he'd ever known. He was determined not to let his new life be snatched away.

CHAPTER 22

Arnie spent the next few days trying to work on his songs, though it was difficult to concentrate after Baskins's visit. Bubba called on Saturday to remind him of their plan to meet at Tootsies the following night, and he drove downtown at nine, grateful for the diversion. Though it was Sunday, the club was packed. After shaking hands with Bubba and giving Sendy a hug, he ordered a round of beers. When the longnecks arrived, he chugged his and waved at the barmaid for another. He couldn't get Baskins's warning off his mind.

"So this is Tootsies?" Arnie said, working on his second beer and examining the club's ancient walls, which were covered with a half-century of autographs, publicity photos and dusty album covers.

"Yeah," Bubba replied. "It's been here forever. The back door upstairs opens onto an alley right across from the stage entrance to the Ryman Auditorium, original home of the Grand Ole Opry. Stars like Hank Williams and Marty Robbins used to slip over here for drinks between performances."

"These old songs sound good," Arnie said, gesturing to the three-piece band onstage, whose repertoire consisted mostly of country standards by traditional artists such as George Jones and Merle Haggard. Every now and then they snuck in an original tune or a rocker like Lynyrd Skynyrd's "Sweet Home Alabama."

"Yeah, they sure do," Bubba replied. "Country music's changed a lot through the years, but it always reflects what's going on in America at the time."

"Is this the group you were telling me about?"

"Nope, they're playing upstairs."

"What are they called?"

"The Appalachian Hellcats," Sendy piped up.

"Cool name for a band. Let's check them out."

Arnie followed Bubba and Sendy up a staircase at the rear of the club to another equally crowded bar on the second floor. On their way to the front of the room, they squeezed by three couples decked in full cowboy and cowgirl regalia. The women were dressed in elaborately embroidered skirts and blouses, and the men wore chaps and sported tooled leather gun belts complete with what appeared to be authentic replicas of pearl handled six shooters. They all wore wide-brimmed cowboy hats and were talking in a language that sounded like some kind of Scandinavian dialect.

Once past the foreign tourists and their hats, Arnie was able to get a view of the stage and the Appalachian Hellcats. The group consisted of two girl singers playing acoustic guitar and mandolin, and three male musicians playing bass, electric guitar and drums. Arnie recognized the electric guitarist by his heavily tattooed forearms, and recalled that his name was Razor—they'd met at the club in Printers Alley. The girl who sang most of the lead vocals was an attractive, if well fed, redhead with a gravelly voice. The crowd was going crazy. The Hellcats weren't as polished as the group playing downstairs, but they made up for it with their energy and the fact that their original songs were great.

When the band finished their set, Bubba brought Arnie and Sendy up to the stage and introduced them to the lead singer, whose name was Sarah, then to the rest of the band.

"I met you with Sam Solstice, didn't I?" Razor asked. "Don't you write for his company?"

"Yeah, I sure do," Arnie replied. "Speaking of writing, I liked the originals you guys played."

"Most of them are mine. I wrote a few myself, and five with Sarah."

"Good tunes," Arnie said.

"Do you do much co-writing?"

"I'm new to it, co-wrote my first song with Bubba last week."

"Maybe we could get together and give it a shot sometime—any plans for breakfast tomorrow?"

"Nope."

"Why don't you meet me at Noshville, say around ten. We could toss a few ideas around."

"Sure."

When Razor returned to the stage to start their next set, Arnie turned to Bubba. "There sure are a lot of talented people in Nashville, aren't there?"

"Yeah," Bubba replied, "but there's only room for ten songs in the top ten. The competition is fierce. That's why you're so lucky to have a song recorded by Stefany. Shit, man, you've only been in town since September."

"She doesn't have a record deal or anything yet."

"Yeah, but Sam wouldn't be working with her if she didn't have a good shot at one. Of course, it may take a while. But you've got your draw to keep you from starving to death in the meantime. That's half the battle in this business, just staying alive."

Arnie had been happily distracted for the last few hours, but Bubba's reference to staying alive brought back his worries about Don Puccini. Almost on cue, his ears imploded with the deafening report of a gunshot immediately behind him. It was followed in quick succession by two more bangs, then a third. He spun to see one of the Western-clad tourists holding a smoking six-shooter. Another was slumped against a wall and in the process of pulling his gun from its holster. The wounded man took faltering aim and fired twice as he slid to the floor. The standing cowboy's body jerked backward as if he'd been kicked by a mule, and he dropped his gun and crumpled over a table of terrified customers with his hands clutching his chest.

Total pandemonium broke loose in the crowded club as the three female tourists screamed and rushed to the fallen men. The Hellcats dove behind their amplifiers and Arnie scrambled behind a tall speaker cabinet, taking refuge with Razor and Sarah. Some bar patrons rushed for the exits while other shrieked and scrambled under tables. A Metro policeman holding a pistol in a double-handed grip over his head forced his way through the mob stampeding out the building's rear exit while yelling into a microphone clipped to his shoulder epaulet.

A few moments later, Arnie heard the faint sound of laughter rising above the din and summoned the courage to peek around the speaker cabinet toward the center of the room. The four surviving tourists, a man and three women, were standing with their arms around each other's shoulders, laughing drunkenly at the two combatants, who miraculously were getting to their feet.

"Is okay!" yelled one of men rising from the floor.

"Love country western music," one of the women added, waving her hat in the air. The cop finally reached them, followed by two other policemen who ordered all six to the floor. The officers pointed their pistols at them while peering warily around the room. More cops appeared at the exits.

Arnie turned to Razor. "What the hell is going on?"

"I think I know," the guitarist said, as the police snapped handcuffs on the tourists lying prone on the floor. All looked to be in perfect health and were protesting in broken English. Arnie made out the words "Roy Rogers" and "OK Corral."

Razor said, "I was on an overseas tour a few years ago, and this same thing happened at a club I was playing at in Oslo. The audience showed up dressed in cowboy outfits. I thought it was pretty cool at first. Halfway through the first set, a gunfight broke out and the band freaked and dove behind the amps. A minute later, the guy who got shot stood up and the crowd applauded. It's what they do at country shows over there—act out scenes from old western movies and shit. The bullets are blanks. Next place we performed, the same thing. We just kept playing."

The police got the handcuffed tourists to their feet and started marching them toward the exit. Razor picked up his scarred Telecaster from the floor and slipped the worn leather strap over his shoulder.

"I think I'll give them a little soundtrack for their adventure," he said. "Make sure they get the full Music City experience. This is a vacation they're going to remember for a while."

Razor stepped to the microphone, strummed a twangy chord and sang loudly, "*You're in the jailhouse now.*" He repeated the line and the drummer and bass player edged out from their hiding places and joined him at their instruments as he launched into a parody of the traditional jug band classic made popular by Jimmie Rodgers.

You're in the jailhouse now,
You're in the jailhouse now,
You won't forget your stay
In ol' Music City USA,
You're in the jailhouse now

A waitress who'd taken refuge behind the bar stood and started singing along. Arnie noticed Bubba help Sendy to her feet, then put his arm around her. Another waitress popped her head up and began passing out free longnecks. Soon everyone joined in except the grim faced Metro cops leading the protesting prisoners to the pokey. Arnie noticed the flash of a camera as he took a long swig of beer. Razor was right, this was a vacation the tourists would remember for a long time to come.

CHAPTER 23

Arnie stopped at a coin-operated box on the sidewalk outside Noshville the next morning for a copy of *The Tennessean*. When he glanced at the newspaper, he couldn't believe his eyes. Centered on the front page was a picture of Razor onstage at Tootsies singing his updated version of "In The Jailhouse Now" with the handcuffed Scandinavian tourists in the foreground. The reporter had a good time with the story, headlined, WILD WEST NIGHT AT TOOTSIES. It turned out that, as Razor had suspected, the tourists' guns had indeed been loaded with blanks and the shoot-'em-up was something they'd acted out many times previously in their home country. The authorities had nonetheless insisted that they accept the hospitality of a night in jail to give their charade a dose of authenticity. At press time, it was still uncertain if formal charges were to be pressed, though the article said it was doubtful.

Razor breezed in at ten-thirty. "Sorry to be late, man. I've been on the phone all morning," he said, sliding into the booth and waving to the waitress.

"I guess you saw this?" Arnie asked, raising the paper after they placed their orders.

"It's *unfuckingbelievable*," Razor replied, nodding. "I've been in town for five years trying to get a record or publishing deal with no luck at all. Then this morning I get calls from one manager, three publishers and two record company A&R people. They all wanted to hear my songs and find out when the Hellcats are playing again. The crazy thing is that just last week I'd dropped CDs off with two of the same dumb fucks who phoned. They didn't even know they had them on their desks. What a fucking business!"

"Did you call them on it? Tell them they already had your CDs sitting in front of them?"

"Naw, I was nice and respectful. Said I'd drop off copies this afternoon."

"You did the right thing. By the way, your band sounded great last night. Sarah has a fantastic voice."

"Thanks," Razor said as their food arrived. "So you write for Sam Solstice's company? How long have you been working with him?"

"Just a few months, I'm new in town."

"I've heard he's quite a character—doesn't leave a reflection when he walks by mirrors."

Arnie frowned. "I don't know about that. He's been good to me so far. One of his artists cut a song of mine a couple of weeks ago, and his checks always clear the bank."

"That's all that matters," Razor said. "I know his records sound good."

"I suppose he does what he has to do, business-wise. I'll tell you one thing, I've seen him work in the studio; he's a great producer."

"Well, I'd love to get a copy of the Hellcat's CD to him."

"Have you got one with you? I'm headed to the office after breakfast."

Razor pulled a CD from his jacket pocket and passed it across the table.

"I'll see that he gets it. And I'm really interested in writing with you when things settle down."

"Thanks, let's do it."

* * *

When Arnie arrived at Sam's office, Starr was on the phone. "That was Stef," she said, hanging up. "Have you heard the good news?"

"What's that?"

"Sam was out on Buzz Corbin's boat over the weekend and played her project for him—he'd just finished mixing it. Buzz loved what he heard and may offer Stef a singles deal on his label."

"What's a singles deal?"

"It's when a record company agrees to put out a single on an artist to test the waters. If it does well, they follow up by releasing an album."

"So she may have a record deal already?"

"Don't get too excited, nothing's been signed yet. Stef gets into town tomorrow and they've got a meeting scheduled for Wednesday."

Arnie saw a *Tennessean* on Starr's desk.

"Did you read about what happened at Tootsies last night?" he asked.

"Yes, in fact Sam called earlier wondering how we could get hold of this guy . . . Razor I think they said his name is. And his band, the Appalachian Hellcats. He thinks there might be a way to wrangle all this publicity into a record deal."

"I might be able to help you with that," Arnie said, handing her Razor's CD.

"Really?" Starr's eyebrows arched in surprise. "You know this guy?"

"I was down at Tootsies last night and heard them. They're great.

"Cool. I'll make sure Sam gets this. That guy Razor would be good to try and co-write with."

"Already planning on it."

CHAPTER 24

When Arnie arrived at Stef's hotel room Tuesday evening to pick her up for dinner, she greeted him with a hug and a kiss.

"Wow!" Arnie said, inhaling her perfume and stepping back to take in the full length of her. She looked magnificent in a merlot turtleneck, black jeans and matching leather jacket.

"So you heard about Buzz Corbin?" she asked in the elevator.

"Yes. Starr said there's a chance he might offer you a record contract—a singles deal."

"I'm so excited. And what's even better is that Sam said Buzz loves 'Last Night Made My Day.'"

"Really? This has all happened so quickly."

"Yeah, most things take forever in this business. I've been coming to Nashville for years, knocking on doors, taking meetings, recording demos and doing showcases hoping to get signed. But nothing's ever come together. Somehow, everything feels right this time, like the planets are finally lining up."

"So you're meeting with Sam and Buzz tomorrow?"

"Yes, we're supposed to go over the terms of the contract."

"That calls for a celebration. Where should we go for dinner?"

"It's so warm," Stef said. "Hard to believe it's almost Thanksgiving. Let's go somewhere where we can sit outside."

"What about South Street?"

"Perfect."

After a short drive they arrived at the restaurant, which was crowded with patrons taking advantage of the unseasonably mild evening. The establishment's wall-to-wall windows, which were mounted on garage door-like tracks, had been raised to let the warm breeze blow through, giving it the ambience of an open air beachfront bar, complete with several dozen Harleys lined up side-by-side along the curb across the street. At Arnie's request, the hostess seated them at a downstairs booth adjacent to the sidewalk where he had a good view of the street.

"I love this place!" Stef said over the din of raucous bikers partying at the bar and wailing blues guitar pumping out of the overhead speakers.

"Yeah. The only thing missing is the ocean."

They ordered crab and shrimp dinners and chatted through the meal about the casino where Stef had performed the previous weekend, and a month-long cruise ship gig she was booked on in December.

When they finished eating, Stef reached across the table and took Arnie's hand. "I've got a feeling about your song. I've had it since the first time I heard it." She leaned to kiss him briefly on the lips, then started singing softly in his ear. "Last night made my day. . ."

Listening to her gave him chills, and he squeezed her fingers. Under the table, she slipped a shoe off and rubbed his upper ankle with her foot.

"What are you thinking?" he asked.

"Probably the same thing you are," she answered with a smile.

"Do you want to go back to your hotel?"

"No, it's too pretty out. Let's take a little ride somewhere."

Arnie took Stef's hand and led her toward the door. As they passed the bar, a shriek almost ruptured his eardrum. He turned to face a busty girl in jeans and a crop-top straddling the leg of one of the bikers sitting on a barstool. She was bouncing up and down and yelling "Giddy up!" while grabbing both his ears and grinding his face into her boobs.

The guy came up for air and caught Arnie's eye. "Sorry about that," he said to Arnie, spanking the girl's butt playfully.

"Don't worry, man," Arnie said, giving him a thumbs up.

The biker winked. "My Daddy would be proud of me—but my Mama'd kick my ass!" he said, giving the girl another smack on the butt, causing her to shriek again and pull his head back between her breasts.

"That's a song title if I ever heard one," Arnie said as they headed to the door.

"No shit!"

"Will you be cold if I put the top down?" Arnie asked when they reached the car. The evening had cooled a bit, but it was still pleasant.

"Not if I can snuggle next to you."

Arnie retracted the Miata's top and made a loop around Music Row. He pointed out his apartment as they passed, then headed toward West End. Between shifting gears he reached over and gently squeezed Stef's knee. She responded by rubbing his forearm through the sleeve of his battered leather jacket and snuggling closer.

"Where are we headed?" she asked.

"There's a neat place that I found while I was driving around the other day, a street called Love Circle. It has a beautiful view."

"I like the name already."

Arnie turned left onto a series of ever narrowing tree-lined streets that corkscrewed up a steep hill. When they emerged onto the summit, a panoramic view of Nashville lay beneath them.

"My goodness!" Stefany exclaimed. "It's like being on an airplane." Below, the glittering city sparkled like a million-candle birthday cake.

"When I have some hits, I think I'll buy a Ferrari and a house on Love Circle."

"Really," Stefany said, batting her eyelashes. "That might be nice—someday. But tonight you've got me, and your Miata. What do you think about that?"

"I think I'm a pretty lucky guy."

Stef leaned toward him and Arnie stroked her hair, then kissed her. She wrapped both arms around his neck and Arnie slipped his hand around her hips and pulled her toward him. His hand accidentally brushed her breast, and she tightened her grip around his neck and kissed him harder.

"Do you want to go back to your hotel?" he asked.

"That would be nice."

He put the car in gear and descended from Love Circle to West End, then drove slowly for two miles until they reached the Vanderbilt Plaza. When they arrived at her room, she turned to face him and leaned against the door.

"Aren't you going to invite me in?" he asked.

"Only if you promise to be good," she replied.

"That might be hard."

"I don't think that's the only thing that's hard right now," she said with a giggle.

Stef ran her key card through the lock and he followed her into the room. They fell onto the bed, kissing and groping each other like teenagers. After a while, Arnie reached gently between her legs and her pelvis rose against his hand. Then, suddenly, she stiffened and pushed him away.

"I wasn't kidding about being good. You promised."

"Okay."

Arnie tried to pull her back toward him, but her body was rigid.

"I think you'd better leave," she said, standing abruptly and walking to the door.

"What?"

"You need to go."

"Did I do something wrong?" he asked, following her to the door. "I'm sorry if . . . I thought you—"

"Just go," she said, her expression blank. "I'll talk to you tomorrow after my meeting."

Arnie stared at her, mystified. It was as if someone had flipped a switch and replaced the girl he was caressing a few minutes earlier with a complete stranger. She gave him a slight push on the chest, and the next thing he knew he was standing in the hallway listening to the metallic *thunk!* of the security bolt being thrown on the closed door.

He remained motionless for several moments, totally confused. Finally, he shook his head and took the elevator downstairs. When he arrived back at his apartment, he still couldn't make sense out of what had happened.

CHAPTER 25

The weather fit Arnie's mood when he awakened the next morning, having turned cold and rainy overnight. He stared out his bedroom window at the leafless trees blowing in the wind, replaying the events of the previous evening and wondering what made his date with Stef go south so abruptly. Frustrated, he turned his mind to what the biker had said as they had left South Street and focused his thoughts on coming up with a way to write a song called "Daddy'd Be Proud, But Mama'd Kick My Ass." By the time he'd finished showering and downed his first cup of coffee, he had most of a chorus running through his head.

He sat with his guitar and notebook and surprised himself by completing the song by early afternoon. Exhausted, he lay down on the couch to take a nap. Within minutes he was awakened by a knock on the door. He rose to unlock it and stepped back in shock as Stef rushed in and smashed her purse on the kitchen table.

"What's wrong?" Arnie asked, alarmed.

"I just got out of my meeting with Sam and Buzz."

"Yes?"

"The contract wasn't anything like what they said it would be."

"What do you mean?"

"It was supposed to be a singles deal. The label would put out a single, if it did well, they'd release an album. If it didn't, I'd be free to walk away. But the contract Buzz presented had me tied to his label for five years with no obligation beyond putting out the first single. If it tanked, I'd be at his mercy. He'd own my ass for five years and I couldn't record for anyone else. I can't believe those scumbags thought they could put one over on me like this."

"What did Sam say?"

"He acted dumb—like he didn't know what was in the contract. But I'm signed to his production company, so he must have known something. Sam's a good guy, and a great producer. But when it comes to business, he's a scoundrel like all the rest."

"Don't you have a lawyer?"

"Yeah, he was there, but I didn't need him to tell me what was going on. My father told me never to sign anything you don't understand yourself."

"It's probably a standard contract the record company starts their negotiations with. I don't think Sam would do anything that would hurt you. The publishing contract he gave me was fair."

"To tell you the truth, I'm so pissed off I'm thinking of telling them all to go fuck themselves."

"You might want to think twice before doing that," Arnie said. "You've been trying to get a record deal for years; you don't want to throw this opportunity away."

"Why the hell not?" Stef asked, glaring at him.

"Because . . . then you wouldn't have a record deal."

"And you wouldn't have a song on my album, 'cause there wouldn't be an album. That's all you give a shit about."

"Bullshit. I'm just saying you should wait and see what happens. You can't blame them for trying to negotiate the best terms they can. You'd do the same thing in their shoes. What have you got to lose by giving them the benefit of the doubt?"

Stef didn't say anything for a minute. "You may be right. Anyhow, Sam wants us to meet him for dinner at Bound'ry at eight. It's Ferrari Princess Night and I promised him last week I'd be there."

"Ferrari Princess Night?"

"You'll see."

"Come here."

Stef walked to Arnie and he took her in his arms. "Everything's going to be fine," he said, pressing her head to his chest as he stroked her hair.

"I'm sorry about last night."

"It's okay. I don't know what happened. I'm sorry if I—"

"I've been under a lot of stress recently."

"Did I do something to make you angry?"

"No."

"Then what was it that made you so upset with me? You know I'd never try to do anything you didn't want me to do. I thought you wanted—"

"Would you like me better if I was more predictable?"

Arnie wasn't sure how to answer. "I'm glad you're here," he finally said.

"I woke up this morning thinking about that first night at the hotel," Stef said. It was so special, you just holding me and all. I kept waking up and snuggling closer to you, drifting in and out of sleep and feeling you next to me. It felt so good to be in your arms."

"That's sweet of you to say."

"You made me feel safe," she said. "The rest of the world doesn't sometimes."

"I'd like to keep making you feel that way—safe against the world."

"That's sweet," Stefany said, tilting her head upward to kiss him. "Now you'll have to write a song for me called 'Safe Against The World.'"

CHAPTER 26

Arnie had to knock several times at the door of Stef's hotel room that evening before she answered. When it eventually opened, his jaw dropped—he simply couldn't believe his eyes. She was wearing a bright red dress slightly bigger than a large handkerchief. The shimmering fabric extended from a fraction of an inch above her nipples to just below her crotch. The top was held precariously in place by two shoulder straps the size of six-pound test fishing line, and her curvaceous figure stretched the garment so tightly that Arnie could see the faint outline of the belly button ring piercing the top of her navel.

"Wow," he finally said. "That looks a little chilly for November."

"Sam asked me to wear it," she said with a slight grimace. "Starr ordered eight of them from Frederick's of Hollywood for Ferrari Princess Night.

"So what *is* Ferrari Princess Night?"

"It's supposed to be a dress rehearsal for some Ferrari Club event at Road Atlanta next weekend. Sam likes to take a bunch of girls along with him to those things, and Starr came up with the idea of ordering matching outfits. I won't be able to make it, but I told them I'd come to the party tonight.

"I thought you were pissed off at Sam?"

"I am," she said. "This'll keep him off his guard."

"Well, I hope you've got a warm coat."

They arrived at Bound'ry at eight. Arnie started to ask the French hostess for Sam's group, but she was already reaching for menus.

"You don't have to ask," she said. "Zee dress eez a dead giveaway."

They followed her up a winding stairway to the second floor, where Sam and his entourage of fifteen or so people were seated. Arnie recognized Sendy, along with Vinnie, Robert, Starr and several others. All the girls were dressed in identical red Frederick's of Hollywood dresses.

"Stefany," Starr shrieked, jumping from her seat between Sam and her date *du jour*, a square-jawed fellow with a long ponytail. "Let me see your dress."

Stefany removed her coat and twirled around for the group. The men whistled and the girls squealed their approval as Sam passed Stef and Arnie flutes of champagne. Starr introduced her date, a drummer with a band that had charted several recent hits. He responded by flexing his arm and chest muscles and rolling his shoulders like a *Muscle & Fitness* magazine cover boy, then turned to Starr and said, "You're beautiful, babe."

Two new girls in their twenties were sitting on either side of Vinnie. One was short and blonde, the other was a bit taller, with hair dyed bright purple. Both were ten or fifteen pounds overweight, wore too much makeup and looked like aspiring hookers. Starr introduced them as Middy and Trayne, Ferrari Princesses, but Middy corrected her. "We're the Ferrari Sluts, don't get us confused with these other chicks!"

The group burst into laughter as Sam introduced his date, Jazz, the Eurasian woman whom Arnie had briefly met at the Ferrari Club lunch at the Loveless Cafe. She bore a striking resemblance to the Disney character, Princess Jasmine, and Arnie wondered if that's where her name had originated. Lars and Buford arrived, along with Lars' doll-like wife. Stef drained her glass of champagne and Sam refilled it, then lifted his own glass in a toast.

"I have an announcement to make," he said. "Stefany has just been offered a record contract, and it's largely because of a song Arnie wrote for her called 'Last Night Made My Day.' We're still negotiating terms with the label, but I have high hopes that the attorneys will work things out and Stef will have a hit record by this time next year. Here's to Stef and Arnie—and next year's Grammy Awards."

As the group raised their glasses and downed their drinks, Arnie reached for Stef's hand under the table and found it balled into a fist. Though she was smiling thinly, the tendons of her neck were clenched into taut ropes.

"So, tell me about Road Atlanta," Arnie said, turning to Sam. Stef's fist felt like a hand grenade with the pin pulled out, and he gripped it tightly, hoping to hold off the impending explosion.

Vinnie answered from across the table. "They've got a world-class Grand Prix style track there. The club rents the course for the day. Each driver pays a hundred bucks to take their Ferrari out."

"Sounds like fun," Arnie said. "Could I try it with my Miata sometime?"

"You couldn't drive it on the track since it's a club-sponsored event," Sam said. "But you'd be welcome to try a few laps in one of the Ferraris."

"Just make sure you've got enough cash to pay for the bodywork if you spin out," Vinnie added with a chuckle.

Appetizers arrived: gourmet pizzas that were passed around the table. Arnie and Stef each took a slice and Jazz took two, but the Ferrari Sluts declined, saying they were only ordering salads. Sam ordered more champagne, and refilled Stef's glass once again as Arnie attempted to chat with Starr's date. When Starr prompted him to reply to Arnie, he responded by jutting his chin forward as if posing for a camera before repeating, "You're beautiful, babe."

The champagne disappeared quickly and Sam ordered two more bottles. Arnie refilled Stef's glass once more and she quickly downed it and thrust it forward again.

"You might want to slow down," he whispered.

"I'm might," she slurred.

"Seriously."

"I'm just trying to have a fucking good time."

"Hey Vinnie," Sam said. "Tell Middy and Trayne the joke about the frog."

Vinnie, who seemed to have recovered from his accident, embarked on a long joke about a guy who walks into a bar carrying a shoebox containing a bullfrog. He takes a seat on a barstool next to a pretty girl, and tells her that the frog has a special talent for performing oral sex. The mechanic's thick Italian accent made the raunchy joke hilarious and somehow less risqué as he described how the man eventually convinces the girl to invite him back to her apartment for a demonstration. She undresses and lies on the bed and he places the frog between her legs and tells it to do its thing. The frog just sits there. After several attempts, he moves the frog aside and says, "All right . . . I show you one more time."

Although almost everyone present appeared to have the joke memorized from previous recountings, the group burst into peals of laughter. The Ferrari Sluts laughed so hard that one of Trayne's breasts popped over the top of her dress.

Trayne started to pull the fabric up, then changed her mind and stretched the dress with her left hand as she scooped her breast out and cupped it in the palm of her right. "I show you one more time Vinnie, I show you one more time!"

The group exploded into wild applause. Buford made a grab for Trayne's boob, but it was already safely, if barely, hidden by the top of her dress. He received a lighthearted slap for his efforts. "You'll get a real spanking if you try that again," she exclaimed.

"Too bad I'm not sitting over there," Sam said from across the table.

"You'll have to wait for Atlanta if you want a spanking, Sam," Trayne responded playfully.

"I think Sam needs more than a spanking," Stef spat. "Maybe you should use a bullwhip."

Her voice had a serrated steel edge, and the table suddenly became silent.

"Gimme a cigarette, Middy."

Middy handed Stef a cigarette from across the table, and Lars' wife reached over and lit it with a rhinestone embedded lighter.

"Relax, Stef," Sam said quietly.

Arnie squeezed Stef's hand under the table, and was about to say something when his eyes met Vinnie's. The mechanic shook his head almost imperceptibly.

Stef took a deep drag from the cigarette and exhaled with a snarl.

"I'll relax when you get my contract straightened out," she hissed.

Everyone was quiet, staring at Sam and Stef.

"Later Stef," Sam said quietly.

"No."

"I'll get it taken care of next week, like I told you."

"I know you will, I'm just amazed you couldn't get it right this afternoon."

"I said I'll take care of it. If you don't like what Buzz comes up with, we'll shop your project and try to get a deal somewhere else. I'm doing all I can."

"Good."

Sam's voice had an odd timbre to it—apprehensive, which was out of character for him. Arnie recalled noticing a similar shift in the producer's demeanor after Stef first heard "Last Night Made My Day." He wondered again what sort of power she had over him.

Suddenly Starr raised her glass of champagne. "I propose a toast. Here's to the Ferrari Princesses, more beautiful than the cars, and the reason men drive them!"

"You're beautiful, babe," her date said.

The group roared in laughter and the playful spirit of the evening was restored.

"I need to get out of here," Stef whispered into Arnie's ear.

They stood and excused themselves, then Arnie helped Stef outside toward several taxis parked by the curb.

"Are you okay?" he asked.

"Help me get a cab back to my hotel. I've got a plane to catch in the morning."

Arnie caught her arm as she tripped and lurched against him.

"Talk to me," he said, spinning her so her face almost touched his.

"It pissed me off that you didn't back me up in there, stand up for what I was saying."

"What?" Arnie was taken back. He'd never met anyone who was more capable of standing up for herself. "But it's none of my business, Stef. The contract is between you and the record company."

"You just watched the whole thing happen," she slurred. "That's what you do. You watch the people around you, me included, and get song ideas. But you don't get emotionally involved. You don't even know that's the way you are."

"What about the way *you* are?" Arnie asked, on the verge of losing his temper. "One minute you're an angel, like when you left my apartment this afternoon, then you turn into a complete stranger. Look at me. I am emotionally involved, can't you tell?"

"You say you are," she answered, pulling away. "I thought I was getting involved with you, too. Now I don't know if I want to be."

"What?" Arnie was surprised by the volume of his voice and realized that they were on the brink of a real fight. Since he was tipsy and Stef was flat out drunk, he decided to back off before any serious damage was done. "Let's get you a taxi, we can talk about this later."

Stef shrugged and teetered toward one of the waiting cabs. When she reached it, she turned and brushed her lips against Arnie's.

"Kissing's you is different tonight," he said.

"Different?"

"It's the cigarette. You were a sweet piña colada, now you're a nicotine martini."

Stef giggled. "Well, here's another nicotine martini." She kissed him again, this time full on the mouth.

"Call me before you leave tomorrow!" he said as she collapsed into the cab.

The door slammed shut and Stef disappeared into the night without looking back.

* * *

Arnie returned to find the party breaking up. Robert and Buford were making a serious play for the Ferrari Sluts, but they walked out of the restaurant with Vinnie, who strode across the street to his Expedition with one on each arm.

"Hey, Vinnie," Robert yelled with a laugh. "You're sixty years old. What have you got that we don't?"

"I got a schlong this long, bambino!" The mechanic broke apart from the girls long enough to hold up his arm and make a chopping motion at the elbow with his other hand.

"He's right. Eat your heart out, Robert," Middy yelled over her shoulder, climbing with Trayne into Vinnie's SUV.

"Vinnie, why don't you drive a Ferrari like the rest of us?"

"Cause American cars always run. But I love Ferraris. They make beautiful music like me and Trayne and Middy are going to make all night long."

The Expedition veered away from the curb, narrowly missing the fender of a limo double-parked in front of the restaurant.

"He'll have fun if he doesn't get pulled over for another DUI," Sam said, shaking his head.

After saying goodnight to everyone, Arnie found himself walking down the sidewalk with Robert, whose black Ferrari 308 coupe was parked by his Miata.

"It's great that Stef recorded a song of yours," Robert said. "Good luck with it."

"Thanks. I've been writing songs for years, but I'm new to Nashville. I know I'm incredibly lucky to have a song cut so quickly."

"It must be a very good song, Sam doesn't screw around."

"I appreciate you saying that. Didn't you mention when we met back in September that you're in the import business?"

"Yes, I import heavy factory equipment, precision lathes and stuff, and refurbish it in my shop in Lavergne. It's a little town about twenty miles south of Nashville."

"That's interesting," Arnie said. "Are you going to Atlanta with the rest of the guys this weekend?"

"Nope, I'm headed to Key West on Saturday for a few days. Do you like to sail?"

"I've only been a few times, but I enjoyed it."

"Give me a call sometime," Robert said, sliding a business card from his wallet. "I keep a boat on Percy Priest Lake."

"Thank you. It's hard to imagine warm weather right now, as chilly as it is tonight." A cold front had followed the morning rain and Arnie was shivering.

"You should think about coming to Key West with me this weekend. I've rented a sailboat to stay on at the marina there—cheaper than a hotel. You'd have your own cabin."

"Hmmm, let me think it over," Arnie replied, remembering FBI Agent Baskins's suggestion that he get out of town. "Could I give you a call tomorrow?"

"Sure," Robert said, getting into his car. "I found a '91 Testerossa for sale in Miami. My plan is to spend a few days in Key West, then check out the car on the way back. If I decide to buy it, you can help me drive it home. We'll have fun. I've got a pile of frequent flier miles getting ready to expire, so I can take care of the plane ticket. I'll be going regardless, and I'd enjoy the company. Let me know."

"I'll do it!"

CHAPTER 27

Arnie woke the next day feeling even more depressed and confused about Stef than he had the morning before. At least yesterday he was optimistic that "Last Night Made My Day" had a chance to be heard on the radio—now even that was uncertain. He played back the events of the last two days in his mind, trying without success to make sense of her volatile mood shifts.

He made coffee and prepared to start work, then came across the phrase "safe against the world" that he'd jotted down. Although he didn't feel safe, or in any way confident of Stef's feelings for him, he couldn't get the peaceful feeling he'd had with her the previous afternoon out of his mind. He strummed his guitar and drifted into a reverie of words and music. Occasionally, he made notes of the lyrics that formed in his head and recorded fragments of melody and chord changes.

He spent the morning in a daze, not thinking about putting the song together, but doing it anyway. The phone rang late that afternoon, just as he finished making a final recording of his days work.

He immediately recognized Starr's voice. "Had a good time last night," he responded. It was nice to meet. . ." Arnie realized that he couldn't remember her date's name.

"Yeah, it was fun. Sam asked me to give you a call. He spoke with Buzz's attorney this morning, and the label will have a new contract ready to fax Stef sometime next week. Sam knew you'd be worried about 'Last Night Made My Day.' I'm sure that whatever happened with the first contract was a misunderstanding. Lots of times, record companies start off with standard boilerplate and negotiate from there. It's just the way they do business. I don't think anyone expected Stef to go for those terms."

"I told her that the publishing contract Sam had me sign seemed fair."

"It was, because Sam drew it up. Stef's contract was drawn up by Buzz's legal department."

"That's what I tried to tell her," Arnie said.

"Arnie?"

"Yes."

"Don't worry about this. I've seen a lot of people come through this town. You're more talented than most. Just roll with the punches, keep writing your songs and getting along with everybody like you do. You've got what it takes to become a great writer. Whatever happens with Stef's deal isn't important, there'll be other songs and other singers."

"Thanks, Starr."

Arnie hung up and looked at his watch. It was five o'clock and he still hadn't heard from Stef. Maybe she just needed some space. He didn't exactly feel as though he'd lost her, it was more like wherever she'd gone, it was somewhere he couldn't chase her to. Picking up the phone, he considered dialing her number, then changed his mind and called Robert.

He was ready for a vacation and Key West sounded like a great idea.

CHAPTER 28

The Jamaican woman's blue silk turban and voluminous curves caught their attention as Arnie and Robert emerged from Key West's tiny airport. Her yellow cotton shift fluttered in the wind as she opened the door of the first cab in line and they slid into the backseat. Robert leaned forward to say, "The marina on the north side of the island, please."

Grinning, she pulled away from the curb as she replied, "Mon, I know hotel you like better—where the nekkid people go."

"We're not gay," Robert said stiffly.

"Honey, they be all kinds of people at the hotel—boys, girls, gay and straight, too. Nice pool and beach. Maybe you visit tomorrow."

Arnie chuckled to himself at Robert's homophobia as the taxi continued toward the marina. Along the way he noticed a sign for the Ernest Hemingway Museum, and made a mental note to try to visit it while in town.

At the harbor, they were directed by the rental agent to a graceful fifty-foot ketch with teak trim moored a few slips from the marina office. Robert inquired about taking it for a sail, and was informed that, because of the boat's size, the owner had insisted that someone approved by him accompany them onboard. The manager promised to check on the availability of a skipper and get back to Robert as soon as she could.

They stowed their bags below deck, with Arnie taking the cozy triangular front cabin, and Robert the larger rear stateroom. After settling in and admiring the ketch's mahogany interior and amenities, they donned shorts and headed for the hi-rise hotel adjacent to the marina. Robert breezed by the hotel guard with a few words in Spanish, and soon they were downing Coronas by the pool.

When the sun began to sink toward the palm trees behind them, both Robert and Arnie showered at the hotel facilities and headed back to the boat. Then, after a change of clothes, they walked a few blocks to Mallory

Square Dock, where they joined several hundred other tourists watching the sunset while being entertained by an assortment of jugglers, mimes and street musicians. Afterward, the two headed into town for dinner and spent the rest of the evening bar hopping. Around midnight they found themselves at Sloppy Joe's Bar, located near the harbor. Arnie went to the restroom and returned to find a husky waitress in denim cutoffs and pink bikini top in front of Robert, who was sucking down the contents of a shooter proffered from between her tanned breasts.

"I think she likes me," Robert said after she left their table. "Her name's Dawn. I asked if she wanted to go sailing with us and gave her my cell number. She said she might call in the morning."

Arnie winced as Dawn repeated her shooter performance for a group of Japanese businessmen on the far side of the room. "Don't hold your breath."

"Oh well," Robert laughed.

At two a.m. they stumbled back to the boat, wasted from their day of traveling and the evening's beers and margaritas. Arnie opened the overhead hatch in his cabin and let the cool breeze and gentle rocking motion of the ketch's hull lull him to sleep. Nashville was a million miles away.

* * *

The sound of activity around the marina woke him early the next morning. Nursing a Texas-sized hangover, Arnie scrounged through the galley and found a bottle of aspirin and can of stale Folgers, but couldn't locate a coffeemaker. He improvised by boiling water in a saucepan and pouring it into two Styrofoam cups through a folded paper towel holding a handful of ground coffee. Soon, he and Robert were enjoying their beverage on the boat's afterdeck, and making plans for the day. Robert's first priority was to check out the hotel and beach "where the nekkid people go." Arnie promised to meet him there after visiting the Hemingway Museum.

Robert took off and Arnie strolled across town until he came to the Nobel Prize winning author's two-story stone mansion on Whitehead Street. After paying the admission fee, he joined a group taking a guided tour of the house and grounds and found himself fascinated by the memorabilia of the writer whose life was as interesting as those of the characters in his works. He particularly enjoyed examining the second floor of the carriage house, which Hemingway used as a writing studio during the years when he produced some of his best-known novels. Because he was a morning writer, he had a catwalk built to it from the main house's second story veranda so he could walk right to his workplace as soon as he got out of bed.

Another item of interest was a copper penny embedded in the concrete border of the swimming pool. The tour guide, a slender Filipina girl in her early twenties, explained that Hemingway's second wife, Pauline, had the pool built when he was out of town. When he returned, he was enraged by the expense and had thrown a penny down into the still damp concrete and stomped it with his heel, exclaiming, "You might as well take my last cent!"

Arnie couldn't help notice a large number of cats lounging around the premises, many of which had six front toes, making them appear to have mittens for paws. The tour guide explained that the fifty or sixty felines who made their home at the museum were descendents of one of Hemingway's favorite pets, a six-toed cat that had been a gift from a ship captain. Arnie approached the guide when the tour was over and asked if any kittens ever came up for adoption.

"The official policy is no," she said, glancing over her shoulder. "Most of the cats have been fixed, but not all of them—once in a while we have an extra kitten. I could let you know the next time we do."

Arnie wrote down his email address and Nashville phone number on the corner of a museum brochure and handed it to her. "It's nice of you to offer to do that. Have you been working here long?"

"About six months. I moved here from Virginia last summer, and just passed the test for my real estate license. I'm working part time at the museum until I sell my first property."

"You're lucky to live in such a special place. What's your name?"

"Camilla. Are you in town for long?"

"Just a few days. I'm visiting with a friend—we're staying on a sailboat at the harbor."

"Well, if you guys need someone to show you around, I might be available." She tilted her head and smiled coquettishly.

"That would be great."

"I get off at five, then I need to run home to change clothes and maybe take a little disco nap—in case we stay out late. But I could meet you somewhere at seven-thirty. There's a place I love on Duval Street called Mangoe's."

"See you there at seven-thirty. I'm looking forward to it."

"Me, too."

CHAPTER 29

The "nekkid people hotel" turned out to be a sprawling, somewhat dilapidated oceanfront structure on the south end of the island. Arnie walked past the office through a concrete breezeway toward the beach, and was surprised to find an attractive rear deck and pier featuring a swimming pool and outdoor bar overlooking the ocean. As the cabdriver had predicted, there were several dozen people in various states of undress frolicking in the water and sunning themselves on lounge chairs scattered around the pool. He ordered a beer and fought to keep from staring at a striking mid-forties blonde next to him as she unbuttoned her blouse. The bartender handed Arnie his change and noticed him glance at a young man emerging from the pool who was adorned with enough rings and studs through his eyebrows, nipples and genitals to make passing through airport security a long and embarrassing process.

"You know what all that body hardware's for, don't you?" the bartender asked.

"Not exactly," Arnie replied hesitantly.

"So his boyfriend can hang him up on a nail when he gets done playing with him."

There was a giggle from his right. Arnie turned as the woman next to him shrugged off her bra to reveal two large perfectly formed breasts riding high on her chest. From the pride with which she was displaying them, Arnie suspected they were a recent purchase.

"So you like girls?" she asked the bartender.

"If they're as pretty as you," he replied.

Arnie left the bartender flirting with the blonde and spotted Robert sitting on a lounge chair next to a slender redhead wearing a barely visible polka dot bikini bottom. As he approached, he overheard his friend, who was in a baggy bathing suit, offer to rub suntan oil on her back. The girl got to her feet, pulled on a T-shirt bearing the caption NICE PEOPLE SWALLOW, and paraded toward the parking lot.

"Did you piss her off?" Arnie asked, taking a seat on the girl's vacated lounger.

"I don't think so. She's a dancer at a club a few blocks away, maybe we can stop by later."

Arnie chuckled and told him about Camilla's offer to meet for dinner and show them around town.

"Sounds like fun," Robert said, pulling on his shirt and rolling up his towel. "I've had enough sun; let's head back to the marina."

When they arrived at their boat, they found a note from the marina operator listing the phone numbers of several skippers who might be available to accompany them sailing. Within minutes, Robert had made arrangements with a fellow named Gabe McEwen to meet them at two o'clock.

Gabe arrived promptly at the appointed time. He was an ultra-fit fellow in his early thirties wearing a Navy Seals ball cap. Robert handed him two crisp hundred-dollar bills and gave him a quick run down of his sailing experience. They cast off and Gabe motored the ketch out of the slip and into the channel leading to open water while explaining a few peculiarities of the boat's rigging. Then he turned the helm over to Robert after cautioning him to watch for small buoys indicating lobster pots that could snag the keel. Soon, the large craft was leaning into a graceful tack into the gulf.

Gabe was impressed with Robert's sailing skills and was soon entertaining them with tales of life on the Key West waterfront. In addition to working as a scuba instructor for the Special Forces Underwater Operations School, he also held a part time job with the harbor police. "Believe it or not, we still have problems with pirates," he said. "Not too long ago, a retired couple who'd been sailing around the islands on a thirty-eight foot sloop came into the station. The night before, the wife had been on watch, while the man slept below deck. He woke when he heard her shouting on deck, then grabbed his shotgun and scrambled topside. When he came through the hatch, he saw a guy dressed in black coming over the transom. He shot from the hip, hitting the man full in the chest with a load of buckshot that blasted him backward into the water.

"Shit!" Robert exclaimed. "Was his wife okay?"

"She was fine. They heard an outboard motor rev up behind their sloop and saw a small inflatable Zodiac with another guy in it take off."

"So what happened to the couple?" Arnie asked.

"Nothing. They tried to find the guy they'd shot, or at least his body, but they didn't have any luck. Since Key West was the nearest port, they came in to report the incident."

"Did you call the police or Coast Guard?"

"Nope. The harbormaster listened to the story and told them to forget it ever happened. Said they probably did the rest of us a favor by shooting the dude."

"Sounds like you have some adventures here," Arnie said.

Gabe thought for a moment. "Yeah, I guess about the wildest thing I've ever been involved with was stealing a boat myself. Well, almost stealing it."

"I thought you were one of the good guys," Robert said.

"I am." Gabe replied with a wry grin. "It all started when a dentist from Cleveland decided to sell his practice and retire. He was in his forties, divorced, and loved to sail. So he bought a boat in Miami and cruised around the Caribbean for a while, then met a girl in Marsh Harbor. She didn't know anything about sailing, but she liked him and his boat so they hooked up and spent a few months together. They were off the coast of Venezuela one afternoon when she came up from below after taking a nap. The boat was on autopilot, sailing fine, but there was no sign of the dentist. She called his name over and over, then searched the boat from stem to stern, but he was flat gone. Must have fallen overboard—there was no telling how far back it had happened. She managed to get the radio working and sent out a distress call. The first person to answer was a ferryboat captain en route to Margarita Island. He and a guy from his crew boarded the sailboat and calmed the chick down, then lowered the sails and towed the boat into Caracas."

"She was lucky he was nearby," Robert said.

"Yeah. The police determined there wasn't any foul play involved, so they sent her home to Vermont or wherever the heck she was from," Gabe continued. "Then it got interesting. The ferryboat captain claimed salvage rights on the sailboat, saying the owner had abandoned it by falling overboard. Since he was the first person on the scene, his claim was theoretically correct under maritime law, and the Venezuelan authorities agreed with him. But the American insurance company who carried the policy on the boat got a contradictory ruling in their favor from a judge in Miami saying the sailboat was theirs. The Venezuelans didn't recognize the authority of the U.S. court, so the insurance company hired me to steal the boat. It was a brand new Hunter—worth about six hundred grand. They offered me ten percent of its value, sixty thousand cash, to get it back—no questions asked."

"Did you do it?"

"Almost," Gabe answered regretfully. "I asked for twenty thousand up front, and put together a team of three other guys, one of whom had a big Bertram sport-fisher that he uses in his charter business. It's got twin fifteen-hundred-horsepower diesels and can cruise at over forty miles per hour. We figured we'd head south to Caracas, anchor offshore, then me and another guy would scuba to the slip, hotwire the sailboat's motor and sneak it out of the harbor before anyone realized what was going down. We could be in international waters in less than an hour—then it would legally be our boat."

"So what happened?" Arnie asked.

"The insurance company chickened out at the last minute. But I got to keep the up-front money—easiest twenty grand I ever made." Gabe paused a moment, his eyes gleaming. "But I was really looking forward to stealing that boat!"

"Sounds like you lead a dangerous life," Arnie said.

"It can be, that's why I always carry this," Gabe said, unzipping his fanny pack to expose the butt of a SIG-Sauer semiautomatic pistol.

By now they'd been sailing for several hours. Robert deftly changed course so that they ran parallel to the island's coast for a few miles, then turned shoreward and gave the command to tighten, then loosen the main and jib sheets. Gabe and Arnie scrambled to obey his instructions and ducked under the mainsail's boom as it snapped over their heads in a controlled jibe. Soon they had cut through the ocean swells back to Key West and were safely docked.

"You guys have been super," Gabe said, shaking their hands and giving them each a business card. "Any time I can do anything for you, give me a call."

"Will do," Arnie said as he walked away. "Thanks."

"He's quite a guy," Robert added. "You never know when having a friend like him might come in handy."

"Yeah," Arnie said, pocketing Gabe's card, and recalling Agent Baskins's recent warning about Don Puccini. "I couldn't agree with you more."

CHAPTER 30

A few hours later, Arnie and Robert sipped beers at a small table in the garden bar of Mangoe's Restaurant while enjoying the view of Duvall Street's tourist-choked sidewalk. After showering and napping, they were rested and looking forward to the evening ahead. At quarter to eight, Camilla buzzed up on a cherry-red Vespa, which she chained to a light pole in front of the restaurant. She pulled her helmet off, shook her long ebony hair loose, then waved when she spotted them.

"Hey," she said. "Sorry I'm late."

"I was hoping you'd bring a friend," Robert said.

Arnie gave him a sideways look. "Camilla's beautiful enough for both of us."

She laughed and ordered a glass of wine. Soon they were escorted to a cozy wood-paneled upstairs booth decorated to resemble the inside of a ship's cabin.

"You're so nice to take me to dinner," Camilla said after they'd placed their orders. "It's not every night I get to have a date with two handsome men."

"I think we're the lucky ones," Arnie replied.

"You're sweet. After dinner, I'm going to take you on a tour of the Key West most tourists never get to see."

"Would that include your apartment?" Robert asked.

"Aren't you naughty. I think we'll stick with a few bars and clubs. After all, this is our first date!"

Their entrees arrived, along with a bottle of wine. Arnie and Camilla ordered red snapper and Robert had conch and vegetable fritters. All were delicious. They polished off their meal with slices of fresh Key Lime Pie and Arnie excused himself for the restroom. When he returned, he saw that Robert had his arm draped around Camilla's shoulder and felt a brief flash of jealousy. It passed when he sat down and she squeezed his knee under the table. He and Robert settled the check, then followed her into the balmy night.

Camilla led them several blocks down Duval Street, then up a rickety stairway attached to a two-story Victorian house with gingerbread trim. They circled the building on a narrow second story veranda, then descended another set of stairs to an exquisitely manicured private garden. Behind a small bar set up in one corner was a bare-chested bartender wearing tuxedo pants and a red bow tie. A dozen people sipped drinks and chatted in the shadows. Arnie ordered beers and suggested they sit on a long stone bench next to two guys in their twenties. Robert nixed the idea when one kissed the other, and Camilla looked amused by his discomfort. When they finished their drinks, she suggested they move on to a nearby dance club, where they ordered more drinks and took turns gyrating with Camilla on the crowded floor.

"This next spot is my favorite," Camilla said as they took places at the end of a line of people waiting to get in a cabaret featuring female impersonators. The line moved quickly and soon they were watching a slender black singer lip-synching Natalie Cole's "Unforgettable." Afterward, they were entertained by a series of equally talented artists, the most impressive of which was the evening's final act. Two male bodybuilders wearing sandals and loincloths rolled a three-foot tall flowerpot sprouting a large artificial rose onto the stage. The opening bars of "Raindrops Keep Falling on My Head" played as the rose swayed back and forth in the pot, rising like a growing flower to reveal the head and torso of a chubby cherubic-faced singer holding an armful of long stemmed red roses. She was joined onstage by an ensemble of the previous performers—all carrying armloads of roses—and together they showered the enraptured audience with flowers as they sang. Arnie caught two of the long stemmed blossoms. He presented one to Camilla and tucked the other in the back pocket of his jeans.

"It's late, but there's one more place I'd like to show you," she said.

"Your bedroom?" Robert asked, slipping his arm around her.

"No, I don't think so," she said attempting to disengage herself.

Robert refused to let go, so Camilla settled for putting her other arm around Arnie's waist as they left the club and strolled further down Duval Street. She led them down an alley, through an unmarked doorway, then up a flight of stairs to a large high-ceilinged room with a semi-circular bar. Sitting at it were half a dozen people, including a striking platinum blonde woman in her late forties wearing an evening gown and staring morosely into a martini. Hanging over the bar was a gazebo-like scaffolding constructed of metal pipes supported by 6" x 6" timbers that resembled a children's monkey bar set. Crawling slowly through the bars was an agile young black man clad in a red leather jock strap. He contorted his gymnast's body in every way imaginable, to the delight of the customers below.

Arnie was feeling a bit thickheaded from drinking all night long, but he still ordered a round of beers and tried to ignore the attention Robert was showering on Camilla. When the drinks arrived, he headed for the restroom. On his way back to his seat, the blonde at the end of the bar touched his arm.

"Hi, I'm Veronica."

She was quite pretty and, Arnie realized, a man.

"I'm Arnie," he said, taking a half step backward.

She nodded toward Robert. "You have a handsome friend over there."

"That's Robert," Arnie replied, as the alcohol coursing through his veins spawned a devilish idea. "He's a very nice guy."

"He looks nice. You can always tell a man by the shoes. Your friend has nice shoes."

"His only problem is that he's terribly shy."

"Really?" Veronica raised an eyebrow. "He doesn't look shy to me." She gestured again toward Robert, who was groping Camilla.

"That's because he's talking to his sister."

"That's his sister?"

"Yep. In fact he was telling us earlier how pretty he thought you looked." Arnie reached to his back pocket and withdrew the rose he still had from the previous bar. "And he asked me to give you this."

"He wanted me to have this rose?"

"Yes."

"Really?"

"Why don't you go thank him. Just remember what I told you. He's shy, so you might have to be a bit forward. But I promise you, you won't be sorry."

"Are you sure?"

"I've seen him in the shower," Arnie said with a wink.

Veronica winked back, then made her way toward Robert, teetering on what Arnie imagined were very expensive high heels. He followed several paces behind and reclaimed his seat as she slipped onto the barstool by Robert. In a low voice, Arnie whispered to Camilla what was going on, then caught Veronica's eye and winked again.

Veronica winked back and placed her hand over Robert's.

"Thank you for the rose, thank you so much."

Robert looked at her in surprise. Before he could react further she wrapped both arms around his neck and kissed him on the mouth. He instinctively returned her kiss, then realized something was amiss and tried to pull away. By this time she had him in a full headlock and was exploring his tonsils with her tongue.

The two of them struggled for several seconds before tumbling to the floor in a clatter of barstools and beer bottles. Robert staggered to his feet first. "You fucking faggot!" he yelled. He balled his fist and pulled his arm back to swing at Veronica, but Camilla grabbed his wrist and spun him around, then slapped him hard in the face.

"Don't you dare call her a faggot, you asshole!"

They stared at each other for several seconds. Robert looked like he was considering hitting Camilla, then Arnie moved between them.

"I'm getting the fuck out of here," Robert finally said. "This place is too weird for me. I'll see you back at the boat, Arnie."

"You should have let him hit me," Veronica said, straightening her dress and giggling after Robert stomped off. "He looks so strong, I might have liked it."

Camilla laughed, and Arnie ordered a round of drinks for the three of them.

"Your friend is wound a bit tight, isn't he?" she asked.

"Oh, he's okay."

"Well, I still think he's a dreamboat," Veronica said. "Here's my card, in case he changes his mind and wants to call me tomorrow. I own the fabric shop around the corner."

They stood and Arnie hugged her.

"Sweet dreams," Veronica said, kissing them each on the cheek.

"Would you mind walking me home?" Camilla asked. "It's a long way back to my scooter, and I shouldn't be driving after drinking so much. My place is only a few blocks from here."

Arnie took Camilla's hand as they made their way down the street. The warm tropical breeze caressed their skin and an almost-full moon cast dancing slivers of light through the canopy of palm trees onto the sidewalk. Soon they arrived at a narrow white clapboard house behind a freshly painted picket fence. Camilla opened the gate and he followed her down the seashell-strewn pathway to the front porch, then gently rubbed her shoulders as she unlocked the front door.

"That feels nice," she said, turning to face him.

Arnie kissed her.

"That feels even nicer."

"Your lips are so soft."

"Other parts of me are, too," she said.

Leading him into her bedroom, she lit a candle on the dresser, then turned and kissed him again, this time for several minutes. They fell onto the bed and she reached to unbuckle his shorts and pull them off. She opened the drawer by the bedside table and withdrew a condom, then helped him roll it on. She slipped off her skirt and thong and lay back on the covers.

Arnie continued to kiss her and after a few moments, he raised himself over her, perched on his elbows.

"Be gentle," she said, guiding him inside her. "Now just be still for a minute." Arnie obeyed and Camilla moved slowly against him. Even through the condom, he could feel the walls of her vagina clutch his penis.

She dug her nails into his back. "Now don't be gentle any more."

He clenched her ass and thrust deeply, moving faster until he was pounding into her with all his strength, driving the frustration of the last few months far from his mind. Camilla came quickly, groaning in a long, shuddering orgasm. Then she opened her eyes and looked at him questioningly.

"Did you. . . ?" she asked.

Arnie shook his head.

"Good," she said, rolling him onto his back. "It's my turn to be on top for a while."

CHAPTER 31

Arnie woke the next morning to the aroma of chicory coffee and the sound of soft classical music. He couldn't recall how many times he and Camilla had made love, but his legs ached and every muscle of his body felt exquisitely drained. He remembered Stef and felt a vague twinge of guilt. It passed quickly when Camilla walked in with two large mugs of coffee. Her hair was pinned up and she was wearing a short Japanese bathrobe.

"I've got to be at work in forty-five minutes, or else I'd crawl back in bed with you," she said.

"Do you have plans for tonight?"

"Actually, I do," she said. "And besides, you're in love with someone, aren't you?"

"Uhh . . . not really," Arnie stammered as he got out of bed and pulled on his jeans. "What makes you say that?"

Camilla smiled. "I can tell. After last night, all I've got to say is that she's a very lucky girl. I'll send you an email when we have our next litter of kittens at the museum. Maybe I'll even deliver one in person. I've heard Nashville is nice."

"Key West is nice, too."

"It really is. So many interesting people visit here."

"I'm sure they do," Arnie replied, buttoning his shirt.

"Could I tell you a secret?"

"Sure."

"I was hoping to get both of you guys to come home with me last night."

"I'll tell Robert," he said, laughing as he swallowed the last of his coffee. "I'm sure he'll be glad to hear it."

Arnie kissed her goodbye and headed out the door, feeling fortunate to have been one of the interesting people in Camilla's life.

He stopped at a bagel shop for a second cup of coffee and enjoyed a leisurely stroll across town, reliving his pleasant memories of the night before and wondering if Robert was still upset about the incident with Veronica. When he arrived at the marina, he eased the ketch's hatch open and tiptoed down the ladder into the cabin. When he reached the lower deck, the door to the head opened and out stepped a top-heavy, completely naked girl with a ring of leaping blue dolphins tattooed around her naval.

"Aieeeee!" she squealed, and darted back into the head. She emerged a few seconds later wrapped in a beach towel and smiling sheepishly. She looked familiar.

"Hey, Arnie, this is Dawn," Robert said, coming out of his cabin in boxers and flip-flops. "You met at Sloppy Joe's a couple of nights ago."

"The shooter girl."

Dawn disappeared into Robert's cabin and came out a few minutes later in cutoffs and a halter-top.

"You gonna come see me later tonight, honey?" she asked Robert, standing on tiptoes to kiss him goodbye while simultaneously winking in Arnie's direction.

"If we're still here."

"Call me."

Dawn gave Arnie a playful side-butt with her plump rump as she walked by, then disappeared up the hatch. He turned to Robert. "So I guess last night wasn't a total loss?"

"No. I stopped by Sloppy Joe's on the way back to the marina and Dawn was getting off work. Turned out she'd had a fight with her boyfriend and needed a shoulder to cry on. So I bought her a couple of beers, let her cry on mine, then invited her to spend the night. Grabbed her crotch before I let her on the boat though—no more chicks with dicks for me."

They both laughed.

"So you're thinking about cutting out of here today?"

"Yeah," Robert said. "I just got off the phone with the guy who has the Testerossa for sale in Miami. There's another buyer interested, so we need to pack and get to the airport."

* * *

Three hours later, they made a perfect three-point landing at Miami International Airport. Outside the terminal they spotted a short man in a tropical suit standing by a white Ferrari Testerossa.

"Hi there, I'm Jon Uhm, Bayside Auto Brokers," he said, handing Arnie and Robert business cards. "Here it is—I just picked the car up from my client this morning, haven't had a chance to have it detailed. But as you can see, it's in pristine condition, a '91 Testerossa with only 34,000 miles."

"That's a lot of miles for a Ferrari," Robert said.

Jon unlatched the rear cowling without commenting and lifted it to reveal the massive twelve-cylinder engine that took up over half of the car's chassis. Robert performed a cursory inspection, then turned to Jon. "So you're asking $48,000?"

"No," Jon said, withdrawing a computer printout from his suit jacket. "Let me see, the blue book on the car is $55,000. We're asking $53,500, with a thirty day warranty included."

Robert frowned. "I thought the price was $48,000. I wanted to make you an offer, but all I brought was $45,000."

"Cash?" Jon raised his eyebrows.

Robert nodded. "I was hoping you might have the title with you, so we could do the deal and I could drive the car back to Nashville today."

"Hang on a minute," Jon said, pulling a cell phone from his pocket and flipping it open. He stepped a few feet away and talked for several minutes. "All right," he said. "I spoke to my office and I can go down to $49,000. I'll take $45,000 in cash and I'm authorized to accept a personal check for the balance.

Robert looked perturbed, then pulled out his billfold and thumbed through it. "I've got $1200 here, plus $45,000 in my bag. That's $46,200— it's the best I can do."

Jon furrowed his brow, then punched the keypad of his cell phone. He snapped the phone shut before the number connected.

"All right, this is gonna come out of my commission, but if you've got cash we've got a deal."

Robert started to unzip his bag, but Jon touched his forearm. "Let's at least go inside. This looks too much like a drug deal."

"Sure," Robert said. "Arnie, watch the car."

Jon removed the keys from the ignition and vanished into the airport with Robert. Arnie opened the Testerossa's passenger door and tossed in his bag. The leather interior was all business, with gauges and dials functionally marked like those of a racecar. A teenage girl in a Camaro convertible slowed as she drove by and flashed a sunny smile in his direction. Arnie smiled back and waved, but she kept driving.

Bored, he opened the glove box. In it were some old envelopes and a large black leather glove with something heavy stuffed inside. When Arnie inserted his fingers, they met hard rubber and steel. He grasped the object, gingerly removed it and found himself holding a thirty-eight caliber snub nose revolver. He thumbed the cylinder release and it fell heavily open, revealing five brass jacketed hollow-point cartridges that gleamed in the sunlight. He hurriedly snapped the gun shut and replaced it in the glove compartment as a security guard stepped out from behind a shuttle bus parked ahead of him.

"Sir, there's no parking or standing here."

Arnie felt his face flush. "I'm sorry, officer, I don't have the keys. My friend stepped inside for a minute. . ." Arnie gestured toward the airport entrance and saw Robert coming out the door. "In fact, here he is now."

The guard watched intently as Robert approached.

"We're good to go," Robert said. He put his suitcase in the small trunk up front and nodded to the cop, then got into the car and inserted the ignition key. The engine coughed once, then roared to life as he shifted into first gear and released the clutch. The rear wheels spun on the oil-slick surface, then the Pirellis gained traction and catapulted the Testerossa away from the terminal.

"First thing we need to do is get some gas," Robert said. "The tank's almost empty."

They found a service station near the car rental lots adjacent to the airport and Robert got out to fill the tank. Arnie had momentarily forgotten the pistol in the glove box due to his concern over the security guard, and realized that it was too late to do anything about returning it to Jon Uhm. He wondered if Jon even knew the gun was in the car, then decided he probably didn't, given the fact that he had just picked up the vehicle that morning and hadn't had a chance to have it detailed.

Robert finished fueling the car and walked to the attendant's booth to pay for the gas. Thinking of the contract Don Puccini may have out on his life, Arnie slipped the gloved handgun out of the Testarossa's glove box and into a side pocket of his carry-on bag.

He'd sleep a lot better in days to come with the thirty-eight within reach.

CHAPTER 32

Robert and Arnie arrived in Nashville late the next night. The Ferrari had run flawlessly. With its racing suspension and spartan amenities, it wasn't designed for extended interstate cruises. But any inconvenience was more than made up for by its breathtaking acceleration and handling, not to mention the envious looks they received from other drivers on the road. When Arnie mentioned how much he loved the throaty whine of the twelve cylinders behind him, Robert informed him that for many years Enzo Ferrari refused to include a radio option on his cars, insisting that to do so would interfere with the music of the extraordinary engines.

Arnie was tired when Robert dropped him at his apartment, but before turning in for the night he unpacked his bag and again examined the pistol he'd found. It was a five-shot Smith and Wesson Airweight, with a concealed hammer and aluminum alloy frame. The Beretta 9mm semi-automatic he'd been issued in the Marines had three times the magazine capacity, but he knew that the first shot was normally the one that counted, and no gun was more dependable than a revolver. A fighter pilot he'd known who carried one as backup—in addition to his service sidearm—summed it up best, "Keep pulling the trigger and eventually something'll happen." Arnie carefully reloaded the pistol and stashed it between the mattress and box springs of his bed, then fell fast asleep.

First thing the next morning, he drove to a coffee shop that offered Internet access, and logged into the anonymous email account the FBI had set up for him. Thankfully, there were no further warnings from Agent Baskins. The Miata felt like a cross between a go-cart and a soapbox racer after two days in the Testerossa and he reminded himself that a Ferrari of his own was just a hit song away.

Back at his apartment, he listened to the recording he'd made of "Safe Against the World" before he'd left town and was pleasantly surprised—

the song sounded even better than he remembered. He spent an hour tweaking it, then worked late into the night making a new recording of the tune, adding several guitar parts and a harmony track.

He called the office the next morning and Starr answered.

"How was your trip?" she asked.

"The perfect vacation—good to be gone, good to be back."

"I was in Key West a few years ago," she said. "There's a hotel I should have mentioned to you. It's on the south end of the island and has a deck and pool out back and it's—"

"Clothing optional?"

"That's the one! Did you find it?"

"As a matter of fact, I did."

"That's my Arnie."

"Any word on Stef's contract?"

"Buzz faxed a new agreement to her, but she's still not happy with it. As it stands now, her record deal is on hold. They've got a meeting set up Monday afternoon at four-thirty. Hopefully they'll get it straightened out then, or if not, at least she'll be free to pursue other opportunities."

"I hope it works out. By the way, I've got a couple of new songs I'd like to play for Sam when he gets a chance."

"I know he'll want to hear them. Call early next week and I'll set something up."

"Thanks!"

Arnie couldn't stop thinking about Stef's upcoming appointment, the outcome of which would determine the future of "Last Night Made My Day." He was tempted to call her, but was reluctant to do so since he had no idea where they stood with each other. That's why he was surprised to receive a voicemail message from her Sunday night. Amazingly, she sounded as if their tiff had never happened. What was even more surprising was that she asked if he'd mind attending her meeting the next afternoon.

CHAPTER 33

Monday dawned cold and gray. Arnie worked on his songs until mid-afternoon and was about to head to Sam's office when the phone rang. It was Stef.

"Did you get my message?" she asked.

"Yes, I was just on my way to your meeting."

"Thanks, I'd like for you to be there."

"Could I ask why?"

"I know that you need to keep a good relationship with everyone and I don't expect you to take sides with me or anything. But I've been considering some of the things you said. I think you have good judgment, and I'd like you to hear what goes down so you can tell me what you think afterward. I don't really trust any of those people."

"Aren't you going to have an attorney present?"

"Yes, but I don't have much confidence in him. I'm worried that he may have other irons in the fire with Sam or Buzz."

"I'll be there. But remember: once you sign, your agreement will be binding. It they present something you don't like, don't sign it. There are plenty of other record companies out there."

"Okay. I appreciate you saying that, even if it means your song may not come out. I know you're concerned. I'll see you shortly. Thanks again."

Arnie hung up and decided to walk to the meeting, reasoning that it might not be a bad idea to let it start without him. Razor had referred to Sam as a slick businessman and Stef had once called him a scoundrel, but Arnie had seen no sign of it. Sam was his boss, and had been nothing but fair with him so far.

Fifteen minutes later, he arrived at the office and heard agitated voices behind Sam's door.

"Starr, would you mind checking with Sam to see if he minds me being here?" he asked. "Stef wanted me to come, but I don't want to step out of line."

"Sure, Arnie, that's not a bad idea."

Starr knocked softly at Sam's door and entered. She emerged a few seconds later.

"Go on in," she said with a smile, then whispered as he brushed past her, "It was good that you asked."

Sam nodded at Arnie from behind his desk. Sitting across from him were Stef and a heavy-set white-haired man in a rumpled gray suit who Sam introduced as Jim Butcher, the record company's attorney. Stef's lawyer sat to her left, a pleasant-faced man in his thirties wearing khakis and a plaid shirt. He stood and introduced himself as Brian Peebles, then sat back down and picked up a freshly sharpened pencil and held it poised over a blank yellow legal pad.

"You know, Stefany, we've made the contractual changes you requested," Jim said as Arnie took a seat at the back of the room.

"You did not make the changes I asked for," she responded, tossing her hair. "Do you think I can't read?"

"Of course I know you can read." Jim smiled condescendingly. "What's the main problem you have with the way the new document is worded?"

"I have two concerns. The first is that the record company has options to keep me under contract for three years, yet is only committed to release one single. You've shortened the term from sixty to thirty-six months, but the company still has the option to keep me tied up if they decide to—and I have no options at all."

Jim looked at her gravely. Arnie couldn't decide whether he was weighing what Stef was saying or trying to decide whether having a wildcat like her on the roster was worth the trouble. "And the second problem?"

"Starr told me this morning that Buzz has decided to release 'Love Drops' as my first single. I wasn't consulted and I'd prefer it to be another song."

"It's not your decision, Stef," Sam said. "Things just aren't done that way."

"But I'm not going to let them put out a piece of shit like 'Love Drops' for my first single," she replied, pulling a cigarette from her purse and lighting it in spite of the "No Smoking" sign on Sam's desk.

"No record company ever gives an artist creative control over what songs are released as singles," Jim said. "The label will always respect your input, but the final decisions are made by company executives based on consultation with their promotion and marketing people."

"You're fucking with my career," Stef hissed.

"It's your career we're *creating,* Stef," Sam said firmly. "All of us together—you, me and the record company. You don't have to sign this contract, but I hope you do, because I think you have what it takes to be a star. And I have to tell you, Buzz Corbin is an experienced record man. If we want to work with him, we've got to do it his way, or it's not going to happen."

Stef cast a venomous stare at Sam.

"The way the contract is currently worded, you don't have anything to lose," Jim said. "We'll put out a single, if it doesn't fly we'll decline to pick up your option, and you'll be free to get another deal."

"Jim's right," Sam added.

"No he's not, goddamn it!" Stef turned to Jim. "What if you don't pick up my option—or even worse, what if you pick up my option and keep putting out shitty songs like 'Love Drops' and I never have a hit? You could keep me tied up for three years and I'll lose all the momentum I've worked so hard to build. I'm twenty-six years old—my record deal clock is ticking."

"She's got a point," Sam said, smiling in spite of himself. He glanced at the ceiling for a moment, then spoke, choosing his words carefully. "Jim, could I ask you something?"

"Sure."

"Stef's right, there's a time element here. Her record deal clock *is* ticking. I know the company won't budge on retaining the right to choose what songs are released as singles. But if Stef is tied up for three years without breaking as an artist, it *would* be tough for her to start over. What if you add a clause that voids the contract after the first year if she hasn't charted a single by then? In other words, the label could release as many or as few singles as they wanted, but if none of them reach an agreed upon chart position within that time, she'd be free to pursue another deal."

Jim thought for a few seconds. "I think something like that might be feasible." He pulled out his cell phone. "Would that make you happy, Stefany?"

"It might."

"Let me make a call." Jim excused himself, walked into the reception area, then returned. "Okay. I can do what you've asked, maybe even better. I can add a clause to the contract that states the company will release a minimum of one single within the first year, plus have the option to release an album. If Stef doesn't have a record that breaks into the top forty in *Billboard* magazine's Hot Country Singles chart within fifteen months, she's released from her deal. The record company retains ownership of the masters, of course, and they'll have the option to put out two more albums down the road if the contract goes full term. This will be a 360 deal, the label will want to recoup their investment in you by sharing in some of your ancillary income from concert and merchandising and so forth, but that's pretty standard these days"

"That's sounds fair to me, Stef," Sam said. "What do you think?"

"Okay," she said without hesitating. "Add that clause, initial it, and I'll sign the contract."

Brian Peebles woke up. "I think we've got a deal."

CHAPTER 34

When the papers were signed, Starr popped her head in the door to announce that Buzz Corbin was in the reception area. Arnie wondered if Stef could have pushed harder in her negotiations. If Buzz was already here, he must have known that she was going to sign the contract before she'd known it herself.

Buzz strode into the room. He was about fifty, short and pudgy, with a coconut tan and brilliant white capped teeth. He walked to Stef and extended his hand with the confident enthusiasm of a used car salesman approaching a pregnant couple eyeing a row of pre-owned minivans.

"Stef, it's wonderful to see you. Jim called earlier, and I drove over to tell you personally how happy I am that we've come to an agreement. I don't think we've ever signed an artist that I believe in as much as I believe in you."

"It's so nice of you to come by," Stef said, smiling demurely. "I think this is the happiest day of my life. When I first started working with Sam, I told him that of all the labels in town, yours was one I most hoped to record for. This is a dream come true for me."

Starr snapped photos of Buzz, Sam and Stef as they went through the motions of signing the contract again. Buzz shook hands all around, and Arnie walked Stef to the parking lot.

"You did well to be nice to Buzz after what he put you through," Arnie said.

She smiled. "You know what they say about show business. 'Sincerity is everything—once you learn how to fake that, you've got it made.'"

"The way he showed up like that, so quickly, I wondered if you could have pushed harder on the contract," Arnie continued. "It was almost as if he knew—"

"Buzz is no fool. Sam and I talked over the weekend and devised the idea of a one year kill clause."

"You and Sam worked that out ahead of time?"

"Yes."

"But aren't you worried about them releasing 'Love Drops' as your first single?"

"That's not going to be a problem. Trust me."

Arnie wondered if he could ever trust her—especially after seeing her cunning performance during the afternoon's meeting. If the company released 'Love Drops' and it wasn't a hit, there was little chance his song would ever see the light of day. Unfortunately, there was nothing he could do about it.

"Well, congratulations," he said as they reached the parking lot.

"Thank you."

Arnie leaned over to kiss her. "Another nicotine martini," he said.

"Yes," she giggled. "But I'm quitting as of today."

"How long will you be in town?"

"My flight leaves at nine in the morning."

"Do you have time to come by my apartment to listen to a new song?"

"I'd love to."

She drove them to his apartment and Arnie played her the latest recording of "Safe Against the World."

"God, I love that!" she exclaimed.

"Really? You're the first person to hear it."

"You haven't played it for Sam yet?"

"No."

"Let me hear it again."

Stef listened again, tapping her foot and singing along with the chorus. "You know, that would make a kickin' duet," she said when it was over. "Play it for Sam as soon as you can. If he likes it, I'll get him to talk to Buzz about hooking me up with a male artist at the label, maybe even Randy Fawcett."

Arnie's eyes lit up. Randy was one of the hottest singers on the charts—his last album had sold more than three million copies. "That'd be fantastic."

"I know; it's almost too much to hope for. But that song might be good enough to pique their interest."

"I promise to play it for Sam this week. Are you hungry?"

"As a matter of fact, I'm starved."

"What about sushi?"

"Sure, we can celebrate the contract."

They chatted through dinner about her upcoming Cayman Island cruise ship gig. She was looking forward to a break from the cold weather, and laughed uproariously at Arnie's recounting of his Key West adventures, especially the story of Robert and Veronica, which he recounted with Camilla carefully edited out.

"Ever had a wasabi kiss?" Stef asked when the story was concluded.

"What's that?"

Stef dipped the tips of her chopsticks in wasabi and touching a small amount to her lips, then leaned across the table and gave him lingering kiss that left his lips burning deliciously. Arnie took her hand under the table.

"That was terrific, how about another?"

Stef dabbed her lips with another dollop of wasabi and they kissed again.

"Arnie?" she said when they separated.

"What?"

"I've missed you."

"I've missed you, too. I thought you were going to call me before you left town a few weeks ago. When I didn't hear from you, I didn't know what was going on."

"I'm sorry. Sometimes I don't even know what's going on with me myself. I was feeling crazy the last time I was here, upset with Sam and Buzz—everyone. But I didn't want to stop seeing you."

"I'm glad."

"Maybe I'm scared because I really do like you. It scares me to miss you, but I do."

"I want to keep seeing you too, and to see if we might have a future together." Arnie's brow furrowed. "But there are some things about me that you should know."

"You haven't killed anybody, have you?"

Arnie hesitated for a second, wondering if New York had a death penalty—if so, it was possible that his testimony could send Tony Bertolini to the electric chair. He managed to crack a smile. "Not yet."

"It took you a while to answer," Stefany said, laughing. "Are you sure?"

"Yes, of course I'm sure."

"Are you in love with someone?"

"No."

"Well, I haven't killed anyone, and I'm not in love with anyone either. Maybe we should leave it at that, and see what happens. I think mysterious is nice It'll make it more fun getting to know each other." She leaned across the table and kissed him. "But I do want you to know that I like you—a lot. And I don't want to let this opportunity . . . whatever it is we have with each other . . . slip away. You mean too much to me."

"That's nice to hear, I feel the same way."

"Then that's all we need to know. Lovers take chances, they close their eyes and leap without knowing where they're going to fall."

"Sounds like another song title."

Stef smiled. "Could I ask you something?

"Sure."

"Would you stay with me tonight? We won't get to see each other until January, and I want to be close to you, like that first night we spent together. I just want to be with you."

"Okay."

When they eventually arrived at her hotel room, they kissed for a while on the bed. Arnie controlled his desire to ravish her, remembering her last reaction. They snuggled together and watched a movie until it was almost midnight, then Stef yawned and walked to the bathroom.

"You can take off some of your clothes if you'd like," she said before closing the door.

Arnie slipped out of his shirt and jeans and crawled under the covers in his shorts and T-shirt. In a few minutes, the bathroom door opened and Stef emerged wearing a short nightgown and translucent robe. Her dark hair fell in waves against the emerald-hued silk that covered her shoulders and he couldn't believe how lovely she looked. When she got to the bed, he rose to kiss her, but she gently pushed him down and slipped into bed facing away from him. He reached around to cup one of her breasts and pull her close. They lay without moving for several minutes with his erection jutting against the back of her thighs.

"You're not going to be able to fall asleep like this, are you?" she finally whispered.

"Uh. . ."

"Wait here for a minute."

Stef went back to the bathroom and returned with a small jade bottle. She removed the stopper and poured some oil into her palm, then pulled down the sheet and began massaging his stomach and thighs with the fragrant liquid. She poured more oil in her hand and held it for a few seconds, warming it, then slowly stroked his penis with one hand while massaging his scrotum with the other. The feeling was exquisite and in a few moments Arnie was writhing with pleasure. When he was about to come she bent her head to his chest and pinched his left nipple between her teeth. "You want this to last, don't you?" she said, licking his nipple softly.

"Yes, but. . ."

Several more times, she brought him to the brink of orgasm until he finally begged her to continue. This time she didn't stop. She continued to stroke him softly afterward, then leaned over to kiss his penis before getting up and returning to the bathroom.

In a moment, she returned with a hot washcloth, giggling as she wiped a dab of cum from her nose.

"That was wonderful," Arnie gasped as she gently cleaned his stomach and groin. When she was finished, he pulled her to him and kissed her. Her lips responded but when he slid his hand between her legs, she stiffened and pulled his arm away.

"No, please. Not tonight."

"What about you?" he asked. "You've made me feel so good—can't I do the same for you?"

"I feel good just being with you. And now you'll be able to sleep, my songwriter. Just hold me, okay?" She kissed him again and pulled his body close to hers.

"Arnie," she said, just as he was about to fall asleep. "Don't worry about 'Love Drops.'"

"What do you mean?"

Stef kissed him again.

"You'll see."

CHAPTER 35

The rest of the week passed quickly. Arnie still didn't know where he stood with Stef, other than he was dangerously close to falling in love with her—and somewhat apprehensive of the consequences if he did. Her manipulative skills were terrifying and he wondered if her career would always be the main priority in her life.

Starr had set up a meeting on Friday afternoon for Arnie to play his new songs for Sam. When he arrived, the producer was returning from lunch with Jazz, whom Arnie had last seen at Bound'ry. She looked stunning, tall and slender with delicious *café au lait* skin, and once again Arnie was reminded of the Disney character, Princess Jasmine. As it happened, she was wearing an indigo baseball cap with the word PRINCESS stitched in gold thread across the front.

"I've been meaning to ask you," Arnie said when she walked in. "Is Jazz short for Princess Jasmine?"

"People call me Jazz here in Nashville," she answered. "In L.A. I have a different name."

"What do they call you in L.A.?"

"I'm in Nashville now."

"Oh," Arnie said. "Will you be in town long?"

"I'm not sure."

"Okay, sweetie," Sam interrupted. "Here're the keys to the 355. See you at the house around six."

In a few seconds, Arnie heard the virile whine of the Ferrari's engine, followed by a screech of wheels and a blaring horn from some motorist who evidently didn't realize that a pretty girl in a Ferrari always has the right of way. Sam's face contorted, but the anticipated crunch of metal on metal never came, just a double toot of the Ferrari's horn accompanied by the fading sound of the 355's engine revs rising and falling as Jazz shifted gears into the distance.

"She's a pretty girl," Arnie said to Sam. "Is she a singer, too?"

"No, she's an actress and model—you may have seen her on TV. She's had a few bit parts here and there, and was a hostess for the Emmy's last year, you know, one of the chicks who hands out the awards and escorts people off the stage. She stays with me while she's in Nashville."

"Hope she's careful with the car!" Arnie said, handing Sam his CD.

Sam smiled. "I'm looking forward to hearing these. Stef called the other day and said that she thought you had one that might make a good duet."

He listened to the first song, "Daddy'd Be Proud," and nodded his head at the end of the final chorus. "Good work."

"Thanks," Arnie answered as the opening notes of "Safe Against the World" began to play.

Sam drummed his fingers on his desk all the way through the song and smiled several times. "That's strong," he said when it was over. He listened to the next two songs without comment, then withdrew the CD from the player.

"You've come a long way in the last few months. I'm not crazy about the last two tunes, but the first two are top notch. I can think of a number of pitches for 'Daddy'd Be Proud,' and I particularly like 'Safe Against the World.'"

"Thanks."

"Stef's right, it would make a great duet, and a duet would help establish her as an artist if we could get someone like Randy Fawcett interested in recording it with her. I'm going to have Starr set up a demo session for you sometime right after the first of the year. We'll record both of these, plus the song you wrote with Bubba last month. Hopefully you'll come up with a couple more good ones over the holidays."

"I'll do my best. I've been writing more with Bubba, and also have plans to work with Razor, the guitarist with the Appalachian Hellcats."

"Good, I liked their CD and may cut a few sides with them."

"By the way, do you know if Buzz Corbin has made a final decision on what Stef's first single will be?"

"It looks like it's going to be 'Love Drops.' I know it's a disappointment for you, and as far as I'm concerned it's not the strongest song we recorded. But I think I explained to you that part of the reason Buzz signed her is because he owns the publishing rights to the tune. Your song is still everybody's favorite, and they plan to release it as the second single."

If there *is* a second single, Arnie thought.

"There's so much politics in this business it's a miracle any music gets made at all," Sam continued. "But don't worry. The good news is that Stef shouldn't have any more contract problems. And there's an upside."

"What's that?" Arnie asked.

"It's tough to break a new artist. If 'Love Drops' does well, your song will follow it and almost surely be a hit. If 'Love Drops' stiffs, the record company probably won't pick up her contract option and we'll be free to pitch 'Last Night Made My Day' to other acts. If your song came out first and died halfway up the charts, other artists might be hesitant to record it."

"That makes sense."

"It's out of our hands at this point. Because Buzz publishes 'Love Drops,' he'll pull out all the stops to make it a hit. If he puts his mind to something, he can make shit happen."

"Really? I mean he doesn't look like he knows anything about music at all. How did he get to run a record company?"

"It's an interesting story. He got his start writing metal songs back in the seventies. Doesn't keep any pictures around, but he looked totally different back then—long hair, even a few tattoos. You'll notice he wears long-sleeved shirts most of the time nowadays."

"He started as a songwriter?"

"Song plugger, actually. Buzz was working for a publisher in L.A. pitching songs, and managed to get his name on a few tunes that did well. He parlayed his songwriting success into offers to produce a few people. His first project was a pop act that wanted to record like Frank Sinatra used to—with a full orchestra playing live all at once in the studio."

"It isn't done that way very often, is it?"

"No. It's ridiculously expensive, and there's too much that can go wrong."

"So what happened?"

"The label hired one of the top arrangers in L.A. for the project, so the parts were all written beforehand and placed on the musicians' music stands the night before the session. The story goes that Buzz bribed a janitor to let him sneak in the studio early the next morning with a pencil and eraser and changed a couple of notes on one of the string player's charts."

"And?"

"Then, when the orchestra showed up later on, he stopped everyone in the middle of the first take, and announced over the talkback microphone, "Excuse me, but there seems to be a problem with the second violin. Shouldn't the third note of measure such and such be an F rather than G, and the fourth note be C natural instead of C sharp?"

"Holy shit!"

"Yeah, no one could believe a human being could hear that well— not with fifty or sixty musicians all playing simultaneously. The violinist checked and found that, sure enough, Buzz was right. So he made the changes and Buzz got the reputation of having phenomenal ears. The next thing you know he was running a record company—he hasn't looked back since."

"What a story!"

"Like I said, he knows how to work the system. I'll never forget what he said when he took his job at the label. Someone asked him if he'd miss being on the creative end of things. He said, 'Hell no, I've spent the last ten years deciding what key or other some song should be in, now I'm ready to decide whether people live or die.' He got a haircut, took the job, and, as they say, the rest is history."

Arnie laughed.

"But he does know talent. He wouldn't have signed Stef if he didn't believe she has what it takes to be a star. Though, like I said before, it certainly helped that she cut 'Love Drops.'"

"I guess we'll keep our fingers crossed."

"That's right," Sam said, standing. "Do you have big plans for the Christmas holidays?"

"Not really, I figured I'd hang around town and work on my songs, especially if you're going to set up a demo session. I'd like to write a couple more killer tunes before then."

"I'm heading to Palm Springs with Nicole next week, most of the music companies close down for a couple of weeks this time of year–, but I'll be back after Christmas. One of the Ferrari guys, Cam, is having a few people over on New Years Eve. I'm sure you'd be welcome to join us."

"I'd love to."

"See you then. Have a great holiday."

CHAPTER 36

Arnie spent the next two weeks happily immersed in his songs. He enjoyed the fact that most Music Row offices were closed for the holidays—there was something oddly appealing about working hard while the rest of the world was on vacation. He spoke with Stef by phone a number of times. She was chatty but somewhat distant, and he was concerned that she didn't return a number of his calls, a fact he hoped was due to her being preoccupied with her performance schedule rather than entangled in a shipboard romance with a cabana boy or a steel drum player.

Bubba also spent the holidays in town and they co-wrote several times. One of the songs they worked on was called 'Lovers Leap,' a title inspired by his last conversation with Stef. He'd started it by himself, then played what he had for Bubba, who was able to pick the strongest parts of what he'd devised and suggest ways to link them together. A few hours later, they completed the song and agreed that it was one of their best collaborations so far.

Sam called a few days after Christmas to let Arnie know that he was back in town, and to invite him to dinner before Cam's New Year's Eve party. Arnie arrived at the restaurant and found his boss at the bar with Nicole.

"How's the songwriting coming?" she asked.

"Great!" Arnie answered. "Thanks to Sam, I've just had my first song recorded."

"That's wonderful, I'll keep my fingers crossed for you."

"Any new Victoria's Secret shoots?" Arnie asked.

"I'm featured in their spring catalogue."

"I'll look forward to seeing it."

Nicole smiled demurely, then excused herself.

Arnie followed her with his eyes until she disappeared, then turned to Sam.

"She's incredible."

"Thanks," Sam answered.

"How long have you been dating?"

"Oh I don't know—three or four years."

"Have you ever thought of marrying her? I mean she's gorgeous, she's acts like she's crazy about you, and she's a Victoria's Secret model for Chrissake."

"Naw," Sam said, shaking his head with a laugh. "There are too many others around. Plus, she's got two kids."

"Really? How old are they?"

"I'm not sure; I've never met them. One's a boy I think. I'm not sure about the other."

"You've been going out with her for three years and you've never met her children—and don't even know how old they are?"

"Besides, she'll be turning thirty-five this summer." Sam gave a mock shudder. "That's old!"

Arnie laughed in disbelief. Nicole was a world-class beauty; a million guys his age would marry her in a minute. "Well, you've got some amazing girlfriends. I don't know how you keep them all straight."

"It's a lot of work juggling them. You've got to keep new ones in rotation—like a movie producer always has new scripts in development. Or a racehorse breeder has new colts in training. You can win the Derby one year, but there's always next year and the Triple Crown."

They both laughed as Arnie imagined a Kentucky horse stable stocked with Ferrari Princesses.

Nicole returned as Robert walked in with Vinnie and the Ferrari Sluts. The hostess soon seated them at a large circular table at the rear of the restaurant. The talk through dinner centered on cars. The group discussed plans to attend various track events in the spring and summer, and Robert had already made hotel reservations to attend the big Southeast Regional get-together in Savannah in the fall. Vinnie was seated between Trayne and Middy, and Arnie noticed him smiling throughout dinner—and occasionally squirming in his seat. At one point the mechanic winked at

Arnie, and he could see Middy's arm angled toward Vinnie's lap under the table. Although neither of the girls' faces revealed anything, Arnie politely focused his attention elsewhere.

After their meal, the group headed to the suburb of Brentwood for the party. Arnie whistled as he followed Sam's Ferrari up the long drive to Cam's home, a palatial brick showplace with glass-enclosed pool and patio in the rear.

The burly insurance executive greeted Arnie with a slap on the back, and introduced him to his wife and to his daughter, Missy, a short brunette who was a sophomore at Ole' Miss University. She and her mother served the group beers and snacks as they lounged around the pool and recounted stories of the holidays.

When the conversation drifted to music, Sam sent Nicole to his Ferrari to get a copy of Stef's session. Arnie didn't know if it was Cam's expensive Bose speakers or a final equalization done by the mastering engineer, but "Last Night Made My Day" sounded better than ever. When the song was over, everyone applauded and assured him it would be a hit.

Cam's daughter was particularly impressed and took a seat next to Arnie. "I just know you're going to win a Grammy with that song," she said. "Do you own a Ferrari like Daddy's?"

"Not yet, but I'm planning to buy one when I get that Grammy," Arnie joked.

"Will you take me for a ride?"

"Of course."

"When I get back to school, I'll have my sorority sisters call every radio station in Mississippi and request your song. I just love it."

"Thanks."

"Would you ever write a song for me? Like, maybe I could inspire you sometime."

"Maybe you already have," Arnie replied, looking into her eyes. Missy had appeared wholesome and innocent to him at first, but now the innocent part seemed questionable. He glanced toward Cam, uncertain about the etiquette of dating one of the club member's daughters.

Missy excused herself to get more drinks for the guests and Arnie set off to find a restroom. He was halfway down the shrub-lined path toward the main house when he noticed a pool house to the left. Sure enough, there was a bathroom inside. After using it, he lingered for a moment to admire several paintings of island scenes in the dressing area.

The door opened and Trayne walked in. "I was just about to leave," he said.

"Come here, there's something I want to show you first," she said, locking the pool house door. She took him firmly by the hand and led him into the bathroom, latching the door behind them.

"I love your song," she said.

Arnie was at a loss for words, not so much from the several beers he'd had at dinner and by the pool, but by the sight of the two large breasts that popped out from under Trayne's tight purple Lycra top as she pulled it up.

"They're beautiful," he blurted.

"But that's not what I wanted to show you," she answered. She lifted her skirt. "What do you think?"

On the inside of her left thigh was a tattoo of unicorn's head with a delicate, spiraled horn that angled upward and disappeared under the lower seam of her purple thong.

"Uh, wow . . . it must have hurt!"

"Not much. Vinnie got it for me for me for my birthday last month. I'll bet you've got an interesting tattoo, too."

"No, actually I don't have any—" Arnie tried to protest, but she already had his belt unbuckled and was pulling down the zipper to his jeans.

"I don't believe you."

Before Arnie could react she had his pants around his ankles, and was on her knees taking him in her mouth. He was hard in a few seconds and she sucked him rapidly. He came in less than a minute and she leaned forward to take almost the full length of him down her throat.

Arnie leaned against the vanity on quivering legs and tried to catch his breath as Trayne stood and grinned. "I think you'd better get back to the pool. Your new girlfriend's going to wonder where you've been."

"Uh . . . okay . . . thank you," he said, pulling up his pants.

"Don't mention it . . . and don't forget to zip up your fly," she said, smiling at him in the bathroom mirror while straightening her hair and dabbing on lip gloss. "I love your song!"

Arnie walked unsteadily back to the pool, where he found Missy waiting for him with a fresh beer. They resumed their conversation, chatting about her favorite bands and plans to spend spring break skiing in Utah. A few minutes later, Trayne emerged from the pool house and rejoined Robert and Vinnie, who both grinned at him from the far side of the pool.

The party broke up just after midnight. Arnie exchanged phone numbers and email addresses with Missy as he left, unfazed by a pinch in the butt he received from Middy as she and Trayne passed behind him with Vinnie and Robert. He followed Sam and Nicole to the driveway where their cars were parked.

"I see you're getting with the program," Sam said.

"What do you mean?" Arnie asked sheepishly, wondering if Sam was aware of his interlude with Trayne.

"Interviewing Cam's daughter for a position as a future Ferrari Princess."

"I'm just learning from the master."

"You guys are terrible," Nicole said, shaking her auburn curls and laughing.

"Give me a call next week," Sam said. "Stef'll be in town Thursday for a meeting with Buzz. And I want to get that demo session set up. I'm anxious to play 'Safe Against the World' for him as soon as I can and see what he thinks about it for a duet with Stef and Randy."

"I'll do it!"

CHAPTER 37

Arnie woke the next morning to the sound of the phone ringing.

"Happy New Year!"

"Hi Stef, same to you."

"Hope you didn't get too crazy last night."

"No. . ." he replied hesitantly, as the details of the previous evening returned. "Not *too* crazy at least. How was your night?"

"We played later than usual, so I'm a bit tired."

"Sam mentioned that you'll be in town Thursday."

"Yes, we're meeting Buzz at one-thirty at his office to discuss marketing strategies for my first single. I was hoping you could be there; I think you might find it interesting."

"Sure."

"I can't believe it's been a month since we've seen each other."

"I know, I've missed you."

"Me too—more than you know."

* * *

Arnie was absentmindedly switching from one radio station to another on the drive to the office Monday when he heard a song that grabbed his attention. It was called "Frazzled" and had a melody and groove that was quite unusual for a country record. When he walked in the reception area he asked Starr if she'd heard it.

"Yes. That's Randy Fawcett's new single," she said.

"Do you know who wrote it?"

"Bob Markum."

"I think I've heard Bubba mention him."

"We've only met a few times—but his song plugger, Alison, is a good friend of mine. In fact, I'm having lunch with her tomorrow. I could check with her and see if he might be interested in co-writing with you."

"I'd appreciate that."

"The fact that Stef recorded one of your songs and has a deal now will help. I'm sure he'd love to have a cut on her album."

"That'd be great."

"By the way, I spoke to Sam this morning about booking a demo session for you and I've got calls in to the musicians and studio."

"Thanks."

"Keep writing those songs."

* * *

Shortly before one-thirty Thursday afternoon, Arnie arrived at the two-story West End Avenue office building that housed Stef's record company. He had read in *The Tennessean* earlier that week that Buzz was in the process of a half-million dollar renovation to the label's state of the art recording studio, and hoped to see it during his visit.

He emerged from the elevator into a reception area dominated by a nine-foot grand piano that had STEINWAY emblazoned in four-inch square gilt lettering in place of the original understated factory logo. As he gave his name to the receptionist, Arnie smiled at the company's advertisement of the fact that it could afford a hundred-thousand dollar instrument for lobby furniture. Soon an intern led him to Buzz Corbin's office, a walnut paneled room decorated with antiques and framed prints of hunting scenes. It looked more like the workplace of a senior partner in a law firm than that of a record company president. Sam and Stef were waiting and she jumped to her feet to hug him. She was wearing a lace bustier, frayed denim skirt and lavender cowboy boots. As usual, she looked beautiful.

They made small talk while waiting for Buzz, and Arnie noticed Stef glancing frequently at her watch as the minutes dragged by. Finally, at a little past two, Buzz breezed through a door cleverly concealed in the paneled wall behind his desk.

"Sorry to be late," he said. "I've been at lunch with George Ng, Randy Fawcett's manager."

"It's interesting that you should mention Randy," Sam said. "Arnie's got a great new song called 'Safe Against the World' that might make a good duet—possibly for Stef and Randy."

"I look forward to hearing it," Buzz replied. "Hmmm . . . a duet with Stefany and Randy. That's an interesting idea. There's a song in my publishing company that comes to mind. . ."

Just then the door behind Arnie opened and an enormous overweight black man wearing a baggy blue warm-up suit and oversized Clark Kent glasses lumbered in. He appeared to be in his mid-forties, was almost completely bald and had at least three chins. "This is Ronnie Dexter, our head of promotion," Buzz said.

"Nice to meet everybody," Ronnie said in the resonant voice of an ex-DJ.

Arnie wondered how many drive-time listeners had ever pictured the man behind the microphone as the gargantuan creature he really was. The door opened again, and a Latina woman in her thirties dressed in tailored jeans and a green satin blouse entered.

"Hi, I'm Nanci Morales, Director of Marketing." She shook hands with everyone, then faced Stef. "I want you to know that I love your music, Stefany."

"Thank you."

"And I particularly like the song 'Last Night Made My Day.'" Turning to Arnie, she added, "I understand that you're the writer."

"Yes," Arnie answered, surprised that she knew the song was his. "Thank you very much."

"We can't have a hit record without a hit song."

"Right," Buzz interrupted. "Speaking of songs, we're here to go over our marketing strategy for 'Love Drops.' We're all excited about it, aren't we Ronnie?"

Ronnie coughed, then said, "Yes, it's got a good beat . . . and it's kind of. . ."

No one finished his sentence for him, and Ronnie was apparently unable to think of anything further to say. Arnie was puzzled, as it seemed like an odd reaction from a promotion man.

"It's not my favorite," Stef said, abruptly.

Sam's head snapped sideways and he gave her a warning look.

"It's a great song," Buzz said. "And it's just what we need to break you to radio. As I said, we're all very excited."

"Is that the only reason you want it to be my first single?" Stef asked bluntly.

"I think it's a hit," Buzz said, rolling the diamond pinkie ring on his right hand with his thumb.

"What about the fact that you personally own the publishing rights to 'Love Drops'?" she challenged. "You'll make a pile of money by releasing it."

Arnie noticed Sam grimace and shift his stare to a painting of a Brittany Spaniel holding a pheasant in its mouth.

Buzz's smile faded a few degrees. "I'm surprised that you're more concerned with how I run my business than you are with your own career."

"My career *is* what I'm concerned about. But, speaking of business, I'm sure you know that in any other profession what you're attempting to do would be considered insider trading."

Buzz cleared his throat and sat up in his chair. "My business is selling records, and I'm damn good at it. If you have a hit with 'Love Drops,' everyone wins: you make money, I make money, the company makes money."

"And if I don't have a hit, I'm back on the street," Stef said. "Wouldn't it make more sense to release 'Last Night Made My Day' as my first single? Everyone loves it—you heard what Nanci just said."

"You should remember what your place is here, Stefany." Buzz leaned back and withdrew a cigar from a humidor on his desk. "There are hundreds of chick singers who'd give anything, do anything, to be sitting where you are right now."

"Then why don't you find one."

"Okay, young lady, this meeting is over," Buzz barked. He slammed his unlit cigar down on his desk and mashed a button by his phone. "You're going to have to leave the building."

"You've got it right, except for one thing—you're the one who's going to have to leave the building."

"What did you just say?"

"I said that you're going to have to leave the building."

"And why would that be?"

"Because I own it."

"You own *what?*"

"The building."

"You own this building?"

"That's what I said. I own the fucking building." Stef crossed her arms. "Actually, my father does. And you're going to have to leave—not now, but next month, when your lease expires."

"What the hell are you talking about?"

An off-duty Metro policeman burst through the door into the office. "Is there a problem, Mr. Corbin?"

"Uh . . . I'm not sure," Buzz sputtered. "Wait outside please."

"What were you saying about the building?" Buzz continued, his face beet red.

"My father bought this building last week," Stef continued. "Your lease expires in February. I know you're still negotiating the terms of your new lease, and at this point only have a handshake deal with the rental agent. You've invested more than a half-million dollars in the recording studio downstairs and if the label has to move, you'll be out every cent of it. I don't think your bosses in Los Angeles would like that."

"I'll have to talk to my attorney about this," Buzz said.

"I've already talked to mine, and he says you'll have to go."

"Brian Peebles?" Buzz said incredulously.

"No, my father's attorney in New York. I know Brian's in bed with all of you guys."

"Okay, Stefany," Buzz said. The used car salesman returned. "Listen, we're all in this for the music. I'm confident that we can work things out in a way that's satisfactory to everyone."

"I hope we can," Stefany said, getting to her feet. "If we can't, I think I'll really like this office."

Buzz stared at her without speaking.

"Once I get rid of all the dead animal pictures on the walls."

Stef turned and marched out the door. Arnie and Sam followed, along with Ronnie Dexter and Nanci Morales. Nanci caught up with Stef down the hall, just as she was about to get in the elevator.

"I can't believe you stood up to Buzz like that," Nanci said. "Whatever happens, let's meet for a drink sometime. It's nice to have an artist with your kind of fire at the label."

Arnie's ears perked up and he added "Your Kind of Fire" to his list of potential song titles.

Stef smiled and shook Nanci's hand. "I'd like that."

Sam followed Stef and Arnie into the elevator. When the door closed, he said, "You'll either get what you want Stef, or I'll never produce another album for Buzz's company. Either way, I think we all could use a drink."

It was an unseasonably warm afternoon for January, with the temperature in the low sixties, and Arnie and Sam took the tops down on their cars and screeched out of the parking garage to a nearby Mexican restaurant. They sat on the outside patio and drank a pitcher of margaritas, then ordered another.

"All right. Let's head back to the office and see if we still have careers," Sam finally said.

It was five-thirty when they pulled into the parking lot. Starr was on her way out the back door.

"What in the hell happened with you guys and Buzz this afternoon?" she asked.

"Did he call?" Sam asked, grimacing.

"No, he came by. Personally. Have a look inside."

They followed her into the office. Perched on the desk, couch and chairs in the reception area were six crystal vases, each containing a dozen long-stemmed red roses. Amidst the containers was a three-foot tall card that read: STEF, IT MAKES OUR DAY TO HAVE AN ARTIST WITH YOUR CONVICTION AND TALENT ON OUR ROSTER. GOOD LUCK WITH YOUR FIRST SINGLE, "LAST NIGHT MADE MY DAY." RELEASE DATE: MARCH 1. LOVE, BUZZ, NANCI AND RONNIE.

"I guess we're still in business," Sam said jubilantly as they all clasped each other in a wild rugby scrum of a hug. Stef picked up one vase of roses and insisted that Starr load the others into her car.

"Some man's going to be very jealous," Stef said.

"Several," Starr answered with a laugh. "It'll be good for them."

CHAPTER 38

Arnie and Stef drove to a cozy restaurant in Hillsboro Village called Belcourt Taps and Tapas for dinner. Though they were still tipsy from the margaritas, she insisted on celebratory martinis and a bottle of cabernet with their meal.

"So tell me about your father," Arnie said as he glanced around at the establishment, whose walls were decorated with gold and platinum records from some of Nashville's biggest stars. "What's he like—and how the hell did he manage to buy the building?"

"He's a businessman."

"What kind of work does he do?"

"When people used to ask my mother that question, she'd say 'he owns things,'" Stef said, laughing.

"I guess he owns that office building now."

"Yes. I told you once that he's offered many times to help me with my career, but I've always wanted to make it on my own. When I told him there might be a problem with Buzz, he made some calls and figured out a way to ensure things worked out in my favor. It's how he does business. He likes to be in control, to get his way, and he usually does. And he doesn't want his little girl to be unhappy."

"You seem pretty capable of taking care of yourself."

"Maybe I got that quality from him."

"What else does he own? I mean, I didn't realize you came from a wealthy family. That building must have cost several million dollars."

"Arnie, let's not talk about my father right now. He's successful, but I don't want you to be after me for my family's money."

"Actually, I'm after you for your beautiful body."

"Then why are you staring at that other woman's boobs."

Arnie realized that he had in fact been glancing towards the bar where the restaurant's buxom co-owner was holding court with several hip-looking characters who looked vaguely famous. "It's sort of hard not to, actually. Especially since I think she just sent us a round of shots. And you know it's been a while since I've had the pleasure of seeing yours."

A waiter arrived with the drinks and said "These are compliments of Rose, she and her husband saw Stefany perform on a cruise last winter and they're big fans."

"So you missed me?" Stef asked pressing her knee against his under the table, after they'd raised their glasses to Rose in appreciation.

"Of course I missed you. I missed you like crazy. Whenever you're gone I can't stop thinking about you. Then, when I see you again, you surpass all my best memories."

"Spoken like a songwriter, but I am very touched anyway."

"It's true."

The pressure from Stef's knee on Arnie's grew and she smiled.

"Then why don't you take me to your apartment and show me how much you've missed me?"

When Arnie stood, the full effect of the afternoon's and evening's drinks hit him, and he was glad his apartment was only a few blocks away. When they arrived, he locked the door behind them. Stef leaned with her back against the wall, placed one of his hands on her breast, then kissed him so hard it felt like his lips were going to bleed. After several minutes she led him to the bedroom and they fell onto the bed.

Arnie lifted her denim skirt and caressed Stef through her panties. The tops of her inner thighs were slick, and she writhed against his hand. He slipped her underwear off, then reached into the night table drawer for a condom, though in his present inebriated state the idea of her becoming pregnant with his child seemed like the most wonderful thing in the world. He unbuckled his jeans and yanked them around his knees and maneuvered himself between her legs, then rolled on the condom.

"No . . . ," Stefany moaned, clutching his arms and pulling him toward her.

Arnie pressed the tip of his condom-clad penis against the moist lips of her vagina.

"No . . . no, I said!"

Stef's body suddenly went rigid and Arnie raised himself on his elbows to catch a vicious slap in the face. Astonished, he gripped her in a boxers clinch as she swung again, rabbit-punching him in the ribcage and kidneys with one hand, and raking his exposed forehead and cheek with the fingernails of the other.

"What's going on?" Arnie yelled as he tumbled out of bed, hobbled by his jeans, which were still around his ankles.

She lurched toward him and started to swing again, but he grabbed her wrists and fell on top of her, pinning her to the mattress and narrowly avoiding being kneed in the balls.

"Don't hit me again, or I'll knock the shit out of you," he yelled, furious. "I thought you wanted to make love."

Stefany struggled to free herself and Arnie held on with all his strength. After several minutes, her efforts grew weaker.

"I'm going to let you go," he finally said. "Don't hit me again. I won't make you do anything you don't want to do. Just tell me what the hell is going on."

She glared at him like a caged rat, then her body went limp. Arnie slowly relaxed his grip while eying her carefully, then finally released her wrists. She ran to the bathroom and slammed the door. He pulled his jeans on, grabbed a beer from the kitchen refrigerator, then returned to the bed and stared at the bathroom door.

When something dripped into his eye, he realized his forehead was bleeding. He returned to the kitchen and checked his face in the toaster's reflection. There were several gouges, one of which appeared to be fairly deep. Soaking a paper towel in cold water, he cleansed them the best he could, then sucked down his beer and opened another. Fifteen minutes later, Stefany emerged from the bathroom.

"Take me to my hotel, or call me a cab if you're too drunk to drive me."

"Not until you tell me what this is all about."

"No."

"I think I'm falling in love with you, and I'm not taking you anywhere until you tell me what just happened."

It was the first time the word *love* had come up between them, and they stared at each other for a few seconds. Stef walked to the night table and picked up the phone.

Arnie rose from the bed and took the receiver from her hand. "Listen Stef, you've got to tell me what the hell's going on. The last thing in the world I want to do is to hurt you. I thought you wanted to have sex . . . the things you said. . ."

Her shoulders drooped and she began to sob. Arnie put his arm around her and led her to the living room couch. "Do you want some coffee?"

"No. One of those would be nice though," she said, nodding at his beer.

He got her one and they sat in silence for several minutes.

"I'm sorry. I'm so sorry," she finally said. "You didn't do anything any other man wouldn't have done. I was sending all the right signals, and part of me even wanted to."

"But we've done other things before . . . like the last time you were in town . . ."

"There's something we need to talk about," she said. The skin around her eyes crinkled as she shuddered and broke into fresh tears.

"Something I did? Something I said tonight?"

"No, something that happened to me a long time ago."

"What?"

"Someone. . ." she paused.

"Someone what?"

"Someone hurt me."

"What do you mean? Like, abused you or something?"

"Raped is a better word. It was my cousin."

"Really?"

"Yes."

"Did you tell anyone about it? Report him to the police?"

"No. When I threatened to, he got a big kitchen knife and shoved the handle inside me. I thought I was going to die. He said he'd do the same thing with the sharp end if I ever said a word to my parents or anyone else. I believed him then and I believe him now. I told my mother I was sick and stayed in bed for a few days. Then I went back to school. That was fourteen years ago. I was twelve and he was seventeen. I haven't been able to be intimate with a man since then. I thought I was going to be able to with you, because I care for you. Maybe I will someday. I just don't know. God, I'm so fucked up."

Stef started to cry again and Arnie put his arms around her. She leaned closer.

"I told you that I'm falling in love with you, Stef. I mean that."

"I think I might be falling in love with you, too," she said, wiping her eyes. "But it scares me. I dated someone when I first started coming to Nashville; he was in the music business, too. It turned out he was married, and—"

"And he wasn't me. Let's try to get some sleep; we're both exhausted. We'll talk more tomorrow."

He swept her into his arms and gently placed her on the bed, where she quickly fell asleep. Arnie stared at the ceiling for a long time, finally drifting off as the first light of morning filtered through the shades.

CHAPTER 39

Arnie didn't know how Don Puccini had found him, but it didn't matter. He was lying on the floor with his wrists and ankles bound tightly with duct tape, staring at three sticks of dynamite wired to an alarm clock placed in front of his nose. No matter how he twisted his head and neck, he couldn't reach the clock. It was ticking and the noise grew louder as the minute hand approached the terminals of a nine-volt battery taped to the top of the dial.

The ticking increased in volume, finally becoming a loud metallic click, and he woke from his nightmare to see Stef by the night table holding the pistol he'd found in the glove box of Robert's Testerossa in an expert two-handed grip. She turned in his direction and Arnie tumbled to the floor on the far side of the bed.

"No!" he yelled in stark terror, knowing the gun's lethal hollow point bullets would penetrate the mattress like tissue paper.

"Don't worry, it's not loaded," she said.

"Yes it is!"

There was another click as Stef pulled the trigger. Arnie slowly raised his head and peeked over the mattress. She was now pointing the gun at the ceiling fan. The revolver's two-inch barrel moved in a barely discernable arc as Stef followed the motion of one of the blades, leading it with the precision of an Olympic trap shooter. "You look like you've done that before," he said, ready to duck behind the bed again.

"Enough to know that it's bad to dry fire a gun too much," she said, lowering the pistol and thumbing the cylinder release. She slipped five shells from her lap into the cylinder and snapped it home with a flick of her wrist.

"But you should find a better place to hide it," she said, stifling a yawn and standing to hand the gun to Arnie butt first. "Haven't you heard the story of the Princess and the Pea?"

"The fairy tale?"

"Yes. Your pistol kept me up half the night, digging into my back through the mattress."

"You really are a princess, aren't you?"

She smiled.

Arnie made his way into the kitchen, stashed the gun in a box of plumbing parts under the sink and set about making coffee.

"Are you angry with me about what happened last night?" she asked.

"No, I'm pretty sure I'm in love with you."

She laughed. "Well, you may change your mind when you look in the mirror. My nails did quite a job on your face." She touched his cheek. "But there's only one bad place. Wait here."

She went to the bathroom and returned with Band-Aids and Neosporin. "You know, I've been crazy about you since the moment I saw you," he said when she was finished and had called a cab. "No matter what happens, I somehow feel closer to you afterward."

Stef took his hand and squeezed it. "I feel the same way."

"We've really gone through a lot in the last twenty-four hours."

"I think Woody Allen or someone once said, 'relationships are like sharks, they've got to keep moving.'"

"Well, we've certainly covered a lot of ocean on this visit."

"The next few months will be incredibly busy for me, but I want to be with you as often as I can."

"I think we can accomplish that."

The taxi arrived and Arnie watched Stef walk down the sidewalk. Just before it drove off, she turned and blew him a kiss. He felt a brief twinge of pain from the bandage covering the gouge on his face and wondered what the hell he was getting himself into, but something in his heart told him it was too late to turn back now.

CHAPTER 40

"What happened to your face?" Starr asked, gesturing toward the bandage over Arnie's eyebrow when he stopped by the office on Monday.

"Uh, I. . ."

"Fell down some stairs?"

"Yeah, that's the excuse the police use, isn't it?"

"Watch out for those flights of stairs, especially the ones wearing high heels and a bit too much makeup."

"Always a good idea."

"I'm glad you came by, I was about to call. I've got dates for your demo session nailed down. You'll be tracking on the first Tuesday in February."

"Great. Any news on Stef's single?"

"It'll be released March 1st, like Buzz promised. The label's got press interviews and photo shoots lined up for her when she gets back to town next week, then she'll be on a two week pre-release radio tour at the end of February. She's got such a magnetic personality, Nanci and Ronnie want to have her meet as many DJs as possible in person before the actual release date."

"I can't wait until it comes out."

"Just be patient, the best thing you can do is keep writing. Speaking of which, I spoke to my friend Alison, Bob Markum's song plugger, about you guys working together. He's booked solid for the next few months, but she promised to call if there's a cancellation."

"Thanks, Starr. I do appreciate your help."

"Sure. Sam's in New York this week, but he'll be wrestling at the Fairgrounds next Friday night with Bobbie. I can't make it, but you should check it out, especially if you've never been to a live wrestling match before. It's quite a spectacle."

"Maybe I'll even get a song out of it."

"You never know."

* * *

Arnie stuck to his routine in the following days, focusing as hard as he could on his work—partly to avoid obsessing about the upcoming release of his song, and partly because he was determined to keep his good fortune rolling. He thought often about the long hours he'd spent rehearsing with his band in New York, and the dozens and dozens of songs he'd written for them—all without success. He was now in a position to make a living from songwriting and he was determined to make it happen.

By the night of the wrestling match, he was ready for a break. The Tennessee Fairgrounds were located in a run down semi-industrial area a few miles south of downtown. The sprawling hundred-acre site included the old Nashville Motor Speedway racetrack and a motley collection of concrete block buildings used for craft fairs, gun and knife shows, and a monthly flea market. A banner announcing WRESTLING TONIGHT stretched over the entrance of one of the larger halls and he spotted Sam's Ferrari 430 parked under the watchful eye of a Metro policeman at the head of the crowded parking lot. The closest space he could find was more than a hundred yards away, and he walked as fast as he could between the dimly lit buildings, glancing furtively around him and wondering if he would ever get over the fear he felt since the shooting in New York. He paid fifteen dollars for a ticket, then entered the main arena, which thundered with the roar of the crowd yelling at the top of their lungs. As he stepped inside, he froze in his tracks. Sprinting toward him from the ring was a deeply tanned seven-foot tall man clad in a leopard skin Speedo and knee-high fringed boots. His sweat-soaked face and shoulder length platinum hair were streaked with blood streaming from an open gash on his forehead.

Chasing close behind the bronze giant was a barrel-chested geezer waving a folding metal chair menacingly over his head. As the younger man approached to within twenty yards of Arnie, he paused to look back over his shoulder and the chair crashed down on his skull with a loud *whack!* that splattered blood and perspiration over the nearby spectators.

Arnie had always heard that the action at wrestling matches was faked, but the blood and cuts certainly looked real, and the blow from the chair had to have hurt like hell. As the giant continued forward and staggered past Arnie out of the arena, Arnie felt the full violence of the crowd's bloodlust focused in his direction for a split second. The sensation was terrifying. The fans then shifted their attention to the wizened older wrestler, who had to be at least sixty, and cheered as he waved the chair in the air, then set it on the floor and leaned on it, wheezing and shaking his head at the audacity of his challenger. Finally, he turned and limped wearily back toward the ring, dragging the chair behind him to the continued applause of the crowd.

When the arena quieted, Arnie spotted some empty seats in the bleachers, but, hoping for a better view, headed toward the rows of folding chairs set up at ground level around the perimeter of the ring. Miraculously, he found a vacant third row seat next to a leather-faced woman in her fifties who informed him that the chair's occupant had "done gone." Arnie thanked her and settled into the chair, noting that sitting on her far side were a chubby girl about six years old and a woman in her thirties who looked like she could squash him like a bug. The women shared similar features, and Arnie realized that he was sitting next to three generations of wrestling fans.

Soon the sound system blared the opening notes of John Cougar's "Hurts So Good" and the referee announced the next event: a ladies title match billed as "Battle of the Boobs," featuring Tits Witless and Badass Bobbie, aka Busty Valentine. A tall and heavily made up blonde with a Barbie-doll-on-steroids figure trotted from the locker room wearing an American flag swimsuit and white knee high lace-up leather boots. She was followed by her manager, a stocky middle-aged woman dressed in combat fatigues and an MP helmet slapping a police nightstick against her palm in time to the music. The two women slipped through the ropes into the ring and paraded in circles to cheers from the crowd.

The music segued to the Donna Summer classic "She Works Hard for the Money" and Bobbie came running to the ring dressed in a streetwalker's outfit consisting of a crotch length black vinyl skirt, fishnet pantyhose and a sheer red tank top that showed off every detail of her new boob job. As an added fashion accessory, she carried a live four-foot boa constrictor draped over her shoulders. Trotting behind her came Sam, dressed in a pimp outfit: a dark double-breasted suit complete with a white velour turtleneck, multiple gold chains, a slicked back black wig, and thin moustache penciled on his upper lip.

Bobbie waved the snake at Tits Witless, who appeared to be terrified of it. Her manager screamed in protest at the referee and swung her nightstick at Bobbie, who continued to chase Tits with the writhing reptile. Finally, the referee got a grip on the constrictor's tail, jerked the serpent from Bobbie's grasp, and handed it to Sam, who stuffed it in a burlap sack and turned to the crowd with his arms outstretched in protest. He got little sympathy. Meanwhile, Tits retreated to her corner of the ring and checked her makeup in a compact provided by her manager.

The bell clanged and Tits and Bobbie circled each other warily, making feinting moves. Bobby grabbed one of Tits's wrists and swung her against the ropes, but Tits came boomeranging back and vaulted high over Bobbie's head with her legs spread wide, drawing cheers from the crowd. She landed and deftly spun around to ricochet off the ropes again with a body block that knocked Bobbie on her ass. Tits dove on top of her, but Bobbie wriggled loose and got Tits in a half-nelson hold. She smashed the blonde's forehead into the canvas, then twisted a shank of her hair in her free hand and yanked it with all her strength. Tits screamed and the ref broke them up, motioning with exaggerated gestures to Bobbie that hair pulling was illegal.

The two women circled, then grappled and tumbled to the canvas once more. Tits got behind Bobbie, placed a knee at the base of her spine, slipped her right arm around her neck, then interlocked the fingers of her left and right hands and snapped Bobbie's head back. Sam yelled at the ref, but to no avail as the chokehold continued for several minutes. Bobbie grew weaker and weaker. Then, just when it seemed she was about to pass out, Bobbie miraculously rose to her feet, carrying Tits upward on her back like a papoose as she bent forward at the waist. Tits's feet left the ground and Bobbie continued to bend forward, finally flipping her over her head. Tits landed on her back with a dazed thud. Bobbie climbed halfway up one of the corner posts and clenched her fists over her head, then made a swan dive onto Tits. She landed with a pulverizing crash, pinning Tits to the mat, and the referee knelt and started to count. "One, two—" Suddenly, Tits's manager reached under the ropes and swung at Bobbie with her nightstick, landing a blow to one of her legs with a loud *thwack!* The referee stopped counting and jumped to face the manager, motioning her away with exaggerated gestures, which she appeared not to comprehend.

Meanwhile, Sam crawled through the ropes from the opposite side of the ring with the burlap sack containing the boa constrictor. He pulled the snake out and waved it at Tits, whom Bobbie still had immobilized. Tits screamed in terror as Sam thrust the snake at her face, and then attempted to force its head down her cleavage.

The referee, who was still facing away from Tits and toward the crowd, feigned puzzlement at their screams of protest, shrugging and cupping his hand to his ear as if trying to comprehend the problem. Tits' manager waved her nightstick, and the ref warned her again, still oblivious to Sam terrorizing the girl just behind him.

As the referee began to turn around, Sam whisked the snake back into the burlap bag and slipped out of the ring, then strolled nonchalantly back to Bobbie's corner, whistling and running his fingers through his hair. Tits's manager took this opportunity to reach through the ropes and bop Bobbie a good one on the head with her nightstick. The ref spun back around to see Tits flip the apparently unconscious Bobbie onto her back and raise a leg high in the air to pin her shoulders to the canvas. He dropped to a knee and counted, "One, two, three!!!"

The crowd cheered and Tits jumped to her feet. The referee raised her hand in victory and paraded her around the ring with her manager following behind holding an oversized championship belt with a gigantic brass buckle overhead. Occasionally the manager paused to kick Bobbie's prostrate body, which was being ministered to by Sam, and Tits admonished her, telling her to "Be good."

Sam couldn't seem to revive Bobbie. Arnie was puzzled by the fact that, unlike other professional sporting events he had attended in the past, there weren't any medical personnel present. After several minutes, Sam and the referee dragged Bobbie's limp form to the edge of the ring and flopped her onto a folded metal chair provided by an usher. Then they slid the chair under the ropes, and Sam and the usher hoisted the makeshift stretcher and carried Bobbie back to the locker room as the crowd chanted "Roadkill, roadkill, . . ."

Arnie waited several minutes, then headed for the portal leading to the locker rooms. Sam poked his head out a doorway down the hall and the rent-a-cop guarding the passageway let him pass. Inside, Arnie found a fully recovered Bobbie sitting on a bench with Tits, laughing and slugging Gatorade.

"Good match, Bobbie," he said.

"Thanks, Arnie. This is Trixie," she said, pointing to her opponent of a few minutes ago. "And this is Karen." She nodded toward Tits's manager, who was changing out of her MP's outfit into jeans and a sweater with no apparent concern for modesty.

"Get any good song ideas tonight?" Sam asked.

"I did. I'm thinking of writing a song called 'Roadkill.'"

"I like that." Bobbie popped. "Sounds like a kick ass song!"

"Well, I guess I'm out of here," Karen said. "I have to be at work early tomorrow."

"I've got to be in the studio myself," Sam said.

"What do you do, Karen?" Arnie asked.

"I'm an attorney with the Department of Human Services. Our work never stops, even on the weekend. I've got to be in my office to take a deposition at eight o'clock."

"Well, you certainly have an interesting hobby," Arnie commented.

Karen laughed. "It's not that different from what I do during the week, fighting the bad guys . . . and girls." She gave Bobbie a wink, then walked over and kissed Trixie on the lips. "See you later, honey."

"Okay, sweetie," Tits replied with a sunny smile. "I'll be home soon, after Bobbie and I finish signing autographs for the fans."

Arnie said goodnight to the group, then headed to the parking lot. As he drove home, a melody began forming in his mind that would be perfect for "Roadkill."

CHAPTER 41

The tune for "Roadkill" was still rolling through Arnie's head the next morning. He sat at the kitchen table, slamming power chords on his guitar and scribbling lyrics, and the song came together quickly—almost as if he'd been unconsciously writing it while he slept. By lunchtime, he had it completed and he spent the afternoon and early evening making a recording to play for Sam. As he did, he envisioned how a full studio demo would give it the kind of AC/DC or Def Leppard arena rock sound he had in mind.

While he was working, Bubba called to say he was performing at a writer's night that evening. When Arnie finished recording, he bundled up and headed across town to the club. His friend ended the evening with the most recent song they'd written, and Arnie was thrilled at the audience's response to it. Sendy was there with two cute girlfriends, and came up after the performance to congratulate Arnie and Bubba, who suggested they all head back to Hillsboro Village for drinks.

Outside the club it was snowing lightly, and Arnie zipped up his jacket and shivered as he waited for his car to warm. When he arrived at the bar, he noticed two familiar looking Ferraris parked out front—a yellow 348 and a red four-seat Mondial sedan. Inside, he found Sam's attorney friend Ted laughing at the bar with Buford and Lars. Arnie re-introduced himself, along with Bubba and the girls.

"Hey, good to see you Arnie," Ted said, slapping him on the back. "How's Sam doing?"

"Fine," Arnie answered. "Saw him last night. In fact, I think he's working in the studio today."

"He called at dinner—but it didn't sound like he was working," Buford said with a chuckle. He had lost weight recently; the gray cashmere turtleneck and tailored wool slacks he wore hung loosely from his lanky frame.

"What kind of work do you guys do?" Arnie asked Buford after their drinks arrived.

"Telecom. Computer systems and stuff," Lars replied.

"We're also putting together an IPO for a new company that's developing a blood sugar monitoring system for diabetics," Buford added. "It'll send out an electronic alert to the doctor's office if the patient is in danger, and has software to communicate back and forth to administer insulin if necessary."

"Aren't there companies that already do things like that?" Ted asked.

"Actually, we're both waiting for our parents to die so we can live off our trust funds." Lars said with a pronounced sniffle as he lit a cigarette.

Arnie and Bubba ordered several rounds of drinks and continued chatting with the group until it was well past midnight. Sendy and the girls were particularly fascinated by Ted's description of the new home he was building in Belle Meade, which featured a four car garage decorated with Ferrari memorabilia and custom painted full wall murals to make it look like a Grand Prix pit stop. He referred to it as his "Ferrari Shrine." As they were settling up with the bartender, Buford's cell phone rang.

He listened briefly, then thumbed in a number. After a few moments, he flipped his phone shut.

"That's odd, Sam just called. He didn't say anything, but there was music in the background, and weird noises, almost like someone groaning.

"Are you sure it was Sam?" Lars asked.

"Yeah, here's his number on my caller ID. But he didn't pick up when I called back. The line just flipped over to voice mail."

"Try calling him again."

Buford tried, then shook his head. "Still no answer. I hope he's okay."

"He's probably boffing some bimbo," Ted said.

"Yeah," Buford said, dialing a third time. "I'm tempted to drive by his place and make sure he's okay. But it's out of my way and I'm afraid of getting pulled over—I can't afford another DUI."

"I'm in the same shape," Lars slurred, and Ted nodded his head indicating he was, too.

"I could run by there, if you think I should," Arnie said.

"It might be a good idea. Those noises sounded weird."

Arnie walked the girls to their cars with Bubba, then headed for Sam's condo. When he arrived, he was surprised to see the front door and several upstairs windows wide open in spite of the frigid temperature. He stood on the doorstep and rang the bell, then stepped inside and called Sam's name.

Not getting a response, he cautiously entered the elegant town home and looked around. Nothing seemed disturbed, though the wind had blown a few papers and magazines from the coffee table onto the floor. He gingerly made his way upstairs, calling Sam's name with each step. When he reached the upper landing he heard soft music and a grunting sound coming from an open door down the short hallway. He inched toward the door, ready to make a swift exit if Sam was with a girl. When he peeked around the doorjamb into the bedroom, he gasped.

Sam was lying face down on the bed, naked, with his wrists handcuffed behind his back and a pair of fishnet panty hose stuffed in his mouth and knotted tightly around his head. His legs were spread wide and secured to the lower bedposts by silk cords attached to black leather cuffs buckled to his ankles. He was shivering uncontrollably, and the skin of his body had a mottled bluish tint, with the exception of his buttocks, which were crisscrossed with crimson welts. Emerging from between his flaming ass cheeks was what appeared to be the handle of a black leather riding crop.

Arnie froze in his tracks, paralyzed by the sight in front of him. Then a muffled grunt from Sam jolted him back to life. He grabbed a pile of bedclothes from the floor and threw them over his boss, then went to work undoing the gag tied around his head. When he got it off, he grabbed the phone from the nightstand.

"No," Sam said.

"I'm dialing 911."

"No, no . . . d . . . don't do that. J . . . just get more blankets from the spare bedroom. And shut that f . . . f . . . fucking window!"

Arnie set the phone down and reluctantly did as he was told, walking down the hall and returning with a thick quilt, which he spread over Sam.

"N . . . n . . . now draw me a hot bath. But f . . . f . . . first, see that string up there?" Sam said, gesturing upward with his head toward the ceiling.

Arnie looked up. Hanging from a wrought iron chandelier over the bed was a partially melted ice cube dangling from a string.

"U . . . u . . . untie that and m . . . melt it under the faucet when you draw the bath, but make sure the drain's closed."

"What?"

"Just do it, goddamnit."

Once again, Arnie did as he was instructed. He started the bath running, then made sure the stopper was in place in the bathroom sink and held the ice cube with string emerging from it under the faucet. It soon melted and revealed several more feet of string frozen inside with a small key tied to the end. Wondering what the hell was going on, he returned to the bedroom with the key.

"That's for the handcuffs. Unlock them and get those fucking ropes off my feet."

Arnie pulled the bedclothes down from Sam's shoulders so that his wrists were exposed and unlocked the handcuffs, then unbuckled the thick leather straps securing his ankles.

"What's going on here? I mean, what the hell happened tonight?" Arnie asked as he pulled the bedclothes back up.

"It's a long story."

Sam's head disappeared under the covers and he wriggled around for several minutes and finally emerged, still naked, but minus the riding crop. As the producer rolled over to face him, Arnie's jaw dropped, and he stepped back. Sam had a gigantic erection, the likes of which Arnie had never seen, even in a porno movie. The producer's swollen penis was almost a foot long and thick as a policeman's flashlight.

"My God!"

Sam smiled as he lurched out of bed and stumbled toward the bathroom, his organ jutting forward like a flagpole over the entrance of a federal building.

"You're not gay, are you?" he asked as he reached the tub and sank into the soapy water with a splash.

"Hell no," Arnie said, keeping his distance. Thankfully, Sam's lower body was now hidden under the deep suds.

"Me neither."

"I, I can't believe you're . . ." Arnie stuttered. "I mean it's freezing cold and you're—"

"Trimix."

"What?"

"It's a shot I give myself sometimes before I have sex. It's better than Viagra. Your dick stays hard as a rock for hours, even after you come. You ought to try it sometime, though you probably don't need it at your age."

"Is that what was going on tonight?" Arnie asked. "Did you have a girl over? Was it Bobbie—did she do this to you?"

"Yeah . . . I like that chick, but she's crazy as hell. God, she's got a temper. We like to play S&M games sometimes, tie each other up and stuff. Tonight it was her turn to be in charge. The plan was that she'd put me in bondage, then go out for a while, maybe buy a bottle of wine or something, then come back. We've done it before. The key to the handcuffs was in the ice cube over the bed, so if she had a car wreck, the cube would melt and drop the key and I could free myself in an hour or so.

"But once she had me tied up, we began arguing. She was pissed off because I canceled a credit card I gave her a couple of months ago, and she started whipping me with the riding crop. We have a rule, a safe word we use. If either of us says uncle, the other's supposed to stop. But when I said uncle, she started hollering, 'Grandpa, don't uncle me grandpa!' I yelled uncle louder, so she opened the bedroom windows and asked if I wanted the whole neighborhood to hear me holler and know what a pervert I was. So I shut up and she whipped me till her arm got tired, then shoved the riding crop up my ass and stomped out of here in the high heels I bought her this afternoon. The last I heard was my Ferrari screeching down the street."

Arnie took the incredible story in. Finally, his tongue returned. "Buford got your call and asked me to come over. I guess I'm glad I did." Actually, he wasn't sure he was glad at all. Rather, he was apprehensive of how this new level of intimacy might affect his relationship with Sam.

"Me, too. I managed to reach the night table with my head and knock my phone onto the floor. It must have fallen on the re-dial key and connected to Buford's number, since he was the last person I'd called. I could hear him trying to talk to me, but all I could do was grunt and moan. I guess Bobbie didn't realize how cold it was—or maybe she did. That ice cube wasn't going to melt until morning with the windows open. I could have frozen to death."

Arnie could tell that Sam was feeling a lot better. The hair on his chest was a tangle of white, but his arms and torso rippled with muscles. He looked to be in great shape for someone his age.

"Well, I guess I'll be heading home," Arnie said, sensing it was time for a graceful exit. "What are you going to do about Bobbie and the Ferrari?"

"I'll wait till morning, then check at the airport. She most likely drove out there and caught a plane back to Syracuse. The Ferrari's probably sitting between two pickup trucks somewhere in the long-term parking lot. I'll send Starr to pick it up."

"I'll see you later then. Uh . . . you don't have to worry about me mentioning this to anyone or anything."

"Good. It never happened. I'll talk to you next week."

* * *

Arnie returned to his apartment, exhausted, but smiling to himself about the evening's events. Stef had called and left a voicemail message saying that she'd be in town in a few days. Although she would likely be working late that night, she said she couldn't wait to see him. It was all Arnie could do to keep from calling her and recounting the evening's adventure, but he knew he would honor his promise to Sam.

CHAPTER 42

Arnie avoided the office for the next few days, sensing that it might be best to give Sam some space. Starr called on Wednesday.

"Good news. Sam's been in the studio with the Hellcats this week and they cut one of the songs you co-wrote with Razor and Bubba, 'Wild Wild Feeling.'"

"Awesome!"

"Yes, he said it turned out really well. And he wanted me to confirm the times for your demo session next week. You'll be tracking on Tuesday and mixing Wednesday. Oops . . . hang on, I've got another call."

Arnie was on hold for several minutes. When she came back on the line, she had more good news. "That was Alison, Bob Markum's song plugger. He's had a cancellation for two weeks from today."

"I'd love to work with him."

"I'll book it. Gotta run—busy day."

"Okay, thanks again." Arnie replied as the line clicked dead.

He hung up with a sigh of relief. Evidently, it was business as usual; things were fine between him and Sam. His second song had just been recorded after being in town for barely six months, and Stef would be in town tomorrow. Life was good!

* * *

Stef called the following afternoon to say that her photo shoot had gotten off to a late start. She called several more times as the evening went on. Each time, there was a further delay, and it was well past midnight before her work was done. She asked him to meet her at her hotel lounge for a drink. When he arrived he found her hunched over the bar, smoking a cigarette and staring into a glass of wine. Her face was pale and drawn and she looked completely drained. She explained that she was unhappy with the record company's choice of photographer, and, to make matters worse, was concerned that having been so tired had rendered her less photogenic than usual.

Arnie tried to assure her that even on a bad day she was more beautiful than most women in America, but it did no good; he was unable to snap her out of her dark mood. After finishing her glass of wine, she apologized for not being in better spirits and excused herself, saying it would be best for both of them if they spent the night separately. Arnie walked her to the elevator and kissed her goodnight, then drove home feeling horrible. He'd been looking forward all week to seeing her.

* * *

Stef phoned the next morning on her way to the airport.

"Sorry about yesterday, I was wiped. I've been performing almost every night for the last ten days, and I guess it caught up with me."

"You sound better this morning."

"I am. I can't believe I was smoking again last night. I'm quitting for good."

"Where are you off to this time?"

"Miami. I've got another cruise, a short one, then a couple of club dates in Georgia. But I'll be back in Nashville two weeks from Sunday and promise I'll have more free time. I really apologize about yesterday."

"No problem."

"I'll talk to you before then."

"Yes." Arnie heard the sound of baggage handlers in the background. "Be careful."

"You, too."

Arnie hung up the phone feeling despondent, though better than he had last night. In spite of Stef's shifting moods, he couldn't wait to see her again.

CHAPTER 43

Arnie arrived for his demo session filled with nervous anticipation. The studio, located in the semi-commercial suburb of Berry Hill, was similar to the one where Sam had worked on "Last Night Made My Day," though smaller. Both the cozy control room and larger recording area were finished in rough-cut cedar paneling and burlap-covered sound absorbing panels that gave the spaces a comfortable, homey feel.

Arnie found Sam in the control room chatting with Robb Lawson, the guitarist who overdubbed "Last Night Made My Day". A young engineer was busy plugging cables into the recording console's patch bay and calling for the drummer in the main studio to play his drum set. When he was satisfied with the sound of the drums, he repeated the process with the other five musicians, who had begun trickling in, calling on them each in turn to play their instruments, and adjusting the controls of the console and racks of outboard gear until he was happy.

Just after ten, the engineer announced they were ready to go. Arnie handed him a copy of the first song, and in a moment the intro to "Safe Against The World" emerged from the speakers. The musicians joked with each other while writing down what appeared to be strings of numbers on pads of paper. When the song ended, the drummer verified the key, and that Arnie and Sam were comfortable with the tempo, then exited the control room with the other players through the thick padded door that led to the recording area.

"What were they writing down?" Arnie asked Sam as the musicians filed out.

"It's called the Nashville Numbers System," Sam said. "What you might call a musician's shorthand. Each number corresponds to a chord. For example: two measures of C followed by one measure each of F and G is written 1145, since C is the first note of the scale, F is the fourth and G is the fifth. It sounds complicated, but it's simpler than writing down the individual chords, and it has the advantage of enabling them to transpose keys if they need to without having to write a whole new chart."

"Cool."

"Yeah," Sam said, pointing to the studio. "Now go to the vocal booth and sing a scratch vocal while the musicians lay down the tracks. It doesn't have to be perfect. We've got singers coming in later this afternoon for the final vocals. Just do the best you can so everyone can hear how the melody goes."

Arnie made his way to a windowed cubicle to one side of the main studio area where he found a microphone, a music stand and headphones. The drummer and acoustic guitarist were enclosed in similar isolation areas, as was the fiddle player. The musicians continued their light-hearted banter as they tuned their instruments, and Arnie tried to quiet the butterflies in his stomach. After a few minutes, Robb asked the drummer to count the track off, and Arnie felt a rush of excitement as his song come to life. There was some confusion and a few bad notes as the band hit the first chorus, but all in all, he was impressed by how well the players captured the feel he had envisioned.

When they reached the end, Sam's voice came through the headphones.

"Sounds like it's coming together. Is everyone clear about the chorus now?"

One of the musicians made a joke about taking up a collection for a Mel Bay guitar instruction book for whoever had made the mistake, and they ran through the chorus again. This time it was much better.

"Okay. Let's go for it," Sam said. "When we get to the instrumental, let the fiddle have the first half and steel the second."

The engineer's voice came through the talkback. "Rolling," he said. The drummer clicked his sticks together and the group again launched into the song. Arnie sang along, delighted with how it sounded.

When they reached the end, Arnie could see Sam smiling in the control room as he again pressed the talkback button. "Sounds great guys. Anybody have anything to fix?"

"Yeah, I need the instrumental again," the fiddle player said. "Let me take it out from there."

"And let me have the second verse and chorus," the piano player said.

"No problem," said the engineer, as Arnie followed Robb and the other musicians back into the control room.

"It sounded super." Sam said, beaming. "We've got a few things to redo, shouldn't take long."

The engineer started the song from the top and re-recorded the parts the fiddle and piano player had requested while leaving the rest of the band's performance intact.

"Pleased, Arnie?" Robb asked when the process was completed.

"I'm blown away. You guys hadn't even heard the song twenty minutes ago, now it sounds like a record—except for my vocal, of course."

"It's what we do."

"Well, you do it awfully well."

"Thanks, man," Robb said, visibly pleased. "Guess we're ready for the next tune."

They repeated the process for the next two songs, and Arnie continued to be amazed by the musicians' intuitive ability to create imaginative arrangements for his compositions. Several times he picked up a guitar to demonstrate a particular lick or rhythm and the players quickly grasped what he had in mind and augmented his ideas with their own. Bubba strolled in just before noon, and they began working on their song "All We Need to Know," which also turned out well, although it took a little longer than the others. It was past twelve-thirty when they finished, and Arnie was concerned about squeezing in the final song before the three-hour session was scheduled to end.

The engineer played Arnie's recording of "Roadkill" and Arnie explained to the musicians that he was looking for a heavy metal/rock feel, quite different from that of the previous tunes. The drummer exchanged his snare drum for a larger one with a deeper, fatter sound and Robb adjusted the controls of his equipment rack, then raked his pick across his black Gibson Les Paul guitar's strings near the bridge. The result was a thickly distorted chord that echoed from speaker to speaker as if bouncing off the walls of a huge auditorium. Pleased with the sound, he signaled the drummer and the band blasted into the tune. Arnie was astounded at what he heard in the headphones as he sang the scratch vocal and the track went down sounding like an eighties rock band in concert. The band nailed it on the first take. Robb overdubbed a screaming lead part and the song was completed with five minutes to spare.

Arnie thanked everyone profusely for their hard work. Then, as the musicians were packing up, Sam announced to Arnie and Bubba that he was buying lunch.

"You did well today," Sam told Arnie when they arrived at the restaurant.

"With your help," Arnie replied. "I was nervous as hell at first. But those musicians are so good—I can't believe how quick they were, and how well everything turned out."

"Like I said, you did fine," Sam said. "The players respect you, and you communicate well with them."

"Thanks."

They chatted through their meal about the vocals to be recorded that afternoon, and discussed who they might pitch the completed songs to. Arnie was delighted that Sam wanted to make sure Stef heard the entire session, and also that he planned to play "Safe Against the World" for Buzz Corbin as soon as possible.

They returned to the studio at two, and Arnie was pleased to discover that the singers Starr had booked were as professional as the musicians he'd worked with in the morning. Each had learned the song they were to sing beforehand, and after a quick run-through or two, laid down a basic vocal track, perfected their performances by punching in any questionable lines, then added harmony and background parts. Sam urged Arnie to make any suggestions he felt were appropriate, and he grew more confident in doing so as the afternoon went by. Even though a couple of the tunes, especially the duet, which required a male and female singer to work together, took a bit longer than he had hoped, Arnie and Sam left the studio late that evening with all five songs completed. Arnie was thrilled with the way every song turned out, and couldn't wait to share his excitement with Stef.

He dialed her cell number when he got back to his apartment and reached her in Nassau. She apologized again for being so tired on her last visit, and seemed as excited as he was about how well his session turned out, especially after he played her "Safe Against the World" over the phone. Though her gig had been going well, she said she'd found herself bored on the trip and had been taking a scuba class in the mornings.

"Next time, maybe you could come with me," she said. "It's really magical to swim around the coral reefs; they're so beautiful—just like you'd see in National Geographic."

"I'd enjoy that."

"I'll be in town a week from Sunday. It's a special day, you know."

"Valentine's Day," Arnie said. "Is there anything particular you'd like to do?"

"Just be with you."

"That's the nicest thing you could say," Arnie said, his ear jarring with static as the connection started to go bad.

"I miss you."

"Me, too—see you then."

CHAPTER 44

Arnie arrived at Sam's office early for his appointment with Bob Markum the following week and found Ronnie Dexter, Stef's record company's head of promotion, chatting with Starr in the reception area.

"Hey there, Ronnie," he said, shaking hands with the big man. "It's nice to see you again."

"You, too, I was just talking about Stef's single with Starr. The release date's still a few weeks away, but right now we're feeling very positive about the record, considering it's a first single."

"I guess that makes it tough—being a first single?"

"Yeah, with an established act, someone like Randy Fawcett, listeners can't wait to hear their next release. But a new artist is an unknown quantity. It's kind of a catch twenty-two situation. Stations don't want to play a song unless it's a hit, but it can't become a hit unless it gets played. On the positive side, listeners are always looking for something fresh and interesting."

"That makes sense. So what's your strategy with Stef?"

"Our plan is to focus on secondary markets at first, and promote it hard there. Most of the big stations nowadays are owned and controlled by a just few corporations, and they rely heavily on consultants for their programming. So we're going to start with the smaller ones, try to establish credibility. Then we can then go to the big guys with evidence that the record might be a hit, and hopefully get a few of them to spin it. If they get good phones, we can go to the other larger stations and continue the process, show them it's proven itself and try to build momentum. There are only about two-hundred stations in the country that report to *Billboard*. Those are the ones we need."

"Sounds like it's as hard for you to get songs played on the radio as it is for songwriters to get them recorded."

"It's similar I guess, but there's nothing like the kick of breaking a new artist with a hit record. The timing is really good here. Randy's current single is doing well, so we'll be able to focus hard on Stef. Also, CRS, the Country Radio Seminar, is coming up in a few weeks. All the important DJs and program directors in the country will be here. Buzz and Nanci and I will get Stef as much face time with them as we can, and she should have several opportunities to showcase her single at the hotel suite parties and downtown clubs near the Renaissance Hotel, where the event is held. I believe in your song and think other people will too, once they have a chance to hear it."

"Thanks for the promotion lesson."

"Anytime."

Ronnie stood and shuffled to the door, still wearing the same blue warm-up suit Arnie had met him in. Though he looked like a loser at an all night craps table, Arnie reflected that, in his own way, he was as gifted at his job as the musicians and singers who made the records he promoted.

Bob Markum arrived a few minutes later. He was about forty—tall, lanky and tanned—and had the goofy, offhand manner of an overgrown college kid. After uncasing their guitars in one of the upstairs writer's rooms, they talked for a while about what kind of songs Stef might need to complete her album, then tossed around several title ideas before settling on one.

Bob's low-key, relaxed demeanor belied a mind that was working full tilt and Arnie was impressed with the focus he was able to bring to the tune. Bob zeroed in on the best way to make use of the title, suggesting a unique approach that Arnie realized never would have occurred to him on his own. Arnie came up with a guitar groove that Bob loved, and in a few hours they had a chorus and most of a first verse written. They took a break for lunch, then returned to the office and had the song finished by mid afternoon. Arnie felt as if he'd just completed an intense graduate-level course in songwriting.

"I'm wondering," Bob said as they were wrapping things up, "Do you think we could use a bridge? Maybe a couple of lines after the second chorus to give the song a lift, followed by a modulation before the last chorus?"

They worked for another half hour without settling on anything, then decided to leave the song as it was and think about it over the next few days.

"Where are you from, Arnie?" Bob asked when they were packing their gear.

"New England, how about you?"

"Southern California—but I've been here fifteen years. Nashville's a good town, except for July and August, when it gets so hot and humid. I bought some property in Colorado a few years ago, and spend summers out there now with my family. Do you like to fish?"

"My grandmother used to take me sometimes when I was a kid, I grew up not far from Cape Cod. It was saltwater fishing, but I loved it."

"You should think about coming to visit in July. We've got a condo in Steamboat Springs and my land's on the Yampa River—the fly fishing's outstanding there."

"Watch out now, I might take you up on that."

"Let's stay in touch then," Bob said as they headed downstairs. "We'd love to have you. And let's plan on getting together and writing again soon. I think our song turned out really well."

"I look forward to it."

Bob left, and Arnie listened to their new tune again before leaving the office. On the way home an idea occurred to him for a bridge. When he arrived, he made a quick recording of the song with the added section.

The next day he listened back and was pleased. He went by the office that afternoon and dubbed a copy for Sam and also one to drop off at Bob's publishing company. Starr poked her head in the office's copy room while Arnie was working.

"I like that a lot," she said.

"Thanks."

"By the way, things are looking good for Stef's single."

"That's what Ronnie Dexter was saying yesterday."

"Those promo guys are always positive, that's their job. But I think the company's fully behind it. Buzz has got full page ads coming out in the trades next week, looks like he's going all out. Have you heard about Nanci Morales's alarm clocks?"

"Alarm clocks?"

"She was in Target a couple of weeks ago, buying an alarm clock for a business trip and came up with the idea of sending out little travel alarms that play your song to radio stations. She bought a couple off the shelf and had an intern insert a chip that plays a few bars of "Last Night Made My Day" instead of their preprogrammed chimes. They ordered a couple of hundred of the clocks and the intern's been working twelve hours a day burning chips and soldering them in."

"That's incredible."

"Here, take a look, she sent one over this morning."

The clock was a few inches square and looked like a regular travel alarm, except for a sticker across the front that said, WAKE UP, STEFANY'S GOT A HIT! Arnie set the alarm for a few minutes ahead of the current time and, sure enough, when it went off, Stef's voice sang, "*Last night made my day. . .*"

"That's unbelievable! Stef'll love it."

Just then, Sam breezed into the office wearing a bright red windbreaker emblazoned with a yellow Scuderia Ferrari emblem.

"That's a great idea, isn't it?" he said, pointing to the travel alarm.

"It really is. Do you think I could get one?" Arnie asked.

"I'll make sure you do," Starr said. Then she turned to Sam. "Arnie's got a cool new song that he wrote with Bob Markum."

"Let me hear it."

Arnie followed Sam into the office and he listened thoughtfully, tapping his fingers on his desk the whole way through.

"I like it . . . a lot," he said when it was over.

"Thanks, I'll let Bob know," Arnie said. "I still can't get over those alarm clocks. The record company is really supporting Stef. Do you think Buzz Corbin is over his anger?"

"It's hard to tell," Sam said with a wry smile. "Buzz is an experienced record exec; he'll tell you whatever he thinks you want to hear. But he's not a bad guy, as far as record execs go. In fact, when he lies to you he's considerate enough to do it with enough sincerity to make you appreciate that he went to the trouble. He'll do whatever's expedient for him, and it's in his interest to have a hit with Stef—we've got that going for us."

Arnie smiled.

"But I have to say this," Sam continued, suddenly serious. "I've known Buzz for a long time, and I've never seen him get behind a new artist like this before. Randy Fawcett's manager called the other day to say Buzz is even planning to have Stef start opening shows for Randy this spring. He's pulling out all the stops—I don't know what's gotten into him."

"Maybe he likes his office." Arnie said.

Sam laughed. "That must be it. By the way, I've been listening to the demos and I plan to play "Daddy'd Be Proud" for him and see what he thinks about it for Randy."

"Thanks!"

"And I'll let you know what he says about "Safe Against the World," though of course, whether Stef goes in the studio again depends on how "Last Night Made My Day" does.

Arnie tried to control the tension in his gut. He couldn't wait for his song to be released. But, if it failed to make a good showing and Stef didn't get to finish her album, well, he didn't want to think about it.

"The Hellcats sessions last week went well, especially the song you wrote with Razor and Bubba called 'Wild Wild Feeling.' I should have the tracks finished soon, and I think you'll dig how it turned out."

"I can't wait to hear it."

"Keep up the good work!"

CHAPTER 45

Stef called at a little past noon Sunday to say she was in town, and Arnie wasted no time heading to her hotel. He found her waiting on the sidewalk outside, bundled in a down ski parka, scarf and jeans.

"Happy Valentine's Day. You look gorgeous."

"You look pretty gorgeous yourself," Stefany answered, getting into the Miata and giving him a long warm kiss. The taste of her lipstick and the scent of her perfume and shampoo had their usual effect, like a head-spinning jolt from an exotic drug. "Thanks for the flowers you sent to my room."

"You're welcome. Have you had lunch?"

"No. I've been up since six and I'm starving—I only had peanuts on the plane."

"I've heard Starr and Bubba mention a place on the river they like called Rock Harbor Marina that has a cool restaurant. Do you want to give it a try?"

"Sure!"

When they arrived at the waterfront restaurant, most of the boats were in their slips, but a few larger ones motored slowly in and out of the small harbor, taking advantage of the sparkling February day.

"Maybe that'll be us next summer after 'Last Night Made My Day' is a hit," Stef said after they'd been seated, pointing to a handsome forty-foot Sea Ray cabin cruiser idling past.

"That'd be nice."

"I thought you might like to see this," Stef said, digging a newspaper clipping out of her purse. "I did a show in Macon Friday night, and the review in Saturday's paper mentioned your song." She handed Arnie the clipping—a short paragraph from the *Macon Chronicle-Herald*, and sure enough, the reporter noted "Last Night Made My Day" as one of the highlights of Stef's performance.

"Maybe I *will* be able to afford that boat—after I buy a Ferrari, of course."

"We'll know soon enough. The release date is only two weeks away."

"Sam mentioned that you may be opening shows for Randy Fawcett."

"Yes, starting next month. I'm leaving tomorrow on a two-week radio tour. Ronnie Dexter wants me to meet as many program directors in person as possible before we actually go for adds on March 1. Then I've got CRS and an interview on WSM-AM here before I start my dates with Randy in mid-March. I'm excited; we'll be playing some big venues."

"Sounds like you'll be busy."

"Yes, but I'm planning to make time for us, too. I'm sorry again for being in such a funky mood last time I was here. I'm a little more human today."

"Don't worry. Speaking of us, is there anything special you like to do? I mean it is Valentine's Day."

"This is special enough," Stef said, taking his hand. "All the restaurants will be packed and to tell you the truth, I could use a break from people. Let's just do something quiet, maybe rent a movie and watch it at your place. We could order a pizza or something. I just want to relax and unwind with you."

"That sounds wonderful."

They lingered on the deck sipping their drinks until the sun settled to the tips of the gray trees across the harbor, then picked up a couple of romantic comedies and some snacks. When they arrived at his place, he loaded a DVD and they kicked off their shoes and snuggled together on the bed. Halfway through the first movie, Stef dozed off. Arnie covered her with a quilt, turned the volume down on the TV and watched the rest of the movie alone. When it was over, he pulled off his jeans, then slipped under the quilt and was soon asleep, too.

Arnie woke at the first light of dawn to the delicious sensation of Stef fondling him.

"Do you have any condoms?" she asked.

"Yes, but—"

"Where are they?"

"In the drawer," Arnie said, rubbing the sleep from his eyes. "Are you sure you want to, because after last time——"

Stef found a condom in the drawer and tore it open, then handed it to Arnie as she undressed. Arnie pulled off his shorts and rolled the condom on. When she slipped under the covers he kissed her and reached cautiously between her legs. Finding her moist and apparently aroused, he guided his penis toward the entrance of her vagina. He gently pressed forward, penetrating no more than an inch, while watching her cautiously. This time, there was no explosion. Instead, her body went limp and tears started to well in her eyes. He started to pull away.

"Don't stop, Arnie," she said clutching him. "I don't want you to stop. I just can't . . ."

Arnie withdrew and rolled next to her. Stef wiped her eyes and put her arm over his chest.

"I'm sorry."

"Don't be."

"I want you . . . I want you to . . . I woke up thinking I'd make it up to you for the last time and——"

"I don't want to make love to you like this. If you're still frightened. . ."

Stef managed a smile.

"But I appreciate you not shooting me for trying," he added.

She laughed in spite of herself. "Take off that condom," she said.

"You don't have to . . . do anything," Arnie said but she was already rolling it off.

"There's an old saying in the *Girl's Rule Book*. 'Never send your man off with a loaded gun.'"

Rather than inquire as to what the *Girl's Rule Book* was, Arnie let Stef take him in her mouth. She cupped his balls in her hand and sucked and stroked until he climaxed. Afterward, he wrapped her in his arms.

"I'm sorry about before," she said. "Someday it'll be better. I know it will."

"Don't apologize, that was wonderful."

"Just because we don't have sex doesn't mean we can't have a sex life."

They both laughed, and Arnie stroked her stomach, then reached lower.

"Just hold me," she said, pulling his hand to her breasts.

"But I want you to enjoy us being together too. It's only fair."

"Don't worry about me for now. I want you inside me and I want us *both* to enjoy it. I think it's more than the trauma of being molested that gets in my way. I think I'm afraid of being hurt, too."

"I'm not going to hurt you, Stef."

"I believe that."

"And we've got all the time in the world."

Stef wrapped her arms around him he stroked her hair until she fell asleep.

CHAPTER 46

Things grew increasingly hectic at Sam's office as the release date for "Last Night Made My Day" approached. The label's marketing and PR departments finalized graphics for trade magazine ads and scheduled an array of media appearances for Stef. Meanwhile, Arnie's angst built to an almost unbearable degree. Though he tried not to, he found it impossible to avoid fantasizing about what it would be like to have a hit record.

When the release date finally arrived, he thought he'd readied himself for any eventuality, but was totally unprepared for what actually happened—nothing. He spent Monday driving around town and switching between Nashville's four country stations without hearing his song once. He did the same on Tuesday and Wednesday, and by Thursday had still not heard it played a single time. On Friday, he stopped by the office to see if there was any news. Starr and Sam were in the reception area examining the printout of an email from the record company, and they waved him over to take a look.

The sheet of paper contained a list of numbers and station call letters that he found hard to interpret. "What does it all mean?" he asked.

"Well, the good news is that over a dozen small stations are playing it," Sam said, "And several reporting stations have committed to adding it in light rotation next week. Both *Billboard* and *Music Row* magazine gave it good reviews. *Music Row* even mentioned your name. Here, let me read it to you, 'Stellar vocal performance combined with outstanding song by Arnie Fortune make Stefany a contender for next year's CMA Horizon Award.'"

"That's awesome!" Arnie said.

"But unfortunately, the single hasn't gotten enough adds—that's the term for stations committing to add it to their playlists—for it to chart, though we really didn't expect that it would this early."

"Well, at least some people like it."

"True. This is actually a pretty fair showing for the first week, especially for a new artist. Stef'll be in town Tuesday for her interview on WSM, hopefully after that we'll have at least one station in Nashville on it. And I know she'll make a good impression at CRS."

"Ronnie warned me that it would be a slow process," Arnie said, following Sam into his office.

"That's right. By the way, Buzz Corbin likes 'Safe Against the World' quite a bit. I had a meeting with him yesterday. He also took a copy of 'Daddy'd Be Proud' for Randy."

"That's terrific."

"Don't get too excited, it doesn't mean Randy will record either one of them, or even hear them. He writes most of his material himself. But at least Buzz likes the songs."

"I guess that's the first step. I'm just beginning to understand what a crazy business this is."

"You're in the best end of it. The great thing about being a songwriter, as opposed to a singer or musician, is that when you have a hit you get royalties for a long time, it's like owning rental property."

"How much will my song make just by being released, assuming it charts, but doesn't make it to the top thirty or forty?"

"Not much. Anywhere from a few hundred to a few thousand bucks. A song has to get up into the top twenty to start making significant money—and the amount becomes exponentially more as it reaches the top ten and then top five."

"Sounds like it's all or nothing."

"Pretty much. A big hit by a well established multi-platinum selling artist like Randy Fawcett could easily be worth half a million dollars or more over the first couple of years. The residual money can be quite substantial, especially if other artists cover the song. 'White Christmas' still makes a fortune every year for the Irving Berlin estate."

"I guess I'd better sharpen my pencils and make sure I've got fresh batteries in my recorder—I want to enjoy the money while I'm alive!"

"Good idea," Sam said with a laugh. "I really like the songs you've been turning in. We'll keep our fingers crossed with Stef's record, but whatever happens, I'm confident you'll have some big hits if you hang in there."

* * *

When Arnie drove to the airport to pick up Stef on the night before her WSM interview, the interstate was down to one lane due to construction. He arrived twenty minutes late to find her waiting on the sidewalk outside the baggage claim area. There were visible bags under her eyes in spite of her makeup, which was applied more heavily than usual.

"You're late," she said.

"Sorry, there was a problem on the interstate." Arnie kissed her. "Nicotine martini?"

"I'm afraid so. Worried about my single, I guess."

"Have you talked to Sam or Buzz or Ronnie? Quite a few stations are playing it already."

"Yes, but not enough to chart. The label could be doing more."

"From what Sam and Starr said, it sounds like they're doing quite a bit."

"It's not enough."

Stef dug in her purse and pulled out a cigarette. Arnie considered asking her not to smoke in the car, but thought better of it. Instead, he punched the buttons of the Miata's radio, hoping by some miracle to catch one of Nashville's stations playing her single. He was stressed and tired, and didn't have the energy to continue trying to cheer her up—especially since she was oblivious to the fact that the record's success was as important to him as to her. They drove the rest of the way downtown without speaking.

"Are you hungry?" he asked as they pulled off the interstate.

"I'm not starving, but I could use a snack."

They stopped for sandwiches and Arnie suggested renting a movie, but Stef was exhausted so they headed to her hotel and turned in early.

He woke the next morning and reached for her, but the bed was empty. In a moment she emerged from the bathroom wearing a low-cut cotton dress and her trademark cowboy boots.

"You're going to look good on the radio!"

"Thanks," she said, kissing him quickly. "I'm running late, could you drive me to Sam's office?"

"Sure."

"So you're just here for two days?" he asked when they were on their way. "When will I see you again?"

"It may be a while, three or four weeks. Today and tomorrow are going to be insane—I don't know how I'm going to get any sleep at all. I'm meeting this morning with Sam to go over songs in case Buzz picks up my contract option and I get to finish my album. Sam says we need to be ready. Next, there's the WSM interview, then I'll spend all night tonight and tomorrow downtown with Nanci and Ronnie, meeting as many radio and media people as possible at the Country Radio Seminar showcases and after-parties. I'm flying to Dallas tomorrow night, and my first show with Randy is Friday."

"I'm going to miss you."

"Me, too. Maybe you could come to one of our gigs sometime, you know, fly or drive to meet me where I'm singing, especially if I have a day off afterward."

"That would be nice."

"I'll let you know when I get my schedule."

"Great. I'll be listening for your interview."

Back at his apartment, Arnie showered and worked on his songs for an hour, then tuned to WSM-AM, home of the Grand Ole Opry. The announcer brought Stef to the microphone and started the interview by commenting on how lucky he was to be sitting next to one of the most beautiful women in Nashville. They chatted for several minutes about her record deal and upcoming tour with Randy, then the DJ played "Last Night Made My Day."

Arnie turned the volume up on his boom box until it was at the point of distortion. His song sounded great! Halfway through, he started dancing around the kitchen. The thrill of hearing it was indescribable, there was just no way in the world that it couldn't be a smash.

"I think you might have a hit on your hands, sweetheart," the DJ said when the last notes faded. "We've already had two calls from listeners who loved it."

Stef thanked him and the interview was over.

CHAPTER 47

Arnie flipped through the country stations constantly during the following week, but never heard his song played again. He stopped by the office frequently, hoping that Starr might have some good news. On Friday, she announced that she had received an email from Ronnie Dexter indicating that a few more stations had added the single, and that the ones already playing it would keep it in light rotation.

The following Friday's email listed several more adds, but included the discouraging information that one of the reporting stations had dropped, or stopped playing, the record. Arnie had a writing appointment with Bob Markum early the next week, and was waiting for him to arrive at Sam's office when Nanci Morales stopped by. The marketing director didn't have much to report.

"We've got over a dozen major stations playing the single now, but that's still not enough to chart. The good news is that almost forty smaller stations are on it and everyone's getting good phones."

"Well, that's good," Arnie said.

"It's going to be a little longer before we know if the record's going to happen or not. Ronnie's close to getting it added in Austin and St Louis. It's frustrating. Everybody who hears the song loves it and the fact that Stef's been touring so hard has been a tremendous help, but we're having a hard time getting any real momentum. I can tell you this though, Buzz is doing everything he can. He's even authorized funds to hire a couple of indie promoters."

"Are those the dudes that show up with hookers and cocaine for the DJs?" Arnie asked.

"I only wish it was that easy," Nanci replied, laughing.

"I guess we'll keep our fingers crossed."

"That's all we can do."

Bob Markum arrived and he and Arnie worked for several hours, getting a good start on a song before driving to lunch at one of Bob's favorite restaurants. On their way back, as Bob was switching between stations on the radio of his Jeep, Arnie caught the tail end of "Last Night Made My Day." He reached for the volume knob and cranked it up.

"That's Stef's single!"

"Sounds good," Bob said, as the song faded. "What I heard of it."

"It's been out for almost a month. This is only the second time I've heard it myself. The whole thing's been driving me nuts. I've got another song that Buzz Corbin may want her to cut as a duet with Randy Fawcett if her album deal goes through, but she'll never get back in the studio if this one doesn't chart."

"I try not to pay too much attention to that stuff," Bob said. "Chart numbers and things like that."

"Really? How could you not?"

"I pay some attention. You don't want to miss out on the rush of it all. But most songs never become hits. If you get your hopes up too much, it can hurt your writing. I try not to get too high with the ups or too low with the downs. Ninety percent of what happens in the music business is out of your control."

Arnie had to acknowledge the wisdom of Bob's words, but it was hard to take his advice to heart. Back at the office, they concentrated on their current song and soon finished it.

"I don't know if this one is all that great," Bob said. "But it's another song under our belt. Sometimes you've got to write your way through the okay ones to get a tune that's special."

"I'll play it for Sam and let you know what he thinks."

"Have you thought any more about visiting Colorado this summer?"

"I'd love to, though like I said before, I don't know much about fly fishing. Guess I need to go to the library and pick up a few books on it."

"Why don't you follow me back to my place this afternoon? I can show you the basics and lend you an old rod to practice with."

"That'd be super."

Arnie followed Bob to his stately home. They parked and Bob searched the garage until he found a chipped fiberglass fly rod and old

Pflueger reel. "It's not as responsive as some of the new graphite rods by Sage and Orvis, but I've caught plenty of fish with it," he said, handing the rod to Arnie. "Come out by the pool and we can try it."

Arnie followed him to the rear of the house and swung the nine-foot rod overhead a few times, trying to get a feel for it.

"Let me take over for a sec and show you how it's done," Bob said. "With a fly rod, you're casting the line, not the lure."

Bob lifted the rod and arched it gracefully back and forth with his right hand while stripping line off the reel with his left. When he had about thirty feet of line circling in a gentle loop overhead, he extended his casting arm in front of him and the line shot forward and dropped softly to the swimming pool with barely a splash.

"Here, give it a try."

Arnie imitated Bob's deft motions but only managed to produce a crack like a bullwhip behind his right ear.

"Move your arm more slowly. If you'd had a fly tied on you would have snapped it off."

Arnie did as he was told, following Bob's instructions to keep his wrist stiff and move the rod in a narrower arc.

"That's better, imagine that your right forearm is the hand of a clock, it only needs to move between the ten and twelve o'clock positions."

After half an hour, Arnie still felt awkward, but was able to lay the line out fairly consistently for a distance of twenty or thirty feet.

"That's all you need to be able to do. With practice, you'll be able to cast a lot farther, but you can catch fish all day the way you're casting now, provided they're biting, of course!"

"What about flies? Don't you need to be an expert on insects to match the different hatches on the river?"

"Not really, at least where I fish. You can get by most of the time with a half dozen or so different patterns. That's one of the beauties of fly fishing, you can easily pick up the basic skills, then spend a lifetime learning the finer points."

"I really appreciate all this."

"Sure, I look forward to seeing you in Steamboat this summer."

As Bob walked Arnie to his car, a green Range Rover driven by a woman about Bob's age pulled into the long driveway. When it came to a stop, he introduced his wife, Sally, and their two handsome middle school aged children, Nathan and Angie. Sally complimented Arnie on the progress Bob said he was making with his casting, and said she, too, was looking forward to his visit in Colorado.

When Arnie reached the end of the drive and was about to pull out on the highway, he glanced in his rearview mirror and saw Bob tossing a football with Nathan while Sally and Angie watched. He carried a picture of the family in his mind all the way back to town.

CHAPTER 48

Six weeks after the release of "Last Night Made My Day," only nineteen reporting stations across the country were playing it, well shy of the number necessary for it to enter the *Billboard* national chart. Arnie tried to keep his spirits up, but found it increasingly difficult. He hadn't realized how much he'd counted on the record making a good showing. The initial sharp pang of disappointment gradually deepened into a dull ache that consumed his waking hours as he resigned himself to the possibility that his song might not make it. He tried to look at the upside. Sam had said if "Last Night Made My Day" didn't chart at all, there'd be a better chance of it being recorded again by another artist than if it got part way up the charts, then died. But it was a small consolation.

He missed Stef. She was performing almost every night, and the opportunity to meet her on the road never materialized. There was nothing to do but heed Bob Markum's advice and focus as best he could on writing more songs. After working with Bubba one afternoon, he realized that it had been a while since he'd checked the email address given to him by the FBI, and drove to a coffee shop that offered Internet access.

He was surprised to find a terse message from Agent Baskins: "Call me."

"Have you been following the news?" Baskins asked when Arnie reached him.

"What news?"

"Tony Bertolini was sentenced last week. Life in prison, no possibility of parole."

"That's good . . . I guess."

"There's some not so good news, too. Roberto Puccini's still got a contract out on you."

"What good can it do to have me killed now, if Bertolini has already been convicted and sentenced?"

"You said you watched *The Sopranos*. Haven't you heard of vengeance? It's a Mafia tradition. The good news is that your new name hasn't come up again on any of our phone taps. But still, I wanted to let you know what's going on. Stay on your toes at all times and let us know if you notice anything unusual."

"I'll do it."

"Keep your eyes open. I mean it."

"I said I will."

Arnie hung up. As the receiver touched down, it rang again. Arnie picked it up, expecting to hear Baskins's voice once more. Instead, it was Stef.

"I've only got a sec, but make sure you watch *The Tonight Show* tonight."

"Okay, but wait . . . how are—"

"Sorry, I've got to run. I'll call later."

* * *

At ten-thirty, Arnie settled on the couch, popped open a beer and tuned to the opening of *The Tonight Show*. After the monologue, the host interviewed a young housewife from Phoenix who was the recent winner of a cable reality show featuring women competing to be porn stars, and then an archeologist trying to halt construction of a downtown Los Angeles office building because of what he claimed were bones from a new variety of dinosaur unearthed at the site.

Near the end of the show, the host stepped out from behind his desk to announce, "Ladies and gentlemen, we've had a change of plans this evening. Country star Randy Fawcett was going to close tonight's show, but had to cancel due to a minor medical problem. But you're in for a treat. We've got a great new talent from Nashville performing in his place. It's my great pleasure to present the lovely Stefany Simmons, singing her new single 'Last Night Made My Day.'"

Arnie jumped to his feet to get closer to the TV. The camera panned to *The Tonight Show* band, then Stef as she stepped to the microphone and began singing his song. When she finished the final chorus, the audience gave her a thunderous ovation. The camera panned over the cheering crowd, most of whom were on their feet. Then it shifted back to the host, who put his arm around Stef and said, "I think she's got a hit on her hands, what do you think?"

The audience responded with more wild applause.

Arnie was in shock. He wished he'd thought to record the show, but there was no way in the world to have predicted this. His phone rang; it was Bubba.

"I hope had your TV on," he said.

"I can't fucking believe it!"

"You just made a couple of thousand dollars in performance royalties, buddy. Plus, this may be what it takes to get your song on the charts."

"I hope you're right! I need to call Stef."

"Good idea. Talk to you tomorrow."

Arnie hung up and dialed Stef's number. He got her voice mail and remembered that *The Tonight Show* had been taped earlier in the day and she was performing a concert that night with Randy at L.A.'s Gibson Amphitheatre. With the two-hour time difference, she was probably onstage. He left a message telling her how wonderful she was on *The Tonight Show*. At three a.m. she called back, waking him up.

"Hi, sweetie."

"Hey," he replied sleepily.

"Sorry to wake you. So I sounded okay?"

"Better than okay, you were unbelievable. What happened to Randy?"

"It's a good story. The last time he did *The Tonight Show*, he had a fling with one of the production assistants. Her husband found out about it and followed her to Randy's hotel during her lunch hour today and beat the hell out of him. The girl's okay, but Randy was in pretty rough shape."

"That's too bad," Arnie said.

"They took him to the emergency room. Turned out he wasn't hurt seriously, no broken bones or anything, but he had a bad gash on his jaw where the husband's Princeton class ring cut him. He was still getting stitches when they started taping this afternoon. The band was set up and Randy's manager suggested I fill in. The network people went for it."

"Wow, that's a miracle. So Randy's okay?"

"Yeah. The doctors patched him up well enough to do the concert tonight, but you should have heard him explain the bandage to the audience."

"What was his excuse?"

"Some bullshit about falling off a bull at a rodeo in Oklahoma. I didn't even know they had rodeos in April."

"Well all I can say is that it's great you got to perform. The audience went nuts."

"They really did. Listen, I know I woke you, so I'll let you get back to sleep. Keep your fingers crossed. Good night sweetie."

"Love you."

"Love you, too."

CHAPTER 49

Arnie woke the next day full of energy and had a productive morning working on his songs. Starr called early that afternoon. She was exuberant.

"Did you hear about Stef and *The Tonight Show?*"

"I saw it!"

"Buzz called a little while ago. Stations all over the country got requests for your song this morning—during drive time no less. Ronnie Dexter thinks we're going to get a bunch of adds this week. And a pile of them will be from big stations too, the ones we need to chart the record."

"That's fantastic. Is Sam excited?"

"Totally. Keep your fingers crossed!"

Arnie waited anxiously to see if the radio stations' promised adds would materialize. Sure enough, on Friday, *Billboard* reported that over seventy of their two hundred or so reporting stations had committed to play Stef's record, and the song would enter their country chart at number forty-two.

Starr called the following week with the good news that it had risen to number thirty-six.

"I'd say we may have a hit on our hands—top twenty at least," she exclaimed when he stopped by the office. "Looks like it's got legs. Stations are moving it up in rotation, and there's been no burn so far."

"Burn?" Arnie asked.

"Listener burnout. Audiences tend to get sick of some records quickly, and the first stations that went on 'Last Night Made My Day' have been playing it for a while now. But the song has such an intriguing melody that people want to keep hearing it. Buzz says downloads have been increasing by fifty percent each week, and he wants to finish recording Stef's album next month."

"He's committed to finishing her album? Is that for sure?"

"Looks that way. He says he wants to have it out by early summer, right after the CMA Music Festival."

"What's that?"

"It's an annual event downtown; a country music extravaganza. For a hundred bucks or so, fans get to see four days worth of shows featuring most of Nashville's top artists. People come from all over the world. Stef will definitely have a featured spot."

"I'll plan to go. I'm sure I'll get some good writing and song pitching ideas."

* * *

Arnie called Stef as soon as he got home.

"Have you heard this week's numbers?" he asked.

"Yes! Have you ordered that new Ferrari yet?"

"I may wait a few more weeks. But Starr is confident the record's going to happen."

"When you do order the car, make sure it's red. I just got off the phone with Buzz's secretary. It looks like he's going to pick up my contract option."

"Starr mentioned that too—congratulations."

"And he wants me to do a duet with Randy. Guess which song?"

"'Safe Against the World?'"

"You've got it. What's even better is that she said he may want to include it on Randy's album, as well as mine. He wants us in the studio in two weeks, as soon as we finish this leg of the tour. I'm so excited! Plus I'll get to see you again. I hope you can be there for the session."

"I wouldn't miss it for anything."

CHAPTER 50

Arnie arrived at Stef and Randy's session to find the studio buzzing with activity. Although the musicians joked around with the same camaraderie he remembered from his demo, there was a special electricity in the air. "Last Night Made My Day" had risen to the mid-twenties in *Billboard*'s Hot Country Singles chart, and a duet between two hit artists was a special event.

He greeted Sam and Zero Thompson, then slipped quietly to a seat on a couch in the rear of the control room. Buzz Corbin arrived a few minutes later to announce that Randy and Stef were running late because their flight had been delayed. Sam, who was co-producing with Buzz, suggested they start working on the instrumental tracks, since studio time was expensive. Also, the musicians were being paid double union scale, a practice common for important master sessions where the record company and producer wanted to make sure they secured the absolute best players possible for the date.

Zero played Arnie's demo of "Safe Against the World," and the players began working on the arrangement. Once they had the general feel captured, their main concern was to determine the best way to switch keys mid-song so that the first verse would be in Randy's vocal range, and the second would be in Stef's. Buzz suggested an abrupt modulation similar to that used in the Kenny Rogers-Dolly Parton duet, "Islands in the Stream." He waved his arms in the air in an attempt to illustrate what he was trying to say and the piano player gave him a funny look.

Suddenly, Robb Lawson played a riff on his Stratocaster which echoed the melody of the last line of the verse, then ascended upward to conclude in the key where the second verse needed to begin.

"That's it! I love that!" Sam yelled, mashing the talkback button.

Buzz jumped to his feet. "I've been trying to get him to do that for the last ten minutes!"

Arnie smiled. Though Buzz lacked Sam's musical sophistication, his enthusiasm was contagious.

The other musicians made notes on their charts and soon worked out an accompaniment to Robb's lick.

"Can you do something like that for the intro, too?" Sam asked Robb.

Robb played a variation of the guitar part in Randy's key, then added a musical phrase to precede it which incorporated the melody of the first line of the verse. The effect was magical.

Sam turned to Arnie. "That's what separates the men from the boys," he said softly. "There're lots of talented musicians in Nashville, but these guys have the ability to be unbelievably creative under pressure. I've never heard that figure before, now it's the hook that'll make your song instantly identifiable on the radio."

After running the track down a few more times, everyone appeared satisfied with their parts and there wasn't much more that could be done until Randy and Stef arrived. Buzz told the players to take a break and sent an intern out for snacks and sandwiches. Finally, at six o'clock, Randy walked in with his arm draped around Stef's shoulder. The famous singer was shorter than Arnie had anticipated, but ex-con muscular and undeniably handsome.

"Sorry we're late," Randy announced. "I wanted to run Stef by my new office to show her how construction is coming."

Stef disengaged herself from Randy and greeted Sam and Buzz, then walked over to give Arnie a hug and kiss on the cheek. "Randy, this is Arnie Fortune."

"Oh, you're the songwriter," he said, nodding at Arnie and turning to Zero. "Let's hear how the track's coming together."

The engineer pressed a button on the console, and played of the most recent run-through of "Safe Against the World".

"Sounds good, but the key's a little high," Randy said. He turned to Stef. "Let's get in the vocal booth and see how it feels."

When they had left the room, Buzz turned to Sam. "I thought we had the right key?"

"We cut it in the key Randy gave us," Sam said. "It's no problem to change it, but if we do, Stef's verse may be too low for her. I hope we can keep that modulation lick that Robb came up with."

The musicians went back to their instruments and ran through the song in a key that was a half step lower as Randy and Stef sang their parts.

Randy was happy with the new key, but Sam was right, the verse was now too low for Stef. Robb turned down the volume of his guitar, and his fingers moved furiously over the frets for a few seconds. When he turned the volume back up, he played a slightly altered modulation part that resolved in the new key. When the band reached the bridge, they modulated again, and Stef's and Randy's voices blended perfectly as they traded lines and harmonized with each other through the end of the song.

Sam nodded to Zero and the drummer clicked his sticks together. Robb kicked the song off with his intro lick and the band launched into the track. Halfway through, the piano player abruptly hit several dissonant chords to signal the group to stop. Sam made a suggestion, and the players again started the song from the top. By the end of the last verse Arnie had goose bumps; the hair was actually standing straight up on his arms.

"Sounds like a hit to me," Buzz bellowed, jumping up from his seat behind the console. "What do you guys think?"

"It felt great," Robb answered. "But it's still a little loose in a few spots. I think we've got a better one in us."

Zero hit the record button again, and the band repeated their performance. When they were done, Sam called everyone into the control room to compare the two tracks.

The piano player said, "The second take is a little tighter, but the first feels better to me."

"I think you might be right," Sam said. "The first take has the magic." He turned to the drummer. "What if you added some percussion, maybe a shaker or something, to glue the rhythm together through the section in the middle where the band starts pushing ahead of the click track?"

Arnie had no idea what they were talking about. He'd listened carefully and both takes sounded flawless.

"Sure," the drummer said. "Lets try a tambourine on the bridge, and keep me in until the end of the song." He went into the main studio and overdubbed the additional instrument while the acoustic guitarist doubled his rhythm part.

The musicians again gathered in the control room to hear the final result. Zero played the track back on the main speakers, and both Sam and Buzz were pleased. Arnie looked for Randy and spotted him in Stef's vocal booth, listening to the playback with his arm again around her shoulder.

"I think we've got it," Sam said. "Anybody hear anything that needs fixing?"

"Nope, it all sounds good to me," the piano player said. "Have we got another song?"

"That's all for today," Buzz said.

"Too bad we don't have a copy of 'Daddy'd Be Proud,'" Sam said. "It's only eight o'clock, and we've got you guys for another hour."

Buzz spoke up: "I haven't played that song for Randy yet, I've been meaning to but—"

"It's up to you Sam," Robb said. "If we had a chart, we could run a track."

Sam turned to Arnie. "Arnie, do you think you could you play it for us live here in the studio?"

"Sure," he said quickly.

Robb passed Arnie an acoustic guitar, and he sang the song through as the musicians jotted down the chord progression.

"Go ahead and write down the lyrics, Arnie," Sam said. "We'll see what Randy thinks."

Arnie printed the lyrics on a pad provided by Zero and handed it to Sam, who walked out to the vocal booth where Randy was still chatting with Stef. They spoke for several minutes. The microphone in the booth was turned off, but Arnie could see Stef pointing toward the paper and mouthing the words to the song. Finally, Randy waved at Zero. The engineer un-muted the microphone and Arnie heard Randy's voice. "Okay, baby, if you think it's a hit, I'll give it a try."

Stef winked at Arnie through the glass as the musicians commenced running the tune down. After rehearsing it twice, Robb looked at his watch.

"Alright guys, it's almost nine o'clock. We've got time for one take."

The drummer kicked the track off with a crashing roll on his tom toms, and the band blazed into the song. When it got to the title line, Randy sang, "Daddy'd be proud, but Mama'd kick my. . ." and Robb bent the strings of his Telecaster in a screeching twang at the word "ass." He repeated the part at each chorus and the band reached the end without a mistake.

"That's freaking incredible!" Buzz yelled.

Randy and Stef followed the musicians back into the control room for the playback. Arnie was beside himself. His song sounded better than he ever could have imagined.

"I think we could even keep most of my lead vocal," Randy exclaimed. "Stef, you're a genius."

Randy gave her a hug that ended with his fingers lingering on the seat of her jeans.

"Are you ready for dinner, baby?"

Arnie groaned. It was driving him crazy to watch Randy come on to Stef, and it pissed him off even more that she wasn't rebuffing his advances. He reminded himself that the singer was one of the biggest stars in country music and had just recorded two of his songs.

"You know, Randy, I'm exhausted," Stef said. "We've got an eight o'clock flight to Philadelphia in the morning. I think I'll just head back to the hotel and get a bite from room service."

"Well, at least let me give you a lift back there, I've got a CD I need to give you. It's a new song I need you to work out a harmony part for—for the show tomorrow night."

"Okay."

Stef walked over and gave Arnie a quick kiss along with a whispered promise to call him later, then followed Randy from the control room.

"Arnie, do you want to join us for a drink and bite to eat?" Sam asked.

"Sure," Arnie answered.

"Everybody else is welcome to come along," Sam said, "I'm buying."

Most of the musicians politely declined, saying they needed to get home to their families, but Robb, Zero and the piano player agreed to join them.

Sam got on his cell phone, and when they arrived at the restaurant, they were met by Sarah and June, from the Appalachian Hellcats.

"I'm so glad you called," Sarah said, hugging Sam as they were led to their table. She was a big girl, with curly red hair that framed her freckled farm-girl face. Arnie had forgotten how pretty she was. June was just as attractive, with a mane of chestnut hair that reached almost to her waist.

Soon, the girls were chattering away about how much they loved Sam's records and how they'd do absolutely anything to get a record deal. Sarah kept rubbing her breasts against Sam's arm, and he seemed quite taken with her. Arnie made a mental note that it wouldn't hurt to keep writing songs with Razor.

After ordering drinks, Robb mentioned that he and his wife had a vacation home in Colorado near Bob Markum's place in Steamboat Springs. It turned out that the Markums were friends of theirs, and Arnie promised to call in July when he was visiting Bob and his family.

Dinner was fun, though Arnie was concerned about Stef and Randy. When the group broke up several hours later, Sam screeched into the night with Sarah and June sharing the passenger seat of his 430.

When Arnie got back to his apartment, he found a voicemail from Stef asking him to call. She picked up after half a dozen rings.

"Hey," she said drowsily. "I'm so glad you called. I was worried you'd get the wrong idea about me and Randy."

"I was wondering a bit. Did you get the CD?"

"Yeah. Don't worry about Randy. He always has to be the center of attention, especially if there's a female in the room. It's not so bad when we're on the road, 'cause there're lots of other chicks around. Tonight I was the only one available."

"Are you at your hotel?"

"Yes, and I'm exhausted, but I'd love to have you come over and crawl into bed next to me."

"I'll be there in a few minutes."

When he arrived at her room, Stef came to the door wearing a short pink nightie. She led him to the bed and he slipped off his jeans and shirt and slid under the covers next to her.

"Are you sure there's nothing to worry about with you and Randy?" he asked.

"Absolutely," she said sleepily.

"Well, I appreciate the way you got him to record 'Daddy'd Be Proud.'"

"You might make a lot of money off it. You'll have to buy me a present if it's a hit."

"Diamonds?"

"Maybe just one."

CHAPTER 51

Arnie tried to contain his excitement the following week as "Last Night Made My Day" rose to the low twenties in *Billboard* and retained its bullet, a chart designation that indicated the song had continued upward momentum. When he called to congratulate Stef, she had a proposition. "I'm doing a show with Randy in Little Rock on Friday at the Riverfest Amphitheater. After that, I'm free until Monday, when I'm due back in Nashville to finish my album with Sam. Why don't you drive down and catch the show, then maybe we could spend a few days together in Hot Springs."

"I've heard that's a great little town."

"Starr'll get you a backstage pass for the show."

Arnie hung up and called the office.

"What a coincidence," Starr said, when he told her about his plans with Stef. "Sam's been talking to some Air Force guy in Arkansas about buying a 348. It's an older model, but Sam needs a beater Ferrari he can use for track events."

Arnie smiled at the expression "beater Ferrari" as Starr continued, "I just got off the phone with him. He was wondering how to get the car to Nashville. Let me see if he wants you to drive it back for him. It'd be fun."

Starr called back late that afternoon. "I've got your pass for the concert and I spoke with Sam. He's decided to buy the car and said you could pick it up Friday and have it for the weekend."

"Awesome."

"I'll stop by on my lunch hour Thursday to take you to pick up a rental car for the drive to Little Rock. I've arranged for the 348's owner to meet you at the airport before the concert to take delivery."

"Okay. By the way, do you know of a hotel in Hot Springs that you can recommend?"

"You should call the Arlington," she said without hesitating. "It has several nice restaurants, and quite a history. Hot Springs was the big gambling spot back in the nineteen-twenties, before Las Vegas was developed. Al Capone and his cronies used to stay there. It has a spa and mineral baths. Stef will love it."

"Sounds fabulous."

* * *

When Starr came by Arnie's apartment later that week, she punched the buttons of her car's CD player and said, "Sam stopped at the office earlier and dropped off a rough mix of 'Safe Against the World.' I thought you'd like to hear it."

"What can I say? It sounds incredible!" he exclaimed when it was over.

"Yes, it's probably going to be a single from the way everyone's talking. And Sam said may cut one of the songs you wrote with Bob Markum on Stef when she goes back in to record next week. You've been very lucky, don't let it go to your head."

"Don't worry, I don't think there's much chance of that."

"Good. Here we are," she said as they pulled to a stop in front of the Budget office on Broadway. She handed him an envelope and small cardboard box. "Here's a cashiers check for the 348. Make sure you get the title and that it's signed and notarized properly. And double check to verify that the serial number matches the one on the car. Some of these Ferrari guys are . . . oh well, never mind."

"What's in the box?"

"It's a Valentine One, the best radar detector made—has a three-hundred-sixty degree scanning radius, and can even ID the cop's location. Don't let on to Sam that I lent it to you. But if you're going to have a Ferrari for the weekend, you might as well enjoy it to the max."

"Thanks," Arnie said with a grin. "Maybe I'll come back with a song called 'Ozark Mountain Autobahn!'"

"Knowing you, I wouldn't be surprised." Starr said. "Have fun."

Arnie stopped at a market on the way back to his apartment and picked up a road atlas. The best route to Little Rock was a straight shot west through Memphis on I-40. As he examined the map, an idea popped into his head. He'd always been curious about Elvis Presley's Graceland Mansion. If he left now he could be in Memphis by nightfall, visit the museum in the morning, and still make it to Little Rock for his appointment. He packed a bag and tossed it in the trunk of his rented Taurus, then hit the road.

Three hours later he arrived in Memphis and checked into a motel near Beale Street. He spent the evening checking out the bars and clubs, getting a particular kick out of a place called Silky O'Sullivan's, where two trained goats in a back room entertained customers by walking up a wooden ramp and guzzling beers.

Arnie had always loved the music that had come out of Memphis, and found that something about the city itself fascinated him. It was almost as if a sweet soulful energy seeped up out of cracks in the sidewalk. At midnight, he had a beer buzz going and drove carefully back to his motel. He fell asleep wondering how the goats at Silky O'Sullivan's were going to deal with their hangovers.

The next morning he rose early and headed to Graceland. Since it was a weekday, the ticket line was short, and he soon found himself being handed a headset and given instructions for the self guided tour by a severe looking young black woman with a wasp waist and enormous rear end.

As he entered the handsome colonial mansion's foyer, he was struck by two tall, stained glass peacocks guarding the entrance to a small music room to his right. Inside, the room housed a beautiful ice-cream-white baby grand piano. He adjusted the volume of the tour narration and strolled through the gracious living room, then continued into the comfortable kitchen and dining area where Elvis and his pals were said to have spent most of their time. The Jungle Room, decorated in an African safari motif, was particularly fascinating, not only because of its décor, but also because it was where Elvis had recorded the vocal for his last single, the classic Layng Martine, Jr. song "Way Down." Behind the sprawling mansion were several outbuildings, including Elvis's original office, and a racquetball facility.

Arnie had often heard Graceland referred to as a garish monument to bad taste, but after seeing it, he didn't quite agree. It impressed him as a home that reflected its owner's pride in his accomplishments and enthusiasm for life. He grinned when he found himself thinking it might be a fun place to live, and laughed as he wondered if Stef might feel the same.

When he reached the Meditation Garden where Elvis and his family were buried, he was surprised to hear the voice on the recording playing through his headset announce that the tour was over. He was disappointed not to see the upstairs of the house, especially the bathroom where the King had met his tragic end, and also the master bedroom closet, which supposedly had a peephole enabling Elvis and his cronies to watch visiting record execs and movie producers cavorting with their wives and starlet girlfriends in the guest bedroom.

He spotted the attendant he had spoken to earlier and inquired about getting access to the mansion's second level. She informed him in a stern voice that no one—not even the tour staff—was allowed upstairs.

"How long have you been working here?" Arnie asked.

"Two years."

"Two years, and you've never been upstairs? Not even once?"

"That's right," she said brusquely, hand on hip.

"So maybe the rumors are true, the King's still up there somewhere singing gospel songs, and eating barbecue and fried peanut butter and banana sandwiches?"

The tour guide broke into a grin, then laughed and waved goodbye as Arnie turned to catch the shuttle bus back to the parking lot. Soon he was back in his Taurus, speeding over the Mississippi River on Interstate 40 towards the rice and cotton fields of Eastern Arkansas.

CHAPTER 52

Arnie arrived at Little Rock National Airport late Friday afternoon. As he stepped out of the Budget office after turning in the Taurus, a gleaming white Ferrari 348 zipped up in front of him, followed by an emerald-green Ford Expedition driven by a woman with a chubby-faced baby strapped into a car seat behind her. He introduced himself to the Ferrari's driver, a fit man in his forties who bore a vague resemblance to John Wayne.

"Hi there, I'm Arnie Fortune."

"Stan Fishman," the man said, pumping Arnie's hand.

"It's a beauty," Arnie said, eying the Ferrari. "Mind my asking why you're selling it?"

"I'm retiring from the Air Force this year and just bought a 355 from a fellow down in Mobile as a retirement present to myself—beats a gold watch."

"Nice. So you're a pilot?"

"Yep, stationed with the 314th Airlift Wing, just north of here in Jacksonville. My wife Laurie and I are getting ready to move to your neck of the woods soon." Her family's from Murfreesboro. I'll be doing some consulting at the Arnold Engineering Development Center in Tullahoma."

"You'll have to look up Sam and his Ferrari buddies when you get to Tennessee."

"I'd love to. Do you own a Ferrari?"

"No, not yet, but they let me hang around anyway."

"There's nothing like 'em. It's like driving an F-16 with wheels," Stan said, handing Arnie the keys. He unsnapped the side pocket of his nylon flight jacket and withdrew an envelope. "Here's the title; it's been signed and notarized."

Arnie walked around the 348 and examined it closely. It was flawless. Remembering what Starr had told him, he checked to make sure the chassis serial number matched the one listed on the title. It did.

"Everything seems to be in order," Arnie said.

"Enjoy the drive," Stan said, shaking hands. "Don't worry about gas, I just filled her up. Try not to get too many tickets."

"Will do."

Stan slid into the Expedition, and he and Laurie waved as they drove off. Arnie strapped himself into the Ferrari and sat for a moment, enjoying the feeling of being in the cockpit of an "F-16 with wheels", then turned the ignition key. The starter whined and the engine turned over for several seconds without catching. Just as he was becoming concerned, it snarled to life. He eased the gearshift forward into first and let out the clutch, then felt like Michael Schumacher leaving the pits at the Monaco Grand Prix as the car rocketed away from the curb into the traffic exiting the airport.

Driving the 348 was exhilarating. Though it didn't have quite the power of Robert's twelve-cylinder Testerossa, it handled like an extension of Arnie's brain, sensing where he wanted to go and arriving there by the time he was conscious of turning the wheel. Soon he spotted the exit for the Riverfest Amphitheatre and downshifted for the ramp, then followed the signs to the venue.

He used the all-access laminate to enter the VIP parking lot, and passed through security into the main arena. Though the show didn't start for an hour, the sold out amphitheatre was already packed and Arnie was struck by the diversity of the crowd, which ranged from designer clad yuppies to farmers in overalls.

Knowing how much pressure Stef was under before her performances, he decided to watch her set with the fans rather than head immediately backstage. He bought a hot dog and beer and strolled through the mass of people, enjoying the mild spring evening until a local radio personality stepped to the microphone. The DJ warmed up the crowd with ten minutes worth of jokes and announcements, then introduced Stef, who ran out on stage as her band kicked off the intro to her first song. Arnie hadn't seen her perform live since Printer's Alley in Nashville the previous fall, and was impressed by the easy rapport she established with the large audience. Soon she had the crowd of several thousand people wrapped around her finger.

Stef ended her seven-song set with "Last Night Made My Day" and Arnie experienced a shiver of pride as a smattering of applause from the audience greeted his song's first few lines. When she finished the tune to a standing ovation, Arnie made his way to the front of the amphitheater, where a security guard nodded at his laminate and waved him backstage to the performer's area. Stef spotted him and rushed over to throw her arms around his neck.

"I'm so glad you're here, did you see the whole thing?"

"Yeah, the crowd loved you!"

"Come," Stef said disengaging herself and taking his hand. "Let's catch Randy's show, I think you'll enjoy it."

They walked forward to the left wing of the stage, where they had a good view of Randy and his band, who had just begun. It was hard not to admire the seasoned showman. Although he must have given the same performance scores of times, Randy worked the crowd masterfully, making them feel like it was the most important night of his career. Not only were his singing and guitar playing great, but his act was full of spontaneous energy; he put every ounce of his being into giving the audience their money's worth.

After doing a string of his past singles, Randy announced that he wanted to try out some new songs from his upcoming album. He started with a mid-tempo ballad that got good response, then called Stef to join him for "Safe Against the World." She trotted to the microphone and their performance drew thunderous applause. Arnie wasn't thrilled about the fact that Randy took her hand during the last chorus, making them appear like a couple in the enormous video monitors, but any jealousy he felt was drowned by the skin-tingling rush of adrenaline he experienced from the crowd's response to his song.

Stef ran back to Arnie's side, rosy-faced and hyperventilating as Randy blasted into the opening chords of "Daddy'd Be Proud." Though the audience was unfamiliar with the song, they reacted immediately, loving it. Randy repeated the chorus twice at the end of the tune, holding the microphone out in front of him for the crowd to complete the line: "but Mama'd kick my . . ." and the entire crowd was on its feet singing along and clapping in unison by the time the song ended.

"Wow!" Arnie exclaimed.

"Sounds like a hit to me!" Stef yelled, clutching Arnie's sleeve and jumping up and down.

"And he never would have recorded it if it hadn't been for you," Arnie said, turning to kiss her.

Randy closed his set with his current single, "Frazzled," then returned for an encore that consisted of a medley of several of his biggest hits. As Arnie and Stef made their way through the crowded backstage area afterward, she was interrupted by the DJ who had been the show's MC and asked to record a brief on-air announcement. He suggested that she be spontaneous, and she gestured for him to raise his iPod's microphone.

"When I'm in Little Rock I keep my radio tuned to ninety-five-point-seven FM and I hear great country music," she said. The DJ smiled as she continued. "And when I'm not in Little Rock I still keep my radio tuned to ninety-five-point-seven FM and I hear . . . whoooooooosh." Stef moved her lips close to the microphone and blew hard, creating a sound like static.

"That's hilarious," the announcer said. "My audience will love it!"

They all laughed, and Stef took Arnie's hand.

"I'm ready to scoot out of here," she said.

"Sounds good to me. We've got a bit of a drive ahead of us to Hot Springs, but I think you'll enjoy the ride."

Stef grabbed her overnight bag from the security station, and they were escorted to the VIP parking lot. Her eyes lit up when they approached the 348, and she clapped her hands.

"Arnie! You got a Ferrari!!!" she squealed. "I told you I wasn't crazy about white, but now I think it's my favorite color!"

"It's only ours for the weekend," Arnie said sheepishly. "I'm driving it back to Nashville for Sam. He bought it from a fellow in Little Rock."

"I don't care . . . I'm just glad we'll get to enjoy it together."

Arnie popped open the hood and tossed Stef's bag into the trunk.

"What's that smell," she said as they accelerated from the service road onto the highway. "Is it gasoline?"

"Now that you mention it, I do smell gas."

Arnie noted that the fuel gauge was reading just above half a tank and was surprised—it had been full before the short drive from the airport. He spotted a service station a few miles down the road and pulled in. After examining the engine, he checked the tank and found the gas cap was missing.

"I think that was the problem," he said to Stef after topping off the tank and plugging the filler pipe with a wad of paper towels. "Stan must have forgotten to put the cap back on when he filled it."

Traffic was light and Stef dozed with her head on Arnie's shoulder for most of the drive. An hour and a half later they descended through the Ouachita Mountains to Hot Springs. Even at night, the Arlington Hotel was an impressive sight—an ornate eleven-story structure at the center of the downtown historic district. They checked in and rode a brass-trimmed elevator to the tenth floor, where they were delighted by their spacious room in one of the twin towers that adorned the front of the building. Exhausted from the long day and drive, they slipped into bed and soon fell asleep.

Arnie woke the next morning and found himself alone in the king sized bed. A few minutes later, he heard the door handle turn and Stef entered with two tall cups of coffee.

"I got up early and thought I'd check the place out," she said, dropping a handful of brochures on the bed. "The rear of the hotel is built into the mountain that contains the springs that supply hot water to the mineral baths and spa. I've made an appointment for a massage at ten."

"Sounds like a great plan. Starr said you'd like this place!" Arnie said, tossing off the covers. He showered and dressed and soon they were downstairs ordering breakfast at the hotel coffee shop.

"I didn't know there was a horse racing track here," Arnie said, paging through one of the brochures Stef had brought along as they waited for their meal to arrive. "It's called Oaklawn Park."

"I love horse races. I used to go with my father to Aqueduct and Belmont when I was little. In fact, he even owned a racehorse for a while, but I was always trying to get him to trade it for a pony."

"Let's go this afternoon."

Stef headed to the hotel spa appointment and promised to meet Arnie back at the room at noon. He spent the rest of morning strolling through the various galleries and shops near the hotel, then returned to retrieve Stef and the Ferrari and head for Oaklawn Park.

When they arrived at the track, a parking attendant informed them that, unfortunately, the season's live racing meet was over—though the Player's Pavilion remained open for simulcast viewing and betting. They entered the large sports-bar style room to find a crowd of several hundred people watching races from other tracks around the country on large wall-mounted TV monitors. After ordering beers, Stef studied the *Daily Racing Form* and deliberated on which of two long-shot horses to wager on in an upcoming race at Hollywood Park. A stooped gray-haired gentleman to her left suggested that if she couldn't decide between the two mounts, she could place a bet called an exacta box, which would pay off if both her choices finished in the top two places, no matter which came in first. She went to the betting window and followed his instructions, wagering four dollars, then returned to the bar as the horses exploded from the starting gate. A few minutes later, she shrieked with delight when her mounts came in first and second, yielding a payoff of two hundred sixty-eight dollars.

"So what made you pick those two?" the older man queried when she'd returned from the betting window with her winnings. "They each went off at thirty-something to one."

"I thought they had cute names," Stef announced. "Cash Advance and On the Money."

Their new friend shook his head and laughed, then went back to chewing his cigar and studying his *Racing Form* as Arnie and Stef finished their beers and headed back to the hotel.

After a short nap they went downstairs for dinner, followed by drinks at the hotel's mural-paneled bar. A four-piece combo was performing and several dozen couples were twirling around the dance floor. Arnie surmised it was a hangout for the local ballroom dancing crowd.

"Come on," Stef said, taking Arnie's hand and pulling him to his feet as the drummer kicked off a Salsa number.

"But I can't dance!" he protested.

"I don't believe you."

"I really can't."

"You can write songs, so you've got to be able to dance," she said.

Arnie allowed himself be led to the floor and followed Stef's instructions to keep his shoulders straight while moving his feet and hips in a mirror image to her own. She was a skilled dancer he was surprised to find himself able to keep up with her, even going so far as lifting her hand in the air for a few twirls toward the end of the tune. The next song was a waltz, and Arnie took her in his arms and managed to circle the floor twice without stepping on her toes a single time.

"I thought you said you couldn't dance," Stef said breathlessly when they returned to their seats at the bar. "You did great! You're a fine dancer."

"Only when I dance with you."

"You're talking in song titles again."

After a few more dances and a final nightcap, they headed upstairs. In the elevator, Stef kissed him, then looked into his eyes.

"Arnie, this has been such a perfect day."

He nodded as his lips met hers again. When they got to the room Stef pulled him to the bed and unbuttoned his shirt. They kissed for several minutes, and when Arnie reached between her legs she responded by unzipping her skirt and shrugging out of her top. Soon they were both naked under the covers. "Rub my back," she said, rolling onto her stomach.

"Didn't you get enough of that at the spa today?"

"It's better with you."

Arnie started with her shoulders, massaging them gently. He rolled her vertebrae between his thumbs as he worked his way down to the small of her back, and soon her muscles felt so relaxed that he wondered if she'd fallen asleep. When his palms reached the base of her spine she sighed loudly.

"Legs, too."

Arnie dug his fingers deep into her sculpted thighs and calves, then raised his wrists and softly feathered his fingertips over the thin skin between the tendons behind her knees. Stef's legs parted and her buttocks rose as his fingernails, still barely touching her skin, traced her tan lines back to the base of her spine.

Stef flipped over. Her lips locked to his and she clutched him to her.

"I want you," she gasped hoarsely. "I want you Arnie."

"Are you sure?" Arnie said, caressing her with his fingers.

"Please . . . just go slow."

"I don't know if I have any condoms."

"That's okay. I'm just finishing my period."

Arnie rolled on top of her and she guided him between her legs. He felt her body begin to tense.

"Stop," she said softly.

He started to pull away and she dug her nails into his ribcage, holding him in place. "No, don't go away. Just stay where you are."

After a few seconds, she relaxed and her legs parted slightly. "Okay, now try again."

He penetrated a little further and she stopped him once more. After a moment, she again directed him to continue. Soon he was completely inside her.

"I want you to come," she said, angling her hips upward.

"What about you?"

"Don't worry about me right now."

Stef raised her legs, locked her ankles around the small of his back, and rocked back and forth as he slowly slid in and out. He felt her body begin to follow his motions, then her hips found a rhythm of their own, which he matched. When he exploded inside her Stef was clasping him so tight that it felt as if his body was part of hers., She held him inside for a long time and afterward he felt as if his senses had totally left him.

"Stef. . ." he said as he collapsed on the sheets several minutes later.

"Don't say anything. Just hold me," she whispered.

Stef kissed him, then turned on her side. Arnie nestled against her back and cradled her breast in his hand while struggling to keep his eyes open. He wondered if he was already asleep and dreaming If not, he wanted to make this moment last as long as possible.

CHAPTER 53

Arnie opened his eyes the next morning to the gorgeous sight of Stef lying beside him with the covers pulled down to her waist. Memories of last night quickly filled him with lust. He ran his palm across her taut tan stomach, then caressed one breast while teasing the nipple of the other until she stirred.

This time there was no hesitation. She kissed him hard on the mouth, reached to guide him inside her, then moaned and bucked till he couldn't control himself any longer. He tried to slow down, but she wouldn't let him, grinding under him until he gave in.

"You know, it was even starting to feel good that time," she said as he held her afterward.

"You could have fooled me!"

Stef punched Arnie's arm, then snuggled close.

"I don't know what I'm going to do with you."

"Whatever it is, don't stop."

After enjoying a lazy brunch, they gathered their bags. A light rain was falling, and they held hands just inside the hotel's heavy double glass doors as the parking valet pulled up to the entrance in the 348, a grin on his face from having piloted the Ferrari to the hotel entrance. As he stepped out of the car and started toward them, Arnie spotted a small flash of flame under the 348's chassis.

A millisecond later there was a loud *whummmmmmmp*, followed by a deafening explosion as a ball of fire raised the back of the car almost vertically off the ground. The shockwave blew the valet through the hotel doors into Arnie and Stef's upraised arms, knocking all three to the floor, and pummeled the front of the building with shrapnel-like shards of metal and debris.

Arnie looked up from the carpet amid screams and shouts from the hotel guests to see the 348 engulfed in flames. Stef tried to get to her feet, but he forced her back down and lay on top of her, protecting her as best he could from whatever might come next.

Miraculously, no one had been standing near the car. The valet, who appeared to be unhurt, got to his feet, grabbed a fire extinguisher from the wall and ran back outside. Soon he and two security guards had the blaze extinguished. Within minutes, three ambulances and half a dozen police cars were on the scene, with cops and paramedics alike shaking their heads in wonderment at the fact that no one had been injured.

Arnie stood in the lobby with his arm around Stef. He was trembling as he stared at the car's smoldering remains in the driveway and shook his head.

Evidently, even a Ferrari wasn't fast enough to outrun his past.

CHAPTER 54

The rest of the day was a nightmare of bureaucracy and red tape. Once the initial trauma of the incident passed, Stef's main concern was getting back to Nashville in time for her recording session the next morning. Meanwhile, Arnie was overcome with fear for himself, and also guilt for having inadvertently exposed her to a situation that could have caused both of their deaths.

They called Sam, and once the producer was assured they were okay, he contacted Buzz, who arranged for a charter plane to fly them back to Nashville that evening. Arnie was worried that Sam would be upset by the loss of the Ferrari, but his boss assured him that it was fully covered by insurance.

As the afternoon wore on, the cause of the explosion remained uncertain. While being questioned by the Hot Springs Police Department, Arnie debated whether to mention anything about Don Puccini, but decided it would be best not to do so without consulting the FBI first. He also decided not to activate his beeper, reasoning that he and Stef were probably safe for the time being, since they were surrounded by law enforcement officers.

That evening, they were driven in a highway patrol cruiser to a chartered Piper Baron at Hot Springs Memorial Field Airport. Stef signed autographs for the two state troopers who'd accompanied them, then huddled close to Arnie on the flight home in a state of semi-shock. Several times he found himself on the verge of blurting out the truth about his past, but couldn't bring himself to do it. To reveal his true identity would likely mean abandoning the career that had been going so well, not to mention their romance.

Buzz had arranged for a limo to pick them up at the Nashville airport, and Arnie, for safety reasons, directed the driver to the West End Marriott rather than Loews, where he booked Stef a room. After helping her get settled in, he explained that he thought it best she spend the night alone and get a good night's sleep before her recording session. As soon as he got to his apartment, he called the emergency number given to him by the FBI. Agent Baskins called back ten minutes later.

"Don't move," was the agent's terse instruction. "Don't leave your apartment until you hear back from me, and stay away from the windows. I'll be back in touch within twenty-four hours."

Baskins called late the next morning. "I don't have much to tell you. I've gone over the incident report with the Hot Springs chief of police and they're ruling it an accident. You mentioned to one of the officers that the Ferrari was missing its fuel cap. They think gasoline vapors may have accumulated in the body cavity like they can in the bilge of a boat, and been set off by a spark from the ignition, or maybe a cigarette butt lying in the driveway—they're not sure what. But they haven't found any residue from explosives."

"It couldn't have been a cigarette butt, it was raining outside."

"The report says the car was parked under the entrance canopy."

"How can you be sure it wasn't. . ."

"We can't."

"Isn't that your job?" Arnie asked, raising his voice.

"Calm down."

"Can you send what's left of the car to a lab or something and figure out what caused the explosion?"

"It's not that easy."

"I thought that's what you guys did. Remember when the space shuttle Challenger blew up? You guys were able to pick up wreckage scattered across seven states and figure out what caused the crash. And that's after it fell out of fucking orbit. The pieces of the Ferrari were all right there in the parking lot."

"We're not NASA, they're rocket scientists."

"I don't give a shit," Arnie said. "You're the fucking FBI for Chrissake!"

"Listen, I can have someone at your door in two minutes and pull you out of Nashville right now. It's your call. We can reassign you anywhere you want, like the grad school program at Pepperdine we talked about last year, or anywhere else you want to go. The bottom line is that the Hot Springs Police Department has ruled the explosion an accident."

Arnie took a deep breath. "What do you think caused the car to blow up? Honestly."

"I think it was either an accident or done on purpose by a real expert."

"Jesus fucking Christ! A *real expert*? The kind of person Don Puccini could afford to hire for fifty grand?"

"If you want to think of it that way, yes. But if it had been an attempt on your life, I think whoever was responsible would have followed with another try by now. They'd figure we'd snatch you out of Nashville and want to get to you before we had the chance. You've been under close surveillance since yesterday, and so far, there's been no sign of anything unusual, nothing at all."

"What should I do?"

"My advice would be to go back to your regular routine. We'll keep an eye on you for a week or two, and if we don't spot anything out of the ordinary, you're probably okay. Like I said, if they were going to make a move they would have done it by now. Keep the beeper in your pocket."

Arnie hung up.

CHAPTER 55

Arnie remained in his apartment for the next two days. In spite of what Baskins had said, he couldn't convince himself that the explosion had been an accident. By Wednesday, he was going stir crazy and decided to drive by the record company studio and see how Stef's recording sessions were coming. The sunny morning lifted his spirits, but didn't stop him from glancing in the rearview mirror constantly and planning escape routes down side streets, should it become necessary. Once at the studio, he took the elevator to the top floor, and while checking in with the receptionist, on a whim, asked if Ronnie Dexter was in. She spoke on the phone for a few moments, then waved Arnie down the hall. Halfway there, Nanci Morales popped out of a doorway.

"Hey there, Arnie. Looks like our girl might go all the way."

"Really?"

"Yes! We're at nineteen in *Billboard* this week."

"That's fantastic."

"Just keep writing more songs like 'Last Night Made My Day' and 'Daddy'd Be Proud.'"

"So you've heard Randy's cut?"

"Yes. Buzz played the staff a rough mix yesterday. We also heard 'Safe Against the World.' They're both great."

Nanci vanished down the hall and Arnie knocked lightly on the door to Ronnie's office, which was cracked open. Ronnie waved him in and motioned toward the couch.

"You're the only station in Dallas that isn't on it," he said into the headset hooked over his ear. He paused and clicked his fingernails on the desk. "Yes, I know she's a new artist, but 'Last Night' is a great record." He paused again. "I'll tell you what, Stefany's opening for Randy at the Astrodome in June. I can get you two dozen tickets for the show, plus a party bus to and from Houston. You can run a contest like you did last year and listeners will be burning up the phones trying to win tickets." Ronnie tapped an unfiltered Camel from a pack on his desk and frowned as he spun the cigarette on his blotter. "Okay, I'll try to get one pair in the first row. But you'll have to find your own date." A few more seconds went by and he laughed. "Hey, hey. Relax, I was just kidding. Didn't I take care of you during CRS?" He covered the microphone and chuckled, rolling his eyes at Arnie. "Yeah, I'm sure she and her friend will be back next year. So you think you can add the record? Just give me a few spins, that's all I'm asking, just a few spins. People are going to love it." Ronnie gave a silent thumbs-up sign to Arnie. "All right then, I appreciate it. Talk to you next week."

The promotion man clicked a button on the console in front of him and slammed his palm down on his desk.

"We got the station!"

"He's going to add the record?"

"Yep, now I've got to convince Buzz to spring for the tickets and party bus, hopefully it won't be a problem. I'll call our last holdout in Houston this afternoon and tell them the biggest station in Dallas-Fort Worth is on it—they won't want to be the only one in the region not playing it."

"It's interesting to watch you work."

"Things have changed a lot since the old days," Ronnie said.

"In what way?"

"I remember my first visit to Nashville. Years ago, they used to have something called the DJ Convention downtown—it was a precursor to the Country Radio Seminar that happens nowadays every February or March. I was a jock back then at a little station in Cape Girardeau and I was talking with a producer from Texas in the lobby of the old Hyatt Regency. A program director from Baton Rouge approached the producer, handed him two keys and pointed to the elevator. When the PD walked off I asked the producer what the keys were for."

"And. . . ?"

Ronnie slipped into a Tex-Mex accent. "One of dem is for de room, de other is for de girl handcuffed to de bed."

"You're shitting me! I guess you couldn't get away with that today."

"Naw," Ronnie said wistfully. "Those were the good old days. It's all business now. But I still make sure these guys are taken care of when they come to town. What's most important is that Stef's got a great record. That's what counts. Once listeners hear your song, they love it. That means they stay tuned to the station. That means advertising dollars keep coming in. That means everybody keeps their jobs. It all works out."

"So things are looking good?"

"Real good. We should have almost all the reporting stations onboard in the next few weeks. If they keep moving it up in rotation, we've got a good chance for a top ten record, maybe even better—not bad for a new artist."

"Thanks for all your hard work."

"Thanks for the song."

Arnie headed downstairs to the record company's recording studio. When he stepped out of the elevator, he couldn't believe his eyes. The facility made Graceland look like a convent. The hallway and lounge were decorated with red velvet wallpaper, matching shag carpet and dim lighting provided by ornate chandeliers and heavy wrought iron wall sconces holding flickering imitation electric candles. It looked like a sailor's fantasy of a New Orleans whorehouse.

The control room and studio itself were slightly more business-like, but still appeared more like a bordello than a workplace. However, work was being done. Arnie took a seat on a plush Victorian sofa at the rear of the room and watched as Stef and the musicians ran down a western swing tune under Sam's direction.

During a break, Stef joined Arnie on the couch. She confirmed that she'd cut one of the songs he'd written with Bob Markum and several others from various publishing companies around town, plus the Patsy Cline standard, "I Fall to Pieces," which Arnie had first heard her perform in Printers Alley the previous fall. After a few minutes, she kissed him and returned to her vocal booth, saying she'd be working most of the night and flying to Chicago in the morning.

Arnie drove back to his apartment, missing her already.

CHAPTER 56

With Stef gone, Arnie settled back into his writing routine. He was excited about one new song in particular, "Only When I Dance with You," inspired by their evening on the dance floor at the Arlington Hotel. "Last Night Made My Day" continued upward in the charts during the next two weeks, jumping to the mid, then low teens. During their frequent phone conversations, Stef was exuberant about the single's success. Her tour was going well, and she was looking forward in particular to a show that Buzz had managed to book for her at a club in Las Vegas the night before the Academy of Country Music Awards were to broadcast from the MGM Grand. It would be a great opportunity to showcase for industry bigwigs in town for the event. Most importantly, she couldn't wait to see Arnie in Nashville when she returned for the upcoming CMA Music Festival.

Meanwhile, Sam spent long hours in the studio overdubbing and mixing her album. Arnie checked his email frequently, and was relieved that there was no further communication at all from Baskins. One afternoon, while at the computer, he Googled Tony Bertolini's name, and a recent article on the *New York Times* website popped up saying that the gangster had been denied an appeal for his conviction, and was now permanently incarcerated in a federal prison in Marion, Illinois.

* * *

When Arnie stopped by the office late the following week, Sam waved him toward a chair in front of his desk. The producer appeared tired, but was in a grand mood.

"Have a seat. I've got some good news, some not so good news, and some great news. I just got out of a meeting with Nanci and Buzz, and the not so good news is that the song you and Bob wrote isn't going to make

Stef's album. We've cut a total of thirteen sides over the last year, and they picked what they felt were the best ten. Unfortunately, your song wasn't one of them."

"Oh well," Arnie said, disappointed for both himself and Bob.

"Don't worry about Bob," Sam said, reading Arnie's thoughts. "These things happen and he's used to it. The good news is that you'll have two songs on her CD—'Last Night Made My Day' and 'Safe Against the World.'"

"That *is* good news."

"And the great news is that the label's also going to include 'Safe Against the World' on Randy Fawcett's new album—as well as 'Daddy'd Be Proud.' Both songs have definitely made it."

"Wow!"

"Stef's album will be out sometime this summer and Randy's should be out in the early fall. His last CD sold over three million copies and they're projecting the new one will do at least that. Having two songs on a triple platinum album is worth a quarter million dollars to you, more than enough to recoup your advances. I'm planning to double your draw, effective next month, to a thousand dollars a week. It'll give you some extra cash and also help you spread out your income for tax purposes."

"That's nice of you, Sam. I know you don't have to do that."

"I *want* to do it. Like I told you when we first met, I believe in win-win business relationships. You'll be getting some very substantial performance royalties in addition to your draw. 'Last Night Made My Day' should earn at least a hundred grand in airplay, maybe even as much as twice that, if it keeps going up the charts. If you get another single with one of the other two songs, which is very possible from the way Buzz is talking, your total income next year could be well into six figures—three or four hundred thousand dollars."

"Really? That's hard to believe."

Sam paused and cleared his throat, then continued. "Listen carefully to what I'm about to say. I want you to make an appointment with my CPA, Phil Hart, as soon as you can. You need to work out some tax strategies—now, before the money comes in—so you can hang onto as much of it as possible. This business is extremely uncertain. You're talented, and you're a hard worker—but you've been unbelievably lucky. You've got a special opportunity here, and I don't want to see you blow it like I've seen a lot of other people do."

"Would buying a Ferrari be blowing it?"

Sam broke into a grin and ran his fingers through his hair, which Arnie couldn't help noticing was showing nearly a quarter inch of gray at the roots. "A Ferrari is an investment. When I think of all the female companionship my Ferraris have gotten me, I have no regrets!"

They both laughed, then Sam continued, "But seriously, I don't think you have any idea how hard this business can be, or how unusual it is for someone to come to town and have the kind of success you've had so quickly. There's no guarantee that you'll ever have another song recorded. I hope you do. In fact, I'm counting on it. But, if you play your cards right with the chunk of cash you'll be making over the next few years, you'll be in good shape for a long time to come."

"Thanks Sam, I'll take your advice and call him. By the way, I've been meaning to ask, what's going on with the Hellcats?"

"I've played the tracks for a few people, but no one's going nuts. We'll know more in a little while. Everyone's so busy now. Most of the A&R folks from the labels are just getting back in town from the ACM awards, and the CMA Music Festival is coming up. Stef's show is scheduled for a week from Friday. I'll make sure Starr gets you get a pass."

"Thanks."

"And don't make any plans for later that night. Buzz Corbin's got a party planned on the General Jackson riverboat after the show. A bunch of the Ferrari guys will be there."

"Look forward to it!"

CHAPTER 57

Arnie met with Sam's accountant a few days later.

"You're wise to have come to me now," Phil Hart said, as he greeted him and motioned to a plush leather armchair across from his desk. His spacious office was located on the twenty-fifth floor of a downtown high-rise that featured floor-to-ceiling windows offering a sensational view of the Cumberland River and LP Field. The accountant was in his sixties and had the gentle demeanor of an old-time country doctor. Arnie found himself liking and trusting him immediately; he reminded him of the grandfather he'd never known.

"Actually, it was Sam's idea," Arnie said.

"Sam's an astute businessman. He's been a good client for many years—and a close friend, too. He's seen a lot of songwriters get in difficulty with the IRS, as have I."

"What do you mean?" Arnie asked, glancing around Phil's office. Between the many gold and platinum records hanging on the cherry paneled walls were framed pictures of over a dozen of Nashville's top stars. Other photos appeared to have been taken at various charity events, including one of the accountant and several civic leaders presenting an oversize seven-digit check to the director of Vanderbilt Children's Hospital.

"Most writers struggle for years without ever making enough money to owe the IRS much of anything. When a songwriter finally has a hit or two, they have no idea what their tax liability will be. He, or she, spends what they earn—sometimes before they even get it—through advances or loans. I'm not talking about extravagant expenditures, they figure they deserve a decent car so they buy one. Then the songwriter makes a down payment on a house, takes a vacation or two and starts eating at nice restaurants instead of Burger King. They believe they've worked hard and deserve these things—and, to be honest, they probably do. But when the tax is due a year later, most of the money is gone and their income is down again. The writer can't pay."

"What happens? Do they go to jail?"

"No, nothing like that," Phil said with a soft laugh. "The IRS wants to keep them working so they'll eventually pay their tax liability. They set up a payment plan that includes penalties and interest on the amount in arrears. Once in debt, a struggling songwriter has a hard time ever catching up. The next time he or she has a hit, if they ever do, Uncle Sam is waiting to take the profit."

"So what's the secret?"

"There is no secret. Wise men plan for the future. The first thing to remember is that you owe the government its share. The second thing is to set aside that money for when it's due. How much do you think you'll be making next year?"

"Sam says it could be $100,000 or more—as much as $300,000 or $400,000 if I get another single."

"Let's assume you make $300,000," Phil said, not blinking at the amount as his fingers danced over a calculator on his desk. "There are some things you can write off: business travel and meals, maybe a new guitar or two. Keep your receipts in case we need to document your expenditures for an audit. Between income and self-employment taxes, you're going to owe the IRS about $93,000."

"I'll owe almost $100,000 in taxes?"

"Yes, and that's if you make the maximum allowable contribution to a tax-deferred retirement plan, $40K."

"You're kidding? So if I make three hundred thousand dollars, I'll only get to spend half?"

"A little more than that—$165,000 or so. As I said before, most people have no idea."

"That's still a lot of money," Arnie said, shaking his head. "What's your advice for what I have left over?"

"You should consider buying a house or condo for the interest deduction. After that, you might want to think about some other investments, but don't forget you've already placed a significant amount in your retirement account. Our firm manages money for quite a few artists and writers. I'd be glad to talk more with you about the services we offer when the time comes. As far as the rest of the money, I'd enjoy it."

"What about buying a Ferrari?"

Phil laughed. "I see you've been talking to Sam. The interesting thing with exotic cars is that sometimes they can be a good investment. Provided you've got the capital to tie up they often maintain their value remarkably well, and can sometimes even appreciate over the years. Plus, you get to drive them in the meantime. But that brings up another point."

"What's that?"

"Sam loves his cars. Money has intrinsic value, but unless it enhances your life, it isn't worth much. There are different kinds of equity a person can have. There's financial equity in things like a home, real estate or investments, and personal equity in things like career, health and family. The trick is to keep a balance. If you can convert your money into something that has value to you, like Sam's cars have for him, it's not necessarily a bad thing. In fact, if you can afford to do so, I'd say, go for it. You only live once, and you don't want to be the richest man in the graveyard."

"That makes sense. I've never heard it put that way before."

"Death and taxes are the only two things anyone can count on. Once you have a sound financial plan in place, invest in yourself, and lead the best, most interesting life you can."

"That's good advice, thank you."

"Anytime," Phil said, standing. "Come to see me in early December when you've got a better idea what your situation is and still have time for year-end planning, if needed. I'll do your tax return for you, and set up a quarterly payment schedule for next year so you get off to a good start with the IRS. We can talk about some investment strategies then also, if you'd like. In the meantime, enjoy yourself—you don't get these days back."

"So you don't think I'd be crazy to buy a Ferrari?"

Phil smiled. "Not if it's what you want to do."

CHAPTER 58

It was raining hard when Arnie picked Stef up at the Nashville airport the following week.

"How have things been with Randy?" he asked as they drove back to his apartment.

"The shows have been great, though he's still the same horn dog he's always been."

"Still barking up your tree?"

"He tries," she said, laughing. "If he starts pawing and snorting too badly, I wave a make-up girl in front of him and he usually takes the bait."

Arnie was quiet for several moments. "I noticed something different when you kissed me tonight," he said.

"I told you, there's nothing between Randy and me," Stef said, squeezing his knee.

"No nicotine martini."

"I've quit, this time for good."

"I'm glad. I want to keep you around for a while."

"It's where I plan to be."

They arrived at Arnie's apartment and fell into each other's arms on the bed. Arnie slipped off her slacks and slowly kissed from her toes up to the moist lace triangle of her underwear. He reached in the drawer of his nightstand for a condom and she helped him roll it on.

"We won't be needing these after another few weeks," she whispered, slipping off her panties. "I've started taking the pill."

Arnie rolled on his back and she lowered herself onto him. He caressed her breasts as she moaned and rose up and down. Several times he had to grasp her shoulders and still her to keep from climaxing.

"I want you to get off," she finally said moving her hips seductively.

Arnie arched his torso upward, raising her high off the bed with deep, rhythmic thrusts.

"Did that feel good?" she asked as they lay together panting afterward.

"Wonderful. But I want it to be good for you, too."

"Don't worry, it'll come."

"So to speak."

Stef laughed, and they were soon asleep in each other's arms.

* * *

Arnie dropped her off at Sam's office after breakfast the next morning, then worked on his songs for a few hours before heading downtown to the CMA Music Festival. The Nashville Convention Center was bustling like a Wal-Mart after-Christmas sale with long lines of fans jostling for autographs and photo opportunities with their favorite stars.

Stef's performance wasn't scheduled until that evening, so he decided to catch the afternoon show at Riverfront Park. The spacious outdoor venue featured ascending tiers of grassy seating areas facing a stage at the edge of the Cumberland River, and was packed with thousands of fans with lawn chairs and blankets. Each of the artists scheduled performed an abbreviated set of twenty to thirty minutes, and as Starr had predicted, it was a great opportunity to sample the music of many top acts in a short period of time.

When the show was over, he spent several hours wandering in and out of some of the lower Broadway honkytonks. People lined the sidewalks ten deep outside the more popular clubs, and several times Arnie had to step out into the street to make his way around the throngs of enthusiastic fans. A number of the club performers at the venues he managed to squeeze into sounded as good as the ones he'd heard on stage earlier in the day, and he wondered if any of them would be part of the Festival's official lineup next June. Anything was possible, he reminded himself. After all, he had a hit song on the charts after being in Nashville less than a year.

He arrived at LP Field just before Stef was scheduled to begin. By the time he'd worked his way through the crowd to the backstage area, Buzz Corbin was stepping to the microphone.

"Ladies and gentlemen," Buzz began, "I want to open the show this evening with an important announcement. Six months ago, I signed tonight's first performer to our label. I've been in this business for many years, more than I'd like to admit, and something told me this artist was a unique talent. Tonight I've been proven right." Buzz raised his cell phone. "A few minutes ago, I got a call from *Billboard* magazine saying that her first single, 'Last Night Made My Day,' will be number nine with a bullet on their national chart next week. Please join me in congratulating a very special singer on the first, of what I'm sure will be many, top ten hits. Ladies and gentlemen—Stefany Simmons!"

There was a swell of applause from the audience as Stef ran to the microphone and hugged Buzz briefly, then launched into her first song. The crowd loved her. She finished her short set with "Last Night Made My Day," and the audience broke into whistles and cheers at the first few lines, then rewarded her with a standing ovation when the last notes of the song faded out into the warm June air.

Arnie was waiting for her when she came backstage. "You were awesome. Congratulations on your top ten single!"

"Congratulations on your top ten *song*!"

They found a spot behind a large speaker cabinet where they had a good sideways view of the stage and enjoyed the remainder of the performers, then strolled hand in hand through the backstage area. She stopped occasionally to pose for snapshots and sign autographs, though most of the people were industry insiders and were too cool to ask. Arnie spotted Buzz chatting with Sam, who was standing with Sarah and June from the Hellcats.

"We're getting ready to cruise up the Cumberland on the General Jackson," Sam announced. "I hope you're coming."

"Sounds like a blast," Stef said. "I've never been on a riverboat."

Buzz turned to Stef and took both her hands in his. "Darling, you were marvelous."

"Thank you, Buzz. I'm so grateful for all the work you've done. I can't believe my single's in the top ten—I'm so excited."

"We're hoping it goes all the way. The fact that you've been touring so hard has been a great asset. An artist like you is a record company's dream."

Arnie tried to keep a straight face. Buzz sounded as if he meant every word that he said. Maybe he did. A few months ago, the executive might have been happy to see Stef's makeup compact packed with anthrax—or ground pepper, at least. But now that everyone was making money, love filled the air.

They followed the group outside to a line of limos parked by the performers exit and were directed by Buzz into an enormous white stretch Hummer. The vehicle inched through the mob of fans outside LP Field, then crossed the Cumberland, where half a dozen gleaming Ferraris were lined up in a roped off reserved parking area near the walkway to the General Jackson. The vessel was an imposing sight: four stories tall and almost as long as a football field. Arnie heard a yell from the second deck and saw Vinnie wave from the railing with Robert, Middy and Trayne.

Several hundred people were already onboard. When Arnie and Stef entered the main salon they were quickly surrounded by well-wishers congratulating her on her single. Bob Markum and his wife walked up and Arnie introduced them to Stef, then headed for the bar with Bob.

"We're leaving for Steamboat next week," Bob said. "Still thinking of coming?"

"Absolutely. Stef's headed back on the road and I'd love to do some fishing. What about the end of July?"

"That'd be perfect. We'll be having family in during the first few weeks of the month, so the third or fourth week would be ideal."

"This is quite a party, isn't it?" Arnie said, gesturing to the throng of jabbering guests. "I guess you're used to these events after all your years in Nashville."

"Yes, but it's not really my scene. I usually let my publisher do my politicking for me. And this crowd is a little wilder than normal."

Arnie heard a peal of laughter to his right as Vinnie and Robert approached with the Ferrari Sluts. Middy dropped an olive from her martini down the front of her dress, Trayne plucked it out with her inch-long fingernails, then popped it into her mouth as the Captain's voice announced over the loudspeakers that they were getting underway.

"Let's take a look outside," Bob suggested.

Arnie followed him up a flight of stairs and emerged onto a second story walkway. They passed by Buford and Lars, who looked as if they were involved in a serious discussion along the railing, and continued on to the front deck. The vessel shuddered as its massive paddle wheel dug into the Cumberland's swirling current, and soon was making headway upstream.

"Nashville's changed a lot since I moved here," Bob said, gesturing to the skyline behind them. "Some of these skyscrapers hadn't even been built then."

"It really looks like the Bat Building from here, doesn't it?" Arnie asked, pointing to the twin spires of the towering AT&T Office Building.

"Sure does."

Arnie heard a shout from the rear, followed by a splash and a woman's scream as someone yelled, "Man overboard!" He spun to see a security guard wrestling Lars to the deck of the narrow walkway behind them. He looked over the railing and in the faint light from downtown could dimly see Buford's head bobbing in the dark water beside the boat.

The swift current and forward momentum of the General Jackson propelled Buford astern and he flailed his arms, attempting to swim away from the hull to avoid the turbulence of the churning paddle wheel bearing toward him. He wasn't able to make much headway, and Arnie lost sight of him as he was sucked into the swirling vortex of foam that preceded boat's wake.

A horn sounded as passengers tossed life preservers over the railing, and the deck shook as the riverboat's engines slowed to a point where it was held stationary against the current. The vessel was obviously too massive for the captain to turn around and attempt a rescue.

"I hope he can swim," Bob said.

"It looked like he was doing okay," Arnie replied. "If he got past the paddle wheel, he might make it."

"It's only June; the water's still cold."

Several small pleasure craft were on the river and a crewmember on the upper deck alerted them with a bullhorn. A few minutes later, a cheer went up from the crowd gathered at the General Jackson's stern and Robert came running up.

"They got Buford. He's okay."

"What happened?" Arnie asked. "How did he fall overboard?"

"He didn't fall. He and Lars were having an argument—I think it had something to do with Lars' wife. Lars knocked the hell out of him and he went over the rail."

"Thank God he didn't drown," Bob said.

"No kidding. Lars may not be so lucky."

By now the General Jackson had returned to the dock, and they spotted Lars, now handcuffed, being led down the walkway by two black-clad security personnel towards a swarm of waiting Metro policemen and policewomen.

"There's probably a song in this somewhere, but I'll be damned if I know what it is," Arnie said, shaking his head. "I think I'll head back downstairs and look for Stef."

He found her in the main salon. The riverboat was underway again, and the inebriated crowd was gyrating to a blues band. Stef was standing with Sam and Buzz, and as before, they were surrounded by a clutch of people offering congratulations and seeking favor. He elbowed his way to her side and she turned to him.

"I wish we could get out of here," she whispered into his ear.

"Considering we're on a boat, that might be tricky," he whispered back. "Although Buford managed to do it."

She laughed. "I heard he'll make it."

"I think so."

"Let's find someplace where we can be alone for a little bit."

They excused themselves from the group, then headed for a stairwell leading to the upper decks.

"Let's see what's down the hallway," Stef said when they reached the third floor. "We might find somewhere . . . private."

On his right was an unmarked door that looked like a closet. He tried the handle, but it was locked. A few feet away he spotted another door. He turned the handle, and as it swung open they were greeted by loud giggles. Inside, leaning against a pile of life preservers, was Trayne with her blouse open and Middy kissing her breasts.

"I see you had the same idea," Trayne said, smiling.

"I guess we'll try to find another closet," Arnie replied, laughing.

"Or you could stay and join us," Middy said, licking her companion's fingers lasciviously.

"We'll find another spot," Stef said, yanking Arnie into the hallway and shutting the door firmly.

They continued to a deserted landing near the rear of the boat. Arnie took her in his arms and Stef tilted her head back to kiss him. "Congratulations again on your record," he said.

"And your song." She ran her fingers through his hair. "You know, I'm so glad I met you before all this happened. When I'm on the road I think of us and it helps keep me sane. You're my anchor. Everything is so crazy now—I can't believe the way all these people are kissing my butt."

"That's my job!"

"Silly! I'm trying to be serious. Everyone I meet wants something from me. I've been coming to Nashville for years, and before I got a record deal most people wouldn't give me the time of day."

"Still, I noticed that you're being nice to everybody—that's good. I once heard there were two important rules in show business."

"Really, what are they?"

"The first is that if someone ever treats you badly, don't ever let on that you remember."

"What's the second?"

"Don't ever forget!"

The General Jackson had been underway for an hour and had reached the Opryland Hotel. They felt a shift in the boat's motion as it began to turn sideways. Then the captain reversed the paddle wheel's direction, and the heavy prow was slowly swept around by the current until the vessel was pointed downstream. The captain again reversed the paddle wheel, completing the impressive maneuver, and before long the lights of downtown were once again glowing ahead.

When they neared the dock, Arnie and Stef wandered back to the main salon, where they found Sam still talking with Buzz.

"Buzz is thinking about buying a Ferrari," Sam said.

"It looks like the company's going to have quite a profitable year," Buzz responded. "Especially with Stef's and Randy's albums coming out in the next few months. Sam thinks he can get me a spot on Ferrari of Atlanta's waiting list for a new 458 Italia so I can take delivery this fall."

"Yeah," Sam said, "a friend of mine from Austin put a deposit on one last year. But his air charter business went under and he's short on cash. I think you might be able to buy his spot on the list for ten or fifteen grand."

"I'm grateful for your help," Buzz said.

"Arnie's thinking of getting a Ferrari, too."

"The way things are going, you might be able to afford two or three," Buzz said.

"I'll keep my fingers crossed, but I think I'll wait till I see the checks."

"And cash them!" Sam chortled. "Arnie's a pretty sharp guy."

Soon the General Jackson was safely tied to the pier, and Arnie and Stef accepted Buzz's offer for limo a ride to the parking lot where he'd left his Miata.

"We're going to grab a drink somewhere, feel like joining us?" Sam said when they were underway. He was seated with Sarah across from Vinnie, Buzz and the giggling Ferrari Sluts. As he spoke, Sarah snuggled closer to him, and slid her hand under his unbuttoned shirt.

"It's almost one-thirty and I'm so tired," Stef said. "Plus, I've got an early flight to Omaha tomorrow. Otherwise we'd love to."

Arnie caught winks from Trayne and Middy as he and Stef bid the group goodnight. Stef laid her head on his shoulder on the drive and they fell asleep soon after they arrived at Arnie's apartment.

The next morning Arnie woke to the sound of "Last Night Made My Day" playing on one of the record company travel alarms, and the delicious sensation of Stef taking him in her mouth. He reached to pull her up to kiss him, but she pushed his hand away.

"Remember the *Girls Rule Book*?" she asked as they were lying together afterward.

"Don't send your cowboy off with a loaded gun?"

"Actually, it was don't leave your man with one."

"I think cowboy sounds better.

"Have I inspired another song?"

"Yep."

Stef giggled and kissed him.

"I saw the looks Trayne and Middy were flashing at you and I wanted to give you something to remember me by while I'm gone."

"I think you can count on that."

"Good," Stef said, getting up from the bed and pulling the covers over him. "Why don't you enjoy a few more hours of sleep. I'll catch a cab to the airport."

"Call me tonight?"

"I promise."

CHAPTER 59

"Last Night Made My Day" continued up the national charts the following week, rising to number seven. Encouraged by the single's progress, and by the fact that Sam had doubled his draw, Arnie decided to upgrade his recording equipment. He visited several music stores and settled on a laptop computer pre-loaded with a multi-track recording program that offered many more capabilities than his current four-track recorder. He also purchased a portable electronic keyboard that included a number of pre-programmed musical grooves and drum patterns that he hoped would help inspire fresh melodic ideas.

The weather continued to grow warmer, with most days in the nineties, and he spent his time sequestered in his apartment, working on songs and learning to use his new equipment. He buried himself in the instruction manuals and soon was able to operate both pieces of gear, though he suspected he would never utilize all their capabilities. In the meantime, he was thrilled that the software-based recorder's additional tracks enabled him to create more elaborate pre-production demos.

Stef called often. She was performing almost every night, either in concert with Randy or alone at club gigs when Randy took breaks from his tour. When she mentioned she had a couple of days off between shows in Kentucky, Arnie jumped at the chance to meet her in Louisville.

He had an appointment to play a new batch of tunes for Sam a few days before their rendezvous and was confident in both his songs and his arrangements. Sam's reaction was also positive.

"These are quite good," Sam said after listening all the way through each song and making occasional comments and suggestions. "Let's book another demo session in August or September. We'll pick the best five songs that you've got at the time. I particularly like 'Only When I Dance with You.' It'll be a good pitch for Stef's next album. And 'Lovers Leap' is fantastic."

"Thanks. By the way, do you have the new chart number for 'Last Night Made My Day?'"

"Yes, I just got it. We go to number six. It's moved up relative to the other songs in the top ten, but there was a slight decrease in its total number of airplays compared to the previous week, so it lost its bullet and may have peaked. The stations that have been on it since the beginning are starting to move other songs into their playlists. It's a natural process. Some of them have been playing the record for over four months."

"Have you told Stef all this?"

"Not yet—we won't know anything for sure until next week. On a good note, for you at least, the money will still be quite substantial, even if it doesn't go higher. If you'd like, I could help arrange for a loan against your royalties to buy that Ferrari you're thinking about."

Arnie laughed. "I may wait a few months for that."

"You deserve every penny you're going to make. Don't forget to enjoy it."

"I'm headed to Louisville to see Stef. We're hoping to spend few days unwinding."

"Don't mention anything about the single peaking; it's probably best if she hears that from me or Buzz," he said with a thin smile. "Just in case she gets the urge to shoot the messenger."

"I'm sure she'll be happy it's done as well as it has."

"Whatever happens, we've had tremendous success. Buzz is confident that Stef can be a big moneymaker for the label. Her album will be released August 1st, and he's talking about releasing another single soon, right after this one peaks. "Safe Against the World" will probably be a single, too. In fact, it may come out later this summer to precede Randy's new album. As I told you a few weeks ago, you're in a position to become quite a wealthy young man."

"Thank you again for everything you've done."

"I'm glad to be part of your success, but don't forget that your songs are a part of mine, too. Keep up the good work. And have a great weekend with Stef."

CHAPTER 60

Arnie whistled softly when he stepped inside the Brown Hotel in Louisville. Another of Starr's recommendations, it was even nicer than the Arlington in Hot Springs, with a graceful brick-and-stone exterior and stunning antique-filled lobby. He strolled across the polished marble floor to the reception desk and paused to admire the molded plaster walls and chandeliers hanging from the coffered ceiling. Starr certainly knew how to pick a love nest.

After being informed by the desk clerk that Stef had already checked in, he took the elevator upstairs. She greeted him at the door to their room with a crushing hug. "I've missed you so much! It feels like forever since I've seen you."

"Three weeks is a long time."

She pulled him to the bed and they tore at each other's clothes. When they were naked, she bit Arnie's chest hard, almost drawing blood, and he entered her quickly. She dug her nails into his back until he grabbed her wrists and pinned them to the sheets over her head. Then, he pounded into her with all his strength until he came. Afterward, she clutched him and panted as their heartbeats slowed to normal.

"I liked that," she finally said. "You holding me and fucking me hard."

"Me, too."

"I like being out of control with you—you taking me like that."

"I think I'm sort of out of control whenever I'm with you. My feelings are at least."

"I feel the same way. God I've missed you." She sighed and snuggled closer. "This is the first day I've had off in so long, I just want to lay here in your arms until morning."

"What about food?"

"We might take a short break for that."

They rested for a while, then made love again, this time slowly, until it was well past dark. Afterward, they showered together and took the elevator downstairs to the hotel's mahogany paneled restaurant for dinner.

"How have your shows been going?" Arnie asked over coffee.

"Great. Everybody says 'Last Night Made My Day' will be number one in the next few weeks and I can't wait. I'm already planning my number one party."

"Whatever happens, you've got a lot to be excited about."

"What do you mean . . . whatever happens?" Stef asked, arching an eyebrow.

"I mean that having your first single just get into the top ten is a tremendous accomplishment."

"It's going to number one."

"I'm sure it will," Arnie said quickly. "Right now I'm just glad we've got a couple of days together. I called Churchill Downs yesterday and found out it's the last weekend of the spring meet. They've got races tomorrow afternoon, live ones with real horses. Would you like to go?"

"Sure, as long as we get to bed early tomorrow night. Randy and I have a TV taping before our show in Cincinnati and then we're working nonstop for the next three weeks. Thank goodness I'm off for ten days after that."

"You're off for ten days? When?"

"The last few days of July and first week of August."

A light bulb went on in Arnie's head. "I'm driving to Colorado in a couple of weeks to visit Bob Markum and his family. Maybe you could meet me there at the end of the month. We could rent a car and drive to Montana or something. Would you enjoy that?"

Stef's eyes sparkled. "What a fantastic idea! I could fly to Denver and you could pick me up and we could see the Rocky Mountains, find some cute romantic lodges to stay in—see how many states we could make love in in a week. It'd be an adventure."

"Let's do it!"

The next morning they explored Louisville for a few hours, then spent the afternoon at Churchill Downs. They sipped Mint Juleps in the historic twin-towered clubhouse and between races sauntered hand in hand to the paddock to watch the horses being readied under the watchful eyes of the jockeys and trainers. Arnie remembered hearing it said once that there were no ugly racehorses and he had to agree—though they found the flamboyantly dressed owners and their entourages as fun to observe as the graceful mounts. When the last race was over, he and Stef tallied their bets and found they'd broken even for the afternoon. Calling the day a success, they headed back to the Brown and turned in early.

In the morning, they enjoyed a hurried breakfast together in the hotel restaurant. Afterward, Arnie walked Stef to her rental car. "So I'll see you in Colorado?" he asked as he kissed her.

"Before that," Stef said. "You know you'll have to fly back for our number one party."

"I wouldn't miss it for the world."

CHAPTER 61

Nashville was hit by a heat wave the following week, with the temperature hovering close to one hundred degrees each day. In anticipation of his trip to visit the Markums, Arnie purchased a fishing vest and waders at Friedman's Army Navy Store on Hillsboro Road, and drove to Centennial Park in the early mornings to practice casting. He was disappointed when his song held its position without rising the following week, but still hopeful that it might continue upward—in spite of the fact that it had been jumped by two other songs.

A few days before he was scheduled to leave for Colorado, Sam called. "Starr said you're headed to Steamboat Springs this weekend and I wanted to catch you before you left town."

"I appreciate you checking in. Any word on Stef's single?"

"That's the reason I called. I spoke to Buzz, and he said it's dropping to eleven."

"Oh . . . well," Arnie said.

"Don't worry. It spent a month in the top ten and you'll have a lot more chances for a number one record. The new songs you've been turning in are really strong."

"Thanks."

"Have a great time out west, and tell Bob hello for me."

Arnie thought he had been prepared for "Last Night Made My Day" not to reach number one, but was surprised by how let down he felt now that it had started falling. He dragged through the rest of the day, knowing he should be happy with his success, but unable to shake the dark cloud hanging over him. Late that afternoon, he bought a twelve-pack of Budweiser and was drinking beer dejectedly in front of the TV in his living room when Stef called. His disappointment paled in comparison to hers.

"I can't fucking believe it," she said.

"Yeah, but at least it went top ten."

"That's bullshit. It could have gone to number one if Buzz wasn't so cheap."

"What do you mean?" Arnie asked, hazy from the beers.

"Buzz could have hired some independent promoters. I'm sure he would have if it was a song he published.'"

"He did."

"Publish it?"

"No, he hired some indies. Nanci Morales told me he hired several, a few months ago."

"Why are you taking his side?" she barked.

"I'm not taking his side," he said loudly. "I'm just as disappointed as you."

"You've got two songs on Randy's album and he never would have recorded either one of them if it hadn't been for me. You'll make a shit-load of money no matter what happens and I'll still be slaving away on the road."

"What could I do, write you a better song?" Arnie said, surprised to find himself losing his temper.

"Maybe it would have helped!"

"What?"

"Maybe a better song would have helped. I'm the one who's been on the road for the last four months. People played the record because I got in their face and made them listen to it. It could have been any song, but maybe a better one might have helped."

"Then why don't you call your Daddy and have him buy every radio station in America—like he bought Buzz's building," Arnie yelled. "Then he could force them all to play your next single twenty-four hours a day."

The line went dead. Arnie got another beer from the refrigerator and sucked it down, then drank another and went to bed. In spite of the beers, he had trouble sleeping, but was too angry to call Stef back.

He went through the next two days without speaking to her. Bubba drove him downtown Sunday to pick up a rental car for his trip and Arnie told his friend about their fight.

"She went frigging volcanic on me. Told me I should have written her a better song. Then I totally lost it. I feel horrible about what happened, but. . ."

"Don't beat yourself up man." Bubba said. "It's not your fault."

"You're right. But shit, she can go from zero to crazy in two seconds flat. I've never seen anything like it."

"Good song title, 'Zero to Crazy!' But seriously, that's why I never date chick singers. They require more maintenance than an Alfa Romeo."

Arnie laughed in spite of himself.

"Their career is always number one. They'll sacrifice anything for it: friends, relationships, even their own health. That's what makes a star a star. They need to believe in themselves to an unreasonable degree to survive in such a tough business."

"She can be a dream come true sometimes—an angel I never imagined could exist. Then something sets her off, and she morphs into this total psycho stranger. I'd almost forgotten how bad it can be. It's as if a switch gets flipped and she—"

"She's a beautiful girl, and she's probably been spoiled rotten her whole life. And you know what they say about beautiful women: no matter how pretty she is, there's some guy somewhere who's sick of her shit."

"In this case, maybe it's me."

Bubba laughed. "Maybe she'll settle down when her career stabilizes and things will work out for you guys—if you can handle the crap in the meantime. Don't let her get you down. You've had a big hit, and that doesn't happen every day. Enjoy it."

Arnie thanked Bubba for his advice, drove the rental back to his apartment, then packed for his trip. He woke early the next morning and headed west, glad for a break from both Stef and the music business.

CHAPTER 62

Arnie made it as far as Oklahoma City the first day of his trip. That night, he was roused from sleep at three AM by a deafening thunderstorm that rattled his motel's windows and flooded his room with bright flashes of lightning. He sat up in bed, transported back to the shooting and firebombing in Greenwich Village the year before. The building shook with crashing peals of thunder for several minutes, then the noise faded as the storm moved off. Wondering if it was an omen, he made his way down to the structure's first floor and logged on to the email account Agent Baskins had given him on the motel's lobby computer. There was no warning of any kind, but he couldn't shake the terror he felt when he was awakened. He chastised himself for being irrational as he returned to his room, all the while envisioning one of the doors lining the dim, florescent-lit hallway flying open to reveal a pistol-wielding thug with a $50K paycheck on his mind.

Knowing that sleep was out of the question, he packed his bag and hit the Interstate, driving in a funk across the sweltering, sun parched plains of northern Oklahoma and Kansas until he reached Colorado. As he ascended into the foothills of the Rocky Mountains west of Denver, the temperature fell into the sixties and his spirits began to lift; the stark grandeur of the pine dotted terrain made it impossible to concentrate on anything else. Following Bob's directions, he arrived at the Markum's stucco and tile condo at the base of the ski mountain, where he found a note saying that the family was downtown at the Friday night rodeo.

Arnie followed signs to the rodeo grounds and parked his car, then threaded his way through the crowd toward the grandstand. After almost a year in Nashville, it was refreshing to see people in cowboy hats and western boots who weren't wannabe country singers. A barrel race was in progress and he paused along the arena railing to watch the quarter horses thunder by, kicking up clumps of earth as their skilled riders guided them through the turns. When the race was over, he spotted Bob and Sally in the grandstand and made his way up to their seats.

"How was your drive?" Bob asked, standing to shake hands.

"Fine," Arnie answered. "Your directions were perfect."

"I see you brought a jacket," Sally said, flashing a pretty smile. "The weather's my favorite thing about Colorado. The kids start school in a few weeks, so it'll be back to the sauna soon."

"Have you been practicing your casting?" Bob asked.

"Yes. I can't wait to see the river."

"We'll be on the water first thing in the morning with my buddy Al. You'll get a kick out of him—he used to be a fishing guide."

"Sounds great."

The Markum's children, Nathan and Angie, scrambled to their seats in time to watch the bull ride, the evening's final event. When it was over, Arnie followed the family back to their condo, where they chatted and watched TV until Bob announced it was time to hit the sack. Arnie cracked open his bedroom window to let in the breeze, then slipped under the bed's down comforter. He tried to prolong the delicious feeling of falling asleep in the cool mountain air as long as possible.

The next thing he knew, a soft knock on the door woke him. He pulled on his jeans and boots, then brushed his teeth and retrieved his fly rod, fishing vest and waders from the trunk of his rental car and tossed them into the back of Bob's Jeep Wrangler. Soon they were careening down the curvy road that wrapped around the base of the ski mountain. They found Al waiting in the parking lot of his condo. He was about Bob's age, powerfully built, with a broad face and muscular forearms.

"Have you been out to Bob's property yet?" Al asked as they pulled onto the highway and headed north.

"Not yet," Arnie answered. "I'm looking forward to it."

"It's a little piece of heaven."

About five miles northwest of town, Bob turned left onto a narrow gravel road leading into a wide green meadow. He crossed over a railroad track, then steered the jeep onto a faint trail leading through the tall grass toward a teepee at the base of a steep bluff several hundred yards away. When they got closer, Arnie caught his first glimpse of the Yampa River, which lay at the base of the one hundred foot tall bluff. The section of water in front of him was seventy to eighty feet wide, mostly slow moving, and shallow, except for several dark green pools. The rest of the river varied in texture from twisting gravel-bottomed riffles upstream to his left, to gentle rapids tumbling through large black boulders that choked the channel a quarter mile downstream.

"Look!" Al whispered suddenly, pointing to his right.

Arnie turned and caught a glimpse of a cow elk and calf standing at the water's edge several hundred yards away. A smoky patch of early morning fog drifted across the river, momentarily obscuring their view. When it lifted, the elk had vanished.

"Wow," Arnie exclaimed, "Do you own all of this property, Bob?"

"Only forty acres—from the highway behind us up to the top of the bluff across the river. It's one of eight adjoining tracts here in the valley and the deed includes exclusive fishing rights."

"It's like a private club," Al interjected. "Property owners and their guests are the only people allowed to fish here, and even guests must be accompanied by one of the eight landowners or their immediate families."

"Couldn't someone wade in or use a canoe to get access?" Arnie asked.

"Colorado law's funny that way," Bob said. "In most states you only own up to the high water line, but in Colorado the property owner owns the land under the river, and the river's surface, too."

"Everything but the water itself," Al added.

"Technically, someone could scuba dive down and fish," Bob said with a laugh, "or maybe take a submarine. But they'd have a hard time making it through the rapids!"

Bob retrieved his rod and waders from a pop-up camper parked by the teepee, and Al made some suggestions about which flies they should try first. Then they split up and waded into the water, taking positions about a hundred yards apart. Arnie was glad he'd had a chance to practice his casting and was able to get his fly out a good twenty feet or so ahead of him on his first attempt. Still, he felt awkward compared to Bob and Al, whose effortless motions sent long graceful loops of line snaking over the river's misty surface to rising trout dimpling the water. After an hour, Bob and Al had hooked and released several fish and Arnie was still waiting for his first strike. It was such a pretty morning that he didn't mind. He let his thoughts wander, hypnotized by the river's magic, until he was brought back to reality by a shout from behind him.

"Watch your line!"

It was Al.

"You just had a strike and didn't even notice it."

"I did?"

"He took it right below the surface." Al waded into the water behind Arnie. "Even if you saw the fish hit the fly, you wouldn't have been able to set the hook because your line was too slack. Let me show you."

Al gripped Arnie's right wrist and raised it up and down three times with a fraction of the motion Arnie had been using, then extended the rod forward. The line shot in a slowly-opening loop that landed gently on the river's surface half again as far out as Arnie had been casting. "That's where you want your fly to be, right at the seam where two currents meet— that's where the fish will be holding."

Arnie tried to absorb the barrage of advice and he cast again. By some miracle he dropped the fly right where Bob had pointed and it danced through the foam where the river's main current met an eddy caused by a partially submerged boulder. As it swept past the glistening black rock, it vanished in a small splash and Arnie instinctively reared back. The line wasn't as taught as he would have liked, but he raised his arms as the tugging weight confirmed his first catch.

The leader zipped through the water as the fish headed upriver. When the trout jumped, it was a nice rainbow, well over a foot long, and Arnie bided his time, letting it make several more runs before easing it close to the bank to be netted by Al. Bob appeared on the gravel bank behind them and pulled a camera from his fishing vest to snap a photo.

"See what happens," Al said as he unhooked the fish and held it in the current to get its strength back. "I teach the new guy to fish and he catches the biggest one of the morning." Al released the sleek trout and it swam slowly for a few feet, then flicked its powerful tail and flashed off over the mossy bottom toward deeper water.

They fished for several more hours, and Arnie hooked and released two more trout. They weren't as big as the first, but he felt like he was beginning to get a handle on the basics of fly fishing.

"Has Arnie seen the 'James Brown Soul Center of the Universe Bridge' yet?" Al asked on the ride back to town.

"I don't think so," Bob answered. "He just got here last night."

Bob turned off the main highway not far from downtown and pulled to a stop at the edge of an unspectacular two lane concrete bridge spanning the river.

"It doesn't look all that special," Arnie said. "How did it get that name?"

"The bridge was built in the early nineties," Al replied. "The local newspaper ran a contest to name it and the winning entry was the 'James Brown Soul Center of the Universe Bridge.'"

Bob chimed in, "The city council thought the name was too outlandish and the newspaper and townspeople demanded a referendum. The people voted and the name stuck."

"What about James Brown? Did he know about it?"

"Oh yeah," Al replied. "They invited him to the dedication and he showed up, even brought two or three long-legged soul sisters with him. You should've seen him strutting around. He gave a speech and promised he'd be back every year to check on his bridge."

"Did he ever make it back?" Arnie asked.

"Hell no, but I'm sure he thought about us all the time."

Arnie laughed as Bob did a U-turn, then drove downtown where they found Sally and the children waiting with Al's wife at a cute deli restaurant on Main Street. After lunch, he and Bob strolled to the local fly shop where he picked up a pair of polarized sunglasses and several flies Al recommended. They talked with the shop's owner about fishing conditions for a while, then spent the afternoon perusing local bookstores and shops before driving back to the condo. Bob grilled chicken for supper on the outdoor deck and Sally tossed a scrumptious salad.

"Robb Lawson's having a bonfire party tomorrow night at his place," Bob said during the meal.

"That sounds great," Arnie replied. "It's quite a life out here."

"We love it," Sally answered. "It's especially good for the kids— there's so much for them to do. And it helps Bob's writing too, you know, to get away from the music business for a while."

"Do you do much writing while you're here Bob?" Arnie asked.

"I don't, but when I get back to Nashville I find the well's full again. Sometimes I really get on a roll."

"I hope the same happens for me."

After dinner, Arnie paged through some of Bob's fishing magazines, then joined him and Angie for a game of Scrabble while Sally and Nathan watched TV. He was surprised when Angie easily won the game. Although she was only eleven, her ability to improvise imaginative word combinations was amazing.

The family turned in about eleven and Arnie spent the next morning on the river again with Bob and Al. Under Al's tutelage, his casting technique and ability to present his fly in a natural fashion continued to grow, and he caught several good fish, including a stocky brown trout almost as long as his first rainbow. As his fly fishing skills improved, he found himself enjoying himself more and more, to the point where he wondered if he might be in the early stages of a new addiction.

They met Sally and the children for lunch again at noon, and that evening drove to Robb's log home in the mountains—a towering two-story A-frame chalet featuring soaring glass windows that offered a picture-postcard view of an aspen choked valley. Robb introduced Arnie to his cute wife Luanne and three small children, and Arnie noticed a photo of an airplane with Robb standing by it on the wall. He asked the guitarist if he was a pilot.

"Yep, that's my Mooney."

"Sweet," Arnie said.

"Thanks. It's only a single engine, but it can cruise at two hundred knots. I can make it to Nashville in five hours if the weather's right. During the summer my sessions slow down a little, and I try to book them in three or four day stretches so I can spend as much time as possible with my kids and my sweetie pie here."

Luanne put her arm around Robb and he kissed her forehead. More guests arrived bearing covered dishes and various musical instruments, and soon there were fifty or sixty people gathered around a roaring bonfire behind the house. At one point, while watching sparks from the fire fly into the starlit mountain sky, he found himself missing Stef. As upset as he'd been with her a few days earlier, he realized he'd give anything to have her with him tonight.

The party eventually wore down and it was after midnight when Arnie and the Markums arrived at their condo. The family slept in the next morning, but Arnie woke early and drove into town for coffee. Halfway there, he pulled over, dug his cell phone from the car's glove box and dialed Stef's number. She answered on the first ring.

"I'm so glad that you called," she gushed. "I'm so sorry about the other night."

It was nice to hear her voice. "Me, too."

"I shouldn't have said what I said."

"I owe you an apology, too. I was upset about the record myself or I wouldn't have snapped at you like I did."

"So, are you having a good visit with Bob and his family?"

"It's been wonderful."

"I didn't know how to reach you and I was wondering if you still wanted me to meet you in Denver this weekend?"

"If you'd like to . . . I was hoping you'd still want to."

"I was hoping you'd still want me to."

"I do. Remember what you said last month when we were on the General Jackson, about me being your anchor?"

"I still feel that way."

"Let's try to be that for each other. It's been good for me to get away from the music business for a few days and be around people—real people—with families and kids. If we're going to make it as a couple, we're going to have to be more important to each other than our careers."

"I'll try Arnie, I really will. But you know how important my work is to me, and yours is the same for you."

"I know, and we're bound to have ups and downs. It'll be hard enough without taking the lumps out on one another."

"You're right, and I can't wait to see you. Let's not talk about it any more right now."

"So I'll pick you up at the airport on Sunday?"

"I'll be there."

CHAPTER 63

Arnie spent the next several days fishing with Bob in the mornings and attending various activities with the Markums and their many friends in the afternoons and evenings. He felt as if he was part of a family, an experience he'd never had before. He found himself loving it, and was sorry when the week came to an end.

On Sunday, against a backdrop of brilliantly colored hot air balloons rising into the sky from the town's annual balloon festival, he reluctantly bid farewell to Bob and Sally and their children, and headed east to pick up Stef at the Denver airport. While waiting for her flight, he marveled at the unique construction of the terminal's roof, a translucent white fabric tent with multiple steep peaks. He asked a ticket agent about it, and was told that the points of the tent both symbolized the state's Rocky Mountains, and enabled snow and ice to slide down during the winter months, keeping weight off the building.

Stef's plane arrived on time and she ran to Arnie at the security gate and kissed him. After a short wait, they collected her suitcases at the baggage carousel, loaded them into his car, then headed north on I-25. Both Arnie and Stef were giddy about the prospect of a week together with nothing to do but explore wherever their whims might lead them.

Stef said she had dreamt of visiting Yellowstone National Park since she was a little girl, and Arnie was curious about Montana, so they formulated a rough plan to drive northwest to Jackson Hole, Wyoming, which was just south of Yellowstone, then explore the park for a few days before wandering further northwest into Montana's Bitterroot Mountains. By nine o'clock they'd reached Rock Springs, Wyoming, where they checked into a motel and had dinner at a nearby Mexican restaurant. Stef seemed to have gotten over her disappointment over "Last Night Made My Day," and when they made love that night it was as if their argument of a week and a half before had never happened.

They rose early the next morning and grabbed coffee and muffins in the motel lobby before hitting the road again. The terrain slowly changed from rolling prairie to gentle hills, followed by the snow-capped peaks of the Grand Teton Mountains. When they reached Jackson Hole, Arnie spotted a hotel called the Wort and pulled over to take a look. Stef loved the rustic lodge, especially the ground floor Silver Dollar Bar and Grill, which featured an antique blackjack table and a long bar with several thousand authentic silver dollars embedded in the top.

They settled into their room, then spent a delightful afternoon browsing the boutiques and galleries that lined the streets near the hotel. The town square was unique, with genuine elk antler arches adorning all four corners. Stef purchased a buckskin vest and skirt at one of the shops and loved a turquoise and silver bracelet she saw at another, but decided it was too expensive to buy. Since she was tired, she decided to take a nap and Arnie took a writing notebook downstairs, hoping to working on some lyrics. Before he began, he returned to the shop to buy the bracelet Stef had admired, eager to surprise her with it at breakfast in the morning.

That night they enjoyed a band at a local cowboy bar, then returned to the Wort where they shed their clothes and slipped under the covers of the four-posted lodge pole bed. Arnie kissed her and she pushed his head to her breasts, then lower. She sighed as his tongue explored between her legs, then moaned and clamped her thighs around his ears, grabbing his hair and keeping him there for a long time. Just when it seemed she was about to come, she pulled him up and rolled him on his back, then straddled and rode him like one of the bronco riding cowboys pictured on the hotel room's wall. When he finally felt as if she was about to have an orgasm, he let himself go.

"That was incredible!" she gasped.

"But you didn't come, did you?" Arnie asked.

"Almost . . . it felt wonderful."

"I thought you were about to, so I. . ."

"Don't worry, I will, soon. I was close!"

They lay quietly listening to the occasional car drive by the square outside until Arnie leaned over and kissed her stomach, then he moved his head lower. Stef trailed her fingers through his hair, then pulled him up and kissed him.

"I want you inside me."

"We may have to wait a little while for that."

"I don't think so," she said, running her fingernails up his inner thigh and smiling at his response.

"I'll make you a bet," she said. "I'll bet I have an orgasm by the time we get to Montana."

"Are you going to ride me all the way there?"

"How did you know?"

CHAPTER 64

Arnie and Stef slept late the next morning, then went downstairs to the hotel restaurant for breakfast. When the check arrived, Arnie handed the waiter his Visa card, then excused himself. He retrieved the turquoise bracelet from their room, and returned to the restaurant to find Stef talking animatedly on her cell phone. She snapped the phone shut as he got to the table and slammed it down, splashing coffee onto the white tablecloth.

"I can't believe it, I just can't believe it!"

"What's wrong?"

"That was Nanci Morales. My next single's going to be 'Love Drops.'"

"What?"

"Buzz waited until he knew I was out of town before making the announcement. It's going out to radio next week. He even had some company from Vancouver put together a video using footage from my live shows and it's already been sent to CMT and GAC. The son of a bitch has been planning this all along. I can't believe it, I just can't fucking believe it. I won't let him fucking do this to me!"

Arnie glanced nervously at the other restaurant patrons staring their direction. "Unfortunately, I think he can do whatever he wants," he said quietly.

Stef gave him a searing look.

"I know it's not your favorite song," Arnie continued. "It's not mine either, but people do like it at your shows. The beat always gets the crowd clapping, and they're usually singing along by the last chorus."

"I don't care. He knows I hate it and he agreed not to put it out."

"He agreed that it wouldn't be the first single, but he didn't agree not to put it out."

"Stop taking his side," she hissed.

281

"Stef!"

"All I know is that I can't let it happen. Take me to the airport; there must be one in this fucking town."

"Calm down. If 'Love Drops' is coming out next week, the machinery's already rolling and it's too late to stop it. Why don't we just relax and enjoy our trip. That's what vacations are for—to forget about business. You can deal with Buzz when you get back."

"No!"

Stef stared out the restaurant window for several seconds, then stood up as if to leave and bummed a cigarette from the waiter who had been hovering behind them. She spun around, sat back down, lit it and exhaled toward the ceiling, and Arnie watched his dream of an idyllic week together go up in smoke.

"So there's nothing I can do but let you go back to Nashville and destroy your relationship with the record company and ruin your career?"

"Think of it however you like," she said, searching unsuccessfully for an ashtray and then stubbing out her cigarette in what was left of the scrambled eggs on her plate. "It's something I've got to do."

Stef had the hotel clerk check on a flight reservation, then she and Arnie packed their bags without speaking. Arnie remembered the bracelet in his pocket and was glad he hadn't given it to her. Then he wondered if he could return it.

Stef had calmed a bit by the time they got to the airport and Arnie offered to wait with her.

"You don't have to do that, Arnie. I'll be okay. I'm no fun to be around when I get like this. I know you think I'm crazy, but I just can't let Buzz get away with what he's trying to do."

"Maybe you are crazy. But I love you, Stef, at least some of your multiple personalities. I wish, I just wish—"

"That's funny—multiple personalities," she said with a tight-lipped smile. "One of them needs to pee. Watch my things for a minute."

Stef walked to the restroom and Arnie slipped the gift-wrapped bracelet from his pocket into her leather carry-on bag. She returned in a few minutes and kissed him on the lips.

"You just go off and have some adventures and call me in a few days," she said with her arms around his neck. "I'm sorry for getting angry with you earlier. This isn't your fault. My career wouldn't be what it is if it weren't for your songs."

Arnie walked back to the car feeling numb and emotionally drained. In spite of the fact that they'd parted on good terms, the fact remained that yet another of her career obsessed mood swings had torpedoed their vacation. As he drove north, his mood darkened, and he tried to untangle his feelings.

As much as he loved Stef, at that moment he had to admit that there were times that he didn't *like* her a hell of a lot. The only problem was that he already missed her like crazy.

CHAPTER 65

Arnie spent the next few days fly fishing in some of the most spectacular wilderness on earth in Yellowstone National Park. In spite of the surroundings and relaxing atmosphere, thoughts of Stef kept throwing him emotionally off balance. Hoping to clear his mind, he decided to call her, but only got her voicemail. He left a message telling her where he was staying and headed out for a beer. When he returned to his room, he found a note on the door from the motel manager saying Stef had called back. He dialed her number.

"When are you going to start leaving your cell phone on?" she asked.

"I suppose I should. But I don't know, I sort of like not being bothered by it, you ought to know that by now. Besides, the reception sucks out here in the wilderness. How are things in Nashville—what's going on with 'Love Drops?'"

"The single's being released Monday. Buzz is in L.A. and won't return my calls. I talked to Sam and he said it's too late to do anything. I guess you were right."

"You don't seem as upset as you were."

"Well, for one thing, I'm wearing a lovely bracelet."

"So you found it . . ."

"Yes, and it made me wish I'd hadn't gone so crazy in Jackson Hole. I'm glad that you called, I thought you were going to break up with me—I probably deserve it."

"Going back was something you had to do."

"Yes, but now I wished I'd stayed and we'd finished our vacation. By the way, Sam had some good news—the label's definitely releasing 'Safe Against the World' as a single later this month. I'm hoping that 'Love Drops' dies a quick death—at least I'll have something on the radio I'm proud of."

"Be nice to Buzz when you do speak to him," Arnie suggested. "Remember the rules of show business we talked about . . ."

"When someone shits on you, don't let on that you remember—but don't ever forget?"

"That's right."

Stef laughed. "So, when will you be back?"

"Soon. I may stay in Montana another day or two, I'm not sure. I love it here, but I'm starting to miss Nashville. And I miss you, too."

"I miss you terribly. I'll be in town for a few more days, I really hope you get back in time for us to see each other." Stef paused. "I want to apologize again for what happened in Jackson Hole. I'm so sorry—I know I'm hell to be around sometimes."

"You're nice to be around sometimes—and have you around me."

"You're making me miss you more. Arnie, I really love you."

"And I love you, too."

* * *

Arnie woke early the next morning and watched the sunrise from a bench on the motel's porch. A girl wearing cutoffs and a halter top walked across the parking lot and he caught a brief glimpse of a multicolored butterfly tattoo at the base of her spine. His mind flashed back to a similar looking butterfly sewn to the jeans of the girl he'd seen on the sidewalk outside of Pizza Pete's in Manhattan a year and a half ago. If he'd followed her to wherever she was going, he reflected, he wouldn't be here today.

It occurred to him that this was one of those rare times in life when he was completely free to do whatever he wanted, unencumbered by any obligation, other than what he felt in his heart. After a last look at the morning fog rising in the valley below him, he packed his gear, checked out of the motel, and headed to Music City.

CHAPTER 66

Arnie drove east from Yellowstone Park through the Shoshone National Forest and Bighorn Mountains, and by mid-afternoon had reached Sheridan, where he stopped for lunch. At one point, while switching between radio stations, he heard the news that Randy Fawcett had suffered a minor concussion in Las Vegas due to a fall. The announcer said that he was expected to recover completely, and miss only a couple of shows. Arnie was glad to hear he was okay—the singer had recorded two of his songs, and he had a vested interest in his continued good health.

As Arnie continued across Wyoming, he was puzzled by the number of motorcycles he saw on the highway, until he heard a local DJ mention that this was "Bike Week" in Sturgis, South Dakota. Arnie checked his atlas. Sturgis was just outside of Rapid City, only a slight detour from his planned route back to Nashville. He headed that way, noting the growing number of Harleys swarming around restaurants and gas stations at the interstate exits. When he finally arrived at Sturgis, a town that, according to Rand McNally, normally had a population of about five thousand people, he was astonished by the spectacle of tens of thousands of bikes clogging the streets. He parked and walked around for an hour, enjoying the parade of leather clad riders and occasional boob flashing babes rumbling by on their V-twin mounts. Then, as the late afternoon sun was settling toward the horizon, he returned to his car and drove south through the Black Hills into Nebraska, where he spent the night.

He covered almost a thousand miles the next day, driving like a man on a mission. The closer he got to Tennessee, the more he found himself jonesing for Stef. When he finally pulled into Music City late that evening the August heat hit him like a hot barber towel slapped in his face. Still, it was good to be home.

Arnie spent the day unpacking and returning phone calls. He was looking forward to getting back in the swing of writing, and setting up appointments with Bubba, Razor and Bob Markum for the upcoming weeks. On the way to Stef's hotel that evening he felt a little nervous—it seemed as if they'd been through several wars in just the last month. Fortunately, she was in a good mood, and loved the cozy Italian restaurant in Franklin that he'd chosen.

"I want to apologize again for the way I acted in Jackson Hole," she said as they sipped wine while waiting for their salads to arrive.

"That's okay—it's in the past," he said. "I like us better like this."

"Still, I'm sorry. You've been nothing but supportive and I acted like a temperamental spoiled chick singer—which I am, I suppose."

"What should I do if it happens again?"

"Just love me through it—if you can."

"I can't help loving you, whether I want to or not." Arnie thought for a moment, then smiled and added, "In many ways you're like a Ferrari—hard to handle, but worth the ride."

They both laughed. "There you go, talking in song titles again," she said, leaning across the table to kiss him.

During dinner, Arnie recounted the details of the rest of his trip after Jackson Hole, and laughed as she shared some of her adventures on the road. Afterward, he put the Miata's top down and they held hands as he drove through the thick summer air back to Nashville. The canopy of lush green trees stretching over the road, combined with the glow from the wine at dinner, made it feel as if they were floating down a tunnel in a fairy tale.

When they arrived at the hotel, Stef walked to the bed, unzipped her dress and pulled it over her head. Arnie tugged off his shirt and jeans. Finding her aroused, he entered her and she rolled on top to straddle him. He felt as if he was going crazy as her vagina gripped the head of his penis like a clenching fist.

"I want you to come," she whispered.

"What about. . ." Arnie gasped.

"Don't worry about me."

It was already too late, Arnie drove into her and exploded. Stef rolled off while he lay panting on the bed and went into the bathroom. Several minutes later, she emerged and walked toward him, her body silhouetted by the light from the doorway. Arnie was startled; For a moment she looked like a stranger, her expression invisible in the shadows, her body a slender ghostly form bulging from left to right with the sway of her breasts. She got into bed and they lay under the covers for several minutes without speaking.

"What's wrong?" she finally said.

"You didn't want to, did you?"

"Didn't want to what?"

"Have an orgasm."

"I just wanted to make you happy. It's nice not to worry about me sometimes."

"But that's not all . . . is it?"

Stef didn't say anything for a moment. "Maybe not. I told you once before that I was afraid. I guess I still am. I've never had an orgasm with anyone. If it happens with you, I'll be tied to you—like what happens when a baby eagle bonds with the first thing it sees after it hatches. That's why they raise motherless eaglets in a special enclosure, so they don't imprint on the people who care for them."

"Well, it may be too late, I think I've already imprinted on you."

"It may be too late for me, too. I love you. Just give me time."

"Is there someone else?"

Stef sat up abruptly and spun toward him. "God, no!"

Arnie slid his hand up her backbone and caressed her shoulders, then pulled her back down to his side. "Are you sure? Sometimes I worry."

"Don't."

"Sometimes I worry about you and Randy."

"He's the last person you should worry about."

"*Is* there someone else?"

"There's no one else," she said, kissing the tip of his nose. "What happened to me when I was a child has me messed up in ways I don't even understand. I'm afraid that if I have an orgasm with you, you'll own me—my heart at least—and it's terrifying to think about us breaking up if that happened. What happened in Jackson Hole was my fault, but it scared me as much as it hurt you. When I didn't hear from you for a few days,

I was sure you'd found someone else, some waitress or other. Someone uncomplicated who would just love you."

He ran a finger down Stef's cheek.

"But she wouldn't be you," he said.

"And that's why you don't have to worry about me being with anyone else—he wouldn't be *you*."

Neither of them said anything more. Arnie pulled her close and closed his eyes, feeling her breath softly pulsing against his neck. As he drifted off to sleep, it occurred to him that her last words might make a good song title, but he decided to keep them as a sweet memory shared only between themselves.

CHAPTER 67

Arnie rose before Stef the next morning and took the elevator downstairs for coffee. He spotted Buzz Corbin sitting at a table across the hotel restaurant with a dazzling girl wearing a low-cut cocktail dress that was definitely out of place for seven a.m. His first instinct was to avoid them, but before he could slip away unnoticed, Buzz waved.

"Hi there, Arnie. This is Desiree."

"It's nice to meet you," she said, tossing back a thick mane of copper and gold ringlets.

"Arnie wrote Stefany's single, 'Last Night Made My Day.'"

"Oh, I love that song," Desiree squealed. "Would you write *me* a song like that someday?"

"I'd love to," Arnie said. Desiree was gorgeous, but something about her expression bothered him—her forehead was frozen, in spite of the smile that lit up her animated countenance. She had to be in her mid-twenties and he wondered if she was already using Botox. He also noticed that her breasts were enormously out of proportion to her tiny frame.

"There's good news about Stef's latest record," Buzz said. "It looks like 'Love Drops' is going to be *Billboard's* most added single next week. I don't have the exact number yet, but Ronnie's predicting it'll chart somewhere in the mid-thirties. And we just got the first week sales figures for her album—it debuts at nineteen with a bullet."

"Wow," Arnie replied, unable to avert his eyes from Desiree. Her décolletage offered him an astonishing view of the top of both of her breasts and the underside of one, while barely keeping the nipples hidden. It was an engineering miracle.

"Stef will be thrilled!" he said, turning to Buzz.

"I know she's not crazy about the song, but she'll get to like it a lot more if it does as well as I think it will."

"All she's concerned about now is getting back on the road and supporting it and the album any way she can. By the way, I've seen the reaction 'Love Drops' gets at her shows—people in the audience go nuts when they hear it."

"Yes, I know. And I'm excited about 'Safe Against the World.' We've got a great video planned. Also, it looks like 'Daddy'd Be Proud' will be coming out as a single in September to coincide with the release of Randy's latest album."

"You wrote all of those songs?" Desiree leaned over a little further, widening her eyes.

"Uh, yes," Arnie stammered, as she exhaled and hunched her shoulders forward slightly. One of her nipples was no longer hidden, and she knew it.

"Why don't you put a CD together of some tunes for Desiree and drop it off at my office when you get a chance? We're looking hard for material for her right now."

"I'd love to. In fact, I'll take care of it this afternoon."

Arnie headed for the elevator, trying to shake the image of Desiree's nipple from his mind. When he re-entered the room, Stef was seated in front of the dresser mirror with a towel wrapped around her, applying makeup. Desiree's memory faded as he told her about his conversation with Buzz. She was skeptical of his prediction for the success of "Love Drops," but was excited all the same. She was especially happy that her album would debut in the top twenty.

"I guess we'll just see what happens," she said as she finished her coffee.

"That's all we can do. 'Safe Against the World' will be out soon, so even if Buzz is wrong and 'Love Drops' dies, you'll have something on the charts. There's no way radio won't play a duet with you and Randy."

"You're right, and at least it's a song that I love."

"So you're leaving today?"

"Yes, but I'll be back at the end of the month for the final edit of the 'Safe Against the World' video."

"I wish we could spend more time together," he said as he stood and kissed her goodbye.

"Maybe that'll change someday."

"I'll miss you."

"I'll miss you, too."

CHAPTER 68

Arnie tried to avoid thinking about the release of "Safe Against the World" over the next two weeks, but it was difficult. The excitement of his first hit song was addictive and he couldn't wait to see what radio's response to the duet would be. The fact that "Daddy'd Be Proud" would be Randy's next single sent fire coursing through his veins, and he approached his writing with a new vigor—the prospect of having two songs in the charts simultaneously was exhilarating.

Amazingly, Buzz's prediction for "Love Drops" proved accurate. In spite of mediocre trade magazine reviews, it entered *Billboard's* country singles chart at number thirty-seven, then jumped to thirty-two the following week. No one Arnie spoke to on Music Row was crazy about the record, but radio programmers and listeners across the country evidently loved its infectious groove. Arnie recalled how hard Ronnie Dexter worked to get that kind of reaction and realized that radio's opinion was all that mattered.

He stopped by the office every few days, and one morning Starr played him the Hellcats album Sam had finally finished.

"That's really good," Arnie said. "Has Sam had any response from the labels?"

"Not from the majors, but he's still shopping it. He'll probably go with an indie if one of the big dogs doesn't bite soon. By the way, I think the song you wrote with Bubba and Razor, 'Wild Wild Feeling' is everybody's favorite."

"Thanks, I'll mention that to them."

"Speaking of co-writing, I've had a number of calls recently from other publishers wanting to hook you up with some of their writers."

"Really?"

"You're about to get hot. More and more people are going to want to write with you and you'll have to be careful—you've only got so much time and inspiration. But it's also important to capitalize on the success you're having. I've kept a list of who's gotten in touch with me, and I can set up a few appointments if you'd like. To be honest, one reason I haven't mentioned it so far is that Sam's a little nervous about losing you to another publishing company."

"What?"

"Well, your contract only has a one year option, and, as I said, you're getting hot—you'll probably be getting offers from some of the bigger companies soon, especially if you start building relationships with their writers now."

"I don't think there's any danger of me leaving here—not after what you and Sam have done for me."

Starr smiled.

The front door opened, and a tall man in his forties strode in. He was wearing a navy blue business suit and tan alligator cowboy boots.

"Arnie, do you remember Jules?" Starr asked, standing and kissing him warmly.

Jules shook Arnie's hand. "Good to see you again." Arnie remembered him—he was the investment banker who had been Starr's date at the Ferrari Club drive a year ago that had ended with Carl's accident. He recalled how much he'd enjoyed the ride Jules had given him in his Porsche.

"Jules just bought a new car," Starr said, reaching under her desk for her purse. "He's taking me to lunch to show it off."

"A Ferrari?" Arnie asked.

"No, another Porsche," Jules replied. "It's parked out back, come have a look."

The new car was stunning, a green metallic Carrera Cabriolet with a tan interior. "I remember how much I enjoyed the ride you gave me in your other Porsche, the blue one." Arnie said. "This looks almost the same, except for the color."

"This is my third. Each one's been better than the last. My lease ran out on the last one, otherwise I'd still be driving it—it only had fifty thousand miles. I know guys with well over a hundred thousand miles on their Porsches and they're still running great."

"I don't know if I've ever seen a Ferrari with more than twenty or thirty."

"To each his own," Jules said, opening the door for Starr. "Ferrari's are fantastic cars, but I'll always be a Porsche man."

"By the way, I won't be seeing you for a few days," Starr said as she slipped into the car. "Jules is taking me to Jackson Hole for a long weekend."

"Sounds like fun. You wouldn't be staying at the Wort Hotel by any chance, would you?"

"Where else?"

Arnie laughed as Starr flashed a smile. He realized with a shock that this was the first time he'd seen her with the same man twice—now a weekend in Jackson Hole, too. He wondered what the world was coming to. The Porsche's engine growled to life, and he stared after the car for a long time as it accelerated out of the parking lot and merged into the busy noontime traffic.

CHAPTER 69

Stef was more exhausted than usual when she returned to Nashville for the final edit of the "Safe Against the World" video. Arnie picked her up at the airport, and after a quiet supper they turned in early. The next morning he dropped her off at the postproduction facility where she was booked, then met Bubba at a demo session that included one of their new songs.

The tune, "Your Kind of Fire," turned out extremely well. Between observing Sam's skills as a producer and being around Bubba and Bob Markum when they'd demoed individual songs, Arnie found himself growing more and more comfortable working in the studio. After a quick sandwich with Bubba, he returned to the postproduction house to check on Stef. She jumped to her feet when he entered the edit suite.

"Arnie!" she said, throwing her arms around him. We just got a call from Ronnie Dexter. 'Safe Against the World' goes into *Billboard* at forty-eight!"

"That's great news!"

He shook hands with Nanci Morales, who was overseeing the edit, and was introduced to the video editor and to the director, a slender black woman from San Francisco about his age. The complex task was almost complete, and the editor cued his workstation at the director's instruction to play the video from the beginning on two large screens. It opened with a long shot of Stef and Randy walking hand in hand on a beach at Jekyll Island, Georgia, then alternated between contrasting scenes of them embracing on a sailboat, and footage of various tragedies. Arnie had mixed emotions. The video for his song was impressive, though a bit over the top—yet he couldn't help feeling jealous about the intimate way in which it portrayed Stef and Randy.

"This is really good," he said, turning to Nanci.

"Thanks. It's a great song and now we have a great video to go with it. I think the record's going to be a smash."

"Are you planning to do a video for 'Daddy'd Be Proud?'" Arnie asked.

Nanci hesitated. "Not at this point."

"I guess you don't do one for every single that's released?"

"We love that song, but right now we're not certain what Randy's next single will be."

Arnie was stunned. Buzz had made it sound like his song's release was a done deal. He chatted with the group for several minutes, doing his best to appear unaffected by the bad news. After making plans to meet Stef for an early supper before driving her to the airport, he headed to Sam's office to see if he might have any idea what happened with "Daddy'd Be Proud."

"Yeah, I spoke to Buzz yesterday," Sam said, waving Arnie to a chair by his desk. "It looks like it isn't coming out in September after all."

"What happened?"

"Two things. The first is that the label's decided to put off releasing any single at all on Randy until they see how the duet does. The other thing is that Buzz said the label's research has determined that "Daddy'd Be Proud" has a high burnout factor."

"Burnout?" Arnie vaguely remembered Ronnie Dexter using the term.

"Record companies test singles with sample audiences—if the test groups tire of a song in what they feel is too short a time, the company figures it won't last long enough in the charts to reach the top ten."

"I thought labels put out songs because they loved them. I mean, I've seen Randy perform "Daddy'd Be Proud" live and people go nuts."

"The business has changed a lot since I first started There's just so damn much money involved in promoting a single. It's too bad, because a lot of classic songs wouldn't have a chance now. Remember 'Rudolph The Red Nose Reindeer?' It was first released as a B-side and some DJ flipped the 45 because he loved the song and it became a hit. Nowadays a jock at a big station could lose his job for doing something like that."

"But Buzz still likes 'Daddy'd Be Proud?'"

"Yes. But he said that at this point in Randy's career, they aren't sure if they can afford to take a chance on a record that might die in the twenties. It's an unusual song, and his bosses, the bean counters in L.A., are always afraid of anything out of the ordinary. But don't worry too much. Once the album's released, your song will get a certain amount of airplay. If listeners start requesting it, they may decide to release it after all. And besides, 'Safe Against the World' is going to be a monster."

"Well, I'm glad to hear you say that. I was a little worried that it only entered the chart at forty-eight."

"It'll probably take a big jump next week. Have you seen the trades?" Sam passed the current week's *Billboard* and *Music Row* magazines across the desk to Arnie.

"Cool," Arnie said after scanning the reviews of the duet. They were stellar, with *Music Row* magazine's review even referring to his song as a "killer tune."

"Don't be concerned that it's getting off to a slow start. You make the most money with a song that takes its time going to the top—that way it spends as many weeks as possible in the chart."

"That's good to know. As long as it keeps going up."

"Right. Speaking of money," Sam said in a serious tone, "I'd like to speak to you about another matter."

"What's that?"

"Renegotiating your contract. As you know, I've got an option coming up to keep you here for another year. I plan to exercise it. If you'd be willing to extend our agreement to include two more one-year option periods, I'm prepared to offer you a substantial advance. You won't have to wait to order that Ferrari."

"What kind of advance were you thinking of?"

"You've got two songs on both Stef's and Randy's albums. Stef's CD is moving up the charts, and will probably go at least gold. Randy's album is shipping platinum next month and will probably be double platinum by Christmas. That means you'll have sales royalties totaling at least two hundred thousand dollars in the pipeline. Of course, I'll have to recoup your draw and demo costs out of that amount. But there should be enough coming in for me to give you a hundred thousand dollar advance now."

Arnie's jaw dropped.

"Think it over if you'd like," Sam continued. "It means you'll be here for three more years. Other publishers will want to talk to you soon, and their offers will be substantial, too."

"I don't have to think it over," Arnie said without hesitating. "I can't imagine writing for another company. Everything that's happened to me is because of you."

"I'm glad you see it that way," Sam said, smiling. "There's very little loyalty in this business."

"That advance is very generous."

"You've earned it. And, like I said, I don't want anyone stealing you away from me. I've had a great year and it will help my tax situation to pay you the money now, so it's a good deal for both of us. I'll have my attorney prepare an addendum to the contract; it should be ready for you to sign in a week or two, along with your check."

"Thanks, Sam."

"Thank *you* for the songs. I hope we can keep working together for a long time."

Arnie was in a daze when he walked out of Sam's office. As he passed through the reception area, he noticed Starr talking softly on the phone.

"How was Jackson Hole?" he whispered across the room.

She pointed to a sapphire pendant around her neck and smiled.

Arnie grinned back and headed home.

CHAPTER 70

Arnie told Stef about his meeting with Sam at dinner. Although he was thrilled about the hundred thousand dollar advance, he was surprised to find himself depressed that "Daddy'd Be Proud" wouldn't be Randy's next single. Stef laughed when he remarked that it made him more sympathetic to her mood swings.

"So now you know how I felt in Wyoming," she said. "But at least you have another record out that will do well."

"I'm a little worried about that, too. 'Safe Against the World' only charted at forty-eight—'Love Drops' went in in the thirties."

"Nanci said they're expecting it to make a big jump next week."

"Sam said the same thing."

"I guess we'll just have to see what happens. I know I'm doing all I can, squeezing as many dates as possible into this tour. It'll be October before I get some time off. Heaven knows I'll need the rest."

"Do you want to do something special then—maybe get away for a few days?"

"That would be fun. Maybe we could rent a cabin somewhere. The leaves will be starting to turn."

"I'll look into it. I've heard Bubba talk about a place near Dale Hollow Lake that's supposed to be nice. So where are you flying to later?"

"Blackfoot, Idaho. Randy and I are performing at the state fair tomorrow. We're supposed to be honorary judges for a livestock competition in the morning, that's why I've got to leave tonight. You're not still worried about him, are you?"

"No, not really," Arnie answered, thinking of the scenes in the video.

"Don't be," Stef said, reaching across the tablecloth to take his hand. "You know, Arnie, we've had some ups and downs—well, I guess that's putting it mildly." She laughed. "But we've always worked things out. Both of us being in the same business is hard, but it's good, too. We understand what we're each going through."

Arnie squeezed her hand as she continued. "And it's funny, when we have a fight or get angry with each other, we always become closer afterward. Like what they say happens when you exercise—muscle fibers break down when you work out, but they grow back stronger. We're the same way."

"Now there's an idea that sounds a little too complex for a song."

"You never know!"

Arnie paid the check, then leaned across the table to kiss her.

"You know, I haven't tasted a nicotine martini in a while," he said.

"And you won't."

"Good."

Arnie felt Stef's knee rub against his. "My plane doesn't leave for a couple of hours," she said with a twinkle in her eye. "Would you like to run by your apartment before you drop me off at the airport—maybe for a quick nap or something?"

"Or something would be very nice. . ."

CHAPTER 71

The month of September flew by in a blur. Sam's prediction for 'Safe Against the World' proved accurate—it jumped from forty-eight to the mid-thirties after Labor Day, then rocketed upward during the following weeks, following 'Love Drops' into the twenties, then high teens.

Under Starr's guidance, Arnie sought to capitalize on his success by expanding his co-writing relationships. The meetings went well, but when he played back the songs he'd completed with the new people, he had mixed emotions. Though they were competently written, they often struck him as being formulaic. The Nashville practice of sitting down with a complete stranger to come up with a heartfelt song remained foreign to him. He resolved to devote substantial blocks of time to writing by himself, since he still got the most satisfaction from completing songs on his own.

On the upside, he learned something new from each writer. One was a talented young artist from Oklahoma named Bobby Rutgers. Arnie met with him several times and they finished two songs that they both loved called 'Always A Woman' and 'The Girl At The End Of The Song.'

Another meeting was with a guy named Gus, and Arnie was looking forward to collaborating with him because of several big hits he'd penned. When he knocked on the door of Gus's apartment on the morning of their appointment, he had to wait several minutes for a response. Finally, the door opened and he was greeted by a tall, cadaverish-looking Texan in his late thirties. He was wearing jeans and a faded denim shirt, and when they shook hands, Arnie noticed a slight tremor in his fingers. Gus brushed a hank of graying blond hair out of his eyes and invited him to sit at his kitchen table. Arnie was surprised that there wasn't a guitar anywhere in sight.

"So what do you want to write today?' Gus drawled, lighting a cigarette.

"Oh, I don't know, I've got a few ideas," Arnie said, paging through the notebook he'd brought with him.

"I mean an up-tempo or a ballad?"

"Either one I guess," Arnie answered, raising his eyes.

"I've had most of my success with up-tempo tunes. Had two songs in the top ten during the same week the year before last, got two BMI awards that year."

Arnie was taken back that Gus was unaware of his own success. Stef's duet was currently in the top twenty, and, between that and "Safe Against the World," Arnie was sure to receive several awards of his own at next year's ceremonies. "Well . . . I guess we could write something up-tempo if you'd like. Do you have any ideas or titles?"

"Not really, I was hoping you'd have something started."

Arnie felt the enthusiasm drain out of him. He continued to page through his notebook as Gus stood and went to the refrigerator and returned with a sixteen-ounce can of Natural Light. Arnie stared at it, wishing for a cup of coffee. Gus popped the beer open and took a long swallow. He noticed Arnie eyeing the can.

"I'd offer you one, but I've only got two," Gus said apologetically.

"Maybe we could write that," Arnie said, putting down his notebook.

"Write what?"

"A song called 'I'd Offer You One, But I've Only Got Two.'"

Gus squinted at him, then raised his beer and took another swig. "That's too long to be a title."

"You know, Gus, I don't think we're going to get a song written today."

"Okay."

Arnie chuckled to himself as he drove off. What Gus had said might be able to be made into a song, but he wasn't going to waste much time working on it. He stopped by the office to see if his new contract was ready, and Starr laughed when he told her about his experience with the Texan.

"That's just the way it goes," she said. "Don't get discouraged. Songwriting's a lot like your fishing trip last July—you've got to keep throwing your line into the water if you want to hook a good one. In the meantime, enjoy the process."

"Speaking of good ones, I think I've got two super songs finished with Bobby Rutgers called 'Always A Woman' and 'The Girl At The End Of The Song.'"

"I'm anxious to hear them, love the titles. By the way, we got a hold request the other day for the new song you demoed with Bubba, 'Your Kind of Fire.'"

"Who asked to put it on hold?"

"Blue Burnside."

Arnie was familiar with the singer; he'd had a couple of singles out in the last year that had gotten some airplay. Although neither record made it into the top ten, Arnie had liked the songs. "How did he happen to hear it?"

"I dropped a copy off with his manager a couple of weeks ago. She called yesterday and said both she and Blue like it a lot. They don't want us to play it for anybody else until the label's had a chance to hear it."

"Thank you."

"If he records it, it'll be a real feather in your cap—your first outside cut."

"What do you mean?"

"In most situations, songs get recorded because the producer or artist or someone involved in the process has an interest in the writing or publishing rights—like Buzz does with 'Love Drops' or Sam does with your songs. It's not necessarily a bad thing. But in this case, Blue and his manager love the tune and think it could be a hit. Having a cut like that will help a lot when I'm pitching your songs to other acts in the future. It means you're moving into the ranks of writers who get songs recorded regardless of who publishes them."

"I hadn't thought of it that way—I've just felt lucky Sam has taken me under his wing," Arnie said, feeling an increasing admiration for Starr's business acumen. "I'm finally beginning to learn how complicated this business is. In any case, thanks again for pitching the song. I'm sure Sam's grateful, too."

"Funny you should mention that. He's talking about taking me in as a partner in the company."

"That's terrific."

"Actually, Jules suggested that I speak to him about it. I don't know if I'd have had the nerve to if he hadn't. I brought it up to Sam a few days ago and he seemed to go for the idea. He just left for a vacation at Rancho La Puerta, a health spa in Mexico, and he promised to let me know his decision when he gets back in town."

"I'll keep my fingers crossed."

"Thanks. Good luck with your demo session next week. I'm looking forward to hitting the street with your new tunes. Oh, by the way, your contract is back from Sam's lawyer." Starr withdrew a sheaf of papers from an envelope on her desk. Arnie glanced over it, then signed his new contract. Starr gave him his hundred thousand dollar royalty advance check, along with a congratulatory hug and kiss on the cheek. He thanked her and headed to the bank.

At the teller's window, he stared at the check for several long moments. Then, on a whim, he pulled out his driver's license, endorsed the check, and told the teller that he'd like to cash it. The plump girl, who was wearing an engagement ring with a barely visible diamond, noted that Sam's account was at the same bank, then cocked her head and gave Arnie a long look before calling her manager. When the manager arrived, he scrutinized Arnie's ID carefully, then spent several minutes on the telephone before directing the teller to place several dozen banded bundles of hundred dollar bills on the counter in front of Arnie.

"What are you going to do with it all this money?" the girl asked.

"Actually, I just wanted to see what a hundred thousand dollars looked like," Arnie answered, weighing the tall stacks of bills in his hands.

"Do you want a sack to put it all in?"

"Nope," he said, pushing the pile of money back toward her. "I'd like to deposit it in my checking account."

"Okay," the girl said, relieved. "But are you sure you don't want to open a money market account? You could be earning a lot of interest on this much money."

"No, thanks. I've got plans for it."

Arnie walked out of the bank with the deposit receipt in his hand, smiling at the thought of the story the cute teller would have to tell to her fiancée that evening.

CHAPTER 72

Arnie's second demo session went smoothly, thanks in part to his hours of preparation. He had specific ideas for the sound he wanted for each song and tried to emulate Sam, dealing with the players as he imagined an experienced jockey might coax a thoroughbred racehorse—presenting them with arrangement ideas, then giving them the reins when they were inspired to run on their own. When he finally finished the overdubs and completed the mixes several days later, he was exhausted, but felt it was his best work yet. Sam agreed when they met at the end of the week.

"These are fantastic," Sam declared. He looked fit and tan from his week at the spa, and was in great spirits.

"Thanks," Arnie replied. "I was a little nervous—it was my first session without your help."

"I'm really proud of you. You did a super job. In fact, I think you've come along quicker than any writer I've ever seen. We'll have lots of pitches for these songs."

"I've been working hard."

"It shows. I'd like to put 'Only When I Dance with You' on hold for Stef right now. If she and Buzz don't want it, we'll hit the streets with it next week. I'm sure you'll get a record on it with someone. I also love 'Hard to Handle, But Worth the Ride.' It's tough to find good up-tempo songs. This sounds like a smash, possibly even for Randy. 'Don't Send Your Cowboy Off With A Loaded Gun' is good as well. A little out there, but I love it."

"By the way, has the label made any decision yet on his next single?"

"Nanci and Ronnie both think that 'Safe Against the World' has the potential to be a major career record for both Randy and Stef—it's already getting airplay on some adult contemporary stations. So Buzz has decided to throw the full weight of the label's promotion and marketing departments behind it. Once it peaks, they'll decide what to put out next."

"That's good news," Arnie said.

"It's *great* news. You may have your first number one record before long."

"That's super. Stef'll be in town tonight, we're headed to Dale Hollow Lake tomorrow."

"I'm getting together with some of the Ferrari folks in the morning. If you feel like joining us before you leave for the lake, we'd love to have you."

"Sounds like fun."

"We're meeting at the Brentwood shopping center at nine for a run through Williamson County, like the one we took last year. Maybe this time we'll keep all the cars on the road!"

* * *

On his way home, Arnie stopped at a coffee shop to log into the email account given to him by the FBI. It had been a while since he had done so, and he wasn't surprised to find that there was no news. The events of a year and a half ago seemed more remote with each week that passed. In fact, he couldn't remember the last time he'd had a nightmare or flashback—or even the last time he'd bothered to carry the beeper agent Baskins had given him.

When he drove to the airport late that night to pick up Stef, he was still basking in the warm glow of Sam's compliments on his session. For once, it felt as if his life was in balance. And he was absolutely starving to see the girl he would soon hold in his arms.

CHAPTER 73

Stef was exhausted when she fell into Arnie's embrace at the airport. When they arrived at his place, they quickly crawled into bed, leaving her luggage in the trunk for their trip the next day. Tired as she was, she still reached for Arnie under the sheets and they made love quickly, then fell into a deep sleep.

When they arrived at the shopping center in Brentwood the next morning, they found almost a dozen freshly waxed Ferraris, along with several other exotic cars of various marques. The one getting the most attention was a silver 1960s vintage Aston Martin DB5—the same model made famous by Sean Connery in the James Bond movie, *Goldfinger*.

Robert walked up as they stood admiring the car. "Haven't seen you folks in a while," he said, shaking hands with Arnie and hugging Stef. "Got your new Ferrari yet Arnie?"

"No, not yet," Arnie said with a laugh, as Stef strolled off to speak to Sam. "Maybe soon."

"There's a big track event in Savannah, Georgia next month. Should be fifty or sixty Ferraris there—maybe you'll have yours by then."

"We'll see. How are things with you?"

"Okay, though I've been stressed recently by a couple of lawsuits— one in South Dakota and another Wyoming. The attorney fees are brutal."

"I hope you get things worked out soon."

"I've always come out all right in the past. Every salesman exaggerates a little—you'd think people'd get used to it. Speaking of lawsuits, did you hear about Buford?"

"What's going on with him?"

"Remember the General Jackson last June?"

"How could I forget?"

"It turns out he'd been carrying on with Lars's wife for the last year. Lars filed an alienation of affection suit against him and they both filed assault charges against each other."

"How could that be? Buford's the one who ended up in the river."

"Lars said he pushed him overboard in self defense. Claimed he had a witness. Then to top it off, his wife dumped Buford in July, right after she filed for divorce. I hear she's living with a chiropractor in Atlanta now."

"What a mess."

"I think it's all pretty much worked out. Both the assault charges got dropped after Buford's family law firm settled the alienation of affection suit. But I heard it cost him over a hundred grand by the time it was over."

"That had to have hurt," Arnie said, thinking not so much of the money, but of the mental anguish of everyone involved.

"Looks like they're both doing okay," Robert said, gesturing across the parking lot at Buford and Lars, who were laughing together and drinking beers with Carl by his new Lotus Seven, identical to the one he'd wrecked the previous year. "Buford's family is loaded. It's not the first time they've had to bail out. And Lars is a hundred grand richer, plus he unloaded his tramp wife. I don't think Buford was the first guy she messed around with."

"Oh well, I hope your own legal problems come to some resolution soon."

"Thanks."

Arnie rejoined Stef and the rest of the group, which had grown to several dozen people, including Stan and Laurie Fishman from Arkansas, who were talking to Vinnie by Stan's recently purchased 355 Spyder. Arnie noted that Ted, the handsome sixty-something attorney who was president of the local club chapter, was still keeping company with the gorgeous young redhead he'd seen him with the previous year. Starr and Jules stood off to the side, fawning over each other like junior high kids at the mall and chattering about an upcoming trip to the Bahamas. Cam was there with his wife, who Arnie noted kept a wary eye on Middy and Trayne, and Sam had his arm around the waist of a new girl—a bouncy brunette just a little older than Stef.

After socializing for a while, the drivers fired up their engines and headed west into rural Williamson County. Stef rode as a passenger in a Dodge Viper, and Arnie accepted an offer to take the wheel of a black Ferrari 360 owned by a stockbroker friend of Sam's. It was a thrilling car to drive—the power was awesome and its handling was even more precise than the 348 he'd driven in Arkansas.

As was the case the previous year, the drivers attacked the winding roads with no regard for the speed limit, and Arnie struggled to keep up, hesitant to wreck the hundred eighty-plus thousand dollar car he was driving, especially with the owner sitting next to him. He managed to keep the tail end of the pack somewhat in sight until they reached the picturesque town of Leipers Fork, where they stopped at a cafe for lunch. When they emerged from the restaurant it started to sprinkle, and the drivers with convertibles raised their tops. Stef rode back to Brentwood in a 550 Maranello coupe driven by a handsome Tennessee Titan. Arnie rode with Sam in his 430.

The pace was much slower on the way back, as the drivers proceeded with caution in what had become a downpour. Arnie wiped the inside of Sam's fogged windshield with his shirtsleeve, and again noted that the attention the Ferrari engineers focused on the superlative performance of the cars didn't always extend to peripheral equipment like windshield wipers and defrosters.

"That's a pretty girl you've got with you today," Arnie remarked as he settled back in the passenger seat.

"Yeah, I met her at the Grammy's last February. She'd been dating a movie producer in Los Angeles, but finally gave up on him leaving his wife."

"You sure know how to get the babes; she's a knockout."

"L.A.'s full of unemployed mistresses—living in their cars, some of them."

"Unemployed mistresses? Living in their cars?"

"Yeah, girls who date a guy for a while who pays for an apartment and a nice set of wheels, then gets bored and moves on. The chick's stuck with a BMW or Lexus and no way to make the rent."

Arnie shook his head and laughed. "I may have asked you this before, but do you ever miss being married and having kids?"

"I was married once, a long time ago. Haven't seen my ex-wife in years—she's probably got as many gray hairs and wrinkles by now as I do. She did give me a son, though. I'm glad for that."

"Really?" Arnie said, surprised. "I've never heard you speak of him."

"He's out in California finishing up law school at UCLA. Smart kid. Don't see him much, but he sure cashes the checks I send him. So does his mom."

"I suppose you wouldn't have any trouble getting married if you wanted to."

"Successful men always attract pretty girls, even when they've been around as many years as I have. I've been lucky that way."

"I guess it's not bad being a guy sometimes. Too bad it's not the same for women—as they get older, I mean."

"We don't make the rules, we just live by them," Sam said, laughing. "The composer Frederic Lowe, who wrote the score for *My Fair Lady*, once said that variety is the only true aphrodisiac."

They drove the rest of the way to Brentwood in silence, with Arnie continuing to wipe the windshield while pondering Sam's words. What Sam had said might be true for him, but he couldn't imagine getting tired of Stef. He wondered if he would in time. It occurred to him that his boss was one of those rare people who both knew who he was, and what he wanted from life—and was at peace with the price necessary to achieve it.

CHAPTER 74

Arnie and Stef bid farewell to the Ferrari Club when they arrived back at the shopping center, then headed for Dale Hollow Lake. They arrived at Standing Stone State Park shortly after sundown and checked into the small log cabin Arnie had reserved. The mountain air had grown chilly, so they donned sweaters and built a fire in the limestone fireplace, then slipped off their clothes and snuggled under the bedcovers until they fell asleep.

Arnie woke the next morning to feel Stef running her fingers through his chest hair, then down his stomach and beyond. She slipped a leg over his waist, then guided him inside her. He caressed her breasts with his left hand, and slid his right hand down her spine to her buttocks, massaging them and feeling her muscles clench like twin cannonballs under her taut skin. Without thinking, he slid his fingertip into the tight opening of her anus. He probed deeper and she groaned, straining rapidly up and down on his penis, then gasped and dug her fingernails into his shoulders as her body stiffened and shuddered. Slowly her spasms subsided, and Arnie rolled her over on her back and drove into her as hard as he could with his finger still inside her, grinding her lower body against his until he came, too.

"God!" she gasped, as they lay next to one another afterward.

Arnie stood and went to the bathroom. When he returned, Stef cuddled close to him and kissed his throat. "See, I told you it would happen," she said, nibbling his ear.

Arnie pulled her close and drifted off to sleep. When he woke, it was to the smell of fresh coffee. He slipped on jeans and a flannel shirt, and poured himself a cup from the aluminum percolator simmering on the cabin's stove. He found Stef on the front porch, sitting on a weathered split cedar bench. A cool breeze moaned through the pine boughs overhanging the cabin and she offered him a blueberry muffin they'd picked up at a grocery store on their way.

"The leaves here are starting to turn. It's so pretty," she said, gesturing to a hillside dotted with yellow tipped oak trees on the far side of the park's small lake.

"I know. Tuesday's the first day of October. It's hard to believe we've known each other a year."

Just then, a Golden Retriever ran up the cabin's stone walkway and scrambled onto the porch. Arnie scratched its ears and fed it a piece of muffin. A few minutes later, a towheaded girl about six or seven years old ran over from the cabin next door.

"There you are," she said, gripping a tattered bandana knotted around the dog's neck.

"Would you like a muffin?" Arnie asked her.

"No thank you," she said, staring at the muffin. The retriever was staring at it, too.

"What's your dog's name?"

"Bullet . . . my brother named him that. His name is Billy Ray, my brother's name is."

"What's your name?" Stef asked.

"Jody," the girl answered, still eyeing the muffin.

"Why don't you take a muffin home with you?" Stef said. "Then you can ask your mommy if it's all right for you to eat it."

"Okay," Jody answered, grabbing the muffin and running down the porch steps with Bullet at her heels.

"Just make sure Bullet doesn't get it first!" Stef called. The girl turned and smiled, then disappeared into the neighboring cabin.

"Do you ever think about having children?" Arnie asked Stef.

"Sometimes—maybe when things settle down with my career. I've always thought it would be nice to have two little boys, twins maybe. But that girl's awfully cute."

"Yes, she is. I guess there's plenty of time to think about it."

"I don't know. My work's important to me, like yours is to you, but it's not everything. That's what life's all about," Stef said, gesturing next door, where Jody was emerging from the cabin with a boy a few years older than her and a couple in their thirties wearing matching NASCAR jackets over camouflage overalls. The man and woman got into the cab of a battered Chevy pickup truck and the two children helped Bullet over the tailgate into the truck's bed, then climbed in after him and waved at Arnie and Stef as they drove off.

"You're right. We're both becoming pretty successful. You've had three hit singles now, counting the duet, and if things keep going the way they have been for me, I'll have enough of a nest egg to retire in a few years."

"Would you do that . . . retire?"

"No. I think I'd always keep writing songs, though I might want to try my hand at some other kind of writing sometime, maybe a screenplay or even a novel."

"My career's kept me busy for so long," Stef said. "Music's all I've thought about for the last ten years. The touring season will be slowing down for winter. It'll pick up again next spring and summer, but after that I should be established enough to take a year off from the road. Nine months at least."

Arnie reached over and held her hand. "It's something to think about, isn't it?"

"I've been thinking about it more and more."

"That's nice to hear."

"Robert mentioned that there's a Ferrari track event in Savannah, Georgia around Thanksgiving. It might be fun to drive down there with Sam and the rest of the folks—if your road schedule allows."

"Oh, that sounds lovely! I read the book *Midnight in the Garden of Good and Evil* a while back. I've wanted to visit Savannah ever since."

"Let's try to do it then."

"Maybe I'll mention it to my father—did I ever tell you he owns a Ferrari?"

"No, you're full of surprises."

"It's an older one he's had since I was a little girl. I think it might be worth a lot of money now. He stays so busy with his business that he hardly ever drives it anymore, but he might like to trailer it down for the event. He used to do things like that a lot when I was growing up. I'll bet he might even know some of the other Ferrari owners."

"You must really like me," Arnie said, smiling and turning to her. "Wanting to introduce me to your father and all."

Stef smiled a Mona Lisa smile and squeezed his hand.

* * *

Later that morning they drove from the park to Dale Hollow Lake and spent the rest of the golden day exploring and fantasizing about what it would be like to own a vacation home there someday. At sunset, they stopped for supper at a funky but charming waterfront restaurant, then returned to their cabin. They made love in the flickering firelight and Stef was even more passionate than she'd been that morning. She climaxed again, easily it seemed, then almost a second time. It was as if something inside her had snapped and opened the door to a new and wonderful world that existed just for the two of them.

CHAPTER 75

Arnie sensed a growing excitement at Sam's office during the following weeks as "Love Drops" and "Safe Against The World" entered the top ten of *Billboard's* Hot Country Singles chart. The strong performance of "Love Drops" continued to baffle almost everyone, but there were no complaints. Radio couldn't get enough of the song and it seemed sure to be at least a top five record. Even more exciting for Arnie was the fact that "Safe Against the World" was getting an increasing amount of crossover airplay, with Ronnie Dexter predicting it would soon break into the top forty of *Billboard's* Hot 100 pop chart. The prospect of the song becoming a multi-format hit was an added bonus that could potentially double his performance royalties.

In early October, the Recording Industry Association of America announced that Stef's album had been certified gold—quite an accomplishment for a new artist who's CD had been out for barely two months. On the day of its certification, Arnie sent flowers to the hotel where Stef was staying in Phoenix.

"I'm so excited," Stef said when she called late that night to thank him. "I talked to Daddy and I think he's going to be able to attend the Ferrari event in Savannah in next month. I can't wait for you to meet him."

"I'll make us a hotel reservation."

"Maybe we should get separate rooms, for Daddy's sake."

"Good idea."

"Just make sure there's a door between them, or at least that they're on the same floor. We get to see each other so seldom, I want to be sleeping in your arms."

"Ditto. So I'll be seeing you on Sunday?"

"I can't wait."

* * *

Bubba called Saturday to say that the Appalachian Hellcats were playing at Tootsies that evening and Arnie arrived to find the place so packed that he and Bubba could barely make their way upstairs. Sam had been unable to get the group a major label contract, but they'd just accepted an offer from a small, but prestigious New England company. The band had been touring for the last six weeks to promote their CD's release and the crowd of loyal Music City fans was excited to see them for their first in town appearance since August. The Hellcats didn't let them down. They sounded tighter than ever after their studio and road dates, and Arnie felt a surge of pride when they performed 'Wild Wild Feeling' to cheers and whistles from the crowd.

When the band's set was over, Arnie and Bubba congratulated Razor and the rest of the group, then threaded their way through the crowd to leave. Halfway to the front door, Arnie spotted Randy Fawcett at the bar with an entourage of several buddies and stopped to say hello. Although they'd met several times, Randy's response was the same as always.

"You're the songwriter, aren't you?" the singer slurred.

"Yep. Good to see you."

"You, too," Randy grunted, looking over Arnie's shoulder to check out a shrieking bachelorette party entering the club.

"Thanks again for recording 'Daddy'd Be Proud' and 'Safe Against the World.'"

"I could sing the phone book and it'd be a hit."

Arnie realized Randy was drunk. Still, he couldn't believe his ears. Reminding himself that the singer had recorded two of his songs, he summoned the effort to be polite. "I know Stefany's thrilled to have a top ten duet with you."

"She's a cute chick, good harmony singer," Randy said. "Nice rack too."

"What?" Arnie blurted.

"You've been dating her some, haven't you?"

"Yeah, I'll be seeing her tomorrow."

"Try sticking your finger in her ass next time you fuck her—she digs it."

Arnie didn't remember throwing the punch, but the next thing he knew, Randy was lying on the floor with blood spurting from his flattened nose and Bubba was pulling him backward by the collar toward the upstairs exit. The throng closed around them and prevented Randy's buddies from retaliating, though they seemed more concerned about Randy's wellbeing than taking on Arnie. A few minutes later, he and Bubba were safely outside. Bubba maintained a tight grip on Arnie's arm, fast walking him down the alley between Tootsies and the Ryman Auditorium while Arnie looked back over his shoulder wishing for another chance at Randy.

"What the fuck did you do that for?" Bubba gasped when they reached Fourth Avenue and slowed to catch their breath. "I mean that was Randy Fawcett. How the hell do you expect to get any more songs cut by him after that?"

Arnie nursed his right hand. His knuckles felt like they'd been run over by a pickup truck with a flat tire, but he didn't mind. "I think he's been with Stef."

"He's been with half the girls in Nashville. But I wouldn't think Stef'd have anything to do with him—she's got too much class."

"I guess that's something I'll have to take up with her."

When they reached Arnie's car, Bubba stood on the sidewalk to make sure he drove off. Arnie headed back to his apartment, stopping to buy a twelve-pack of Budweiser along the way. He dug his cell phone out of his pocket when he arrived home and found a voicemail message from Stef saying how much she was looking forward to seeing him the next day. He didn't return her call. Instead, he paced back and forth in his kitchen, drinking beer after beer and kicking himself for the fool he'd been.

CHAPTER 76

Arnie woke at noon with a brutal hangover that half a pot of coffee and four aspirins couldn't blunt. Thinking that some sugar might help, he drove to the grocery for a two-liter bottle of Coke and returned to find a message from Stef wondering why she hadn't heard back from him. She was in town at the Vanderbilt Plaza, and asked him to pick her up for dinner at seven.

At seven-fifteen Arnie knocked at the door of her room. She opened it and threw her arms around his neck as he stepped inside, but he pulled away.

"What's wrong?"

"What do you think is wrong?"

"I have no idea," she said, stiffening and taking a step backward.

"I ran into Randy Fawcett last night. Or maybe I should say my fist ran into his face." Arnie held up his still swollen hand.

"My God," Stef gasped, taking Arnie's hand in hers and examining his knuckles, two of which were split open. "I'd hate to see what his face looks like."

"I think you've seen a lot more of him than that."

"What in the world are you talking about?" she asked, looking shocked.

"You know exactly what I'm talking about."

"Arnie, there's nothing between Randy and me. I've told you that before."

"There's nothing more between us either."

Arnie spun and strode out of the room, slamming the door behind him. He took the elevator downstairs, cursing to himself with every breath, then drove a few blocks to Blackstone, the closest bar he could think of. After a few beers, he remembered the restaurant was the site of his and Stef's first date, and he couldn't keep memories of that night from playing back in his mind. He headed back to his apartment, picking up a twelve-pack on the way. After turning off the ringer on the phone, he drank until every beer was gone, then staggered to the bedroom and passed out in his clothes.

* * *

A loud banging jarred him to semi-consciousness at six a.m. He rolled out of bed and lurched to the door to find Stef standing outside— her face Goth-chick white and streaked with tears. She was shaking in the chilly air.

"I've been calling you all night," she said, forcing her way past him into the apartment. "Why haven't you answered?"

"You lied to me."

"I've never lied to you."

"You've been lying to me all along about you and Randy."

"No, I haven't."

"You've slept with him. You're still sleeping with him!"

"Arnie, you've got to believe me, there's nothing between us."

"Bullshit!"

"I'm telling you the truth."

"I saw him the other night he said . . . he told me that . . ." Arnie grimaced. "He knows things about you that only a lover could know."

Stef's shoulders dropped and her face lost all expression.

"God, I feel like such a fool," he said, slamming his fist into the wall. "Such a goddamn fucking fool."

"Listen to me, Arnie," Stef said, taking his hand in both of hers. "Sit down. We need to talk."

Arnie remained on his feet, shaking his head and muttering to himself.

"I've never brought this up before; there was no reason to. But remember I told you that I dated a man in the music business when I first started coming to Nashville, someone who was married? A long time ago?"

"How long ago? Last week?"

"No, years ago."

Arnie jerked his hand from hers.

"Well, that man was Randy. I was new in town, green as could be. He said he believed in me and my voice, and promised he could get me a record deal. I fell for his bullshit, and I fell for him—for a while at least. A very short while. We saw each other for a few months. Then I found out he wasn't really separated from his wife and getting a divorce like he said he was, and I broke it off. And I never did . . . you know. . ."

"What?"

"Have sex with him."

"Bullshit," he yelled. "I don't believe a fucking word you're saying!"

"Stop it!" Stef shrieked. "Stop swearing at me!"

"I'll stop when you stop lying to me."

"I'm not lying to you, damn it. Randy and I spent the night together a few times. And sure, we fooled around some, like you and I did at first. We were dating, what do you expect? But we never made love, had intercourse. You're the first one I've done that with since what happened to me when I was a child. I told you that before. It's the truth."

"How long ago did you say all this happened?"

"Three, maybe four years ago. All his talk about helping me get a record deal was nothing but smoke he was blowing up my ass. He never followed through on any of his promises. I don't know if he could have, even if he wanted to, as his own career was just getting rolling back then."

"And you haven't done anything with him since?" Arnie rolled his eyes. "Not in all the time you've been out on the road together?"

"God no! In fact, touring with him has been incredibly awkward. He tried for a while when we first went on the road, but not since last summer. Remember the news story about him getting a concussion last July—from falling down in a bathroom in Las Vegas?"

"Yeah, I do." Arnie remembered hearing about it while on his trip out west.

"He didn't fall down."

"What do you mean?"

"He's got a good publicist—the press release was a total whitewash job. Randy asked me to meet him in his room after a show we did at the

Hilton one night . . . I can't remember what his excuse was. When I got there he started coming on to me, saying that now that he was divorced it could be different with us. He'd been drinking and tried to pull me onto the bed. I pushed him away, and he knocked me down and got on top of me. I thought he was going to rape me. I managed to crawl out from under him and I made damn sure he'd never try it again."

"How?"

"With his 1962 Fender Telecaster—his favorite guitar. Or more accurately, his ex-favorite guitar. It was lying on the bed. I grabbed it by the neck and swung it at his head as hard as I could and he went down. There was a lot of blood."

"Shit, did you call an ambulance?"

"Hell no. I was trying to kill him. I knew the guitar was worth a lot of money, so I took it in the bathroom and smashed it over the toilet, then threw the pieces into the bathtub and turned the water on. Then I wiped my fingerprints off the doorknobs and faucets, and beat it back to my room as fast as I could. I was actually hoping he was dead."

"But he survived?"

"Like I told you, there was a lot of blood, but they say that happens with head wounds. His road manager showed up half an hour later and got him to the hospital. It turned out he only had a minor concussion."

Arnie believed her. Even he, a songwriter, couldn't come up with a story that good.

"Arnie, I love you," Stef said, clutching his shirt. "I haven't been touched by another man since the first time we kissed."

Arnie reflected that he'd done a bit more than touch a few other women during his and Stef's first few uncertain months together. Even in his befuddled state, he realized that it might be wise to change the subject. But before he could think of anything to say, Stef locked her arms around his neck and kissed him hard on the mouth. A few minutes later they were making love on the hallway floor.

CHAPTER 77

Arnie had a writing appointment with Bubba a few days later and stopped by Sam's office on his way. Starr smiled and said, "'Love Drops' goes to number three next week. It looks like it's going to be Stef's first number one record. The only thing that could get in the way is if it gets jumped by 'Safe Against the World,' which goes to number five. All the reporting stations are on it now, and it got a good bump in airplay last week."

"That's fantastic," Arnie said.

"Just keep up the good work." Starr beamed. "Now that I'm a partner in the company, I'm counting on you to make us all rich."

"Congratulations! I'm on my way over to Bubba's now to do just that. By the way, how was your trip to the Bahamas with Jules?"

Starr raised her left hand and waggled her ring finger, which sparkled with a huge diamond.

"I'm meeting his family in December. His parents own a chalet in Gstaad. We're planning to spend the Christmas holidays there."

"His family owns a chalet in Switzerland?"

"I remember when I was a little girl growing up in Bugtussle, Kentucky, Grandma told me: 'Sweetie, it's just as easy to love a rich man as a poor one!'" Arnie laughed as Starr continued. "But I'm crazy about him. I really am. We're talking about setting a date in April or May."

"I'll have to write a special song for the wedding."

"I couldn't ask for a nicer present."

* * *

Arnie drove to Bubba's office and found Sendy sitting behind the reception desk.

"Hey Arnie, what's going on? Still seeing Stefany?"

"Yep."

"I should have grabbed you last year."

"You had your chance, princess, but we couldn't afford to date each other now."

"What do you mean?"

"Stef would stop recording my songs and I'd go broke. Your father wouldn't let you marry a poor songwriter."

Sendy giggled. "Sometimes playing hard to get can get a girl in big trouble."

"Besides, you and Bubba have been seeing each other, haven't you?"

Sendy smiled coyly as Bubba stepped through the front door. Arnie followed him upstairs to his writing room.

"How's your hand?" Bubba asked as they unpacked their guitars.

"Not bad. It still hurts, but in a good way."

"By the way, maybe I shouldn't tell you this, but I wrote with a friend of mine yesterday—— he plays steel guitar in Randy's band."

"Yeah?"

"And I think there might actually have been something between Randy and Stef a while back."

Arnie felt his neck getting hot.

"Randy still chases after her when they're on the road. But my buddy said she won't have anything to do with him. She's evidently got quite a temper. In fact, he told me a story about her busting his Telecaster over his head in Vegas last summer when he got out of line."

"That's interesting," Arnie said, rubbing his chin. "Stef said the same thing."

"I think the story's true. The Tele was Randy's favorite ax, a 1962 model, cream colored, with half the finish worn off—worth twenty-five or thirty grand. His new album cover shows him playing a different guitar. Still a Fender, because of his endorsement deal, but a different model—a black Strat, shiny and new."

"Hmm. . ."

"Maybe we could get a song out of it somehow," Bubba said.

"Good idea," Arnie said, cracking a smile.

CHAPTER 78

Arnie got a call from Sam a few days later. "I just got next week's chart numbers. 'Love Drops' goes to number one, and 'Safe Against the World' is number three with a bullet."

"That's great!"

"Also, Stef's album jumped to number five this week. The label's predicting it'll be platinum by Christmas. Randy's CD has been certified double platinum, and they're predicting triple platinum for it by then. And there's more!"

"Good news or bad?"

"Good, really good. Buzz changed his mind again and decided to single 'Daddy'd Be Proud' on Randy. I think he means it this time. It's set to be released right before Thanksgiving."

"Wow, what a Christmas present!"

"Enjoy it, you deserve every penny you're going to make. Starr said you're planning to come to Savannah in a couple of weeks?"

"Yes. Stef, too."

"Super, I'll keep you posted on 'Safe Against the World.'"

Arnie hung up, happy for Stef about "Love Drops" and thrilled that his song would be Randy's next single. But he felt as if there was a gorilla inside him waiting to explode. He was dying for a number one record, and there wasn't anything he could do but wait to see if "Safe Against the World" would continue up the charts.

Arnie tried to focus on his songs through the rest of the week, but it was almost impossible. He remembered Bob Markum's advice from several months before about the importance of detaching himself from things in the music business that were beyond his control, but it was impossible not to wonder whether his song would continue upward. When he saw the office number on his caller ID a week later, he grabbed the phone. It was Starr: "Sam asked me to call you. Ronnie Dexter phoned a few minutes ago, 'Love Drops' stays at number one and your song moves up to number two. The label's planning a number one party for Stef at the Flying Saucer next Thursday, right before Savannah."

Arnie was silent for a moment. "Did he say anything more about 'Safe Against the World?' Does it still have its bullet?"

"Yes."

"Thanks, I'll look forward to the party."

"I've got my fingers crossed for you, Arnie."

* * *

The days dragged by like congealed molasses. Stef gushed with exuberance during their daily phone conversations. She was ecstatic to have 'Love Drops' remain at the top of the charts for two weeks in a row, and Arnie was tremendously happy for her. Still, though he felt a bit guilty about it, he was disturbed that her single was preventing his own song from reaching the top slot.

On the morning of Stef's number one party, he got a surprise call from Sam.

"Hey, Arnie. Are you sitting down?"

"Yep."

"Are you sure?"

"I said yes, didn't I?"

"Congratulations, 'Safe Against the World' goes to number one next week."

"No shit, really? How'd you find out?"

"Buzz pulled some strings at *Billboard*, got the news a day early. He's going to make tonight's party at the Flying Saucer a double number one celebration for both songs. It should be quite an event. 'Love Drops' dropped to number two when your song jumped it so Stef still has the top two songs in the country this week—for the second week in a row."

Arnie hung up, tingling from head to toe. A few minutes later, his exuberance dropped a notch when he realized that Randy Fawcett would probably be at the party. But his apprehension faded quickly. He had a number one record and no one was going to steal his thunder. Besides, he thought with a smile, Randy would remember him now not merely as "the songwriter"—but as "the songwriter who kicked his ass".

CHAPTER 79

Arnie arrived with Bubba and Razor at the number one party to find the celebration already going full tilt. The Flying Saucer was a great choice for the event. It was a spacious beer hall housed in Union Station—a beautifully renovated, century old structure that had once served as Nashville's train station. Several hundred people were in attendance, ranging from politicking industry executives sipping mineral water to up-and-coming songwriters and musicians guzzling drinks from the open bar and scarfing down free sandwiches and hors d'oeuvres.

Arnie kept a watchful eye for Randy and made sure Bubba remained nearby in case of trouble. Starr introduced him to a string of successful producers and writers whose names he was familiar with. He accepted their congratulations on his song, and watched admiringly as she used his accomplishments to lay the groundwork for future song pitches and co-writing appointments. When he spotted Nanci Morales and Ronnie Dexter at the bar, he thanked them both at length for their hard work. Stef was with Sam and was mobbed with well-wishers, but when she saw Arnie, she ran to embrace him. Shortly afterward, Buzz tapped on a microphone on a small stage set up in a corner of the restaurant and the crowd quieted.

He made a short speech congratulating Stef for having the top two songs in the nation, then called her and Sam and Arnie to join him onstage. Arnie hadn't noticed Randy in the crowd, but he appeared as if by magic behind Buzz as they made their way to the front of the room. Buzz congratulated Sam for producing the two hit records, and the crowd applauded as he presented plaques to Stef and Randy, along with additional awards celebrating their gold and multi-platinum albums.

Stef spoke briefly, thanking everyone involved for making her childhood dream of becoming a recording star a reality. Then Randy stepped to the microphone and congratulated Stef for her part in making "Safe Against the World" a hit. His cool graciousness in the awkward situation astonished Arnie. Since the songwriters of "Love Drops" lived in California and were unable to attend, Buzz accepted their awards on their behalf.

When it was Arnie's turn to speak, he thanked Sam and Buzz for producing the record, then Stef and Randy for recording his song. He was again taken aback when Randy reached across the stage to shake his hand, then smile his famous ten-gallon smile and thank him for the great song. Anyone in the crowd would have thought they were best buddies.

Randy's demeanor throughout the event was so genuine that Arnie found himself wondering if the star had been so shit-faced when he slugged him at Tootsies that he didn't remember it. He recalled Randy's canceled appearance on *The Tonight Show*, and it occurred to him that getting punched over a woman might be not be that unusual an event. In any case, the singer was evidently too professional to let a personal matter damage his public persona as America's favorite cowboy. Buzz wrapped up the presentation a few moments later and Randy disappeared soon afterward without speaking further to Arnie, though not before posing arm and arm with the group for the every last trade magazine photo.

CHAPTER 80

Stef was anxious to hit the road for Savannah the next morning and was puzzled when Arnie said that he needed to make a stop along the way.

"I've got a surprise," Arnie explained as he drove across town.

"A surprise for me?"

"For both of us. It'll make the trip more fun."

"Your surprise wouldn't have four wheels, would it?"

"It just might."

Arnie turned south at Eighth Avenue and soon reached the showroom of JPA Nashville, Music City's premiere exotic automobile dealership. He parked the Miata under the canopied front entrance next to a stunning white convertible. Stef sucked in her breath.

"Arnie, it's gorgeous," she exclaimed as they approached the car. "Is it yours?"

"It will be in a few minutes."

"I think it's the prettiest Ferrari I've ever seen!" Stef gushed. "But it looks different than Sam's Ferrari."

"That's because it's not a Ferrari."

"What? It's not a Ferrari?"

"No, it's a Porsche."

"A Porsche?" Stef said, breathless as she examined the glistening 997 Carrera. "Well, I still think it's the most beautiful car I've ever seen in my life. And I love the color, white with tan leather—my favorite. I'm so glad you got a convertible."

"Cabriolet, actually," a voice said from behind them. "That's the correct term for a Porsche convertible."

They turned to see a handsome balding gentleman in his fifties approach. He was wearing a charcoal gray pinstripe suit and looked more like a university professor than a car salesman. "Congratulations," he said, shaking hands with Arnie and handing him a set of keys.

"Thanks!" Arnie said. "Peter, this is Stefany Simmons. Stef, Peter Grimes."

The salesman nodded to Stef. "Congratulations again," he said turning back to Arnie. "I see you've got a girl who's even prettier than the car— that's quite an accomplishment with a Porsche!"

Stef blushed at the compliment and Peter helped them transfer their luggage into the Carrera's front trunk. When they were done, Arnie handed the salesman the Miata's keys.

"Thanks again for your help. Someone from Sam Solstice's office will be by to pick up the Mazda later today."

"It's been my pleasure," Peter said. "I think we went over everything about the car when we took care of the paperwork yesterday, but don't hesitate to call if you have any questions. You've got my mobile number."

"Will do. Thank you again."

Arnie drove away from the building, inhaling the scent of the new leather upholstery and reveling in the feel of the clutch and precision six-speed gearbox. He pulled into traffic on Eighth Avenue and continued to proceed cautiously until they reached I-65. Halfway up the entrance ramp, he punched the accelerator. Stef's head snapped back against the headrest as he revved the engine to five thousand rpm in first gear, the limit for the one thousand mile break in period, then shifted to second and did the same. When he reached the upper limit in third gear, Stef cautioned, "You'd better slow down. We don't want to get a ticket or have a wreck before we get out of Davidson County."

Arnie glanced at the speedometer. They were doing almost ninety, and he still had three gears to go. He lifted his right foot and depressed the clutch, then gently up-shifted to sixth. Soon they were loafing along at sixty-five with the rpm's barely ticking above idle. Even with the top down, the ride was so smooth and quiet that it felt like they were doing no more than thirty.

"Arnie, this car is unbelievable," Stef said. "But I thought you were going to buy a Ferrari."

"I was planning to, and I almost did. But I changed my mind."

"Why?"

"Ferraris are wonderful. In fact, I'd like to have one some day. But I discovered I love Porsches."

"Why a Porsche?"

"Well, for one thing, they always run. It's true that Ferrari's are a little faster. Sam's 430 will do a hundred eighty-six miles an hour and the top speed of mine is only a hundred seventy-eight. But I figure that's fast enough to get me into all the trouble I need."

"Is that all?"

"The other thing is that I figured out that I'm not really a Ferrari guy."

"What do you mean?"

"Well, I love the Ferrari folks. They're entertaining—like a good movie or something. But they're all . . . I don't know how to put it . . . such hustlers and scoundrels. You know, getting into lawsuits and chasing young girls and running off with each other's wives and stuff. Maybe I shouldn't be so hard on them. The only guy I know that's actually run off with someone's wife is Buford. Most of them are fun people, but they're just not who I want to be when I grow older. I love Sam. He's been wonderful to me, but I don't want to be his age and dating female wrestlers and unemployed mistresses. I want to be like Bob Markum and raise a family and write worthwhile songs and have a happy life."

"That's so nice to hear, Arnie," Stef said, leaning over to kiss his cheek. "That's what I want too . . . with you."

"I'd like to have it with you, too."

"I know something else you'd like to have." Stef said with a coquettish grin, unlatching her safety harness and reaching across his lap to undo his belt buckle.

"What's that?"

She smiled and unzipped his jeans.

CHAPTER 81

Arnie and Stef arrived in Savannah Friday evening just as the sun was setting. Stef was charmed by their quaint hotel, which faced one of the many lush live oak and azalea filled squares that adorned the city's downtown historic district. They checked into adjoining rooms and, on the advice of the concierge, drove to nearby Tybee Island for supper at a restaurant called the Crab Shack.

The establishment, advertised by a sign saying WHERE THE ELITE EAT IN THEIR BARE FEET, was well worth the thirty-minute drive. It was located at the site of an old fishing camp by a tidal creek on the marshy western end of the island, and appeared to be a local hangout, with regulars arriving by both car and boat. During their meal, Stef informed Arnie that her father would be arriving sometime the following afternoon, and wouldn't be bringing his Ferrari because he had to leave early Sunday morning. He was however, looking forward to meeting Arnie.

After dinner, they decided to explore, and drove several miles to the eastern shore of the island, where they strolled to the end of Tybee Pier. The almost full moon cast a shimmering pathway across the waves that followed them as they walked, stopping occasionally to chat with fishermen who had rods propped along the pier's railing. Afterward, they drove slowly back to Savannah for a quiet drink at a bar a few doors from the hotel. When they got back to the hotel, they made love tenderly in Arnie's room's antique four-poster bed, then feel asleep in each other's arms.

The next morning they enjoyed a leisurely breakfast at a coffee shop by the harbor, then headed to Roebling Road Raceway. When they arrived at the entrance, the guard at the electric chain link gate waved them to a stop. As he spoke, a multi-colored string of Ferraris appeared at the far end of the straightaway to their right. The cars screamed toward them at what appeared to be well over a hundred miles an hour. One by one, the vehicles braked and darted into a sweeping series of turns and vanished into the back half of the course. Several minutes later, they came into view again after rounding the track and Arnie thought he recognized one of them as Sam's 430.

After several laps, a flagman signaled that the heat was over and waved the cars into the pits. The gate official used his walkie-talkie to verify that the track was clear, then opened the barrier and allowed Arnie and Stef to drive across to the shady infield, where they spotted Vinnie and Robert by Sam's car. Sam emerged from the 430, along with Nicole. Both were outfitted in identical Ferrari Red jumpsuits, matching Piloti racing shoes, and looked like they'd stepped out of the pages of *Cavallino* magazine, the Ferrari Club of North America's glossy bimonthly journal.

"Wassamatter, Arnie?" Vinnie said with a throaty laugh as he eyed the sparkling Porsche. "Couldn't afford a Ferrari, so you had to buy a Kraut car?"

"That's right, I'm just a poor songwriter," Arnie fired back good-naturedly.

"You might be a smart man," the Italian mechanic said, chuckling and turning to Sam and Robert who were circling Arnie's Carrera and whistling. "Hope you guys don't get the same idea and put my shop out of business."

Everyone laughed. Hardcore Ferrari snobs that they were, they couldn't help drooling over the new Porsche. After chatting for several more minutes, the group headed to the concession pavilion for hot dogs and Cokes.

Arnie and Stef feasted their eyes on scores of Ferraris as they strolled through the infield. Even at rest, the cars exuded ferocious power and grace—their exquisitely contoured bodies undulated with the might of their massive engines. The cars ranged from older models built in the fifties and sixties to more current ones such as 360s, 430s and a black twelve-cylinder 612 2+2 Scaglietti. There was even an Enzo, with a list price of almost $750,000 and a limited production run of only a few hundred cars. It was fascinating to observe the evolution of the automobiles—all were designed and built without compromise to be as fast and beautiful as the outer limits of human imagination and technology permitted.

Arnie and Stef stopped to take a closer look at a particularly impressive car, which Sam identified as an F-40 built in the late eighties to commemorate the anniversary of Enzo Ferrari's ninetieth birthday. It was similar in ways to the more modern Enzo—a barely street legal racecar devoid of even the most basic luxuries, such as carpet, radio or proper door handles. Arnie inquired about the engine, and the owner, a surgeon from Atlanta, raised the lightweight Kevlar and carbon-fibre body to reveal a gargantuan 478 horsepower power plant that took up nearly two thirds of the interior, leaving barely enough room for a steering wheel and two Spartan seats bolted to the front of the chassis. After lowering the body of the half-million dollar car, the doctor offered to take Arnie and Stef for a spin around the track.

Stef donned a racing helmet provided by the surgeon, and he helped her buckle herself into the F-40's safety harness. Ten minutes and several laps later, she emerged from the car on trembling legs, smiling palely. When it was Arnie's turn, he held his breath as the car accelerated hard down the straightaway to the first curve, braking only when a crash seemed inevitable. Miraculously, the wide tires kept their grip on the pavement, and the Ferrari leapt like a cheetah into a series of switchback S curves. The doctor kept his foot on the throttle through most of the back half of the circuit and when they emerged again onto the main straightaway, the full power of the engine plastered Arnie against the thin, padded seat like an astronaut on a space shuttle launch.

After several laps, the car returned to the pits and Arnie queasily unbuckled his harness and removed his helmet, his heart pumping like an eight year old's after his first roller coaster ride. He and Stef thanked the surgeon profusely, then rejoined Sam and Nicole. By the end of the afternoon, they'd become acquainted with quite a few of the owners and had the opportunity to ride in several more cars. Arnie couldn't decide whether his favorite was the F-40 or a brand new twelve-cylinder 599 GTB Fiorano. Stef voted for a graceful 1959 250 GT that she said reminded her of her father's Ferrari, but whispered into Arnie's ear that his Porsche was still her first choice because of the man driving it.

It was a great day. As it drew to a close, Arnie mentioned to Sam that he'd never seen so many spectacular automobiles in one place.

"You should think about coming to Palm Beach in January for the Cavallino Classic," Sam answered. "It's the crown jewel of East Coast Ferrari events. Takes place at the Breakers Hotel. If you like this, you'll go nuts over the cars there."

"Really?"

"Hundreds of Ferraris are on display, cars from all over the world. Some of them are one of a kind—rare models, only a few ever manufactured. I'm sure the hotel has a parking garage where you can hide your Porsche."

Arnie laughed at the jibe. "Sounds like fun."

"So you'll be at the club banquet this evening?"

"Seven o'clock, right?"

"Yes, it's at the Bistro Restaurant on Congress Street."

"We're looking forward to it!"

CHAPTER 82

Arnie and Stef returned to their hotel in time for a short nap before dinner. When they woke, Arnie dressed carefully in clean jeans and a freshly ironed shirt, hoping to make as favorable an impression as possible with Stef's father. Stef looked ravishing in a black leather skirt and matching wool turtleneck sweater. They strolled down Congress Street and arrived at the Bistro a little after seven to find it crowded with event attendees enjoying pre-dinner cocktails. The restaurant was subdued and elegant, with high ceilings, heart-pine floors, and gray brick walls decorated with paintings by local artists. They spotted the surgeon who had given them rides in his F-40 earlier in the day and were chatting with him and his wife at the bar when Stef grabbed Arnie's arm.

"There's Daddy! Let's go say hello!"

The man who Stef pointed out as her father was standing with his back to them, speaking with a group of people by the front door.

"What's your dad's first name, Stef?" Arnie asked as they approached him. "Or should I just call him Mr. Simmons?"

"His first name's Roberto. Just use your judgment about how you address him, he can be sort of formal sometimes. By the way, Simmons isn't my real last name, it's just the one I go by in Nashville."

"Really, what's your—"

"Sweetheart!" her father exclaimed, interrupting Arnie.

"Hi Daddy!" she said, throwing her arms around his neck.

Her father was a distinguished looking gentleman in his late sixties or early seventies, balding and bespectacled. Though he was still facing away from Arnie as he embraced Stef, something about him was familiar, and Arnie's skin tingled inexplicably. He struggled to put his finger on the source of his *déjà vu*. After a few moments, her father disengaged himself from Stef and turned to face Arnie.

"Daddy," she said, "this is Arnie Fortune."

Stef's father smiled thinly and grasped Arnie's hand in a talon-like grip.

"It's nice to meet you, Mr. . ." Arnie responded.

"Puccini," Stef's father said softly.

Terror paralyzed the muscles of Arnie's face and body, freezing his nervous system like a thousand volt jolt of electricity. The older man's grip relaxed, and Arnie's arm dropped to his side. He took a step backward, and felt the restaurant's rough brick wall against his shoulder blades. Stef's father's eyes never left Arnie's. They were as black and cold as a dead man's, and completely disconnected from the broad smile that spread slowly across his leathery face.

"I see your Arnie's a little nervous about meeting me."

"He's not usually so jumpy," Stef replied.

"He must like my sweetheart quite a bit then," her father said reaching to stroke his daughter's hair, his eyes still locked on Arnie.

"I . . . yes, I. . ." Arnie stammered.

"That's not a bad thing you know," Stef's dad continued. "It's good to see a young man nervous around the father of a girl he's courting. It shows respect."

"Uh . . . thank you, sir." Arnie said.

"You may call me Roberto."

"Yes sir."

"Look, everyone's sitting down for the meal." Stef's father placed an arm around Arnie's shoulder and pulled him away from the wall. "Let's join them."

Arnie's shoes felt like fifty-gallon cement-filled drums as he let himself be led to one of the banquet tables. His mind raced, and was on the verge of short-circuiting. Stef being Mafia Don Roberto Puccini's daughter was impossible. Yet here he was. Arnie wondered if he'd stepped into a nightmare. He pinched his leg through his trousers, but nothing changed.

Slowly, as they traversed the crowded restaurant, the pieces began to fall into place. Sam's deferential treatment of Stef, Buzz Corbin's abrupt turnaround regarding her first single, even her vague description of her father's occupation as "he owns things" after he bought Buzz's office building. Shit, Buzz was lucky not to have woken up with a severed horse's head in his bed.

Stef's father squeezed Arnie's collarbone as they neared their table.

"I've heard a lot about you from Stefania. You've written the wonderful songs that have made her dream of becoming a recording star come true. That makes me very happy. She's my only daughter, you know." Stef smiled, and her father touched her shoulder.

"Uh, thank you sir," Arnie stammered.

"Stef said you own . . . things . . . businesses . . . I mean a Ferrari . . ." Arnie's voice trailed off.

"Yes, I own a number of businesses and a Ferrari too. Several, in fact. But let's not talk about business tonight."

"Yes, sir."

A wave of relief swept over Arnie when he saw that the seating cards at their table had Stef placed between him and her father.

"Here," he said, pulling out Stef's chair and pushing him down into it. "Sit next to me."

Arnie reluctantly took a seat between Stef and one of the most feared men in North America, a man whose nephew he had sent to prison for the rest of his days.

"What's wrong, honey?" Stef whispered into his ear.

"Nothing . . . my stomach's a little upset," he replied. "Maybe it was the hot dog I had at the track."

"Well, you can always go back to the hotel," she continued softly. "But Daddy flew all the way from New York to meet you and has to leave early tomorrow morning. I was hoping you could get to know each other better."

The last thing in the world Arnie wanted was for her father to get to know him better. "I'll do my best to stay," he mumbled. "But I really don't feel well."

The server brought salads and Arnie cringed as Don Puccini reached for his steak knife.

"False teeth," the Don said, noticing Arnie eyeing the broad serrated blade as it flashed under the light of an overhead chandelier. "I've even got to cut up vegetables. Carrots are the worst. One needs to make the most of life while one is young. Old age is a tough thing." Stef's dad chuckled and glanced sideways at Arnie. "Though it beats the alternative."

Arnie gulped. His face itched where he'd had his plastic surgery a year and a half before, and he reflected that he wasn't enjoying what might be the final moments of his young life at all. At the same time, it occurred to him that it didn't seem to be in danger of ending immediately, or the Don would have cut his throat already. Slowly he gathered his wits and peered around the room. At the far end of the long banquet table was a dark haired man in a loose fitting shirt that Arnie didn't recognize from the track, and standing by the front door was another unfamiliar man wearing a buttoned windbreaker. Both were built like tree trunks and neither appeared to have any neck at all, though they must have, since their heads never stopped swiveling between the Don and the front door. Arnie considered excusing himself to go to the restroom, then ducking into the kitchen in hope of finding a rear service exit, but then realized that someone was probably watching that, too.

Their entrees arrived and Arnie picked at his food, thinking about his beeper and pistol—both were back in his apartment in Nashville. Maybe it was a good thing. A swarm of FBI agents descending on the banquet could be disastrous. And a five shot revolver would be no match for the hardware carried by the two goons at the far end of the room. Shit, he'd never even fired the gun. Still, he wished he had it—it might buy him some time.

Fortunately, Don Puccini's attention drifted away from Arnie to the other guests. A real estate developer from Philadelphia seated across the table remembered Stef's father from a Ferrari event in New England several years earlier and asked him if he still owned his 1962 Ferrari 250 GTO. Arnie recognized the model, recalling that Buford and Lars once fantasized about owning one as it was among the most valuable cars in the world, worth at least $6 million.

"I still have it, and was going to bring it down for the weekend," Stef's father answered. "But I have to be back in New York tomorrow. Maybe I'll trailer it to Palm Beach in January. It's a shame to keep a car like that in the garage. It should be out in the sunshine, driven by a young man like Arnie, with a pretty girl like my Stefania beside him."

"I used to love riding in it with you, Daddy," Stef said.

Don Puccini beamed and turned to Arnie. "Do you think that you and Stef will come to Palm Beach in January?"

"Uh, I'm not sure," Arnie replied.

"Try to make it. I have a house there, and a boat too. You'll enjoy yourselves."

A club officer rose from his seat across the room to make awards presentations for the day's track events. Halfway through the ceremony, a waiter dropped a tray of deserts behind Stef, and Arnie jumped in his seat.

"I see you're still nervous," the Don said as Arnie settled back in his chair. "And you've barely touched your food."

"I'm sorry, sir. I'm really not feeling well."

"You have nothing to be nervous about," Stef's father said, touching Arnie's forearm with a gnarled finger. "I promise you."

Arnie didn't reply.

"But you need to work on your appetite. You want to stay healthy, don't you?"

"Yes, sir," Arnie gulped.

"A young man needs to eat if he wants to stay healthy and marry a beautiful girl like my daughter."

Stef blushed at the mention of marriage. "Arnie isn't feeling well," she said quickly. "He's normally quite a bit more talkative."

The Don smiled. "I'm beginning to like your Arnie. Sometimes it's good for a man to know when to hold his counsel."

Arnie reflected that this was certainly one of them. His testimony at Toni Bertolini's trial had been pre-recorded by the FBI, and the timbre of his speech disguised. But he didn't know for sure how effective the equipment had been.

Don Puccini resumed his conversation with the developer across the table after the brief awards ceremony concluded. A few minutes later, the apologetic waiter delivered fresh desserts, but the Don pushed his away and glanced at the bodyguards across the room.

"I'm feeling a little tired," he said. "I think I'll head back to my hotel."

"So soon, Daddy?" Stef asked. "Don't you want dessert?"

"My appetite's not what it used to be, and my energy isn't either. I'm going to get some rest and leave you young people to enjoy the rest of the evening."

"We'll see you at breakfast tomorrow, won't we?"

"Of course," the Don said, rising. Both bodyguards stood as well and Arnie saw the one by the front door mash the keypad of his cell phone with a sausage-like finger.

"It was good to meet you, Arnie," the older man said, shaking his hand. "I'm glad to see my daughter so happy. Be careful with her."

"Yes sir, I will." Arnie caught a glimpse of Vinnie staring at him from across the room and wished he'd paid more attention when the mechanic told him the same thing a year earlier. "I'm sorry I wasn't better company."

"Don't worry." Don Puccini smiled and locked eyes with Arnie for a brief moment, then clasped his shoulder briefly with his free hand.

Then he was gone.

Stef excused herself and Arnie exhaled deeply, then slumped down in his chair. Suddenly, he was knocked forward by a blow from behind and terror exploded in his veins. He spun to see Vinnie behind him. The mechanic grinned and pushed him down in his seat.

"Looks like you passed the test," Vinnie said. "He likes you. I can tell. It's good when Mr. Puccini likes someone."

"I don't know," Arnie answered shakily. "He doesn't know me very well."

"What's to know?" the mechanic asked with a shrug. "Let me buy you a drink—you look like you could use one. Then we'll hit some night spots with Sam and Nicole."

Arnie drained the glass of wine Vinnie ordered, then asked the waiter for another and gulped it as well. His head was spinning. The good news was that he was still alive; the bad news was that he didn't know for how long. Stef's father didn't seem to have recognized him, but he couldn't be sure—and he couldn't forget the indecipherable look he gave him just before he left. If the Don or one of his bodyguards had made him, they probably wouldn't have done anything in front of the hundred or so people at the banquet. The real danger would come later, most likely that night at the hotel. He'd have to bail out of Savannah as soon as possible.

Stef returned and said, "You really aren't feeling well, are you? Look, you're trembling."

"I need go back to my room and lie down. Vinnie's going bar-hopping with Sam and Nicole. Why don't you join them—have some fun."

"I'd rather come back to the hotel and be with you, good company or not," Stef said. "But maybe I will have a drink with them. I'm glad you got a chance to meet Daddy."

"When you come in later, it might be best if you went straight to your room without checking on me—you know, with your father nearby and all. Plus, I don't want to wake up and not be able to fall back to sleep."

Stef gave him a questioning look. "Arnie, are you OK?"

"I love you."

"I love you, too."

Arnie walked Stef outside to where Sam, Vinnie and Nicole were waiting on the sidewalk, then kissed her goodbye and headed toward his hotel. Halfway down the block, he turned to catch a final glimpse of her. She looked more beautiful than ever, and he held the image in his mind as he hurried down the street.

CHAPTER 83

Back at the hotel, Arnie took the elevator upstairs to his room, double-locked the door behind him and packed his bag with shaking hands. He wondered again if Don Puccini had recognized him at dinner, then realized it didn't matter. It was only a matter of time before his past caught up with him. And it might be a very short amount of time indeed.

He considered calling Agent Baskins, but decided against it. First, there were some loose ends he needed to tie up in Nashville. And if the FBI hadn't figured out he was dating Don Puccini's daughter, he doubted that he could count on them to pull him out of Savannah without getting him killed in the process. The most important thing now was to put as many miles as possible between himself and Don Puccini.

He spent several minutes trying to compose a letter of explanation to Stef, then gave up and scrawled a one-sentence note asking her to catch a ride back to Nashville with Vinnie or Robert. Then he opened the door to his room and glanced down the hallway in both directions. Seeing no one, he trotted to the fire exit, took the stairs to the lobby and handed the note to the night clerk, asking that it be delivered it to Stef in the morning. He walked across the lobby, took a deep breath and stepped outside.

The sidewalk was empty, and he fought the urge to run as he slipped through the shadows to the parking garage where he'd left his Porsche. On the way, he removed the battery from his cell phone, crushed the device into pieces with his heel and tossed the remains into two separate trash bins. When he got to the car, he threw his bag behind the seat, and activated the internal locking system before turning the key. The car's tires screeched on the slick concrete as he raced to the exit. He forced himself to stay under the speed limit as he drove through the ominous streets of downtown Savannah that had appeared so charming a few hours earlier. Each red light lasted an eternity, but he soon reached I-16 and accelerated hard up the entrance ramp, glad that there was no sign of danger in his rearview mirror.

* * *

Four hours later, Arnie passed through Atlanta. His terror had subsided somewhat with the passing miles, and he struggled to collect his thoughts and assess his predicament.

Without question, he had to assume that his true identity as Andy Baxter had been, or soon would be, discovered by Don Puccini. He realized with a wrenching ache in his gut that his career as a Nashville songwriter was over. So, in all likelihood, was his romance with Stef. Shit, he'd sent a member of her family to prison and her father had a contract on his life.

The only logical course of action was to bail out of Nashville—and he'd have to do it quickly. Fortunately, his financial situation was good. He still had the $200K investment account set up for him by the FBI. In addition, according to Sam's estimate, he'd have several hundred thousand dollars in royalties coming in over the next year or two, possibly even as much as half a million if "Daddy'd Be Proud" did well as Randy Fawcett's next single—as it almost surely would. He would also have substantial residual royalty income for many years to come. His brief songwriting career had put him in an enviable position. For all practical purposes, he was financially set for life—provided his life lasted long enough for him to spend the money.

As he approached Chattanooga two hours later, a vague plan began to take shape. He remembered his visit to Key West. It might be a good place to get lost in. He still had the business card their sailboat skipper, Gabe McEwen, had given him, and he recalled the stories he'd told. Maybe he could help him sign on as a crewmember on a yacht sailing around the Caribbean for a few months. It might even be fun. He wouldn't need his Porsche—he could stop in Miami and sell it through Jon Uhm, the auto broker Robert had bought his Testerossa from.

The more he thought about his plan, the better it sounded. He didn't have to live in Nashville to write songs—hell, look at Jimmy Buffett. He'd miss his co-writers, but writing alone had always been his first love. He was thirty years old, and hopefully had a lot of good years ahead of him.

It was Sunday morning. In order to put his plan into effect, he'd need to retrieve Gabe's and Jon's business cards from his apartment. He'd also need his guitar and notebooks, the Smith & Wesson and the FBI beeper. He could get them tonight. Then, first thing in the morning, he'd contact Sam and his accountant, Phil Hart, and arrange for his royalties to be paid into an escrow or trust account at an offshore bank that couldn't be traced by the Mafia. With any luck, he'd be on his way to Florida by noon tomorrow.

CHAPTER 84

Arnie arrived in Music City two hours later. He checked into a motel by the interstate, paying cash and using a false name, then collapsed onto the bed in his room.

Though he was exhausted from his all night drive, sleep eluded him. Tattooed on the inside of his eyelids was the image of Stef standing on the sidewalk in Savannah. His mind jumped out of control, synapses firing randomly from too much caffeine and no sleep. He'd escaped with his life, but the thought of living it without her was crushing beyond belief— almost impossible to conceive.

He didn't remember falling asleep, it was only when he awoke that he realized he must have done so. The clock by the bed said it was midnight. He showered and put on fresh clothes, then called his voicemail from the motel phone. There were several frantic messages from Stef. The last one was hysterical. She was in Nashville and begged him to call her as soon as possible. The sound of her voice hit him like a bullet, but the thought of real bullets from Don Puccini's gunmen shredding his ribcage prevented him from dialing her back. He zipped his bag and checked out of the motel.

Arnie had parked his Porsche behind an office building several blocks away to avoid giving away his whereabouts. He approached the car cautiously, then got on his hands and knees and peered underneath it. Not noticing anything bulky enough to be a bomb, he stood behind a telephone pole and activated the remote key button to unlock the doors. The Carrera's lights flashed briefly and there was an audible click as the locks released. He gingerly settled in the driver's seat, took a deep breath and closed his eyes before turning the ignition key. When the engine roared to life, he relaxed a little, then drove to an all night Waffle House for breakfast.

Every time he thought about Stef, his heart sank deeper. If by some miracle she still wanted to have anything to do with him after learning the truth about his past, she'd have to give up her singing career. He knew what he was considering was impossible—she'd devoted her life to her music, and could never sever ties with her family. He mulled over his dilemma as he ate, continuing to rack his brain for a solution that would allow them to be together, but after a full pot of coffee found himself no closer to an answer.

He paid his check, then drove to a twenty-four hour Kinko's and bought a half-hour of Internet access time. He logged into the email account the FBI had set up for him and found a message from Agent Baskins marked urgent. He at first was relieved that it made no mention of Savannah, but the feeling evaporated when he read the news that Tony Bertolini had been stabbed to death in prison. Baskins warned him to be extremely vigilant and Arnie broke out in a sweat. If Tony Bertolini was the Don's nephew, that made him Stef's cousin. Not only had he sent Roberto Puccini's nephew to jail, he had, in effect, caused his death. For all practical purposes, he'd murdered the cousin of the woman he loved.

Any lingering fantasies of a life with Stef vanished. Blood was thicker than water, especially Italian blood. When she discovered the truth about him she'd be seeking vengeance, too. Arnie's heart raced as he checked his watch. It was four a.m. and he'd have to move fast.

He drove to Music Row and cruised slowly past his apartment, then parked several blocks away and stole up the alley, avoiding the overhead street lamps and carefully examining the parked cars he passed. When he neared his back door, he stopped behind some shrubbery and examined it for a full five minutes. The kitchen light he'd left on was still burning, and there was no sign of movement. With a stout tree limb in his hand, he tiptoed up the steps, unlocked the door and swung it inward. He then flattened himself against the outside brick wall. Hearing nothing, he took a deep breath and entered.

Everything appeared to be as he had left it. He retrieved the pistol from under the kitchen sink, checked to see that it was loaded, then slipped it into the back pocket of his jeans. Feeling a bit better, he gathered his guitar, notebooks and beeper and was searching through the bedroom bureau drawer for Gabe's and Jon's business cards when the phone rang. He glanced at the caller ID screen and saw Stef's cell number. The phone rang twice more. Though he knew it was a mistake, he reached for the receiver.

"Arnie!" Stef's voice was frantic.

He didn't respond.

"Are you there? Is that you?"

He took a deep breath. "Yes."

"I was so worried."

"You got my note."

"Arnie, we need to talk."

"Stef, I've got to leave town for a while."

"Arnie, please. Please! We have to talk. You don't—"

"We can't, not now. I'm about to—"

"Arnie, you can't leave. I'm coming over right now."

"I'll be gone."

"If you never do anything else, please do this one thing for me."

Arnie wondered if it was a trap. Loving her as much as he did, he owed her an explanation. Her father might never give her one, and it would look as if he'd abandoned her for no reason at all. He cared for her more than he imagined a person could ever care for anyone, and might never see her again. He started to hang up, but his hand refused to obey his brain. He made a decision. "Okay. We can talk, but not here or at your hotel."

"Anywhere you want, just tell me."

"I'll meet you at Centennial Park in the big parking lot in front of the Parthenon."

"I'll be there in twenty minutes."

* * *

Arnie arrived at Centennial Park ten minutes later and parked in the shadows behind a row of shrubs near the children's playground. The Parthenon was a block or so away and the breaking light of dawn gave him a clear view of the building and broad lawns surrounding it. He

357

withdrew the Smith & Wesson from his back pocket and held it in his lap, after checking again to make sure that it was loaded. A few minutes later, Stef pulled up to the Parthenon. She got out and stepped away from the vehicle. He watched her carefully for a few minutes, then drove slowly to where she stood, prepared to accelerate away at the first sign of danger.

When he was almost to her, he slipped the pistol under his left thigh, then pulled to a rolling stop and opened his passenger door. She got in, and before she could fully close the door, he slammed down the gas pedal. The Porsche's rear end briefly slipped sideways on the dew-slick pavement, then the car shot forward. He circled the Parthenon and parked by the duck pond, where once again he had a clear view for several hundred yards in every direction.

"Arnie, I'm so glad you came," Stef blurted when he turned to face her. "I didn't think you were going to."

"There're some things I need to tell you, Stef. I owe you an explanation before I leave town."

"You don't have to go." She took his hand in hers.

"When you hear what I have to say, it'll make it easier to forget me when I'm gone."

"Arnie, I could never forget you. But I will listen."

Arnie looked around, then took a deep breath and told her his entire story, from beginning to end. A couple of times she tried to interrupt, but he stopped her and continued. When he got to the part about the FBI's email saying that Tony Bertolini had been killed in prison he braced himself in case she slashed at his throat with her French manicured nails. But, inexplicably, she started to smile.

"So that's it," he said.

Stef was still smiling.

"Arnie, may I speak now?"

"Sure. I've murdered your cousin and your father wants me dead. You'll want to kill me too, once you have a chance to think about it."

"Arnie, I had a long talk with Daddy after I got your note. I was going crazy—"

"Not as crazy as I was after realizing who he was."

". . . and I know your story, every bit."

Arnie felt the pressure of his pistol under his thigh and resisted the urge to reach for it. "You know all of my story?"

"And you only know part of mine."

"Which part don't I know?"

"The most important part is that I love you and always will, no matter what. But there's more."

"What?"

"Remember what I told you happened to me as a child? That I was sexually abused—by a relative?"

"Yes."

"It was my cousin who did it."

Arnie stared at her. "And. . . ?"

"His name was Tony Bertolini."

Arnie didn't respond. His mind raced as he again scanned the park. Only a couple of early-morning joggers and a group of people doing exercises were visible on the far side of the pond. His left leg was tingling and on the verge of falling asleep from the pressure of the thirty-eight under his thigh and he shifted his weight.

Stef spoke again. "Tony Bertolini's the one who raped me."

"Tony Bertolini? The same Tony Bertolini I testified against and sent to prison?"

"Yes. I never said a word to anyone. But he bragged about it to the wrong person and word got back to Daddy." Tears welled in Stef's eyes. "Daddy couldn't let Tony get away with what he'd done. But he couldn't just kill him either, because he was family. The shooting at the Pizza parlor was a set-up. Daddy made sure the police were tipped off to what was going down and were there to arrest him afterward. Daddy is probably responsible for him being stabbed in prison last week, too. He didn't tell me that, but I wouldn't be surprised."

Arnie shook his head, trying to take it all in.

"So I was just . . . I was just a player in your father's game? Part of his plan?"

"I wouldn't say you were part of his plan. You were just in the wrong place at the wrong time—or maybe the right place at the right time, depending on how you look at it. A year and a half ago, you were working in a pizza parlor. Now you've got a career as a successful songwriter—and you've got me."

Arnie rubbed his jaw. "How long have you known this?"

"I didn't know anything until I talked to Daddy yesterday. He said he'd been planning to tell me, but was waiting for the right time. He wanted to make sure I was serious about you."

"So . . . so he's known about me all along—where I've been living, my new identity, and that I've been dating you for the last year?"

"I think so. Probably. Not much gets past him."

"Who else knows?"

"Sam might know a little bit, maybe Vinnie too. Daddy's had business dealings with Sam for years because of the radio stations he owns. I'm not sure who else knows."

"What about what happened in Hot Springs . . . when the car blew up?"

"An accident. Daddy had it looked into, something to do with gasoline fumes and a bad ignition coil."

"And your father really doesn't hate me?"

"Not at all."

Arnie stared at her, then took her hand. For the second time in two months she had told him a story too unbelievable not to be true.

"In fact, Daddy likes you a lot," Stef said, wiping her eyes. "Especially the way you didn't talk much during dinner in Savannah. He likes a man who can keep quiet about certain things. In fact, he told me to mention that to you specifically."

Arnie smiled in spite of himself.

"And he knows I love you very much. He wants me to be happy, and you make me happier than I ever thought a girl could be."

He stared into her eyes. For a moment, it seemed they were the only two people on earth. He took her in his arms, and they kissed for a long time.

When he tried to restart the car, his left leg was numb, and he had trouble pushing down the clutch pedal. He withdrew the Smith & Wesson from under his thigh and snapped the cylinder open, allowing the shells to fall into his lap.

"I guess I won't need this anytime soon," he said, tucking the gun under his seat and dropping the bullets into the Porsche's glove box.

"Oh, I wouldn't say that," Stef said.

"Really?"

"I always carry one."

She lifted the hem of her blouse to reveal the butt of a tiny pearl-handled Beretta twenty-five caliber automatic pistol tucked into the waistband of her jeans.

Arnie kissed her again.

EPILOGUE

Three months later, Arnie popped open a beer on the afterdeck of Don Puccini's seventy-foot Hatteras yacht as it sliced through the waves toward Palm Beach after a spectacular day of marlin fishing. The previous weekend's Cavallino Classic had exceeded even Sam's predictions. He and Stef had enjoyed heart stopping Ferrari rides at Moroso Motorsports Park, nightly banquets, and the thrilling annual Cavallino Classic polo match. But the highlight of the weekend was the *"Concorso d'Eleganza"*— the "Ferraris on the Lawn" event held on the grounds of the luxurious Breakers Hotel and Resort.

The hundred and fifty vehicles on display had come from as far away as England and Argentina, and none attracted more attention than Don Puccini's 1962 250 GTO, parked next to an immaculately restored 342 Cabriolet built in 1953 for King Leopold of Belgium. Arnie overheard several people speculate that the cars in front of the hotel were worth more than the palatial building itself, and he didn't doubt that it might be true.

Stef strolled around looking more beautiful than any of the automobiles, and Arnie happily noticed that she wasn't at all shy about flashing the two and a half carat Tiffany engagement ring he'd given her for Christmas. The people they'd met had been as fascinating as the cars, the majority being self-made entrepreneurs from remarkably diverse fields. All present shared a passion for the legacy of Enzo Ferrari.

Arnie sipped his beer and basked in the glow of the descending sun and excitement of his second number one record. Randy Fawcett's recording of "Daddy'd Be Proud" was in its third week at the top of the charts. He'd hooked and lost a big blue marlin that morning and the adrenalin still raced through the aching muscles of his arms and shoulders. He wasn't about to give up trout fishing, but it paled next to the rush of being attached to a fish powerful enough to drag a man overboard. He finished his beer and was about to throw the can into the trash when Stef stopped him. "Why don't you toss it over the back and see if I can hit it with my pistol?"

"Sure."

Stef pulled out her Beretta and Arnie threw the Heineken can over the transom. The little gun barked three times and the can sank into the waves. Arnie recalled that the Beretta twenty-five was James Bond's original gun of choice, Ian Fleming evidently knew his stuff. Fortunately, Bond had never been pitted against an adversary like Stef.

"Care to give it a try?" she asked.

One of the Don's bodyguards watched from the yacht's bridge as Arnie removed his Smith & Wesson from his duffel bag and loaded it. Stef lofted another can overboard, and he managed to get off two shots before it was swept out of range in the boat's wake, missing it by more than a foot the first time and a good six feet the second time.

Don Puccini emerged from the saloon door as Arnie was reloading the revolver.

"I was trying to take a nap and came out to see if someone was trying to shoot me," Stef's father said, smiling and making a show of rubbing his eyes.

The bodyguard on the bridge didn't smile at all.

Arnie held the reloaded thirty-eight gingerly with two fingers, the barrel pointed at the teak deck.

"*Mia cara figlia*," the Don said, putting his arm around Stef. "She can shoot the eyes out of a tin can, eh?"

"Yes sir. She never ceases to amaze me."

"Here, you try Daddy," Stef said, disengaging herself from her father's embrace and picking up an empty Diet Coke can.

Arnie handed Don Puccini the pistol. The Don raised the gun with both hands, then nodded to his daughter, who tossed the can high into the air. Arnie was surprised at the speed of the Don's first shot. The bullet caught the can while still airborne and sent it pinwheeling upward. Stef's father squinted through his bifocals and fired again, and the second slug drove the can rearward and down toward the water. When it touched the waves, the Don hit it a third, fourth and fifth time in rapid succession before the perforated remains sank.

Arnie was awestruck. "Wow!" he said as Stef's father handed the empty pistol back to him, "You're a great shot!"

The older man's face crinkled into an enigmatic smile. He laid a weathered arm around Arnie's shoulder and squeezed it firmly.

"And you," Don Puccini said. "You're going to make a great son in law."

THE END

COMING SOON!

Don't miss *Beat The Devil*, sequel to *The Ferrari Club*. Arnie's world implodes and he faces financial ruin when Sam Solstice marries his dominatrix girlfriend Bobbie and his diabolical son Luke takes over his business. Randy Fawcett reenters Stef's life, and Arnie fights to salvage his marriage and claw his way back to the top of the charts. But he soon learns that nothing comes without a price—and that the Devil is a sneaky bastard who wears many hats. Will Arnie crash and burn—or will he outwit his adversaries and confront the demons within himself in time to rebuild his life, reclaim his career, and finally *'Beat The Devil?'* Visit www.steveobrienmusic.com or www.ferrariclubthebook.com for the latest updates!

ABOUT THE AUTHOR

Steve O'Brien is a Nashville songwriter whose songs have sold over ten million copies. His compositions include the Brooks & Dunn hit "Rock My World (Little Country Girl)", a staple on country radio, and additional songs recorded by platinum-selling singers such as John Michael Montgomery, Larry Stewart and Don Williams. Steve co-wrote "Here Comes The G Man", which was used as a theme song on the G. Gordon Liddy radio show, and has had his compositions featured on TV shows ranging from *Late Night With David Letterman* and *48 Hours*. To learn more about Steve visit www.steveobrienmusic.com.

9080483R0

Made in the USA
Charleston, SC
08 August 2011